PRAISE FOR *FALSE WITNESS* AND OTHER NOVELS BY RANDY SINGER

"In this gripping, obsessively readable legal thriller,
Singer proves himself to be the Christian John Grisham."

PUBLISHERS WEEKLY

"Great suspense; gritty, believable action . . .
make this entry Singer's best yet."

BOOKLIST
STARRED REVIEW

"*False Witness* is an engrossing and challenging read. . . .
Part detective story, part legal thriller—I couldn't put it down!"

SHAUNTI FELDHAHN
BESTSELLING AUTHOR, SPEAKER, AND NATIONALLY SYNDICATED COLUMNIST

"Get ready to wrestle with larger themes of truth, justice, and courage."

CROSSWALK.COM
ON *FATAL CONVICTIONS*

"A solid, well-crafted legal thriller."

BOOKLIST
ON *FATAL CONVICTIONS*

"A book that will entertain readers and make them
think—what more can one ask?"

PUBLISHERS WEEKLY
ON *THE JUSTICE GAME*

"Singer artfully crafts a novel that is the perfect mix of
faith and suspense. . . . [*The Justice Game* is] fast-paced
from the start to the surprising conclusion."

ROMANTIC TIMES

"At the center of the heart-pounding action are the moral dilemmas that have become Singer's stock-in-trade. . . . An exciting thriller."

BOOKLIST
ON *BY REASON OF INSANITY*

"Readers will be left on the edge of their seats by Singer's latest suspense-filled thriller."

CHRISTIAN RETAILING
ON *BY REASON OF INSANITY*

"Singer hooks readers from the opening courtroom scene of this tasty thriller, then spurs them through a fast trot across a story line that just keeps delivering."

PUBLISHERS WEEKLY
ON *BY REASON OF INSANITY*

"[A] legal thriller that matches up easily with the best of Grisham."

CHRISTIAN FICTION REVIEW
ON *IRREPARABLE HARM*

"Singer hits pay dirt again with this taut, intelligent thriller. . . . [*Dying Declaration*] is a groundbreaking book for the Christian market, with well-drawn characters . . . and ingenious plotting."

PUBLISHERS WEEKLY

"*Directed Verdict* is a well-crafted courtroom drama with strong characters, surprising twists, and a compelling theme."

RANDY ALCORN
BESTSELLING AUTHOR OF *SAFELY HOME*

FALSE WITNESS

TYNDALE HOUSE PUBLISHERS, INC., CAROL STREAM, ILLINOIS

RANDY SINGER

Visit Tyndale's exciting website at www.tyndale.com.

Visit Randy Singer's website at www.randysinger.net.

TYNDALE and Tyndale's quill logo are registered trademarks of Tyndale House Publishers, Inc.

False Witness

First printing by Tyndale House Publishers, Inc., in 2011.

Previously published as False Witness by WaterBrook Press under ISBN 978-1-4000-7334-4.

Designed by Dean H. Renninger

Published in association with the literary agency of Alive Communications, Inc., 7680 Goddard St., Suite 200, Colorado Springs, CO 80920, www.alivecommunications.com.

Some Scripture quotations or paraphrases are taken from the Holman Christian Standard Bible®, copyright © 2003, 2002, 2000, 1999 by Holman Bible Publishers. Used by permission. All rights reserved.

Some Scripture quotations are taken from the Holy Bible, New Living Translation, copyright © 1996, 2004, 2007 by Tyndale House Foundation. Used by permission of Tyndale House Publishers, Inc., Carol Stream, Illinois 60188. All rights reserved.

Library of Congress Cataloging-in-Publication Data

Singer, Randy (Randy D.)
  False witness / Randy Singer.
    p. cm.
  ISBN 978-1-4143-3569-8 (sc)
  I. Title.
  PS3619.I5725F35 2011
  813'.6—dc22   2010051598

Printed in the United States of America

17   16   15   14   13   12   11
7   6   5   4   3   2   1

AUTHOR'S NOTE

PEOPLE OFTEN ASK ME, "Where do you get the ideas for your books?"

This one came at a funeral.

The deceased was David O'Malley, a good friend and former client. His wife had asked me to give the eulogy. I talked about David's generosity, his big heart. He was always inviting someone to live at his house until they could get back on their feet. He ran a used-car lot and hired people down on their luck. David believed in second chances.

And he was a character. He had this larger-than-life personality that made people laugh. He sang in a gospel quartet. Everybody had a David O'Malley story. Heads nodded as I shared mine.

David's pastor followed me in the pulpit. He spoke about a man named Thomas Kelly. The man was a scoundrel. Involved in organized crime. He turned on everyone he knew.

Jaws dropped and the mourners stared in disbelief at this pastor. The man had clearly lost his mind!

"You don't think you know Thomas Kelly, but you do," the pastor insisted. "David O'Malley *was* Thomas Kelly before he went into the witness protection program. Before he came to the Lord."

Prior to that moment, the only people who knew about David's past were the government, his family, myself, and his pastor. The men he had testified against had died in prison. His wife had obtained the government's permission to reveal his past.

There was utter silence as the pastor concluded with a line I will never forget.

"The government can give you a new identity," he said. "But only Christ can change your life."

That would make a good book, I thought.

I hope I was right.

A false witness will not go unpunished,
and one who utters lies perishes.

PROVERBS 19:9

THE
PROFESSOR

Courage is fear that has said its prayers.

PROLOGUE

IF ANYTHING HAPPENED TO THIS KID, the professor would never forgive himself. The young man was more than just a brilliant protégé; he was like a son. He reminded Professor Kumari so much of himself at that age. Too much, sometimes. Except that Rajat was brasher, bolder than Kumari had ever been.

Rajat Singh possessed his mentor's gift for complex mathematical theories, but he had something more. At heart, Rajat was a businessman. A risk taker. A part of India's new generation of entrepreneurs. He had grown restless as a teaching assistant at the university; Kumari could see that. Rajat stayed out of respect for the professor.

When Professor Kumari told his protégé about the Abacus Algorithm, the young man's eyes burned with entrepreneurial fire. To Rajat, it was more than a math formula. It became an opportunity to piece together a historic agreement that might help millions of other Dalits, India's caste of untouchables, achieve the same kind of success Rajat had obtained. Though discrimination against the Dalits had been outlawed, the vestiges of the caste system were everywhere. Professor Kumari preached patience, but Rajat would have none of it. He proposed a plan with such zeal and attention to detail that the professor couldn't say no.

This meeting was the culmination of Rajat's plan.

Kumari said a prayer, his head bowed as he sat in the driver's seat of the Ford Escape he had rented. He had a bad feeling about this meeting, something he just couldn't shake. He had insisted on elaborate security precautions to protect the algorithm.

"You worry too much, grasshopper," Rajat said from the passenger seat, trying hard to inject a worry-free tone into his voice. Kumari had once asked Rajat about the grasshopper reference; it was an allusion, as best Kumari could remember, to some old American movie or television show, the type of thing that didn't interest the professor in the least.

"That the birds of worry fly above your head, this you cannot change," the young man continued with mock solemnity. "But that they build nests in your hair, this you can prevent."

Kumari did not smile. He was known for being jovial and outgoing, having a type of mad-professor personality, which, he had to admit, was a reputation he did little to dispel. But this was not a time for smiles.

"Be careful, my son," Kumari said.

Rajat took the cue, nodded solemnly, and instantly became the earnest young businessman. He looked professional in his dark blue suit, white shirt, and red tie. Professional—and almost American. Still, he was so inexperienced to be handling such a sensitive transaction.

Kumari wanted to give Rajat a lecture, one of Kumari's patented professorial pep talks, more about life than about academics. But Kumari sensed that the young man had already surpassed his teacher in so many matters of life and faith. The time for lectures had passed.

"God be with you," Rajat said.

"And with you."

The young man climbed out of the van, grabbed his briefcase, and strode confidently toward the MGM Grand. He did not look back to see the lines of worry etched into his mentor's face, the birds beginning to nest in the professor's hair.

"Protect him," Kumari prayed. He pulled away from the front of the casino, cutting off other drivers and ignoring their horns.

◁▷

Twelve minutes later, Kumari entered his apartment, breathless from his climb up the outdoor steps. He disabled the alarm system, locked the dead bolt, and pulled the chain lock into place.

The living room and dining area, one long, L-shaped open space, was littered with twenty-four interconnected desktop computers and enough wiring to make the rooms look like a den of snakes. There were no pictures on the walls and no couch or recliner or television set. Just twenty-four desktop units, a small card table set up in the dining area, two folding chairs, and a beanbag.

In the single bedroom were two air mattresses.

Kumari had chosen this unit twenty days ago because it met all three criteria on his list: high-speed Internet access, a monthly lease, and anonymity. He paid cash in advance and signed the application using a phony name.

He hustled across the room, accidentally kicking one of the computers. He checked the lock on the sliding-glass door that led to a small patio, then pulled the blinds on the glass door and placed his laptop on the card table so he could hook it up to his improvised network.

Each computer had been maxed out with memory upgrades, according to Rajat, and then linked in such a way that the total network capacity exceeded 256GB of RAM. The network was protected by three separate firewalls.

Kumari's screen flickered to life, and he entered his password. He connected immediately to the Internet and opened the program that gave him remote access to Rajat's computer screen. Kumari typed the words **I'm on** so that they showed up on a document opened on Rajat's desktop. Then Kumari opened a second window on his computer that pulled up the video and audio feed from Rajat's computer. When the MGM Grand conference room came into focus with the same grainy resolution that Kumari had witnessed during the trial runs, he began to relax a little.

Rajat, the more electronically savvy of the two, had wired his laptop with a hidden video camera on the back, inside a port that looked like an Internet connection. He squeezed a corresponding microphone into what appeared to be an expansion port on the side. His computer now fed Kumari a live, blow-by-blow broadcast of the meeting.

Though the resolution was not the best, Kumari could make out three business executives within range of the wide-angle lens. They sat across from Rajat, separated from him by a large, polished-wood conference table. The man in the middle had dressed casually; the others wore suits. All three appeared younger than Kumari had anticipated.

The Chinese American man on the right looked more like a thug than a businessman. He had a low brow and thick neck, with veins bulging from a too-tight collar on his shirt, as if he couldn't afford a custom fit. On the right side of his face, a scar started at his sideburn and ended at his jaw. His right ear was smaller than the left, as if he had lost part of it in a knife fight and a plastic surgeon had just sewn up what was left. A tattooed cobra was coiled on the left side of his neck, poised to strike at any moment.

Kumari pegged him as security.

The man on the left, pale-skinned and tall, seemed infinitely more sophisticated. Eastern European perhaps, with ice blue eyes and short, Nordic-blond hair. He slouched in his seat, a cool, disinterested look on his face.

In the middle, the position of influence, sat a young man approximately Rajat's age, probably the CEO, dressed in a black linen shirt, with long dark hair, a trim goatee, and dark, brooding eyes that seemed to pierce Kumari's screen.

Kumari had missed the introductions and casual conversation, if any had taken place. Rajat was sketching out the logistics of the transaction, a complicated matter since Rajat had insisted on having the fifty million dollars in the bank before the algorithm was transferred. The men opposite Rajat were employed by a deal-brokerage agency that represented the three largest Internet security companies in the world. Understandably, they wanted to test the algorithm before any money changed hands.

"You will forgive my skepticism," the middle man said, his expression difficult to read, "but the implications of your claims are enormous. Not to mention the fact that our top consultants believe rapid factorization into prime numbers is a mathematical impossibility."

"Did you bring the numbers?" Rajat asked calmly. His voice came across louder than the others, based on his proximity to the mike. Kumari could discern no wavering in it, no hint of the frayed nerves that surely had to be racking his young partner.

"Of course."

"Then we can talk theory or we can talk application," Rajat said. "I mean, why bother finding out the true facts if we can just sit around and speculate based on the opinions of your experts?"

"We can do without the sarcasm," the Nordic man said.

The CEO betrayed no emotion as he consulted a folder. He dictated a long number that Rajat typed into the open document on his screen. Next, Rajat read back the digits to the CEO, all 197 of them, double-checking them slowly. It took nearly two minutes just to verify the number.

Kumari smiled. Child's play. Using his algorithm, he should have the answer in less than five minutes. His laptop could process this one by itself. He copied and pasted the number into his formula.

As Kumari's computer crunched the algorithm and Rajat plunked away on his own keyboard, plugging in phony numbers and functions, the conference room grew remarkably quiet, tension filling the air, as if the executives didn't dare jinx this moment by making a sound. From miles away, Kumari could almost tell what they were thinking: *If this works—if this really works—it would destroy the foundation of Internet encryption.* The RSA protocol, used extensively to secure transactions on the web, would be a sieve. It was, as Rajat had exclaimed when Kumari first told him about the breakthrough, "The key to every lock!"

Kumari had started working on his formula nearly twenty years ago as the result of a challenge from a fellow professor. Kumari called it a serious academic pursuit, a scholar's desire to break new ground. Others called it an obsession. Whatever the label, he dedicated his best and most productive years to accomplishing something unprecedented: discovering an order in the sequence of prime numbers. Most theorists believed that the numbers sprang up like weeds among the natural numbers, obeying no law other than the law of chance. It was impossible to predict where the next prime number would sprout, they said.

But where others saw chaos, Kumari saw the faintest outline of order. Over time, the outline became more discernible, the order more predictable, his convictions more resolute. He ultimately developed a complex mathematical algorithm, stunning in its reliability, which could quickly and accurately generate the prime factors of any number, no matter how large.

Delighted, Kumari wanted to publish the formula in a respected, international mathematics journal. But his protégé immediately saw the tragic consequences of such an approach. The Internet would be thrown into chaos until encryption technology evolved in a different direction. When it did, the algorithm would be useless in a matter of months.

Instead, Rajat talked Kumari into selling the formula to a conglomeration of the top global encryption companies. "It could help them see the Achilles' heel in their encryption techniques," he argued. "They could take steps to make Internet transactions more secure, to provide better protection for privacy." Then the clincher: "We could use the proceeds to help the Indian church provide Christian schools for the Dalits. An education in English for thousands of children. A way out of caste-based shackles."

It seemed like a good idea at the time. There were already hundreds of such schools in existence, but they needed thousands more. Otherwise, the children would be relegated to the plight of their parents—degrading work on the fringes of society. Going through life with their heads down, cleaning the bathrooms of the upper castes. This money could be a good start.

Kumari jolted back to the present when the answer popped up on his screen after only three minutes of computation. He typed in the results for Rajat.

Not surprisingly, Rajat decided to add a little drama. He had not been pleased to learn that the brokerage company was owned by the Chinese. The least he could do was have a little fun with them. "If I remember correctly," he said, his voice gaining confidence, "a recent attempt to find the prime factors of a 193-digit number took more than three months, with eighty different computers working simultaneously. Altogether, about thirty years of computer time was utilized. Is that what you gentlemen recall?"

The three men all looked at Rajat stone-faced; they did not like being mocked. "And this number," Rajat continued, "roughly the same length, has just been factored in the amount of time it might have taken you to go to the bathroom."

"And the answer?" the CEO said. His voice had an aggressive, no-nonsense edge to it.

Rajat read the prime numbers while the CEO checked his folder. He shot a glance to his Nordic friend, received a barely perceptible nod, and flipped the page to another enormous number. "This time," the CEO said, "we'll use a number the size our clients would typically use in their protocol. According to the deputy director of the National Security Agency, it should take all the personal computers in the world on average about twelve times the age of the universe to solve it by a traditional sieve method. We'll see if your formula can do it in a few minutes."

For ten minutes, they read and checked the digits of the new number. When everybody was satisfied, Kumari plugged it into his formula. This time, Kumari put his entire little network on the task.

Twelve minutes later, Rajat read the answer to the astonished men—two prime factors, each over two hundred digits long.

The business executives no longer tried to act unimpressed. The CEO called an impromptu meeting, stepping behind the chairs, where the men formed a little huddle, holding their folders in front of their mouths so Rajat couldn't read their lips. When they slid back into their seats, the Nordic man eyed Rajat the way a spectator might eye an illusionist at a magic show—scrutinizing, confident there was some sleight of hand that eluded the normal eye.

"We'd like to try one more thing," the CEO said, "just to prove our own firm's security hasn't been breached by someone on the inside providing the answers in advance. We're going to call a consultant for another test number, different from the ones we brought to this meeting. It could take a few minutes to get this one last beta."

Twenty minutes later, after Rajat had factored the third number even more quickly than the second, Kumari noticed a final change in demeanor on the other side of the table. Even through the grainy resolution, he could tell Rajat was now dealing with converts—men who had seen something that the foremost experts in the world had assured them was impossible.

"Who else has access to this formula?" the man on the right asked.

"Why is that relevant?" Rajat responded.

"Our price is based on exclusivity. If we're the only ones with this formula, it's worth fifty million dollars. If others have it, the value diminishes substantially."

"Only one man has seen this formula," Rajat replied. That part was true, Kumari knew. But the person wasn't Rajat.

The men across from Rajat nodded at each other, and Kumari breathed a sigh of relief. It looked like they might actually have a deal. "Praise God," he murmured. Rajat had been right. *No worries.*

"I think we've proven the concept," Rajat said. Kumari could hear Rajat rustling papers, probably the draft contract he had negotiated by phone prior to this meeting. "Let's get this signed so you can wire the money."

The CEO nodded but was no longer looking at Rajat. Instead, he seemed to be focused on a spot directly above and behind Rajat. Kumari heard another noise—a door opening perhaps, or someone entering the room?

The CEO gestured toward the apparent newcomer. "This is another one of our colleagues, Dr. Johnny Chin," the CEO said, not bothering to stand. "He's one of our firm's best troubleshooters."

Alarm bells went off in Kumari's head as he watched the Nordic man smirk and heard Rajat say a casual "Nice to meet you." Kumari was fairly certain that Rajat had remained seated, and Kumari wanted to write a warning on Rajat's screen. But he couldn't risk it if the man was behind Rajat, possibly watching the screen that very second.

A troubleshooter? For what?

Without warning, Kumari heard a frantic "Hey, what's going—?" followed by a sickening sound like a snake's tongue darting through the air, the deadly hiss of a gun silencer. Red liquid and white fragments spattered the far wall and sprayed the shirt of the young CEO. Kumari heard a thud, the sound of bone hitting something.

The CEO sprang from his seat, shouting, leaning forward, his slacks taking up the full screen of the video feed now.

"Get his head off the keyboard," he shouted. "Blood will fry that thing."

PART I

THE BOUNTY HUNTER

Every morning in Africa, a gazelle wakes up. It knows
it must run faster than the fastest lion or it will be killed.
Every morning a lion wakes up. It knows it must outrun the
slowest gazelle or it will starve to death. It doesn't matter
if you're a lion or a gazelle: when the sun comes up,
you'd better be running.

HERB CAEN,
FORMER SAN FRANCISCO CHRONICLE COLUMNIST

1

THE LONGEST THREE DAYS of Clark Shealy's life began with an expired registration sticker.

That was Clark's first clue, the reason he followed the jet-black Cadillac Escalade ESV yesterday. The reason he phoned his wife, his partner in both marriage and crime . . . well, not really crime but certainly the dark edge of legality. They were the Bonnie and Clyde of bounty hunters, of repo artists, of anything requiring sham credentials and bold-faced lies. Jessica's quick search of DMV records, which led to a phone call to the title holder, a Los Angeles credit union, confirmed what Clark had already guessed. The owner wasn't making payments. The credit union wanted to repo the vehicle but couldn't find it. They were willing to pay.

"How much?" Clark asked Jessica.

"It's not worth it," she replied. "That's not why you're there."

"Sure, honey. But just for grins, how much are we passing up?"

Jessica murmured something.

"You're breaking up," Clark said.

"They'd pay a third of Blue Book."

"Which is?"

"About forty-eight four," Jessica said softly.

"Love you, babe," Clark replied, doing the math. *Sixteen thousand dollars!*

"Clark—"

3

He ended the call. She called back. He hit Ignore.

Sixteen thousand dollars! Sure, it wasn't the main reason he had come to Vegas. But a little bonus couldn't hurt.

Unfortunately, the vehicle came equipped with the latest in theft protection devices, an electronically coded key supplied to the owner. The engine transmitted an electronic message that had to match the code programmed into the key, or the car wouldn't turn over.

Clark learned this the hard way during the dead hours of the desert night, at about two thirty. He had broken into the Cadillac, disabled the standard alarm system, removed the cover of the steering column, and hot-wired the vehicle. But without the right key, the car wouldn't start. Clark knew immediately that he had triggered a remote alarm. Using his hacksaw, he quickly sawed deep into the steering column, disabling the vehicle, and then sprinted down the drive and across the road.

He heard a stream of cursing from the front steps of a nearby condo followed by the blast of a gun. To Clark's trained ears, it sounded like a .350 Magnum, though he didn't stay around long enough to confirm the make, model, and ATF serial number.

◁▷

Six hours later, Clark came back.

He bluffed his way past the security guard at the entrance of the gated community and drove his borrowed tow truck into the elegant brick parking lot rimmed by manicured hedges. He parked sideways, immediately behind the Cadillac. These condos, some of Vegas's finest, probably went for more than a million bucks each.

The Caddy fit right in, screaming elegance and privilege—custom twenty-inch rims, beautiful leather interior, enough leg room for the Lakers' starting five, digital readouts on the dash, and an onboard computer that allowed its owner to customize all power functions in the vehicle. The surround-sound system, of course, could rattle the windows on a car three blocks away. Cadillac had pimped this ride out fresh from the factory, making it the vehicle of choice for men like Mortavius Johnson, men who lived on the west side of Vegas and supplied "escorts" for the city's biggest gamblers.

Clark speed-dialed 1 before he stepped out of the tow truck.

"This is stupid, Clark."

"Good morning to you, too. Are you ready?"

"No."

"All right. Let's do it." He slid the still-connected phone into a pocket of his coveralls. They were noticeably short, pulling at the crotch. He had bought the outfit on the spot from a mechanic at North Vegas Auto, the same garage where he borrowed the tow truck from the owner, a friend who had helped Clark in some prior repo schemes. A hundred and fifty bucks for the coveralls, complete with oil and grease stains. Clark had ripped off the name tag and rolled up the sleeves. It felt like junior high all over again, growing so fast the clothes couldn't keep up with the boy.

He popped open the hood of the wrecker, smeared his fingers on some blackened oil grime, and rubbed a little grease on his forearms, with a dab to his face. He closed the hood and walked confidently to the front door of the condo, checking the paper in his hand as if looking for an address. He rang the bell.

Silence. . . . He rang it again.

Eventually, he heard heavy footsteps inside and then the clicking of a lock before the door slowly opened. Mortavius Johnson, looking like he had barely survived a rough night, filled the doorway. Clark was tall and slender—six-three, about one-ninety. But Mortavius was tall and bulky—a brooding presence who dwarfed Clark. He wore jeans and no shirt, exposing rock-solid pecs but also a good-size gut. He didn't have a gun.

Clark glanced down at his paper while Mortavius surveyed him with bloodshot eyes.

"Are you Mortavius Johnson?"

"Yeah."

"You call for a tow?"

Mortavius's eyes narrowed suspiciously. The big man glanced at the pocket of Clark's coveralls—no insignia—then around him at the tow truck. Clark had quickly spray-painted over the logo and wondered if Mortavius could tell.

Clark held his breath and considered his options. If the big man caught on, Clark would have to surprise Mortavius, Pearl Harbor–style, with a knee to the groin or a fist to the solar plexus. Even those blows would probably just stun the big man momentarily. Clark would sprint like a bandit to the tow truck, hoping Mortavius's gun was more than arm's length away. Clark might be able to outrun Mortavius, but not the man's bullet.

"I left a message last night with the Cadillac dealer," Mortavius said. *The Cadillac dealer.* Clark was hoping for something a little more specific. "And the Cadillac dealer called me," Clark said, loudly enough to be heard on the cell phone in his pocket. "You think they've got their own tow trucks at that place? It's not like Caddies break down very often. If everybody could afford a Caddie, I'd go out of business."

Clark smiled. Mortavius did not.

"What company you with?" he asked.

"Highway Auto Service," Clark responded, louder still. He pulled out the cell phone, surreptitiously hit the End button with a thumb, then held it out to Mortavius. "You want to call my office? Speed dial 1."

Mortavius frowned. He still looked groggy. "I'll get the keys," he said.

He disappeared from the doorway, and Clark let out a breath. He speed-dialed Jessica again and put the phone back in his pocket. He glanced over his shoulder, then did a double take.

Give me a break!

Another tow truck was pulling past the security guard and heading toward Mortavius's condo. Things were getting a little dicey.

"I left some papers in the truck you'll need to sign," Clark called into the condo. But as soon as the words left Clark's mouth, Mortavius reappeared in the doorway, keys in hand.

Unfortunately, he glanced past Clark, and his eyes locked on the other tow truck. A glint of understanding sparked, followed by a flash of anger. "Who sent you?" Mortavius demanded.

"I told you . . . the Cadillac place."

"The Cadillac place," Mortavius repeated sarcastically. "What Cadillac place?"

"Don't remember. The name's on the papers in my truck."

Mortavius took a menacing step forward, and Clark felt the fear crawl up his neck. His fake sheriff's ID was in the tow truck along with his gun. He was running out of options.

"Who sent you?" Mortavius demanded.

Clark stiffened, ready to dodge the big man's blows. In that instant, Clark thought about the dental work the last incident like this had required. Jessica would shoot him—it wasn't in the budget.

A hand shot out, and Clark ducked. He lunged forward and brought his knee up with all his might. But the other man was quick, and the knee hit rock-solid thigh, not groin. Clark felt himself being jerked by his collar into the foyer, the way a dog might be yanked inside by an angry owner. Before he could land a blow, Clark was up against the wall, Mortavius in his face, a knife poised against Clark's stomach.

Where did that come from?

Mortavius kicked the door shut. "Talk fast, con man," he hissed. "Intruders break into my home, I slice 'em up in self-defense."

"I'm a deputy sheriff for Orange County, California," Clark gasped. He tried to sound official, hoping that even Mortavius might think twice before killing a law enforcement officer. "In off hours, I repo vehicles." He felt the point of the knife pressing against his gut, just below his navel, the perfect spot to start a vivisection.

"But you can keep yours," Clark continued, talking fast. "I'm only authorized to repo if there's no breach of the peace. Looks like this situation might not qualify."

Mortavius inched closer. He shifted his grip from Clark's collar to his neck, pinning Clark against the wall. "You try to gank my ride at night, then show up the next morning to tow it?"

"Something like that," Clark admitted. The words came out whispered for lack of air.

"That takes guts," Mortavius responded. A look that might have passed for admiration flashed across the dark eyes. "But no brains."

"I've got a deal," Clark whispered, frantic now for breath. His world was starting to cave in, stars and pyrotechnics clouding his vision.

The doorbell rang.

"Let's hear it," Mortavius said quietly, relaxing his stranglehold just enough so Clark could breathe.

"They're paying me six Gs for the car," Clark explained rapidly. He was thinking just clearly enough to fudge the numbers. "They know where you are now because I called them yesterday. Even if you kill me—" saying the words made Clark shudder a little, especially since Mortavius didn't flinch—"they're going to find the car. You let me tow it today and get it fixed. I'll wire four thousand bucks into your bank account before I leave the Cadillac place. I make two thousand, and you've got four thousand for a down payment on your next set of wheels."

The doorbell rang again, and Mortavius furrowed his brow. "Five Gs," he said, scowling.

"Forty-five hundred," Clark countered, "I've got a wife and—"

Ughh . . . Clark felt the wind flee his lungs as Mortavius slammed him against the wall. Pain shot from the back of his skull where it bounced off the drywall, probably leaving a dent.

"Five," Mortavius snarled.

Clark nodded quickly.

The big man released Clark, answered the door, and chased away the other tow truck driver, explaining that there had been a mistake. As Mortavius and Clark finished negotiating deal points, Clark had another brilliant idea.

"Have you got any friends who aren't making their payments?" he asked. "I could cut them in on the same type of deal. Say . . . fifty-fifty on the repo reward—they could use their cuts as down payments to trade up."

"Get out of here before I hurt you," Mortavius said.

◁▷

Clark glanced at his watch as he left the parking lot. He had less than two hours to return the tow truck and make it to the plastic surgeon's office. He speed-dialed Jessica.

"Highway Auto Service," she responded.

"It didn't work," Clark said. "I got busted."

"You okay?"

He loved hearing the concern in her voice. He hesitated a second, then, "Not a scratch on me."

"I told you it was a dumb idea," Jessica said, though she sounded more relieved than upset. "You never listen. Clark Shealy knows it all."

And he wasn't listening now. Instead, he was doing the math again in his head. Sixteen thousand, minus Mortavius's cut and the repair bill, would leave about ten. He thought about the logistics of making the wire transfers into accounts that Jessica wouldn't know about.

Pulling a con on pimps like Mortavius was one thing. Getting one by Jessica was quite another.

2

TWO HOURS LATER, back in his jeans and ostrich-skin cowboy boots, grease stains still lining his fingernails, Clark Shealy walked into a nondescript, three-story, brick medical building dedicated to outpatient surgery. He checked in with the receptionist, inhaling the sterile odors of hospital antiseptics and freshly scrubbed tile floors. Clark hated the smells and the memories they conjured. Needles made him squeamish, and just thinking about the precise slicing and peeling back of skin that accompanied plastic surgery turned his knees to rubber.

Though he had visited Dr. Silvoso's practice three times in the past two years, Clark Shealy was definitely not the plastic surgery type. It wasn't that Clark couldn't use a few minor improvements—who couldn't? Though Clark never had trouble attracting women—Jessica blamed it on his sky blue "bedroom eyes"—he did have a slight crook in his nose resulting from a junior high fistfight. Not to mention a scar above his right eye that extended the eyebrow line toward his ear, like errant eyeliner applied by a drunken rock star. Based on the nose and scar, his high school buddies had accused Clark of chasing parked cars.

But in Clark's opinion, real men didn't go to plastic surgeons. Real men played out the hand fate dealt them, scars and all. Besides, who wanted a nose like Michael Jackson's?

He found a seat and leafed through a well-worn magazine. Glancing around the waiting room, Clark could easily spot the regular patrons of Silvoso's practice—young, attractive females with Barbie-doll figures, puffed-up collagen lips, or skin stretched so tight between the eyes and jaw, it looked like it might tear at any moment.

They were a sharp contrast to the stooped and older patients waiting for some kind of orthopedic operation or the athletic kids who hobbled in on crutches.

Within minutes an assistant fetched Clark and escorted him into a sterile presurgery waiting room, empty except for a vinyl armchair, a portable tray table, and a few machines to monitor vitals. Clark had done this drill with Silvoso before. One of the nurses would roll the fugitive patient, sedated and prepped for surgery, into the room across the hall. As soon as the nurse left, while the unsuspecting patient waited for Silvoso, Clark would burst into the room, flash his credentials, and arrest the dazed man. Clark would make a scene, with Silvoso protesting loudly even as Clark hauled away his skip in handcuffs.

Later, Clark would quietly send Silvoso 25 percent of the bounty. Other plastic surgeons settled for 20 percent, but Silvoso was a tough negotiator. Even so, it was a good deal for Clark, helping him nail a skip who might otherwise never be caught. Plastic surgeons were a bounty hunter's best friends.

As Clark waited, he pondered the money, dollar signs clouding his thoughts. Johnny Chin, arrested for wire fraud and RICO violations, had posted bond of 1.5 mil and then promptly skipped. Rumors had him serving as a hit man for the mob, though Clark knew better than to believe everything he heard on the street. One thing that wasn't rumor—the bounty for Chin was a hundred and fifty Gs. In his mind, Clark had already spent his share of the money.

Precisely five minutes after Clark entered his room, he heard someone wheel a bed into the room across the hall. Clark waited until the footsteps retreated, then poked his head out the door, watched a nurse duck into a room a few doors down, and dashed quickly from his own room to the one designated for Chin. He closed the door behind him and immediately sensed that something was wrong.

The man in the bed, resting peacefully, eyes closed, bore little resemblance to the photographs of Chin. He was Asian—yes. But the recent mug shot of Chin showed a shaved head, and this guy had a full head of jet-black hair. The man in the bed had a scar on the right side of his jaw and was stockier than Clark expected, based on his recollection of the photos. The nose was flatter and the right ear seemed deformed, another feature not shown in the photographs.

Clark felt the hair on his arms bristle, his instincts flashing red. He retrieved his gun from the small holster attached to the top of his left boot. He prepared to check the room's small bathroom, swinging his gun in front of him, like a police officer checking out a perp's vacant apartment.

But a grunt from the patient startled him. "Can you get me some water?" the man asked, his voice hoarse and dry. His eyelids cracked open ever so slightly, revealing bloodshot eyes and a vacant stare. Clark checked the bathroom first. Clear. He kept the gun in his right hand as he approached the bed and handed the patient a plastic mug of water from the tray table.

The man's eyes fluttered open again as he sipped the water and muttered, "Thanks." Standing over the patient, Clark noticed a small tattoo on the left side of the man's neck, a coiled snake ready to strike, as though at any moment it might lash out and sink its fangs into the man's left ear. It was a metaphor for Clark's own nerves, coiled tighter than a spring, warning Clark to abort the mission.

The patient stopped drinking and looked at Clark through bleary eyes. Abruptly, the eyes popped open with a glint of excitement just as Clark felt a sharp stab in his neck, right above the left shoulder blade. He pivoted quickly, bringing his elbow up and back, hoping to connect with the facial bone of his attacker, but it felt like he was moving through oatmeal.

A spiderweb of pain followed by paralysis spread quickly across his body and down his arms. A faded image of a maniacal smile flashed through Clark's mind as he stood face-to-face for a fleeting moment with the man who had slipped into the room and stabbed Clark in the neck . . . and then the fog engulfed Clark's brain. Before he could launch another blow, his entire world went black.

3

CLARK REGAINED CONSCIOUSNESS propped up in the driver's seat of his Taurus, his head feeling like it might explode at any moment. He grimaced and tried to focus, but his thoughts collided with each other like a pileup at the NASCAR tracks. *Where am I? What time is it? What happened?*

He blinked twice, sat up a little straighter, and herded a few stray thoughts into formation while an invisible jackhammer pounded his skull. He was in a parking garage, alone in his car, sweating profusely in the stifling heat. The windows had been cracked to keep him from suffocating.

Vegas. Dr. Silvoso. Johnny Chin. Events came rushing back to him: time and place, Silvoso's double cross, the strange man in the outpatient prep room, the elusive Johnny Chin. Clark rubbed his neck where the tranquilizer had entered. It felt like he had been stuck with an elephant dart.

He noticed a yellow sticky taped to the steering wheel. *Use the cell phone on the seat. Speed dial 1.* He picked up the phone but paused as a little more fog lifted from his brain. *What if dialing the number triggers an explosive device?* But then again, if they wanted him dead, why was he still alive now?

He put the phone down and stared at it for a long moment. He started the car and cranked the AC to full blast. The outdoor temperature readout said ninety-eight degrees. He convinced himself the phone was safe, his curiosity beating back his survival instincts. He held his breath and speed-dialed 1.

No explosion. Clark exhaled, listening as the phone rang twice before somebody answered.

"Good afternoon, Mr. Shealy," a man's voice said. It had a slight Asian lilt, though the man had obviously worked hard at his diction. "I trust you had a peaceful nap."

"Who is this?"

"Why don't you leave the questions to me?" the voice said. He was calm. Frustratingly calm.

"Why don't you tell me why you drugged me?" Clark replied. He felt like he had landed on the set of *Mission: Impossible*—maybe the phone would dissolve in a puff of smoke when the conversation ended.

"I understand that you're a bounty hunter, Mr. Shealy. One of the best."

Clark scoffed. "Can't prove it by today."

"Yes, you did get in a little over your head on this one. But nevertheless, we would like to hire you."

This is so bizarre. Clark wondered if he was still dreaming, lingering under the effects of the tranquilizer. "You can't afford me," he said, more out of habit than clear thinking. It was his standard opening line for negotiations.

"Perhaps," the mystery man said, pausing ominously, "it will be you who cannot afford to say no."

This was getting old. "Get to the point," Clark demanded. "Because if I ever find out who you are—"

"Clark?"

The new voice jarred him. Confusion gave way to fear as he processed the possibilities.

"Jess? Is that you?"

"Yes. And I'm okay, Clark," she said, though she sounded terrified. "I love you."

"I love you too, hon." He said the words on instinct, his mind racing to make sense of this, his skin bristling with anxiety.

Jessica's next words came out in a rush. "They're Chinese, Clark. The man talking with you they call Huang Xu—" A dull thud, the sound of fist on bone, interrupted the words. Then an exaggerated clunk—perhaps the phone on a hardwood floor? Clark heard muffled shouting and loud commands in Chinese. He felt sick. Helpless.

"Jessica!" he yelled into the phone. "Hold on, babe. Are you okay?"

"Your wife is quite spirited," the voice said, monotone as before but breathing harder. Clark assumed it was the man Jessica had named. Huang Xu. Clark would never forget the name. "We have ways of calming her down."

Anger pulsed through Clark's body as he spit curses into the phone, threatening Xu. He suddenly felt boxed in. Pressured. Like his head might explode in rage. He opened the door and stepped out of the car. Dizzy, he braced himself. "I won't sleep until you're a dead man. Nobody hits my wife."

"Done?" Xu asked.

"So help me God, I'll kill you."

Xu let the silence hang for a few seconds before he spoke. "If you're finished with your empty threats, I have a deal to propose." He waited a few beats again, proving that he was in control of the conversation. "You're a bounty hunter, Mr. Shealy, and you have connections to numerous other bounty hunters. There's a man who has something that's very important to me. You bring him to me, and I'll pay you a handsome bounty: your wife, unharmed."

"Touch her again and you die." Clark no longer shouted. This was not a threat but a promise.

"Yes, yes, I get all that. Now here's how the deal works. Under the car seat you'll find a dossier with relevant background information about an Indian mathematician named Professor Moses Kumari. We believe he is hiding in the Las Vegas area, though we've been unable to locate him. We thought perhaps your vast network of bail bondsmen and bounty hunters might help.

"Time, Mr. Shealy, is of the essence. The rules are simple. You have forty-eight hours to locate Professor Kumari and call us by speed-dialing 1, using the phone in your hand. If you call us before you locate Kumari, your wife will suffer the consequences. Bring Kumari in alive and your wife lives. If he dies, she dies. If you don't find him, she dies. If you contact the authorities in any way, she dies. Are those rules all clear?"

"You're insane," Clark snapped, rubbing the back of his neck. "I can't find somebody in forty-eight hours."

"Then take your time, Mr. Shealy. But missing a deadline has consequences. At forty-eight hours, we start cosmetic surgery on Mrs. Shealy. The first day, we work on that beautiful smile. The teeth appear to be a little crowded, so we'll be extracting four teeth from the front. Without novocaine, of course, since we don't have a certified anesthesiologist."

Clark blistered the phone with more cursing. Empty threats, he knew, but he couldn't control the anger. He wanted to strangle Huang Xu with his bare hands—slowly, painfully. He vowed vengeance, whatever the cost.

"The next day, at precisely seventy-two hours, we start the incisions for her face-lift—a little slash here, another cut there. We think you'll find it quite an improvement."

Clark pounded his fist on the roof of the Taurus, then shook the pain from his hand and tried to think. The world spun—fury and the lingering effects of the tranquilizer taking their combined toll. Jessica *needed* him calm. He inhaled. He clenched his teeth.

"The next day, at ninety-six hours, we start with the breast reduction—"

"Stop!" Clark shouted. "That's enough. What do you want from me?"

There was another pause, and for a brief moment Clark thought Xu had hung up. "I thought we already covered that," Xu said. "But I did neglect to mention one other deal breaker. If you contact Dr. Silvoso or go anywhere near him, your wife dies. Just so you know, Silvoso didn't double-cross you voluntarily. We applied the same kind of pressure to him that we're applying to you."

Clark grunted his assent but made a mental note to circle back and exact his revenge on Silvoso once Jessica was safe.

"Do we have a deal, Mr. Shealy?"

Clark swallowed hard. Hesitated. He pictured Jessica duct-taped hand and foot, surrounded by leering men. They would be dead men soon. *So help me God.*

But for now, he needed time. These were events he couldn't control; an unfamiliar sense of helplessness and panic threatened to overwhelm him.

"Yes, we have a deal."

4

CLARK OPENED the folder he'd found under the car seat and flipped through the information on Professor Kumari, his hands trembling with rage. He couldn't pry his thoughts away from Jessica—what Xu and his cohorts might have already done to her. He thought about ways to trace the phone number he had just dialed but knew it would only lead to a stolen cell phone or one registered in a bogus name.

His mind began to clear. Why did they leave a cell phone instead of just a number to dial? He realized that the phone itself was probably planted with some type of tracking device—an electronic leash of sorts. He thought about tossing it but didn't want to make a move that might result in retaliation against Jessica.

He looked around the parking garage for signs of suspicious activity. Nothing. It was now 1:45 p.m. He set the timer on his wristwatch. Things had suddenly turned frenetic. Time was the enemy. Each second wasted could mean the difference between Jessica's surviving or not. He had less than forty-eight hours.

It took every ounce of will to focus on the documents in front of him. He needed to *do* something. Race down the road, fight the bad guys, crack somebody's head. Anything. The frustrations and tension knotted every muscle. The adrenaline demanded *action*.

Instead, he read. From the plane tickets, debit card receipts, and other data in the file, Clark quickly reconstructed Kumari's most recent activities. The man entered the United States on a research visa exactly twenty-five days earlier. He landed at Newark, spent a day on the East Coast, and then flew to Las Vegas, leaving a trail of debit card receipts in and around Sin City for four days.

He bought twenty-four desktop computers, top-of-the-line models with the fastest processing chips and maxed-out RAM. He bought cables and routers and a burglar alarm system. He bought cell phones and a GPS system with a tracking device. After this flurry of purchasing activity, he closed out the debit card account and went underground—as if he had dropped off the face of the earth. He could be anywhere by now. Clark wondered if the professor was even still alive.

What if he wasn't? What would happen to Jessica?

Clark didn't want to know.

His first call was to a personal friend who owed Clark a few favors. The man promised to use his local connections to check the Vegas hospitals and morgues, though he warned that his hospital sources didn't violate the privacy laws for free. He offered to let Clark use an office computer for Internet access so that Clark could research the typical databases.

Clark drove to his friend's office, his mind racing every second of the way, the dreaded possibilities nearly paralyzing his thought processes. This was too real to be a nightmare. Too concrete. Too devastating.

For an hour and forty-five minutes, Clark sat at his friend's computer and ran into one dead end after another. He could hardly sit still. Every time the computer showed its hourglass wait symbol, it reminded Clark of the fleeting seconds. He had never felt such enormous pressure, as if the walls of the borrowed office had started closing in on him like a car crusher, compacting his body inch by inch.

He was going crazy. But if he knew that, did it mean he was still sane?

At 4:00 p.m., Clark pulled up his Outlook database through the web access feature and generated a list of the twenty best bounty hunters in the L.A. and Vegas areas. He added the names of a few notorious Vegas bondsmen who had a reputation for trouble, then e-mailed pertinent information from Kumari's file, including a scanned-in photograph. Technically, he was asking them to skirt the law. Bounty hunters, or "bail-bond enforcers" as the title read on the cards of his more sophisticated friends, derived their power from a bond agreement. Every felon released on bail signed such an agreement, giving the bail bondsman power to arrest the felon if he or she skipped a court appearance. The bondsman would then assign this power to bounty hunters like

Clark, granting them a derivative power to arrest the skip and bring the felon back to face the judge. But licensed bounty hunters had no more authority to make apprehensions of members of the general public than a soccer mom would.

Who gave a rip? These men were bounty hunters, not the type to get hung up on legal technicalities, especially when the Green Lady whispered seductively in their ears. Clark would be coy in his e-mail; his friends could read between the lines.

Every bounty hunter would immediately run a background check on Kumari and realize there were no criminal charges pending and, thus, no bond contract. Still, for the right reward, Clark's friends would produce Kumari and risk a wrongful arrest charge. To do so, each bounty hunter would e-blast his or her own database of shady characters, offering to split the reward with anyone who found Kumari. That layer of greedy individuals could be expected to do the same, until half the pseudo–law enforcement characters on the West Coast would be looking for one man. The trick, of course, would be a bounty large enough to attract their interest.

Clark ran down a mental list of available assets—his business accounts and credit line, his checking and stock accounts, a home-equity loan he could take out, even the twenty thousand or so he had secretly squirreled away for some home improvements Jessica had been hinting about. The total came to nearly three hundred thousand dollars. He would also need to borrow from friends or talk his banker into an unsecured loan. It would take half a million to get the undivided attention of the top bounty hunters. His e-mail offer was simple: *Attached is information about Professor Moses Kumari, a man I have been contracted to bring in. Within thirty-six hours of this e-mail, bring him to me ALIVE or provide information leading to my apprehension of him and earn $500,000 U.S.*

By 4:05 p.m. the hunt was on.

◁▷

In less than thirty minutes, Clark received his first call, an unknown number with a Vegas area code that made his heart jump. It turned out to be Joe Peters, from the repair shop where Clark had left the Cadillac that morning. *Was that just this morning?* It seemed like a different life.

The car was ready, Peters said. With the clock ticking for Jessica, the Cadillac had been the last thing on Clark's mind. But the next step in Clark's investigation required a return trek to L.A., and Peters's garage was only ten minutes out of the way. Clark might need the ready cash the Cadillac could provide. Besides, Clark could make up the ten minutes during the three-and-a-half-hour drive, testing the Cadillac's upper limits. If he averaged ninety, he could do it in three.

His stopwatch showed an elapsed time of two hours and twenty-six minutes. The vise in his stomach tightened.

5

CLARK ENTERED his house by the side door, covering the doorknob with his shirtsleeve so his fingerprints wouldn't smudge those of the last person to touch the door. It felt surreal: his own house a crime scene—one that couldn't even be reported to the cops. He stepped into the mudroom and called out her name.

"Jess?"

His voice echoed in the stillness. He waited, not even breathing, as if the whole thing might be a bad dream after all. Maybe somehow Jessica would come bounding around the corner and wrap her arms tightly around his neck, kissing him eagerly, expectantly, the way she did when he had been gone too long.

But he knew in his heart it wouldn't happen. He walked slowly from room to room, accompanied by the sound of blood rushing through his ears, heartbeat by heartbeat, as the reality of his desperation took root. He didn't even really know what he was looking for. Perhaps he'd see some small hint of where she might be now. Anything out of place.

It all looked depressingly normal. The mail haphazardly spread on the counter as if Jessica had pulled a prized magazine out of the batch and left the bills unopened, hoping they would pay themselves. A blanket wadded up on one end of the couch, the pillow on the other armrest—vestiges of Jessica nestling down for a television show the night before. An exercise ball tucked away in a corner of the room, evidence of his wife's infatuation with flat abs.

He surveyed every piece of furniture, every trinket and paper, and the sandals that had been kicked off next to the back door. The house looked exactly like it did on every other day. And every detail reminded him of Jess.

He slipped into the first-floor office and checked the computer. The last e-mail had been sent at 9:05 that morning. She had not logged off. The computer file on Johnny Chin remained undisturbed, as far as Clark could tell. He checked the front door and the back, confirming that both were locked. Jessica's car was still in the garage. It seemed as if somebody had just transported her away—as if she had vanished without leaving a trace.

He imagined the scene: a UPS truck pulling into the side driveway and the driver knocking on the mudroom door with a package. Jessica, who never met a stranger, greeting him with a smile. "Sign here," he says, and while she scribbles her flowing signature, he elbows inside and overwhelms her. Not without a fight, of course. His Jess would definitely have put up a fight.

But he couldn't find any evidence of it.

Clark climbed the stairs to the bedroom, struck by the tranquility of the scene there. The setting sun illuminated the room through the window on the west wall, silhouetting particles of airborne dust in their evening minuet. The bed was made, and Jessica's worn teddy bear, the one her mom said had been Jessica's favorite since first grade, rested contentedly against the pillows. As was her habit, Jess had neatly folded her pajamas and placed them next to the bear. Clark picked them up, held them to his face, and breathed in Jessica. Clutching the pajamas with both fists, he promised himself that nothing would happen to her. He wouldn't let it.

I already have.

He rejected the thought and placed the pajamas back on the bed. He wanted to collapse and weep, or maybe go ballistic and punch the wall, but this was no time to get emotional. "I'll get her back," he said to her teddy, as if the words could make it happen. "She'll be all right."

He headed out to the fenced-in backyard and nearly came unglued. Here, too, everything was in order, but he had let his emotional guard down a little when he stepped out back. And now, staring at the trampoline, the tears started rolling down his face.

He remembered her the way she might never be again. Confident, effusive, untroubled by the cares of their dysfunctional lives.

Jess, bouncing on the tramp and displaying the form from her competitive diving days, doing full layouts and back twists, her body ramrod straight as she flies through the air. "Come on, you big baby," she taunts. Clark, his manliness challenged, mounts the trampoline and tries to muster the courage for a single backflip.

"I've got you," she says. "Trust me." One strong hand is on his right hamstring; her other hand rests against his lower back. She stands beside him, gently bouncing. "Remember: get good height and then pull your knees up and kick back. I'll throw your legs around if I have to."

One minute Clark is trembling, bouncing, Jessica urging him higher. The next she's counting: "One . . . two . . . three." He jumps and pulls his legs in, losing all balance and perspective, while Jessica whips his legs around. Next thing he knows . . . he's landing on the trampoline feetfirst. Off-balance, he falls forward, but Jess grabs his shirt and catches him, laughing. They hug . . . kiss.

She breaks it off. "Next time, get a little more height. And jump straighter up, not backward so much."

"There's not going to be a next time," he says, climbing down.

After a few minutes the memory was gone; Jessica's blonde hair had morphed into the twilight haze of a Los Angeles night. She was a thirty-two-year-old kid, the trampoline her one release. He wondered if they would ever be that carefree again.

6

AFTER CLARK FINISHED canvassing the house, he checked with the neighbors. Nobody had seen Jessica since early morning. Nobody remembered any delivery trucks or strange cars or other visitors to the Shealy house. Two of the neighbors hadn't been home all day. Clark thanked them, his throat growing tighter with each visit, then returned to his house to think.

He slumped into the desk chair in the cluttered office he shared with Jessica. He glanced compulsively at his watch, the tenth time in the last few minutes. It was nearly nine o'clock. He changed modes to the stopwatch: 7:13:23. He wrestled with the idea of calling the police, letting the experts start their own investigation. But the threats of Jessica's captors kept him from doing so.

Though he had watched his mirrors all the way and found nothing when he checked the house for hidden cameras, Clark still had a sense he was being monitored. Based on their capture of Jessica, these guys were pros. They had left a cell phone to track his whereabouts. Somehow, they would know if Clark called the police. Besides, he had worked with law enforcement enough to realize that speed was not their specialty. The investigation would be out of his control.

He couldn't take that chance. Instead, he decided to take a chance of a different sort. He pulled up Outlook and e-mailed the bounty hunters he had contacted that afternoon, increasing the bounty on Kumari from five hundred thousand to a million. He would figure out where to get the money later. He also broadened the net. He attached pertinent information and a photo of Johnny Chin, offering a bounty of five hundred thousand. He finished the e-mail with the biggest gamble of all.

> In addition, for information concerning the present whereabouts of a man named Huang Xu, believed to be in the Los Angeles area, I will pay $500,000 U.S.

Clark corrected a few words highlighted by the spell checker, promised God he would do anything God asked if Jessica came back safely, then hit the Send button.

The replies were almost immediate. *Xu is high-level Chinese mafia,* one read. *I don't do mafia.* Another came back more bluntly: *Take me off your distribution list.* And another: *Xu and Chin are members of the Manchurian Triad. I don't mess with the triads, even for a million bucks.*

Clark replied to everyone, asking questions and prying out more information. *How do you know that Xu's with the triads? What businesses are connected with him? Where does he live? Where is his office?*

I'm a bond enforcement agent, not 411, a man called Cyclone wrote back. But Clark was making progress. He learned that Xu was reputedly a lieutenant in the Manchurian Triad and that he was basically responsible for United States operations. Xu was young, tattooed, cold-blooded, and a martial arts expert, like a younger, evil brother of Bruce Lee. *He has a thing for women,* one e-mail said ominously, *especially American blondes.*

Clark deleted it immediately.

The e-mails seemed to indicate that Johnny Chin didn't instill the same level of fear that Huang Xu did. Chin was just an independent contractor for the mob, a hit man with no personal loyalties. Apprehending Chin would not guarantee a mob contract on the bounty hunter's head, though several of Clark's contemporaries still thought someone would have to be an idiot to try it. Others seemed to believe that, for the right price, they could probably be talked into finding Chin.

Five hundred grand was apparently the right price. The same guys who had turned up their noses when Clark had been hunting Johnny

Chin for a bounty of a hundred and fifty were suddenly interested. Chin liked hanging around the Vegas casinos, they said, and had been known to go on gambling binges for weeks on end.

By ten thirty, Clark had collected all the information he could gain online and started going stir-crazy again. He spent the next thirty minutes putting together one-page information sheets featuring pictures and identifying information for both Kumari and Chin. He ran off two hundred copies of each.

He stuffed the tools of his trade into the back of the Escalade—handcuffs, a stun gun, a large black luggage trunk big enough to stuff an entire body inside, a slim-jim for breaking into cars, a baseball bat, glass cutters, pliers, screwdrivers, a ratchet set, his laptop and printer, a laminating kit for fake identifications, two handguns, and a Kevlar vest. He grabbed a Coke out of the refrigerator and pointed the Escalade toward Vegas.

He couldn't just sit around. He would be back in Vegas by 2:30 a.m., not too late to begin canvassing the major casinos. If he worked straight through the night and the next morning, he could speak to the security firms for most of the major gambling establishments on the Strip.

He would find Johnny Chin no matter the cost.

7

BY 9:00 A.M., Clark had been to more than half the major casinos, passed out dozens of photos of Johnny Chin and Professor Moses Kumari, and still had nothing to show for it. He dropped onto a barstool at the New York–New York casino and checked his stopwatch: 19:13:54. Bone weary, he put his forehead in his hand and tried to think. His nerves had caught fire, the seconds ticking away with Jessica's life on the line, while Clark kept striking out.

If anything happens to her, I'll hunt down Xu if it takes me the rest of my life. Kill him. Then kill myself. Through twelve years as a bounty hunter, Clark had never been forced to kill a man. But he had no doubt he could do it now. The pain and the hatred were feeding on each other. It felt like another man, cold-blooded and vengeful, had taken control of Clark's body.

"Can I get you anything?"

Clark looked at the bartender. "Coffee. Black." It would be his third within the last few hours. Even before this new shot of caffeine, his hands had started trembling a little. But he couldn't afford to sleep. Not with the clock ticking.

As the bartender retreated to the coffeepot, Clark caught his own reflection, just above the liquor bottles, in the mirror that lined the back of the bar. He looked like death on a bad day. Matted blond hair. Bloodshot eyes underscored by dark circles. Bagging eyelids. In his younger days, he had been something of a ladies' man. Now, at age thirty-six, an all-nighter made his haggard face look like it belonged on a hostage. Even the piercing sky blue eyes, accentuated by colored contacts, seemed hollow and lifeless. He needed to get the contacts out, but his glasses were in the rental car. Dry eyeballs were the least of his worries.

Two sips into his coffee, Clark decided to take a step he had been contemplating all night. If nothing else, he had to at least know that Jessica was still alive. He blew on the coffee, took another sip, and played out the next conversation in his mind. He ran through it three times, then placed a five-dollar bill on the bar and took a few steps away. He felt his gut tense, the coffee and bile working overtime. He pulled out the black Motorola Razr phone that had been left on the seat of his car and speed-dialed 1.

"I assume you found Kumari," said the same voice he heard yesterday. Perfect diction. Huang Xu.

Clark took a breath, told himself to stay calm. "I'm making progress, but I'm going to need more time. And first, I need to speak with Jessica."

"I told you to call when you have Kumari," Xu replied firmly. "Not before."

"If you want your man, let me speak to my wife."

Xu scoffed at the suggestion, waited a beat, and lowered his voice. "This call will cost you twelve hours. We start pulling her teeth tomorrow morning at 1:45 a.m."

"Wait!" Clark shouted, his mind reeling. He hadn't anticipated this. He swallowed the curse words, reaching for something that might stop the madman. "I've got a lead, but these things take time. If you touch her, even one small cut, I'll stop hunting Kumari and start hunting you. I'm willing to do this deal, but I've got to have a little more time."

"Nineteen seventeen thirty," Xu said. He paused. "Nineteen seventeen thirty-five. . . . Nineteen seventeen forty."

Clark cursed loudly into the phone, threatened Xu again, and drew a number of concerned stares from those around him. He took a breath and listened. Dead air had replaced the counting, but the relentless march of seconds continued unabated in Clark's mind.

Nineteen seventeen fifty-five. In less than seventeen hours, they would start on the teeth.

8

OUT OF OPTIONS, deep in despair, Clark climbed into the Escalade and made his way toward the North Vegas police station. His instincts told him this was a bad move, but he knew that if he wanted the police to help, he couldn't wait until the last minute. He had thought about trying to contact Silvoso but rejected that idea. Jessica's captors would probably be watching the plastic surgeon like hawks.

Driving north on the Strip, just past the Riviera Hotel, Clark received a text message on his cell phone. **I've got the drop on Johnny Chin,** the message read. **Call me.** It was signed by a bounty hunter named "Bones" McGinley, one of the add-ons to Clark's original list, a notoriously shady operator who made his reputation hunting down reprobate Vegas gamblers. Clark dialed the number and felt the adrenaline surge through his sleep-deprived body.

"Quad-A Bail Bond Office," said a deep female voice at the other end.

"I need to speak to Bones McGinley."

"He's not in right now. Can I take a message?"

"This is Clark Shealy. He just sent me a text message. Can I get his cell phone number?"

"Mr. Shealy!" the woman exclaimed as if they were old friends. "He said to put you right through."

The bounty hunters quickly exchanged greetings. "You know where Chin is?" Clark asked.

"They say he's got mob connections," Bones replied. He had a gravelly smoker's voice, but higher pitched than Clark expected. Clark had heard that Bones weighed in at over three hundred. "You know anything about that?"

"Every hit man has mob connections," Clark said, trying to sound casual. Bones himself was rumored to have connections with a few Italian mob families in the casino business. He probably wanted to avoid a conflict of interest. "But I don't think Chin's are anything special. He was apparently working for the Russian mob when he first got busted." Clark deliberately left out Chin's suspected connections with the Manchurian Triad.

"Russian, huh?" Bones paused, apparently mulling it over. "Here's the deal. I'll drop a dime on this guy on two conditions. First, you keep my name out of it. Period. Nobody ever knows where you got your tip." Bones paused and coughed.

"Done," Clark said. He would agree to anything. This was his first and only lead.

"Second, you wire the five hundred K into my account. Angel will give you the wiring instructions. I'll call back when it shows up."

Clark, of course, didn't have the money and suspected Bones knew it. "He might be gone by then," Clark said quickly. "Tell me where he is. I bust him. Then you get paid."

Bones laughed—a big, throaty, taunting laugh. "I was born at night, but not last night. Call me back after you make the wire transfer."

For the second time in half an hour, someone holding all the cards hung up on Clark.

Clark called him back immediately.

"Quad-A Bail Bond Office—"

"Get me McGinley," Clark interrupted.

"Who is this?" Angel asked, sounding perturbed.

"Clark Shealy."

Without comment, she put Clark on hold. A long minute later, she was back on the line. "Mr. McGinley asked me to give you wiring instructions for our account," she said. "Do you have a pen and paper?"

Clark felt his temper flaring again but beat it back. He needed some allies right now. "I can only do a hundred fifty thousand right this minute," he explained. "I'll do the rest later today after Mr. McGinley gives me the information I need. Ask him if that'll work."

"Please hold."

When Angel came back, she was all business. "Mr. McGinley says we need all five hundred thousand before he'll talk to you. Do you want those wiring instructions or not?"

Clark bit his tongue and wrote down the wiring instructions. "I'll need your tax ID number and business address for tax purposes," he explained. After he hung up, he entered the address into the Escalade's onboard GPS.

"Turn left at the next light," a sexy female voice instructed him.

"My pleasure," Clark said.

9

THE AAAA BAIL BOND OFFICE was located about two blocks from the city jail, across the street from the Bad Boyz Bond Office. The neon sign for Bones's operation was larger, though the modular trailer that served as an office couldn't compete with the real brick building that the Bad Boyz called home. Bones plainly didn't believe in burning money on overhead.

There were only two cars in the parking lot—a Lexus that undoubtedly belonged to Bones and a run-down foreign car. Clark parked the Escalade, stuffed his Glock into a shoulder holster, and threw on a blue sports coat to cover the gun.

He barged through the door and surveyed the seedy waiting area. A few wooden chairs. A messy reception desk manned by a chubby lady with too much red lipstick—Angel Sparkman, according to the nameplate. She had a phone stuck to her ear and was looking at her computer. She motioned for Clark to sit down.

He tried to get her attention. "Clark Shealy. I'm here to see Mr. McGinley."

Without looking, she frowned and gave him an exaggerated sit-down motion.

"Thanks for your help," Clark said. He marched past Angel and down the narrow hallway toward what he assumed would be McGinley's office.

"Can you hang on a second?" Angel said loudly into the phone. Clark heard the sound of her desk chair wheeling back and the huffing of an indignant Angel behind him.

"Sir. Wait just a minute."

He turned into a large, cluttered office and stared into the wide-eyed amazement of a man who could have passed for George Foreman's Anglo twin brother.

Bones stood and narrowed his eyes.

"I'm Clark Shealy and I've got your money," Clark managed to spit out before Angel came barreling into the office behind him.

"I tried to stop him, Mr. McGinley. He just barged right on past—"

Bones held out a beefy palm, stopping Angel midsentence, though his eyes never left Clark.

"You've got the money?"

"Yes."

Bones turned to Angel. "Two coffees," he ordered. To Clark: "How do you like yours?"

Just what Clark needed—another cup of coffee. "Have you got any bottled water?"

Bones snorted. "This is a bail-bonds office, not a gay bar."

"I'll take it black."

Angel lumbered out of the room, mumbling something about it taking a few minutes to brew a new pot. Bones asked Clark to take a seat in one of the wooden chairs facing the metal desk. Clark reached over and casually shut the office door, then settled into the unpadded chair.

The office looked like Bones had never thrown away a piece of paper in his life. Stray piles of paper and folders covered his desk and spilled onto the floor and credenza, as if a tsunami of bond files had flooded his office and left this chaos in its wake. His desk also featured at least four foam cups, three grimy glass mugs with varying amounts of coffee in them, and about fifty yellow sticky notes with chicken scratch on them. A monitor sat on the credenza behind Bones, its screen saver building multicolored crisscrossing pipes. The walls had nothing on them except a few water stains from an apparently leaky roof.

Clark leaned forward and began pleading with Bones for help. He was not above begging for Jessica's life. "The Chinese mafia is using my wife as a hostage," he explained. He quickly told Bones about his attempt to nab Johnny Chin and how that led to the current hunt for

Moses Kumari. "I've got sixteen hours," Clark said, glancing at his watch and feeling the panic tingle down his vertebrae, "or they start torturing my wife."

Bones watched impassively, his beady gray eyes giving nothing away.

"I've got my checkbook right here," Clark said, pulling it out of his sports coat pocket while cautiously shielding his holster. "I can write two checks right now. One for a hundred and fifty thousand, which will clear today. The other check, for three hundred and fifty thousand, you can cash by Friday. That will give me time to get my wife back and liquidate a few things. If it bounces, which it won't, you'll have a rock-solid lawsuit against me based on the check itself."

Bones leaned forward, his solid forearms resting on the haphazard piles of paper littering his desk. "Maybe you don't understand who I am," he said slowly, contempt riding on every word. "Or what I do. I enforce bail bonds. I get sad stories every day from felons who tell me about their poor little children or an innocent wife or a mother who will starve to death. I don't operate on sympathy, Mr. Shealy. I operate on Mr. Green—cash, wire transfers, not bogus checks." He leaned back in his chair again, point made. "Now, get out of my sight. And don't come back until you have the money."

Maybe it was a carryover from the tranquilizer or the three cups of coffee—or the fact that his wife could be raped or tortured any minute. But Clark didn't have time for arrogance, and he wasn't in the mood. He had always prided himself on being that rarest of bounty hunters—a gentleman. A fast-talking genius who seldom resorted to violence.

But something snapped.

Clark bolted out of his seat and halfway across the desk. He grabbed Bones by the collar with his left hand and jammed his gun into Bones's temple with his right.

"Listen, you fat, arrogant slob. They've got my wife." Clark pushed the gun a little harder into the big man's temple and watched the beads of sweat begin to form above his eyebrows. "You think I won't kill you if you don't help?"

Clark sounded crazy. Heck, he *felt* crazy. Even *he* wasn't 100 percent sure he wouldn't pull the trigger.

"I hear you, man," Bones managed, croaking the words out, the high-pitched voice going even higher. "Put the gun down."

"Where is Chin?" Clark demanded. He squeezed the trigger ever so slightly.

"Put it down, man! Are you crazy?" A sheen of sweat covered Bones's entire forehead. He trembled slightly, the bravado gone.

"Three seconds," Clark said.

Bones squared his jaw, his eyes at once frightened and defiant.

"One . . ." The big man didn't move. "Two . . ." The trembling increased, the eyes widened in disbelief. "Three . . ."

"Okay, okay," Bones said quickly. "Let go of me, man. The file's yours."

Clark pushed him back in the seat but kept the gun aimed at Bones's forehead. "Put your hands behind your head," Clark ordered, "and tell me where the file is."

Bones interlaced his fingers behind his head, his wary eyes fixed on Clark. "It's on my computer. If you let me take my hands down, I can print it out for you."

Clark nodded his assent, and Bones turned slowly toward the keyboard and monitor behind him. He pulled his hands down cautiously, scrolled through to an e-mail, and hit Print.

Clark moved to the printer and grabbed the document, keeping his gun trained on Bones. "Behind the head," he barked, and Bones did as he was told.

The e-mail was from jhenriques@bha.com.

> Johnny Chin is registered at the Mirage, room 8127,
> under the name Peter Chang. He checked in on August
> 9 and registered for three days.

Clark folded the e-mail and stuffed it in his sports coat pocket. He sat down in front of the desk, placed his gun in his left hand, and took out his checkbook with his right. Pointing the gun at Bones, he used the butt of the gun to hold the top of the checkbook open as he wrote out the check.

"How much?" Bones asked, his hands obediently locked behind his head.

"One-fifty. That's all I've got right now."

Clark placed the check on the desk and returned the checkbook to his pocket. He would have to detain both Bones and Angel until he could make his move on the hit man. He couldn't risk having them tip off Chin.

"Take one hand down, and dial Angel on the speakerphone," Clark said. "Tell her to bring some packaging tape into the office."

Bones reached down and pressed the Speaker button. As he did, Clark noticed a subtle change of expression—a brief glint in Bones's eyes, a smirk starting to play on the lips, and then, too quick for Clark to move . . .

Ka-bam!

It felt like the bullet hit his chest before Clark even heard the noise. The pain shot through him and drove him over backward, the chair and Clark crashing to the floor.

"Gullible moron," he heard Bones say.

10

CLARK OPENED HIS EYES and flinched at the sight of the stubbled red face of Bones, inches from his own, exhaling like a panting dog. "Don't mess with me, boy," Bones snarled, leaning over Clark. "I knew you were wearing Kevlar. Next time, I'll aim a little higher and blow your face apart."

Lying on his back, Clark felt light-headed, as if an air bag had just exploded in his face. His whole chest ached from the force of the blow, but the Kevlar vest had saved his life. Bones must have had a spring gun cocked and loaded in the leg well under his desk. He probably aimed it with his knee and maybe even triggered it with some kind of foot pedal. There would have to be a small opening in the desk for the nose of the barrel. Clark should have seen it coming.

He moaned and kept his eyes nearly closed, watching through slits while Bones smirked, then relaxed a little and rose to one knee. Clark saw his opening, reached up, and grabbed Bones's head, pulling it down violently. At the same time, Clark ducked his chin and delivered a brutal head butt to the bridge of Bones's nose. He heard the big man scream, then felt the warm blood spurt all over him. Clark grabbed his gun and pistol-whipped Bones, heard the crunch of gun on cheekbone, and saw Bones crumple to the floor.

Angel came screaming into the office, and Clark grabbed her, threw her into the vacant wooden chair, and yelled for her to calm down and stop her hysterical crying. Meanwhile, Bones had struggled into a sitting position, holding his nose as the blood rolled down his hands and dripped on the floor. Clark shifted his Glock back and forth from Angel to Bones. "Nobody move," he barked. "Angel, hands on your head!"

She cried and shuddered but raised her hands. Clark grabbed Bones's cell phone from the desk and stuffed it in his pocket. He yanked the desk phone out of the wall.

He now had a big problem. Two hostages, no rope. Angel sobbed loudly, making it impossible to think. Clark had left his plastic FlexiCuffs in the Escalade, never expecting it would come to this.

Clark turned to Bones. "Where are *your* handcuffs?"

Bones lifted a middle finger. Angel wailed, stopping intermittently to yell at Clark.

"Shut up!" he yelled back. Then he tossed a box of Kleenex to Bones. "Stop the bleeding!" he ordered.

Bones pulled his hands away from the bridge of his nose, and Angel shrieked even louder. Blood flowed not just from the nose but from a huge gash below Bones's left eye, ten to fifteen stitches, Clark estimated. The right cheek was also bruised, bloodied, and swollen.

"Look what you've done!" Angel cried. "You're lucky he's not dead!"

Bones cursed at Clark and yelled at Angel to shut up. She quieted a little, but not much. Moving quickly, Clark used scissors to cut the pull cords from the miniblinds, all the while keeping his gun on Bones. Using the cords and some packing tape he found on the shelf of the credenza, Clark bound them both, hand and foot. He positioned them next to the desk and anchored them to it with generous layers of tape, using almost the entire roll, saving just enough to tape their mouths shut. The cursing from Bones turned into muted grunts.

He inspected the sheet of computer paper in the left pocket of his sports coat. The bullet had pierced the upper corner of the folded paper, but Clark could still read the room number for Johnny Chin. Looking at the bullet hole lessened the guilt pangs he felt. A few inches higher, and Clark would have been dead.

He knelt in front of Angel and looked into her tear-rimmed eyes. She still cried uncontrollably, but the sound was muffled by the tape.

"My wife is being held hostage by the mob," Clark said, feeling sorry for the terrified woman in front of him. "Your boss wouldn't tell me where to find the one person that might lead me to my wife unless

I paid him five hundred thousand dollars. So I pulled a gun on him and wrote him a check for a hundred and fifty thousand, which is basically all I have. That's when he shot me with that spring gun in his desk." Clark tapped his chest. "Kevlar," he said. "Needless to say, I survived and turned the tables. That's when you came in."

Clark stood. He thought he saw a flicker of understanding through Angel's tears. "The check is still on the desk. As soon as I get custody of this man, I'm going to call 911 and send the cops out here."

Angel nodded, and Clark felt a tinge of vindication. Then he checked his stopwatch: 20:12:14.

He used the bathroom to wash off the blood and then grabbed a change of clothes from the Escalade. He left Bones's cell phone on Angel's desk.

He left without saying another word.

11

IT WAS NEARLY 11:00 A.M. when Clark slid into the grandiose lobby of the Mirage wearing running shoes, baggy shorts, and a "What Happens in Vegas Stays in Vegas" T-shirt. He had taken off his wedding ring in case flirting was required. He had parked the Escalade in the adjacent garage and then went for a hard run for a few blocks down the sidewalk of the Vegas Strip away from the hotel and back again. At a drinking fountain inside, he splashed some water on his hair and forehead, adding a little on the underarms of his T-shirt for pit stains. He jumped into a check-in line, shifting his weight from one foot to the other, anxiously checking his watch.

A dozen clerks stood in front of a huge aquarium set into the wall behind the check-in counter. It was filled with colorful coral and exotic sea creatures of all types—black-and-white-striped angelfish, orange and yellow puffer fish, tiger fish, tangs, and some kind of see-through fish that Clark had never seen before. And of course . . . sharks. The other fish were all swimming with the sharks. Clark knew the feeling.

He stepped up to the counter and checked the name tag on the pleasant-looking blonde with unnaturally white teeth. *Clarisse Robins.*

"How big is that tank?" Clark asked.

"About twenty thousand gallons of saltwater."

"How many times a day do you get asked that question?" Clark inquired, flashing his best smile.

"About twenty thousand." She smiled back. Perfunctory, but still a smile.

"Well, here's something else you probably get a lot. . . ." This time he gave her a sheepish, I'm-an-idiot grin. "I went out for a run and forgot my keys." He pulled his license from a pocket on the gym shorts. "Room 8127." He held his breath.

"Happens all the time," she said pleasantly. Clark watched Clarisse perform a few keystrokes and then glance at his California driver's license. She did a double take.

"I'm sorry," she said pleasantly. "Our records show someone else in that room." She tilted her head. "Are you sure that's the right room?"

"Positive," Clark responded. "8127. Peter Chance." He had figured the Chinese surname that Johnny Chin used—Peter Chang—might give a desk clerk cause for concern if an Anglo like Clark waltzed up to the desk claiming to be that man. But he wanted Clarisse to figure out the "typo" on her own, making it more believable.

"C-h-a-n-c-e," he said slowly, his stomach flipping.

Suddenly a light came on in Clarisse's eyes, and Clark wanted to hug her. "I'll bet somebody just typed it in wrong," she said. "The guest's name is listed as Peter Chang." She nodded, and Clark nodded along to encourage her. "That's pretty close to Peter Chance."

"It's probably my handwriting," he said. "But you'd think they'd notice that I'm not a Chang."

Clarisse smiled and coded in a new card. "I'll change it in our records," she offered.

Clark thanked her, took the key, and strode casually away from the front desk. He was grateful she didn't notice the credit card securing the room was also under the name of Peter Chang. Though he had an excuse for that as well, he wasn't sure even Clarisse would buy that one.

Clark headed in the general direction of the casino floor and elevators. When he assumed Clarisse would be busy with the next patron, he took a left and exited through the revolving doors. Ten minutes later he was back wearing jeans, his Kevlar vest, a T-shirt, and a new khaki sports coat since his blue one was now stained with Bones McGinley's blood. He was dragging a large, black trunk behind him, using both hands, though it really wasn't that heavy. Yet.

He pulled the trunk through the atrium with its tropical rain forest decor, including palm trees, a sixty-foot waterfall, and a wooden bridge over a lagoon. People snapped photos and milled about, paying no attention to the man with the oversize luggage who probably had a clotheshorse for a wife. He snaked his way across the casino floor in order to reach the elevators strategically located on the other side of the sprawling gaming area. He envied the people mindlessly gambling their money away—their cares limited to the mundane things of life, their spouses holding their hands or standing beside them or tucked away safely by the pool. He nodded at the security guard as he reached the elevator area and rode the elevator to the eighth floor. Room 8127 was the first room on the right-hand side of the hallway. He glanced up and down the hall to confirm he was alone.

There were three possibilities. The best—Johnny Chin would not be in the room. Clark could hide out, wait for Chin to return, then jump him when he least expected it. A close second—Johnny Chin would be in the room sleeping. Under that scenario, Clark could sneak up on Johnny and take him without a fight. The worst—Johnny Chin would be in the room awake. *That* could get ugly.

Clark slid the key in the door and saw the green light flash. He cracked the door and listened. The television was on. He quietly pushed the door a few inches further and felt resistance from the small metal chain that Chin had slid in place for double-locked protection.

Chin was in the room.

Clark pulled out his gun, took a few steps back, lowered his shoulder, and thought about Jessica. He charged with all his might, crashed against the door, and felt the chain give way as the door flung open. Clark plunged into the room, doing a quick dive and roll, and came up in a crouched shooting position.

"What's going on out there?" he heard somebody shout from the bathroom.

Clark paused for a split second, heard the shower running, and smiled. He quickly grabbed the trunk and pulled it inside the room, closed the door, and burst into the bathroom.

He drew a bead on Johnny Chin. The hit man was naked and wide-eyed, standing in the shower with the curtain drawn to the side, water dripping from his body.

"You'd better dry off," Clark said.

Maybe his luck was beginning to change.

12

CLARK'S LUCKY STREAK was short-lived. Thirty minutes later, heading north toward the mountains on I-15, the frustration set in again. He needed complete privacy—someplace where he would not be disturbed as he did what had to be done. But the flat desert stretched before him on all sides like a giant stage, as if God himself was trying to prevent Clark's intended act against humanity.

Exhaustion and lack of sleep weakened every muscle in his body and frayed every nerve. He had knocked Chin out in the hotel room, bound and gagged him with FlexiCuffs and duct tape, then carted him out to the car in the black trunk. A few minutes after he left the parking garage, Clark called 911 and left an anonymous tip about Bones and Angel. The cops probably had an APB out on Clark by now, but they wouldn't know he was driving the Escalade.

Clark eventually took the exit for the Great Basin Highway and headed northwest. The barren mountains rose in the distance before him, but they seemed to back farther away with each passing mile. He was on a two-lane road now, flat stretches of asphalt that tapered into the horizon as far as the eye could see, bounded by the nothingness of desert sand, shrubs, and brown weeds.

He passed by the immense Silverhawk Power Plant on his left and then noticed some dirt paths for off-roading that wound toward the foothills. He took a left at the next set of tire marks, popped the Escalade into four-wheel drive, and climbed the small embankment up to the desert path. A bone-jarring mile and a half later, the path narrowed and curved around the backside of a major ridge that shielded the path from the highway. It was exactly the type of spot Clark had been looking for.

At the base of the ridge, a large flat area was pockmarked by the charred remains of campfires and littered with spent rifle shells and shotgun casings. An old heater and refrigerator riddled with bullet holes, a set of bedsprings, and hundreds of beer cans and plastic pails had doubled as targets. Clark stopped the vehicle and opened the back.

He hauled the trunk out, ignoring the muffled protests of Chin as he rolled the trunk across the rocky ground, coming to a stop next to the refrigerator. The thermometer on the Escalade had said the outdoor temperature was 102 degrees, but it felt even hotter. The sun radiated off the desert floor, sending waves of heat in every direction, turning the entire landscape into a blast furnace. Clark opened the trunk and pulled his captive out, removing the duct tape and sock gag but leaving his captive's wrists bound.

That's when the battle of wills started.

Chin was short, lean, and athletic, with square shoulders and trapezius muscles that stood out like steel cables. Both arms were covered in tattoos, and a tattoo of the sun peeked out from behind the white T-shirt Clark had forced Chin to put on in the hotel room. Chin wore jeans and no shoes, his dark eyes leaving no doubt that he would break Clark's neck with his bare hands if given half a chance. Chin's egg-shaped skull was clean-shaven, adding to a menacing look accentuated by black eyebrows that formed an inverted V above his eyes.

Clark started by offering money for Xu's whereabouts. After all, Chin was a hit man, a mercenary, and every mercenary had his price. But Chin scoffed at the notion, as if trading information for cash was somehow beneath his dignity. Next, Clark told Chin about Jessica and about Xu's threats to mutilate her. A sly smile was Chin's only response.

Such insolence! This cocky little jerk owed every breath he took to Clark's forbearance. How dare he mock Jessica's plight?

Clark held the gun to Chin's temple, counted slowly to ten as he stared into his captive's hardened eyes, and pulled the trigger.

The gun clicked, the sound of an empty chamber.

Chin never flinched.

"You *will* talk," Clark promised. He drove the butt of the gun into Chin's kidney, eliciting a groan as Chin fell to his side and curled into a fetal position. Clark kicked him hard in the gut, and Chin groaned again as he slid a few feet on the ground.

"This is no game," Clark snarled. "He's got my wife."

Clark leaned over and pulled Chin back to a sitting position, then knelt in front of the hit man.

"Don't make this hard on yourself," Clark pleaded. "I don't have any choice here. I'll go as far as I need to go."

Chin grimaced and caught his breath. He raised his eyes, told Clark where he could go, then spat in Clark's face.

Blood rushed like a torrent to Clark's head, detonating his fury like nitroglycerin. Chin became the symbol of everything that had happened to Jessica, the personification of the faceless men who held her. Clark raised his gun to pistol-whip Chin, anticipating the satisfying thud of metal on bone, then caught himself. He allowed the anger to dissipate for a moment, wiped the spit from his cheek, and slowly rose to his feet.

Anger would not make his captive talk. Nor would money or promises of freedom. Only pain might work. But it would have to be a calculated, unyielding pain, administered by someone totally in control, someone who would stop at nothing to get what he wanted. Chin would need to believe that Clark had the guts to do the unthinkable.

Only then might the steel will of Johnny Chin bend to Clark's demands.

But when the initial surge of anger passed, Clark didn't know if he had it in him to carry through. This was a human being on the ground at Clark's feet. How could Clark methodically torture someone, regardless of what he had done? Even if Clark could force himself to do it, the guilt would haunt him forever.

But then a second wave of guilt hit, more powerful than the first. They were probably torturing Jessica at this very moment. What kind of man wouldn't do this for his wife? Could he ever live with himself if he backed off now?

His watch gave him the last fiber of nerve he needed: 23:41:15.

He pulled the extra roll of duct tape out of the trunk, dragged Chin to the refrigerator, and taped him to it, wrapping the heavy-duty tape several times around Chin's body. For extra measure, he taped Chin's head to the refrigerator as well, running a strand across Chin's forehead and another strand securely across the man's neck.

In less than thirteen hours, Xu and his men would begin pulling Jessica's teeth, one at a time. Two could play this game.

"I'll be right back," Clark said, heading toward the Escalade. "I need a pair of pliers."

13

CLARK WAS NO EXPERT on torture, but this much he knew: it was the psychology, not the pain, that would break a man. Walking back to the car gave him time to cool down and put together a workable plan. He would explain each grizzly step of his plan to Chin and follow through without hesitation. If Chin saw Clark flinch even once, exposing weakness, it would steel his captive to remain silent.

Clark nearly hurled just thinking about what lay ahead. Though he worked hard to project a reputation as a heartless bail enforcer, in reality Clark couldn't even bring himself to hunt. He couldn't imagine skinning a deer he had shot down in cold blood. And now he was thinking about the best way to torture a fellow member of the human race.

Does love for Jessica justify torture? He struggled with the thought as he walked back to his prey, sickened by the job ahead. But he also knew he couldn't dwell on it. This was no Senate intelligence hearing—lawyers debating the ethics of torture under international law. Lives were at stake. *His wife's* life was at stake.

These men were evil. Clark would meet force with force.

He knelt in front of Johnny Chin again, inches from his face. The heat of a thousand demons breathed down Clark's back, egging him on. He checked his watch.

"In about twelve hours, they start torturing my wife," he said coldly. "In five minutes, I start torturing you." He searched Chin's eyes for even a sliver of fear. He found nothing.

He pulled out a file folder and Sharpie he had brought back from the Escalade. "Here's the plan," Clark continued calmly. "I'll start on the teeth. They're pulling four of Jessica's; I'll pull eight of yours."

He wrote two headings on his sheet, one labeled *Time* and the other labeled *Torture*. He filled in the first row with a 5 in the left column and *teeth* on the right.

"I'll give you ten minutes to recover. In fifteen minutes, I start on the fingernails and toenails, pulling them out one by one." He made two more notations on the chart: *15—denailing*.

Chin just stared ahead, focusing beyond Clark's shoulder.

"After that, we're done with the pliers." Clark gave him an icy smile. "Ten minutes after step two, I'll put my Glock on the backside of your knee and shoot out your kneecap. First one leg, then the other. I'm told this blows the kneecap completely off the leg, crippling a person for life. I guess we'll find out." He glanced at his watch. "Four minutes to starting time."

While Clark made another chart notation, he noticed a slight sheen of sweat forming on Chin's bald scalp. He prayed the man would crack.

"And if that doesn't slow you down, there's always hamstringing. That's when you slice right through the tendons on the back of the leg. I wouldn't be surprised if you've done that to your victims a time or two, so I won't even bother to describe how painful it is."

Clark made his final notation and mumbled, "Three minutes. If you're still conscious after step four, we'll think of our next procedure."

He stood and grabbed an old plastic pail, placing it a few feet in front of Chin. He taped the list to it. "Can you see that okay? I wouldn't want anybody to accuse me of ambushing you."

Clark looked down at his watch. "Two minutes," he announced, noticing that Chin had broken into a full-body sweat.

14

CLARK'S STOMACH ROILED as he moved toward Johnny Chin, pliers in his right hand, trying to look impassive. "Time's up," he said bluntly.

"I know nothing," Chin said defiantly. It was the same song he had sung earlier. "Those who hire me call on cell phones. The money gets wired from anonymous bank accounts. Why would they tell me where they live or work?"

He sounded more desperate than before, more sincere, but Clark still wasn't buying it. Chin had been arrested for RICO violations and skipped bail. Jessica's kidnapping had been carefully orchestrated by the mob and triggered when Clark had tried to apprehend Chin. The mob and Chin had to be working together.

Clark clamped down on Chin's sweaty scalp with his left hand, trying to hold his captive still. But Chin kept his mouth closed and jerked his head back and forth, small spastic movements limited by the duct tape holding his head in place, yet still enough to prevent Clark from grabbing a tooth with the pliers. They struggled for a moment before Clark slapped Chin hard across the cheek, stunning his captive. Chin gasped, and Clark latched onto a front tooth.

He squeezed the pliers with both hands and told himself to pry hard and fast. But he hesitated, relaxing his grip a hair, which allowed Chin to jerk free.

"I'm telling the truth," Chin stammered. "Why would I protect them?"

Frustrated, Clark stood, turned his back, and walked away, trying to get a little distance. He felt disoriented, like a medical student performing his first autopsy.

How can I do this? Does Chin really know anything?

Clark walked to the Escalade and placed his left palm on the hood, leaning there for a moment, the pliers dangling from his right hand. He took a few deep breaths, fueled his resolve, and returned to his victim. *This is for Jessica.*

He reached for Chin's head again, but the man jerked more violently than before, choppy movements limited by the constraints of the duct tape. Chin made it impossible to get a good grip with the pliers. He cursed at Clark, promising to kill him, protesting that he didn't know anything.

Clark stood. This wasn't working. It was too personal. Too sadistic. There had to be a better way to get this information.

As he thought about the next move, Clark felt a vibration in his right front pocket. *The cell phone from Xu.* His heart slammed to a stop, and he pulled the phone out quickly. It was a text message: **Twelve hours.**

Clark checked his watch and thought about how little progress he had made. Even if he could get Chin to talk, what did he know? Suddenly Clark noticed a picture attached to the message and clicked it open as well. A photograph of Jessica, a head shot from the shoulders up. They had shaved her head. The sight of it shocked him—the pale skin of her scalp, the gaunt eyes, the fear and humiliation of her expression. She had no clothes on as far as he could tell. The rage boiled over, consumed him, the cell phone trembling in his hand.

"How can they do this?" he cried.

He pulled out his gun and turned on Chin, holding the cell phone in front of Chin's face. "This is my wife!" he screamed. "You see this! You did this!"

This time Chin's eyes went wide, his lips quivering. "I don't know anything, man," he said, more adamant than before. "What they did—it's not right. But I don't know anything about it."

"You're lying!" Clark shouted. He pressed the point of the gun against Chin's kneecap.

"I don't know anything! I've never even met your wife, man!"

"You're lying!" Clark repeated. He hesitated and gave Chin one last chance—a pleading look into the hit man's eyes. *Don't make me do this.*

"I don't know where they're at," Chin repeated, but Clark chose not to believe him. This man *did* know. He *had to know*, or Clark was nowhere. This criminal, this man who killed others for money without thinking twice about them or their families, had to know precisely where Jessica was this very moment. Getting her head shaved. Being humiliated and prepared for torture as if she were some kind of lab specimen.

Clark tried not to dwell on what she might be going through, but the images kept popping into his head. He had purposefully *not* allowed his thoughts to go there before, but now his mind raced heedlessly ahead, considering the possibilities. Her shoulders were bare. Was that something they had done just for effect, knowing it would drive him crazy? Or was it a more sinister signal? How far had they gone—a defenseless woman held captive by remorseless men with twisted minds?

What if, God forbid, they have already raped her?

He turned his attention back to Chin. This man was one of them! This man *had to know*.

Enraged, Clark pulled the trigger.

15

JOHNNY CHIN HAD LIED. He confessed as Clark counted down to zero with his gun pointed at Chin's *other* kneecap. Writhing in pain, Chin admitted that he knew the cell phone numbers and the names of the leaders in Xu's organization. He begged Clark not to shoot again, swearing that he didn't know where Huang Xu was holding Jessica. But he could give Clark the cell phone numbers and an account number from a bank that had wired him money for the last job he completed for the Chinese mafia.

"These men are shadows," Chin gasped, the pain and fear creasing his brow. "They don't ever show their faces."

Convinced, Clark put the Glock back in its holster. He didn't have the nerve to use it again anyway. He loaded Chin into the passenger seat of the Escalade, fastened the seat belt, and duct-taped Chin's mouth, muzzling the hit man's moaning and cursing. As he drove back toward the city limits, Clark felt guilty, watching Chin squirm in an effort to decrease the pain, using his bound hands to support his wounded leg as much as possible, emitting muffled groans of agony every time he moved. The hit man was pale and looked like he might pass out at any moment.

Clark hardly trusted his own judgment now. He was beyond tired, his neck aching from the tranquilizer injection, or possibly from being thrown against the wall by Mortavius Johnson, or possibly from the head butt he had given Bones McGinley. He had a splitting headache. And he had that jittery feeling that comes from no sleep, no food, and too much caffeine. He was like a college student pulling all-nighters during exam week, living on energy drinks and coffee, his stomach churning up acid.

And he had just finished torturing another human being.

He needed to concentrate. His stopwatch now registered 24:17:12. He could send out another notice to bounty hunters listing the two new names of triad leaders Chin had provided—Li Gwah and Victor Chi. Given time, his network might locate one of them. But he didn't have that kind of time. Complicating matters, Chin's cell phone, containing the phone numbers of the leaders, and the bank account information were still in Chin's hotel room. *How could I have left that cell phone behind?*

Clark knew he was out of options. Xu had warned him that bringing in the authorities would cost Jessica her life. But Clark had no chance of rescuing her alone. He still didn't know where Professor Kumari was hiding. Or even if the professor was still alive. Or where Jessica might be. What little information he could gain from going back to Chin's room—cell phone numbers and bank account information—was useless without the feds. The FBI could call the cell phones and triangulate the locations. They could get a warrant for the banking information. But that, too, took time.

Still, it was his only hope.

The small matter of Clark's own desperate crime spree also suggested that calling the feds might not be a bad idea. So far, he had been involved in kidnapping, malicious wounding, forging a driver's license, theft of an automobile, and probably a few more violations that he couldn't remember. If he went to the feds first, explaining the entire mess, he might be able to trade cooperation for immunity.

Might being the key word.

He dialed the U.S. attorney's office for the district of Nevada. After a few minutes of getting shuffled around from one staff person to another, he finally reached an assistant U.S. attorney.

"My wife's been kidnapped by the Chinese mafia," Clark began.

"Who is this?" the attorney interrupted.

"Just listen," Clark said, his voice testy. "In less than twelve hours they begin torturing her. They've told me if I contact you, they'll kill her."

Chin moaned loudly into his duct tape. Clark glared at him, but Chin only increased the volume.

"They're demanding that I find and kidnap another person and trade him for my wife." Clark switched the phone to his left ear and made a chopping motion with his right hand.

Chin ignored him again and kept moaning.

"I need your name. Your wife's name. And the names of the persons who kidnapped her." The attorney sounded calm, methodical.

"Will you grant me immunity?" Clark asked.

"Immunity for what? What crimes have you committed? Federal or state? How serious are they? What are you offering in return?"

This was getting too complicated to handle over the phone. And Chin, who suddenly seemed to have a second wind, wasn't making things any easier with his defiant moaning.

"Do you know where the side entrance is for the Mirage?" Clark asked the attorney.

"Yes."

"Be waiting there in your vehicle in exactly twenty minutes. You might want to bring an FBI agent." He paused for a beat and glanced at Chin, who quieted down a little, his eyes glazing over. "And have an ambulance waiting nearby. I'll need your cell number and your name."

The attorney sighed. "My name is Magdalena Sorensen. But this isn't the movies, sir. In real life, you come to our offices and talk with me here. If you'd like, I can have my assistant give you directions."

"No, wait. Listen, they've kidnapped my wife." Clark raised his voice, trying to make this woman understand. "If they see me walk into your office, they'll kill her."

"Who are you talking about? And what is *your* name?"

Clark shook his head in frustration. "I can't tell you that on the phone."

"Then I can't help you."

Clark blew out a breath. "Wait!" *What choice do I have?* "My name is Clark Shealy. And there's probably a state warrant out for my arrest already." He paused for a beat.

"I'm listening," Magdalena said.

◁▷

Five minutes after hanging up with Magdalena, Clark's cell buzzed with a number he didn't recognize. His stomach clenched as he answered.

"Clark Shealy."

"My name is Dennis Hargrove." The name meant nothing to Clark. "You looking for a Indian man named Moses Kumari?"

Clark's heart leaped to his throat. When he spoke, he barely recognized his own breathless voice. "Yes. Do you know where he is?"

"As I understand it, Mr. Shealy, you're offering a sizable reward."

"A million dollars. Where is he?"

"In the backseat of my car."

16

CASH FLOW. Being a bounty hunter was not about manhandling bad guys the way Dog the Bounty Hunter did on A&E. It's about cash flow. Cash greased the palms of the bounty hunter's stringers and inside sources at "partner" companies—banks, the DMV, plastic surgeons, casino security guards. Cash kept the cops from throwing your sorry carcass in jail when you overstepped your bounds on a pickup. If you got busted by a clean cop, cash posted the bond to bail you out that same night. Cash paid the overhead. Cash made the bounty hunter's world go round.

For that reason, Clark had his banker on speed dial.

He called Harry and swore the man to secrecy before explaining what happened to Jessica.

"Did you call the police?" Harry asked. He had the instincts of a banker—play it safe; trust authority.

"I called the U.S. attorney, and I'm sure she called the FBI. They're on it. But in the meantime, I'm going to need as much cash as I can get my hands on. Liquidate everything I've got, increase the credit line, and consolidate it all in one account. I'll need at least three hundred thousand."

Clark's request was met with silence by Harry. Even Chin had calmed down and was now barely conscious, staring straight ahead and emitting pitiful little groans only occasionally.

"Harry, we're talking about my wife here. You want it on your head if something happens to Jessica?"

"That's not fair, Clark." Harry hesitated as if hoping that Clark might apologize for going too far. Clark waited him out. "I'll see what I can do," Harry promised.

"You can't let me down on this one, Harry. I'll pay back every penny. You know that."

"I'll try, Clark."

"You've got to do better than try."

"Call me back in an hour."

"Oh. And one other thing. If you get a check presented for a hundred and fifty thousand from an outfit named Quad-A Bail Bond Office, don't pay it."

"You mind telling me why?"

"You don't wanna know."

Next, Clark called the company that had posted bail for Johnny Chin and told them he had Chin in custody. "I need the money wired into my account immediately," Clark said.

"We'll pay you at his next court appearance, Mr. Shealy. That's the way it works."

"I need an advance."

"We're a bonding company, not a bank."

Clark demanded to talk with Mr. Russo, the owner of the company. Clark explained to Russo that he had blown out Chin's kneecap. "If I turn him over to the authorities, it could be trouble," Clark explained. "Lots of questions about reasonable force, how much Chin resisted— you know the routine.

"If I just let him go, it would take care of a big headache for me," Clark continued, "though you might stand to lose one and a half million if somebody else doesn't pick him up."

By the end of the phone call, Russo Bonding Company had agreed to wire half the bounty—seventy-five thousand—as a refundable deposit for capturing Chin. Clark still wasn't close to a million, but he had quickly accumulated enough money to at least entice Hargrove into a meeting. Even if Harry the banker didn't come through with the three hundred thousand Clark had requested, Clark would have enough money to get his foot in the door. Brute force or a loaded Glock should do the rest.

In the passenger seat, Chin's breathing had become more irregular and strained. He gagged a few times and fell silent. Clark immediately pulled over, checked for a pulse, and removed Chin's gag. The hit man was alive and breathing, but he was out cold.

Clark pulled back onto the highway and drove like a madman, powering the Caddy through turns and around Vegas traffic. With one eye on the road, Clark reached over and programmed the GPS system for the nearest hospital.

He would dump his captive off at the emergency room exit, flash a badge, explain that Chin had violated his bond, and tell the hospital security guard to keep an eye on Chin until the feds arrived. Clark would immediately call Magdalena and tell her there had been a change in plans. She could pick Chin up at the hospital. But Clark wouldn't stick around to meet with her—rescuing Jessica would be a one-man show once again. The feds would only mess things up, panic Huang Xu, and maybe get Jessica killed.

Clark couldn't afford to get bogged down in hours of questioning and mind-numbing federal procedures right now. He had turned to the feds as a last resort. But with the call from Hargrove, everything had changed. Kumari was in the backseat of Hargrove's car less than forty-five minutes away.

When he called, Hargrove had demanded that Clark wire a million into Hargrove's account before they met. But Clark had calmly refused. "You don't get a penny until I confirm that it's Kumari," he said. "Standard operating procedure."

Reluctantly, Hargrove agreed. He selected the turf—a paved parking lot across the street from the Green Valley Ranch Casino, an upscale resort in Henderson.

Time still ticked by unmercifully fast, but Clark suddenly felt energized. This wasn't the caffeine-laced fear he had been living on for the last twenty-four hours; it was something more substantial now. Adrenaline. And a twinge of hope. He wasn't in control—far from it—but he had drawn a few aces.

Yet he still needed a few more. His stopwatch read 24:47:36. And the minutes continued to disappear, as if on fire.

17

WAITING WAS NEVER Clark's strong suit. But now, with every second potentially meaning the difference between torture or release for Jessica, he was going insane. He sat in the driver's seat of the Cadillac, engine running, his loaded gun next to him. His leg bounced with nervous energy.

He was parked in the lot across the street from the Green Valley Ranch Casino, just as Hargrove had instructed. From the northwest corner of the lot, he could still see the city of Las Vegas, its skyline barely visible on the hazy horizon. It was a desolate corner—no other cars parked this far away from the resort. Clark had backed the Escalade into an outside spot next to the green plastic fence that bordered the parking lot, separating it from construction taking place on the adjacent dirt site. On the far side of that site, perhaps a hundred and fifty yards or so from Clark's vehicle, construction workers were pouring concrete.

Clark looked out over the black asphalt, the heat scorching its surface. He kept his eyes peeled for Hargrove. He called the man four times in ten minutes, listening to the same frustrating message every time. A generic female voice, repeating the number Clark had dialed, instructed him to leave a message at the tone.

The fourth time he cursed loudly and demanded that Hargrove call him back. "You're ten minutes late, and I don't *have* ten minutes! Pick up the phone!" He punched the End button and felt the frustration pounding in his temples. Hargrove had no idea how precious each second had become. The cost of Jessica's life could be measured now in hours, even minutes. Running late could result in her torture—the marring of her perfect features. Yet here he sat. Helpless. Frustrated. Furious.

In the fifty-five minutes since speaking to Hargrove, Clark had gone from elated to something just short of despondent. Even if Hargrove did have Professor Kumari, there were still a thousand unanswered questions. What would Hargrove do when he learned that Clark had only a few hundred thousand dollars rather than the million he had promised? And even if Clark gained custody of Kumari, how would he work the prisoner exchange to ensure Jessica's safety? He was, after all, dealing with the mob. And finally, if all of those issues could be solved, what would keep the mob from killing Jessica and Clark when they least expected it? Or keep the feds and local authorities from prosecuting Clark for what he'd already done?

He had a bad premonition about the next twelve hours. This was not going to end well. How could it? There were simply too many things that could still go wrong.

One step at a time, Clark reminded himself. His predicament was too complicated for a master plan. In some respects, he had already made more progress in twenty-four hours than he ever dreamed possible. Maybe somebody up there was looking out for him. Maybe somebody up there owed Jessica a favor.

The phone rang. Hargrove's number.

"It's about time."

"I'm pulling into the lot now, the white Explorer."

Clark waited a few seconds until the vehicle came into view. "I see you."

Hargrove backed into a spot about three rows away, toward the middle of the parking lot, facing Clark and the black Cadillac. The sun ricocheted off the Explorer's front windshield, turning the glass into a mirror.

"There's no warrant outstanding for Kumari," Hargrove said on the phone. "I checked."

"It's all legit," Clark answered. He tried to sound relaxed. Hargrove hadn't raised this issue earlier, and Clark couldn't afford to let him panic now. "He's an illegal. The Indian government wants him back, and they're willing to pay." Clark carefully slid the Glock into his shoulder holster, hidden by the khaki sports coat he had put on once he arrived at the lot.

"A million dollars to extradite an illegal? Don't play games with me." Hargrove paused, and Clark tried to size him up just from the voice. He sounded young. Insecure. Articulate but tense. "I'm about two seconds from pulling out of here and taking Kumari with me," Hargrove continued. "But first, I'll give you one more chance to level with me."

"All right," Clark said reassuringly. His stomach had balled into a tense knot. He stepped slowly out of the Caddy, phone to his ear. "But it's sensitive. I can't talk about it on the phone."

"Not one more step!"

Clark froze. He hadn't even closed his door yet. "I just want to see Kumari. I'll bring my checkbook."

"Take off your sports coat and shirt," Hargrove snapped, "and put them in the vehicle."

Keeping his eyes glued on the Explorer, Clark placed the cell phone on the hood of the Caddy and hit the Speaker button. He glanced quickly around the parking lot and then removed his sports coat, exposing his shoulder holster and the Glock.

"The gun, too," Hargrove said.

Clark placed holster and gun inside the vehicle and took off his short-sleeved oxford shirt. "A Kevlar vest?" Hargrove sniffed arrogantly. "You planning on going into battle?"

Silently, Clark removed the vest and threw it into the vehicle.

"Now the socks and boots. And roll the pants up to the knees."

Clark complied once again, placing his boots and socks in the car. The black pavement scorched the soles of his feet.

"Turn your pockets inside out."

"This is ridiculous," Clark said, emptying his pockets.

"Now, close the door and turn around once so I can see your back."

"I've got another cell phone in the car that I've got to bring with me," Clark said loud enough to be picked up by his phone sitting on the hood. "Somebody's kidnapped my wife, and they use that phone to call me."

There was silence for a moment as if Hargrove was trying to make up his mind. "Okay. Get the other phone. Then close the door and do a three-sixty."

Clark complied, hooking the kidnapper's cell phone on his belt as he picked up his own. He shifted from one foot to the next, heel to toe. He turned completely around. He stood in the shadow from the Escalade, but the pavement still felt like a bed of hot coals.

"Step into my office," Hargrove said and hung up the phone.

18

DENNIS HARGROVE looked more like a stockbroker than a bounty hunter. He had wavy black hair, moussed and slicked back, matched by long sideburns that tapered into thin lines, meeting at the chin. He had a slender nose and sharp brown eyes that radiated nervous energy. Thin, bronze, and midthirties, Hargrove gave the impression of a guy who worked the casinos all night and spent his days at the pool or in the gym or maybe a little of both.

He wouldn't have seemed nearly as intimidating without the gun he had leveled at Clark's midsection.

"You roughed him up pretty good," Clark said, nodding toward the man in the backseat. In real life, Kumari looked more thin and frail than he appeared in the photos. He had a flat face with worry lines that spiderwebbed away from the eyes, others etched deep into his forehead. He sported a three-day stubble and his left eye had a large gash above the eyebrow, while the eye itself had turned a nasty shade of purple and was nearly swollen shut. There was a smaller bruise on his right cheek, and he had a swollen lip. Hargrove had taped the old man's ankles and wrists, wrenching his arms behind his back. To Clark, the professor looked like a malnourished POW.

"Thought he might know martial arts, so I didn't take any chances."

"Yeah, he looks real dangerous," Clark said.

"You said alive. Check his pulse if you want."

Clark studied Hargrove for a beat, confirming Clark's earlier assessment. Hargrove seemed scared—insecure, yet still resolute. Nervous. Trigger-happy. The worst kind. "Why don't you put that gun down so we can talk?" Clark asked.

Hargrove handed Clark a sheet of paper. "Money talks," he said. "Here're the wiring instructions."

Not so fast. "Where'd you find him?" Clark asked.

Hargrove hesitated as if deciding whether answering the question might reveal too much. "I'm a niche player for several Vegas bond enforcers. I have connections with the folks who manufacture false IDs. Mr. Kumari here apparently decided to become Charan Jadhav. Once we found that out, the rest was easy."

Clark noticed a nervous twitch in Hargrove's right eye. He had probably never been this close to a million bucks before. "What bail bondsman are you working with?" Clark asked.

Hargrove flinched like a junior high student caught cheating. "I'm on my own."

In other words, for a million bucks, I'm cutting out my partner.

"You licensed?" Clark asked.

"Enough questions. Call the bank." Hargrove inched the gun closer to Clark's gut.

"I can wire a quarter of a million right now," Clark explained matter-of-factly. He made it sound like buying a loaf of bread. "But I'll need to personally go in and handle the rest."

"What does that mean?" Hargrove's face clouded over, his eyes narrow. "You don't have the money?"

"I've got it. I just need to liquidate a few stocks."

"You should have done that before you made the offer." Hargrove put both hands on the gun and waved it toward the car door. "Get out."

Clark swallowed hard and took a deep breath. Hargrove was strung tight as a piano wire—the high notes—and Clark didn't want to set him off. "I need to tell you a few things first." He nodded toward Kumari. "Can we step outside and talk?"

"He doesn't speak English."

"How do you know?"

"I pistol-whipped him. He begged me to stop in some other language. Must have been Hindi or something."

Without waiting for permission, Clark launched into an abbreviated explanation of everything that had happened since his visit to

Dr. Silvoso's plastic surgery office. Even as Clark recited the facts, they seemed surreal, and Clark found himself getting emotional as he talked about what he had done to get Jessica back. He left out irrelevant details, like his torture of Johnny Chin, and he embellished a few of the financial particulars to make it sound like he could come up with a million bucks in no time. But otherwise, it was an accurate and painful portrayal of how desperate Clark had become. At first, he intentionally dramatized it a little—selling his point. But by the end, the raw emotions had surfaced, and Clark couldn't even finish.

There was a long silence as Hargrove considered his options. "Give me the phone," he said.

Puzzled, Clark handed over his cell phone.

"Not that one."

Clark put his hand over the other cell—the one given him by the kidnappers. It was his only link to Jessica and now Hargrove wanted it. There could only be one reason.

"Nobody calls them but me."

Hargrove tensed. He raised the gun and aimed it at Clark's temple. "You've got a sad story," he said. "But I've got a sad story, too. I lied to you about working alone. I've got a bail bondsman expecting two-fifty of my cut. I've got a company that specializes in false IDs and breaking bones for past-due accounts expecting another two-fifty. A quarter of a million doesn't even cover my expenses." Hargrove was talking fast, his voice tense. "I'm sorry about your wife, man, but that's not my problem."

Clark *couldn't* let him have the phone. The last call had cost Clark twelve precious hours. "Nobody calls them but me," he repeated.

"Listen, pal, you're not making the rules anymore. I'll call them and tell them I'm holding you at gunpoint and I've got Kumari as well. If they're willing to kidnap your wife in exchange for a chance at finding this guy, they'll cough up a million. You get your wife back; I get paid."

"That's insane." Clark shuddered at the thought of Hargrove bargaining with Xu. Jessica's captors would start the torture immediately. Clark's mind flashed to Johnny Chin—the look of stark primal pain after Clark shot out his kneecap. The fear in Chin's eyes when Clark threatened him again. He *couldn't* let Jessica go through something like that.

"Give me the phone!" Hargrove pressed the gun against Clark's temple. Thoughts of Jessica flashed through Clark's mind like a movie on fast-forward. Jessica on the trampoline. Jessica with heavy eyelids in the morning. Jessica with tears streaming down her face the day of the miscarriage. Jessica. Jessica. Jessica. He would die before he handed over the phone.

"If I have to kill you, it only makes my bargaining position stronger," Hargrove said. His voice sounded mechanical, disembodied. "Think about it. They'll know I couldn't care less about your wife. Their leverage will be gone. I could probably get two million."

"You're going to kill me in this parking lot in broad daylight?"

"No. You're going to give me the phone."

A loud moan from the backseat momentarily distracted them both. Kumari cried out in Hindi, then flopped on the seat, his mouth open, gasping for air, a fish out of water. His eyes seemed to pop out of their sockets.

"It's a heart attack!" Clark ignored the gun at his temple and jumped out of the vehicle. He threw open the back door and leaned in, quickly twisting Kumari's body around so he lay supine on the seat. This man—*alive*—was Clark's only connection to Jessica! Kumari's eyes rolled back in his head. He stopped gasping for air. His body went limp.

I can't lose him!

"Call 911!" Clark shouted. He climbed into the backseat and covered Kumari's mouth with his own lips, ignoring the taste of salty perspiration and the feel of the old man's stubble. He pressed down tight to create a seal. He pinched Kumari's nose and desperately pumped a few short breaths into the dying man. He placed both hands on Kumari's chest and applied pressure. He felt the fragile chest compress and expand. He did it twice more.

"Don't you dare die on me!" Clark gasped. But Kumari just lay there, limp. Clark tilted Kumari's head back, pinched Kumari's nose, and blew in a few more breaths, praying for a miracle. He would gladly swallow the old man's vomit if Kumari would just breathe again.

"Call 911!" Clark shouted again, pumping in another breath. "If he dies, we both lose everything."

Clark pushed once more on the old man's chest, but Kumari still didn't respond. Clark pushed again . . . harder. He checked quickly for a pulse and thought he felt something. He placed his ear next to Kumari's mouth.

It seemed like he felt a breath. *Wishful thinking?* Hope surged through him. He blew two more breaths into Kumari and listened again.

Clark's own heart nearly stopped at what he heard.

19

CLARK TRIED TO CONTROL his shock, though the words had stunned him. He needed a second to react, so he blew another few breaths into Kumari's mouth and continued pumping his chest, though not as forcefully as before.

"I can't call 911!" Hargrove cried. "Look at him!" Hargrove had twisted in his seat and gawked at the sight before him, the gun still in his right hand.

Clark checked Kumari again for breathing. This time, the words were unmistakable.

"Grab the gun," the old man whispered. In English. Plain English, with perfect diction.

"Okay, okay," Clark huffed as if responding to Hargrove's comments.

Clark had climbed fully inside the Explorer, kneeling in the leg space of the backseat. He placed his hands on Kumari's chest and stole a quick glance at Hargrove. Clark would have one chance to make this work.

He blew a few more breaths into Kumari's mouth. This time, the old man's breath seemed more pungent. Or maybe Clark just noticed it more, knowing Kumari would be okay. He knelt again and pushed down twice on Kumari's chest.

He recalled the instructions of a bounty hunter colleague who hung out on the more-violent side of the profession. Make the first blow count. Drive the heel of your hand into the tip of the nose with all your might, forcing the bridge of the nose up into the skull. With the right amount of impact, the blow would disable. If the angle was right, it could kill.

Clark didn't want Hargrove dead, but the man had a gun. Jessica's life hung in the balance. Clark had already tortured for Jessica, lied for Jessica, defrauded people for Jessica. If he had to kill for her, this was no time to hold back. He could sort it all out later.

He would twist and, with his left hand, grab the wrist of Hargrove's gun hand, pushing the gun away. Simultaneously, Clark would use his right hand to land the debilitating blow, driving Hargrove's nose out the back of his skull if he had to.

He took a quick breath, the calm before the hurricane. *This one's for you, Jess.*

He twisted and grabbed for Hargrove's gun hand but didn't get a good grip. The bullet whistled by Clark, shattering the back window. In the same instant, Clark drove the heel of his right hand into the tip of Hargrove's nose, pulling back a little at the last possible moment, almost involuntarily, his instincts somehow keeping him from landing the blow with all his pent-up fury. Still, he heard the crunch of collapsing bone and saw Hargrove's eyes roll up in shock. Clark grabbed the gun.

Hargrove buried his face in both hands and slumped in the front seat. Blood flowed in a stream from his hands, down his forearms to his elbows, dripping on the seat. Another rivulet dripped from his chin. He made small gurgling noises, his eyes vacant.

What kind of animal have I become?

Clumsily, with his wrists still taped together behind his back, Kumari scrambled to an upright position in the backseat. "Maybe *you* should call 911," he suggested.

Clark grabbed his cell phone from the front seat. Hargrove pulled his hands away from his face for an instant, and Clark gaped in horror at the damage he had done. Hargrove's nose was nearly collapsed; it protruded only slightly from his face, skewed to the left side. Blood poured from the nostrils.

"Don't let him die," Clark said to nobody in particular. Hargrove stared back in shock. He was losing consciousness fast.

The adrenaline rush that fueled Clark's attack gave way to pity. He called 911 and gave the operator directions to the site. Next, he stuffed the cell phones in his pocket and flung Kumari over his shoulder. The old man wasn't that heavy, maybe a hundred forty pounds max, but still, he could have made things a lot more difficult by resisting.

Clark half jogged, half walked to the Caddy and threw Kumari in the passenger seat. Construction on the adjacent site had stopped as the men turned and stared at the strange scene. A few of them were on cell phones. Clark hopped in the driver's seat, fired up the engine, and beat it toward the parking lot entrance. Kumari had his eyes closed, his lips forming silent words.

"What are you doing?" Clark asked. He careened around a row of cars, throwing Kumari onto his side in the middle of the front seat.

"I was praying," he said.

"For what?"

"Dennis Hargrove, the man you nearly killed."

Clark focused on the road ahead of him as he exited the parking lot and sped past the casino. At Green Valley Parkway he took a right, away from the interstate and the sound of distant sirens. "If you wouldn't mind, say one for Jessica, too."

20

AFTER TWO BLOCKS of glancing in his rearview mirror, Clark took a right into a quiet residential area. He zigzagged down a few streets, keeping a constant watch on the road behind him. The police would soon have a description of his vehicle. He had nearly killed two men today and defrauded a third. He had alerted the U.S. attorney's office to a kidnapping scheme involving the mob and had then fled Las Vegas. Everyone would be looking for him—the feds, the locals, the mob.

He felt like a cornered fox with the hounds baying at his heels, the red-coated aristocratic hunters on their galloping steeds in pursuit. Or maybe, more accurately, like a rat in a maze. He turned left, then right, then left again at the next stop sign. He had no idea where he was going. He needed time and space to figure out his next move. But his frazzled mind was misfiring, the neurons short-circuited by pure exhaustion and fear about what was happening to Jessica.

"Why did you help me back there?" he asked Kumari.

"You, my friend, were the lesser of two evils," Kumari responded softly. "Within minutes of Mr. Hargrove's telephone call to these kidnappers, they would have murdered your wife and overtaken us."

A fist of anxiety squeezed Clark's heart, wringing out any confidence gained from this most recent getaway. Something about the way Kumari said it, as if it were a foregone conclusion, made it more real.

"Two lives would most assuredly have been lost. Mr. Hargrove did not have—what would you say?—the street smarts to deal with the triads. I decided to take my chances with you."

Clark made a mental note about Kumari's assumption that the

triads were involved. When Clark had recited his story to Hargrove in the Explorer, he intentionally chose not to mention the possibility that the Chinese mafia was behind this.

Clark surveyed each street, looking for just the right vehicle. "How can you be so sure they would have overtaken us?" he asked. "And who do you think 'they' are, anyway?"

At this Kumari seemed to nod a little, as if a slow student forced to stay after school was finally asking the right questions. "I have two questions, Mr. . . ." Kumari paused, and Clark had the feeling he would have extended a hand if both hands weren't taped behind his back. "I don't believe I have your name."

"Doe. John Doe."

This generated a polite smile from the professor, swollen lip and all. "Yes, of course, Mr. Doe. I believe my first abductor may have called you Shealy during the phone call, but he was probably mistaken.

"In any event, the answer to your first question is contained in the cell phone the triad gave to you. Unless I am mistaken, that phone will have an LBS system built into it. Such a system, if I am correct, works in the same way as the Global Positioning System that keeps car navigational systems on course. That phone, Mr. Doe, is your electronic leash. As soon as you call the triad and tell them you have located me, they jerk your leash and reel you in."

Goose bumps formed on the back of Clark's neck. In the chaos of locating and gaining custody of Kumari, he had forgotten that the mob would be tracking his every movement.

"Second, I have a history with this group of men who abducted your wife. They will do whatever it takes to get what they want. Human life means nothing to them."

They were now in the heart of a quiet, residential neighborhood with its small, one-story adobe homes on neat little postage-stamp lots. Each house had a few trimmed shrubs in the otherwise-barren patch of desert that comprised the front yard. It was too hot for anyone to be outside, except for a single older man about a hundred yards away, sweeping the sidewalk leading up to his house.

Clark pulled over to the curb a few feet behind a gray Durango, one of the few SUVs he had seen in the last several blocks. He programmed the Escalade's GPS system and wrote down directions to the interstate. He checked the rearview mirror and did a quick three-sixty of the neighborhood.

Clark quickly pulled on his Kevlar vest, T-shirt, socks, and shoes. He fastened the shoulder holster in place and holstered the Glock. He struggled as he twisted into his sports coat in the driver's seat, pain shooting through his sore neck.

"Would you like my advice?" Kumari asked.

"Not particularly."

Clark jumped out of the Escalade and hustled to Kumari's side. After another quick look around, confirming that the old man sweeping his sidewalk was not watching, Clark pulled Kumari out of the front seat and stuffed him into the backseat. Using plastic handcuffs, he linked one of Kumari's taped wrists to the inside door handle. "Just in case you had any ideas of reaching the horn," Clark explained.

As Clark pulled some tools out of the cargo space, a car drove quickly past. The driver and passenger were two young women, both wearing sunglasses, probably in their twenties. Hardly the mob profile.

Clark grabbed his slim-jim, a knife, and a pair of pliers. It took him less than five minutes to hot-wire the Durango. The man down the road finished sweeping his sidewalk and went inside his house. Clark transferred his tools, his prisoner, and his directions. As Kumari settled back in the passenger seat, he gave Clark a worried, quizzical look.

"Are you a professional thief?" the professor asked.

"I don't know where you got that idea," Clark said, pulling away from the curb.

Clark tried to ignore the stares of the professor as he followed the directions back toward the main road. "*What?*" he finally asked, exasperated.

"You kept the cell phone," Kumari noted.

"I'm going to call them with it."

"Write down their number and use your other phone. Discard the leash."

"I can't risk that. They might take it out on Jessica."

"If you keep the phone, they will know where to find you. When they locate you, what is your plan?"

Who knows? Clark hadn't gotten that far yet. He was following a make-it-up-as-you-go plan. "I guess I'll put a gun to your head and demand that they free Jessica before I give you up."

Kumari didn't flinch, as if this were all just one huge math problem. "What if they do not bring Jessica?"

"I'll figure that out when the time comes."

"What if the triad shoots you, takes me, and kills Jessica?"

"That would be a very bad day."

"Maybe I should have taken my chances with Mr. Hargrove."

Clark ignored the comment and turned left onto Green Valley Parkway, conscious that the area was crawling with the Henderson police force and possibly a few triad members as well. He had placed the mob's cell phone in the center console, where it now seemed to pump out evil sound waves like the throb of a telltale heart, revealing Clark's every turn. Until he called them, they probably wouldn't know that he had found Kumari. But once he told them he had the professor . . .

"Let us assume something for the sake of an illustration," Kumari said. "Let us assume the triad brings your wife—I believe you say her name is Jessica—to a place you select for an exchange of prisoners, so to speak. How, Mr. Doe, do you and Jessica escape alive? Even if you put a gun to my head, as you say, once I become a prisoner of the triad, what prevents them from shooting you and Mrs. Doe?"

"I haven't figured that out yet, but improvising is my strong point."

"Improvising?" The professor shifted in the front seat so he was facing more toward Clark. For a moment, Clark thought he didn't recognize the word. Turns out it was the concept Kumari was struggling with. "With foes like Huang Xu," the professor said, "we need a plan."

Clark checked the mirrors. He saw at least three dark sedans, possibly full of murderous Chinese mobsters. Possibly full of federal agents. Possibly full of Vegas vacationers. The pressure was making him crazy. "With respect, Professor, so far your advance planning has not exactly paid off."

"You have a point," the professor said softly.

Something about the answer made the professor seem more like an ally than an adversary. Maybe it was the matter-of-fact way the man acknowledged his failures. Or possibly Clark felt like he owed Kumari because the professor had helped him earlier. More likely it was the small man's quiet dignity, the humble way he accepted these circumstances yet still maintained the voice of gentle authority.

Or maybe Clark had no other choice.

"What do *you* suggest, Professor?"

Kumari closed his eyes and took a deep breath, like Yoda in *Star Wars* preparing to offer profound insights about the Force. "Pull into the McDonald's parking lot up there on the right. Next to the Dumpster. We start by throwing away the triad cell phone. Afterward, we head to my apartment. I have some tools there that may help level the playing field, as you say."

"That cell phone has Huang Xu's number. It's the phone he told me to use." And for Clark, it was also something more. He had heard Jessica's voice on that phone—the last fragile strand connecting them. He dreaded to think what Xu's reaction might be if he threw it out.

"If you want to rescue your wife, Mr. Shealy, you must change how you think. You must begin first by trusting me. Also, you must take charge with Huang Xu. No longer should you blindly follow what your wife's captors have suggested. With me, you now have what *they* want. *You* should issue the orders, not Huang Xu."

Clark thought about this for a moment. Kumari had gone from calling him *Doe* to *Shealy*, undoubtedly the old man's way of signaling a new partnership, a willingness to work together. But Clark hadn't made his reputation as a bounty hunter by trusting others. He lived by the law of the jungle. And the very first precept of that law was to trust nobody. He wouldn't be in this spot to begin with if he had applied the law of the jungle to Dr. Anthony Silvoso.

He drove past the McDonald's and noticed Kumari slouch a little lower in the seat. "Do it your way, Mr. Shealy."

Two blocks later, Clark pulled into a Wendy's parking lot and stopped next to its Dumpster. He recorded Huang Xu's phone number and stepped out of the car. He tossed the phone into the Dumpster, listening as it clanged against the far wall before it nestled among the food scraps and debris. The stench of garbage drifted over the car roof.

It smelled like Clark felt.

When Clark climbed back into the car, Kumari gave him a satisfied nod. "Would you like to hear the rest of my plan, Mr. Shealy?"

Until he had actually captured Kumari, Clark hadn't thought twice about the ethics of exchanging Kumari for Jessica. The only question had been how to do it.

But now, with the realization that Kumari might actually be a good and decent human being, shame joined the other emotions wreaking havoc with Clark's tired psyche. He would still trade this man's life for Jessica's if he had no other choice. But if he had an alternative?

"What have I got to lose?" Clark asked as he pulled away from the Dumpster and headed out to the main road. "And while you're at it, why don't you fill me in on what you have that belongs to Huang Xu. If I'm going to risk my life over it, I might as well know what it is."

The professor closed his eyes again as if collecting his thoughts, breathing in deeply. "It is a long story, Mr. Shealy. I do not suppose you would be open to discussing this over lunch someplace?"

"Don't push your luck, Professor."

21

"WHAT DO YOU KNOW about the men who have your wife?" Kumari asked.

"Not much," Clark said. For the most part, Huang Xu and the members of his triad remained a mystery. "Chinese mafia. They're probably involved in heroin or cocaine trafficking. They hire professional hit men. The leader's name is Huang Xu."

"At the next light, you turn left," Kumari said. "I've done a fair amount of research in the past few days. These men are not like the American mafia. The triads, as they are so called, are not generally violent, using instead fear and intimidation to get their way. Turn left, Mr. Shealy. Stay on this road for one mile. But if you cross them, they become brutally violent, sometimes using ancient torture rituals on triad victims."

The matter-of-fact way Kumari described it made Clark shiver. Though he hadn't talked to Jessica in hours, she was still part of every conscious thought. The picture of her—head shaved, shoulders exposed, eyes frightened but determined—had seared itself into his mind. He checked his watch: 25:18:43. Less than eleven hours before they started the torture.

If they hadn't done so already.

"The Manchurian Triad is linked to ancient religious practices and rituals. They detest your Western influence for creeping into their country, and they especially detest Western-style Christianity. Their leader, Li Gwah, has become a cult hero. Huang Xu is one of Li's most promising lieutenants."

As Kumari talked, Clark stole a sideways glance at his captive. *Can I trust this man?* The cut over Kumari's left eye had wedged further open, outlined by a crusty border of dried blood. The eye puffed out like a balloon, matching the purple coloring of the bruise on his right cheek. Sympathy pangs kept poking at Clark's conscience, though he tried to keep them at bay.

Clark could imagine this energetic man pacing the front of a classroom, scribbling on the board, getting all fired up about advanced mathematical concepts while his students yawned. Now he was trapped in this mess just like Clark.

"Why do they want you?" Clark asked. "What do you have?"

Kumari shook his head ruefully. "It is my bad fortune to possess the world's most valuable algorithm. I came to America for the purpose, so I thought, of executing a deal with a—what would you call it?" Kumari stared at the ceiling for a moment, but Clark couldn't help him. "A combination . . . a conglomeration—yes, that is the word—a conglomeration of Internet security companies." Kumari paused and a tone of sorrow seeped into his voice. "It was instead the Manchurian Triad posing as a deal brokerage company."

"All this over a math formula?"

"Not just a math formula, Mr. Shealy." He perked up again, warming to the subject of his beloved mathematics. "An algorithm that rapidly factors numbers into prime components. A process that for years most mathematicians thought was impossible." He paused and looked at the street sign as they passed it. "You should have taken a left turn there."

"Thanks for the warning." *A math formula.* Clark was having a hard time wrapping his mind around the fact that his entire life had been turned upside down, his wife kidnapped and possibly tortured, over a *math* formula. "So you discovered how to do this factoring stuff, and now the triads want you working for them?"

"Something like that."

Clark pulled a U-turn, cutting off an oncoming driver who leaned on the horn. "Jessica's life is in danger over a math formula." Repeating the fact made it no more comprehensible.

"This formula, Mr. Shealy, would allow someone to break most encryption codes in use today on the Internet," Kumari said, his voice conspiratorially quiet. "It is the key to every lock."

Clark gave him a sideways look requesting further explanation.

"Internet encryption mostly uses public-key cryptography based upon what is called the RSA protocol," Kumari said, his tone switching to lecture mode. "And the security of this protocol is based upon the mathematical assumption that there exists no fast way to factor large numbers into prime components."

Kumari rambled on about the ancient problem of key exchange—the challenge of somehow communicating an encryption key from one person to another without having it stolen or compromised—interspersing his lecture with directions to his apartment. The public-key encryption system used today on the Internet, Kumari explained, was like being able to telepathically pass the key back and forth so that messages could be encrypted without fear of some third party discovering the key.

It was based, he said, on the unique complexities of one-way mathematical functions, and at that point he totally lost Clark. Even when math teachers wrote stuff on the blackboard, Clark struggled. But when a math whiz of Kumari's caliber talked about algorithms without writing anything down—Clark had no chance.

"A prime number," Clark interrupted. "That's a number that can't be divided by any other number except itself and one. Is that right?"

"Of course," Kumari responded, as if Clark had just pronounced that one plus one equals two. "And they have unique . . . what is the word? Personalities? Um, characteristics . . . that computer encoders have used to secure almost every one of the political, financial, diplomatic, and criminal justice secrets on the Internet. With a regular computer, you can multiply two huge prime numbers together in seconds. But if I give you the *same* computer and a number which is the *product* of two huge prime numbers, you could not calculate what two prime numbers were multiplied together to get that number. Not in your lifetime, Mr. Shealy. Not in one thousand lifetimes. Not unless—" and here Kumari donned a self-satisfied smile as if he had just cured cancer—"you use my algorithm."

Ever since Clark had used his head as a battering ram on Bones McGinley, he had nursed a dull headache. Kumari's lecture sharpened the pain.

"For example, a more recent effort to locate prime factors of a two-hundred-digit number took three months with many computers operating together. Altogether, Mr. Shealy—more than *thirty years* of computer time. And two hundred digits are nothing in comparison to the length of the numbers encoded today using PGP technology. Without my formula, if all personal computers in the world were put on the same network, you would still require twelve times the age of the universe to factor such a huge number."

Kumari paused for a moment as if awed by the power of his own accomplishment. Even Clark's mathematically challenged brain was starting to seize the possibilities. "So you could hack into bank accounts . . ."

"Of course."

". . . criminal records, medical documents, school records."

"Yes, yes. All secrets would be exposed."

"You could steal millions before anybody would know."

"With a coordinated attack, you could steal billions."

"And once people found out that the Internet encryption systems didn't work . . ."

"Ah . . . now you understand, Mr. Shealy. Chaos. The Internet, and the world, would be in chaos."

Clark let out a low whistle. "Who else has this algorithm?"

"Turn right at the next street. We are almost there."

"Who else knows?"

Kumari waited a few seconds before answering, perhaps so the impact could sink in. "Only me."

This was bigger than Clark had imagined. Way bigger. "Why didn't you just sell it to the government? They would have paid a fortune."

"Until this year, my government was dominated by the BJP, a party supported by Hindu nationalists who will do everything in their power to preserve the caste system that has oppressed millions of my Dalit brothers and sisters. The BJP is still strong at the national level and controls many of our states. Violence against Christians, of which I am one, has become commonplace in Orissa, Karnataka, and Gujarat. Pastors are thrown in jail for supposedly violating anticonversion laws. Houses are burned. Daughters are carried away and never seen again.

And your government, Mr. Shealy, stands by and accepts the myth of 'India shining,' choosing to believe that our human rights laws actually mean something. Besides, your government hardly needs one more tool for world domination."

"And the mob does?" Clark took a right onto a side street and checked his watch. He pondered the fact that his hostage might be one of the planet's smartest men. And still Clark would trade Kumari's life for Jessica's without thinking twice.

Kumari remained silent, apparently too smart to be drawn into an argument.

"Do you have a name for this formula?" Clark asked.

"I label it the Abacus Algorithm, Mr. Shealy. Or rather, my former partner called it that." Kumari paused for a beat as if he had stepped on sacred ground. "Such a name provides a mental picture of the power of my algorithm. As the abacus transformed multiplication, so my algorithm transforms the process of prime factoring."

A few minutes later, they were driving through a run-down neighborhood on the east side of Vegas where Kumari's apartment was located. The information about the algorithm had certainly given Clark a new perspective about the stakes involved in his predicament, but it hadn't solved the fundamental problem of hostage exchange. Not surprisingly, the same man who had studied and mastered secure exchanges of encryption keys had some ideas about the hostage-exchange issue as well.

"To have any chance of rescuing your wife, Mr. Shealy . . . and hopefully saving also myself in this process, we must use the same concept that prevented nuclear holocaust between your United States and the Soviet Union for so many years. You call it mutually assured destruction." The small professor paused, clearing his throat. "Yet there is one problem.

"For this to work with success, we will need someone who looks exactly like me to act as a potential suicide bomber." He turned to Clark, and Clark noticed that Kumari's somber demeanor had been replaced by a hint of teasing in the swollen eyes. "Do you happen to have any suggestions?"

22

WHEN THEY ARRIVED at the stucco building that served as Kumari's apartment, Clark grabbed a knife from his tools and cut the tape at Kumari's ankles. Both men climbed out of the vehicle.

"I'll need my hands in front of me," Kumari said. Without waiting for Clark's approval, he blithely looped his wrists under each leg and brought his hands to the front.

Kumari wrenched his wrists a little, trying to wiggle some slack into the duct tape, then looked pleadingly at Clark. "Could we not just use conventional handcuffs, sir?"

Clark shrugged. He kept the little man at gunpoint as he slapped a pair of metal handcuffs on his wrists and cut off the duct tape. He noticed the lines on Kumari's wrists where the edge of the tape had bitten into the skin.

"Thank you," the professor said, wiggling his hands around. "Much better."

The professor was unfailingly polite. But watching him, even with a gun pointed at him, Clark couldn't shake the foreboding thought that he had somehow just let a lion out of its cage.

◁▷

Kumari's tiny apartment reminded Clark of a school computer lab. He counted twenty-four desktop computers and one laptop, all hooked together with black cables and powered by a maze of cords that snaked to various outlets around the room. The only furniture was a small card table, two folding chairs, and a beanbag.

"Nice place," Clark lied.

Without responding, Kumari immediately walked to something that looked like an alarm panel and punched in a bunch of numbers.

"Security alarm?" Clark asked.

"Yes."

"Since you're in hiding, I'm guessing it doesn't actually call the police."

"That is correct, Mr. Shealy. It dials my cell phone."

"Clever." Clark wandered around a little, checking out the various computers.

"And if I do not dial a certain number within three minutes, it triggers an explosive device."

Clark stopped in his tracks. "Explosives?"

"Yes, Semtex explosives. The blast would take out this entire building."

"And you disarmed it, right?"

For the first time, the professor smiled. "Yes, Mr. Shealy. I believe I remembered the code correctly."

Before they called Huang Xu, Kumari scurried around and fired up the computers, plugging in some information that looked like Greek to Clark. After about five minutes, Kumari looked up and pronounced the machines "almost ready," then headed to the refrigerator in the small adjoining kitchen.

Clark followed, glancing at the nearly empty refrigerator shelves— a half-drained gallon of milk, half a cold pizza, a jar of pickles, and several twelve-ounce cans of Coke.

"Pizza?" Kumari asked as if he had invited Clark over for dinner.

Clark's face must have registered his surprise.

"Perhaps you were expecting curry?" Kumari asked.

Clark smiled at the little man. In truth, Clark was starving. He hadn't stopped to eat one thing all day. It took Kumari and him no more than five minutes to devour the leftover pizza and chase it down by chugging milk straight from the half-empty jug.

When they finished, it was time to make the call.

Kumari took his post in front of the laptop computer on the card table. Clark needed to pace, stepping over and around the tangle of cords and machines. "Ready," Kumari said, and Clark felt his hands go cold.

Clark pulled the cell number out and began dialing. His stopwatch registered 25:42:12. He had captured Kumari with more than ten hours to spare. He could only hope it was enough time to save Jessica.

The number rang four times without an answer. Finally a recorded voice kicked in—instructing Clark to leave a message at the tone.

"I've got Professor Kumari," he said. "Call me back immediately. I want to speak with Jessica."

Clark hung up and tried to control a cauldron of emotions. "Voice mail," he said, more to himself than Kumari. He stared at his phone as if it had betrayed him. "What does that mean?"

"He will call back," the professor said. Clark noticed the professor had opened some type of e-mail program.

"What are you doing?" Clark asked.

"Getting ready."

"For what?"

At that second, the phone rang. Clark nearly dropped it as he fumbled to answer.

"Hello."

"Nice work, Mr. Shealy." It was the grating voice of Huang Xu. "But why did you discard the phone I told you to use?"

"I was tired of being tracked with it."

As was his custom, Xu paused. These conversations drove Clark mad, but he supposed that was the whole point. "Very well, Mr. Shealy. Let us see if you truly have the professor. Write down this number . . ."

Clark nodded at the professor, letting him know the plan was on track. "Ready," Clark said.

"4-9-2-7-9-5-4-2-8-7-9-8-2-9-1." Xu repeated the number twice and had Clark read it back to him. "That number is the product of two prime numbers, Mr. Shealy. Professor Kumari should be able to factor that number in a matter of seconds and tell us the primes. Call us back when he does. And, Mr. Shealy?"

"Yes."

"The next time you take unilateral action, like tossing away my phone, you might want to consider the effect such actions have on your wife."

"Keep your hands off her," Clark warned, but he was speaking to dead air. Incensed, he restrained himself from calling back until he had the answer. The professor hunched in front of his computer, formulas scrolling back and forth on the screen.

"We do not need the network for this one," Kumari bragged. "A fifteen-digit number?" He scoffed, as if Xu had insulted his intelligence.

"How long?" Clark asked.

"Would this very minute be soon enough?" Kumari wrote the numbers down and handed the paper to Clark. *10245751* and *48097541*.

"You sure?" Clark asked.

Kumari nodded.

"This is my wife's life on the line. You don't want to double-check your math?"

Kumari looked insulted.

"Okay," Clark said. He dialed Xu.

This time, the triad leader answered immediately, and Clark read the numbers. "That's a good start," Xu said.

"Let me talk with Jessica," Clark said firmly.

"You don't make the demands," Xu replied, his voice low but threatening. "But just for your information, even after the way you treated Johnny Chin, I have chosen not to retaliate against your wife. However, if you insist on making demands and acting against my instructions, I will."

The reference to Chin momentarily threw Clark. How did Xu know these things? His words were not empty threats; Clark could feel that much in his bones. Worse, his mind pictured it vividly. He couldn't afford to say or do *anything* that might set this man off. "Okay," Clark said reassuringly, "give me the next number."

"You want to hear from your wife?"

"No, no. Just tell me the number."

Without warning, Clark heard Jessica shriek in the background. His blood turned to ice. "Stop," he insisted. "Just give me the number."

There was another scream, louder than the first. He closed his eyes, balled his fist, and ground his teeth. He felt like he might literally explode from the tension. He had never hated anyone, *anything*, as much as he hated this man on the phone right now. Clark would kill him with his bare hands, spitting in his face as he died, or Clark would die trying.

"Make it stop," Clark begged, his voice despondent.

The response was silence. No screaming, no answer from Xu. Nothing.

"Please!" *Oh, God, please!*

More silence. A few seconds stretched into a minute. Clark hardly dared to breathe, much less talk. What had they done to her? Where had they taken her? What were they doing to her still?

"I will not let them hurt her, Mr. Shealy. But you must play by *my* rules, not yours. Now . . . are you ready for the next number?"

23

THE PHONE CALLS CHANGED the mood in the cramped apartment. Kumari apparently divined what was happening from listening to Clark's side of the conversation and didn't say a word other than to offer a sincere apology. In silence, the professor put his machines to work processing the second number that Huang Xu had provided, over three hundred digits long. Clark paced the apartment, lost in introspection as the professor plugged numbers and letters into some kind of formula. At one point, Clark glanced at the screen and thought he saw a digital Bible open, one with English and some other language side-by-side. But Kumari quickly shrank that window. As long as the formula worked, Clark didn't care.

But even if the formula *did* work, the harsh realities were almost unbearable, though Clark needed to face them. Denial would serve no purpose; it sure wouldn't save Jessica. No matter how well things went from here on out—and he had serious doubts about Kumari's plan—it was already too late to keep Jessica from harm.

Jessica was young and strikingly attractive, though she would be the last to admit it. When Clark called her beautiful, she would correct him. "I'm cute. Maybe attractive," she would say. "But you're the only one who says I'm beautiful." She thought her nose was a bit too broad, her lips a little too thin.

She was wrong about that, Clark knew. He had always been pleased when men swiveled their heads as Jessica passed. But now, the thought of those leers made him sick. Since the triad members undoubtedly planned to kill both her and Clark anyway, there was little chance they would resist molesting her in the meantime.

Jessica. He might get her back, though even that was a long shot. But she would never be the same. Emotional scars would replace the innocence. Clark had always heard that women needed security more than anything else from their husbands. He had failed her at her deepest point of need. He felt a crucial part of himself dying along with her. He was quickly losing hope.

It took nearly ten minutes for Kumari to generate the answer. When he was sure he had the right factors, he gave his seat in front of the laptop screen to Clark. During the ensuing call, both Clark and Xu were all business. Clark swallowed the words he wanted to say and instead recited with precision the digits in each of the prime factors. Xu congratulated him on the correct answers, then said, "It is time for us to exchange prisoners, would you agree?"

"Yes."

"What will you be driving?"

"A gray Durango."

"At 7:00 p.m., bring Professor Kumari to the third level of the parking garage at the Bellagio. Pull your vehicle into a spot facing the south wall and lift the back gate. A white Lincoln Navigator will pull behind you and stop momentarily. Follow that vehicle at a safe distance. It will lead you to our meeting place."

Clark had a million questions, but he knew better than to ask even a single one. He wanted to meet sooner—to get Jessica away from these men as quickly as possible—but he knew a little more time could work to his advantage.

"If you involve the authorities or anyone else, Mr. Shealy, you know what will happen to your wife?"

"I know."

"Maybe you ought to say it, Mr. Shealy, just to make sure."

"You will kill her," Clark said softly.

Xu laughed, the mocking laughter of a bully taunting his victim. "She should be so lucky," he said. "Death has a way of dulling pain and ending humiliation. No, for a beautiful woman like that, death would be a squandering of her many, many talents."

Xu immediately hung up, and Clark stared at his phone. He felt weak and helpless, desperation crowding out his saner emotions. He thought about what he had done to Johnny Chin, the look of anguish when he blew out the hit man's knee, the wailing when they hit the bumps in the dirt road a few minutes later.

These phone calls had changed Clark. Something had snapped. He suddenly found himself proud of what he had done to Chin. While Kumari typed away on his computer, Clark fantasized about what he would do to Huang Xu. He would blow the man's head off his shoulders for making Jess scream. He would protect his wife.

Clark was not the same man who had crawled out of bed yesterday morning, focused on chasing the American dream while living on the slippery outer slopes of legality.

He had a killer's mentality now. And as he and Kumari made their preparations for the next phase of battle, Clark no longer wondered whether he would have the guts to take somebody's life in order to save Jessica. The only question now was whether he'd be able to stop.

24

LATER THAT EVENING, following the white Navigator north on I-15, Clark felt neither fear nor anger, just a surprising sense of grim determination. Feelings of revenge and desperation had been torched into a solid weld of fate—a sense that tonight he would either save Jessica or die trying. Tonight could be his own personal Alamo—he was outgunned and outmanned, but honor allowed him no way out. It didn't hurt to have the optimistic little professor, the smartest man Clark had ever met, riding shotgun.

Earlier today—what seemed like an eternity ago—Clark had been on this same interstate, looking for an obscure place to torture Johnny Chin. As they drove north now, Kumari told the story of Rajat Singh, the professor's young protégé who lost his life to Huang Xu and his cohorts. Kumari stared out the window as he talked, his voice thick with emotion. They were going about eighty-five, but with the scorched desert flatlands stretching out on both sides of the interstate, it seemed like they were barely moving.

"Rajat was only a young man," Kumari said. "Young and full of promise. I gladly would have traded my life for his."

What could Clark say? It seemed that this algorithm had already caused so much pain. "You should be proud of him" was the best that Clark could offer. He was not good with comforting words.

They rode in silence for a few minutes, each lost in his own thoughts. Clark pondered the reality that the triad would kill for the algorithm. *Had* killed for the algorithm. What chance did he and Kumari really have?

He glanced at the charismatic man in the passenger seat. Clark respected the professor, even felt a growing attachment to him. But in a few minutes, perhaps an hour, Clark would be required to act. Mercy, pity, and remorse could cost him split seconds of decision time, the difference between success and failure. For Jessica's sake, he would remain unemotional . . . and unattached to his accomplice.

"In my apartment, I sent the algorithm to your e-mail," Kumari said. Clark looked at the professor in total surprise, as if Kumari had just pronounced himself an alien, but Kumari pretended not to notice. "I found your business address on the Internet when you were on the phone with Xu. I have used a protocol that will delay delivery for forty-eight hours. If our plan works, I will recall the e-mail before then, Mr. Shealy."

Kumari's voice became frail, barely audible. "If not, you will be receiving the algorithm, but I have encrypted it with a code that will be impossible to decipher. I also sent a second e-mail from a remote server. Later this year, a man I trust more than any other will contact you with the key. Until the two of you make a connection, both pieces will be worthless. The triads have been known to use torture—but you cannot reveal what you do not know."

The Johnny Chin sequence flashed in front of Clark's eyes again. Defiance. The gunshot. Agony. Fear. Like PowerPoint images, one after the other.

"Make me a promise, Mr. Shealy, please. When you understand completely the formula, you will sell it to the top Internet security companies. You keep 10 percent for a commission. Send the rest to the church in India so that they might build more schools for the Dalit children who will otherwise have no chance."

"How can I do that?" Clark asked, dumbfounded by the request.

"This man who contacts you. He will know."

"You're going to make it," Clark said, though the words sounded hollow. "We both are."

"Does that mean yes?" Kumari asked. "Is this how Americans promise?"

"I'll do it," Clark said. "If anything happens."

Kumari's face was deadly serious, the swollen eyes staring straight ahead. "Thank you, my friend."

25

CLARK FOLLOWED the Navigator down the exit ramp toward the small town of Apex, close enough to Vegas that you could make out the shapes of the casinos in the rearview mirror, the Stratosphere Casino towering above the rest. As Clark pulled up behind the Navigator at the end of the exit ramp, he could make out the backs of only two heads inside—both in the front seat. Jessica could be lying down, of course, and in the backseat of that vehicle. Or maybe not.

The thought of her possibly being that close made his skin tingle, a combination of anxiety and excitement.

The Navigator turned left onto a small paved road that headed back under the interstate. After a few hundred yards, the vehicles made another left, this time next to a large mound of rock that sheltered the area from I-15. A sign warned against trespassers and declared the land to be a blasting area owned by Las Vegas Paving.

The Navigator continued around to the back of the rock and gravel pile, driving on a wide swath of packed soil and compacted rock that looked like it had been scraped clean by a bulldozer. To Clark's left, standing on top of the large rocky hill, two men stood watch. One used binoculars to keep an eye on the interstate; the other drew a bead on Clark with a sniper's rifle.

The vehicles came to a stop in the middle of a flat plateau about the size of a football field, discreetly tucked away behind the rocks. An abandoned set of railroad tracks ran across the back of this property. Clark's cell phone rang—a different number from the last time he had talked with Xu. Kumari had his head bowed in prayer.

"Step out of the car, Mr. Shealy. Have Professor Kumari step out on the other side. Keep your hands on top of your head and tell him to do the same."

It was not Xu's voice this time. "Where's Jessica?" Clark asked.

"You'll see her soon. But only if you follow instructions."

Clark hung up the phone and nodded at the professor.

"God be with you," Kumari said.

"Thanks," Clark replied. "Same to you."

Clark dialed the number programmed into his cell phone, and Kumari's own phone chirped in response. Kumari picked up the phone, connected the call, and hooked it on his belt. He opened his car door, grabbed his laptop computer from the floor, and climbed out of the car, holding the laptop in front of him. Around his chest, taped outside his shirt for all to see, were several small plastic containers connected by thin wires. The hunch-shouldered professor looked small and frail as he took a few steps toward the back of the Navigator.

He might have been the bravest man Clark ever knew.

Two large men, dressed in black and wearing ski masks, jumped out of both sides of the Navigator. They crouched next to the car, aiming a pistol at Kumari, another at Clark's front windshield. *That's two guns aimed at my head, maybe more.* Kumari stopped in his tracks. The gunman on the left side of the Navigator pulled out a cell phone, and Clark's phone buzzed.

Clark put Kumari on hold and picked up the call.

"I said out of the car!" the man hissed.

"Change in plans," Clark said calmly. "I'm not getting out." He could almost feel the red dot on his temple, the sharpshooter on top of the rocks taking aim. Clark wondered if he would even feel anything when the bullet ripped through his skull. He had only a few seconds to convince this clown on the other end of the phone to call the sharpshooter off.

"The professor is a walking suicide bomb," Clark said quickly, rushing through the script. "He's wired with enough Semtex to blow this entire gravel pit off the map. My finger is on the trigger of the detonator." He took a quick breath. This next part was a lie, but it would take too long to explain the truth—and the truth was just as deadly. "If you shoot me, we all die together."

The goon in the ski mask barked some instructions in Chinese to his companion on the other side of the car and the sharpshooter on the mountain. Clark hoped it was an order not to shoot. Kumari took a few steps closer to the Lincoln, and Clark saw the gunman on the right side of the Navigator stiffen. Clark put his own car in reverse and backed up a few feet.

"Where are you going?" the gunman shouted into the phone.

After thirty yards, Clark stopped, leaving Kumari standing by himself, halfway between the Navigator and Clark's Durango.

"Where's Jessica?" Clark asked the gunman. He could sense that the element of surprise had given him a fleeting advantage. "If I don't see her walking toward my car in thirty seconds, I'm detonating this baby."

With that, Clark ended the call. The fact that Clark was still alive—that the sharpshooter hadn't blown his brains into the passenger seat—showed that the mutually assured destruction plan was working. At least so far. "They won't kill me until they have the algorithm," Kumari had insisted when he told Clark about the plan. "For you and Jessica to survive, we must tie your lives to mine."

Clark tried to see into the backseat of the Navigator, squinting behind his sunglasses, ignoring his splitting headache and the pounding of his own heart. Clark knew that the next few seconds would determine whether Jessica lived or died. And along with her, a brilliant mathematician from India who happened to possess the world's most important secret.

With events frozen at the gravel pit, and Clark's thirty-second ultimatum quickly running its course, Clark received another phone call. Again, he put Kumari on hold and picked up the call, this time from Huang Xu. There was a loud motor and the sound of wind in the background. Clark could barely make out what Xu was saying. "Jessica's with *me!*" Xu yelled into the cell phone. There were some other things that Clark couldn't quite make out, but he did hear a time. "Five minutes! We'll be there in five minutes!"

"Tell your goons here to do what I say in the meantime—all of them!"

"What!"

Clark screamed louder into the phone. "Tell your men here to drop their guns and do what I say!"

"Five minutes, Shealy! I'll be there in five minutes!"

The phone line went dead just as Clark realized what the background noise meant. The loud engine, the whirring of blades, the sound of buffeting wind.

A helicopter! Xu and Jessica were arriving in a helicopter!

He and Kumari had been rehearsing hostage exchange scenarios for the last three hours. They had planned countermoves for every contingency. They had put themselves in Xu's shoes—predicting how he would react—and then worked out the best response. "We have thought of everything," Kumari had said. "We will be ready."

But each of their scenarios had Xu and Jessica arriving in an automobile. They had rehearsed everything *except* a helicopter.

26

THE TRUTH ABOUT the Semtex was a little more complicated. Kumari had indeed wired himself with explosives. He used Semtex because it could be poured into any mold—in this case a small plastic compartment the size of a computer battery. It was what Kumari had been using to protect his apartment: the spare "battery" in his laptop was actually a Semtex bomb, complete with its own detonation device, lethal enough to destroy the entire building. The three plastic containers taped to his chest were filled with household cleaning fluids.

According to Kumari, the suicide bombers in the movies, with explosives strapped all the way around their vests, were typical Hollywood overkill. "That much Semtex would take out half a city block."

The Nokia phone in Clark's left hand was the detonation device. Speed-dial 2 and watch Kumari, and anybody within a hundred feet of the computer, become pieces of shrapnel. They had bought the Nokia that afternoon and programmed the explosives to be triggered only by a call from that cell phone, a programming trick that Kumari had learned from Rajat.

They would have preferred to program the explosives so that detonation would occur whenever Clark lifted a finger *off* the Nokia phone. But Kumari was new to this business, and Clark didn't have the foggiest idea how to do any of it. So Clark decided to do what he did best—bluff that part. As long as the triads *thought* Clark's death would automatically trigger the explosives, Kumari and Clark might be okay.

With Kumari in sight, Clark had sole discretion over the trigger.

Whether to dial it, or when, would be his call and his alone. Once Jessica was safe and Kumari was taken away, the plan changed. If Clark lost connection with Kumari on Clark's regular cell phone, he would try to reestablish the connection for fifteen seconds—no more, no less. If he was unsuccessful, he would place a call with the Nokia. In effect, this meant that Kumari could rain death on himself and those around him at any time by simply disconnecting the call from Clark's cell phone and not answering the return call for fifteen seconds. And if, by some stroke of fortune, the triad members had separated Kumari from his computer, the bomb would be detonated without killing the professor.

As they waited for the helicopter, Clark gained confidence just by watching the unwavering dignity of Professor Kumari. The little man stood there in the baking heat of the early evening sun, his gaze calmly shifting from one gunman to the other, his confidence at death's door probably unnerving them.

Clark stepped out of the Durango, cell phones in each hand.

"They're coming in a helicopter!" he said, reconnecting to Kumari's cell. "They'll be here in five minutes."

The professor nodded. He had his phone, still hooked on his belt, in speaker mode. "Not a problem," Kumari replied, but Clark knew the professor was only being brave. A helicopter would soon rise out of cell coverage. The detonation device would be useless. Their leverage would disappear.

To make matters worse, Xu came early. About two minutes after Xu's call, Clark heard the distant whip of helicopter blades. His eyes shot to the horizon—a small, insect-size dot grew into a gleaming black monster, roaring toward the gravel pit. The helicopter kicked up a cloud of desert dust as it landed, like a giant vulture, swooping down on the flat plateau about a hundred yards behind the Navigator.

When the roar of the engine and whir of the blades shut down, the silence was overwhelming, like the eeriness of a calm breeze before the hurricane arrives. A slender man jumped out of the passenger seat and started walking toward the Navigator. He was shorter than Clark and lithe like a panther, his face shielded by a black ski mask. His T-shirt showcased slender arms and the cablelike muscles of a martial arts expert. He approached the gunmen quickly, confidently. He gave a few commands in Chinese and then started walking toward Clark.

Clark knew he was looking at Huang Xu.

"Where's Jessica?" Clark shouted.

"In the back of the helicopter, unharmed." The man kept coming, covering the territory between the Navigator and Clark's Durango quickly. He kept his dark eyes fixed on Clark, not wasting so much as a sideways glance as he walked past Kumari.

"I want to see her."

"In time."

"Now!"

The man didn't respond but just kept coming, his audacity unsettling Clark. The sharp eyes of a predator peered through the ski mask, oblivious to the world around him.

"That's far enough," Clark said, his finger poised on the Nokia.

Xu took another few steps, calling Clark's bluff.

"One more step," Clark warned. He faced straight into the demonic eyes and held out the cell phone, unwavering. He made himself think about Jessica's screams—the torture. If Clark had to, he would blow them all into eternity right now, himself included.

To Clark's surprise, Xu stopped. Twenty feet away, max. Clark's heart felt like it might pound straight through his chest. Xu was still too far away, Clark hoped, to successfully use his martial arts expertise. Clark held the Nokia closer, relaxing a bit.

"Clever, this plan of yours," Xu said.

"I'm just trying to make sure Jessica gets out of here safely."

"What's to prevent you from driving away and then blowing up the professor and all of us around him?"

"This exchange can't work unless somebody trusts somebody," Clark responded, trying not to sound intimidated. In truth, his hand now trembled a little at the unblinking stare of Xu and the rifle leveled at his forehead from the top of the rock pile. He thought about reaching for his Glock but rejected the idea. "And between you or me, I'd prefer to trust myself."

The dry lips behind the ski mask smiled, displaying perfect rows of whitened teeth. *A showman.* Xu nodded toward the Nokia. "You're using cell technology to trigger the explosives?"

Clark nodded.

Xu studied Clark for a moment, as if through some trick of Eastern meditation he could peer into the dark corners of Clark's mind. He licked chapped lips. "But the helicopter," Xu said. "You didn't plan on the helicopter. Once Kumari is on board and rises out of cell coverage, your detonation device is useless."

Clark glanced toward Kumari, thirty yards ahead of him, still standing between the two vehicles like a soldier on watch. The professor stared at them as Xu and Clark talked, sealing the little man's fate by their negotiations.

"He's not getting on that helicopter," Clark said.

"Then you must not want your wife to get off."

They stood there for a few moments longer, a game of bluff with two lives hanging in the balance. Clark couldn't imagine selling the professor out after everything the strange little man had done for him already. But if the alternative meant losing Jessica, what choice did he have?

Besides, Kumari's plan could still work, even with the helicopter. An hour earlier, the professor had swallowed a small GPS device, shrink-wrapped in plastic, that would transmit his location using satellite technology. The plan was for Clark to escape with Jessica and immediately contact the FBI. Kumari and his captors could be located using the GPS device, and the feds could swoop in to rescue him. *If* he survived that long.

Xu took a few steps forward, and Clark carefully slid his regular cell phone into his pocket, his left hand still poised on the Nokia. He reached inside his sports coat for the Glock. "What is it to you?" Xu asked softly. "You get your wife back. As I promised, she has not been molested. I leave with the professor. He is not your concern."

Clark kept his hand on the gun but didn't remove it from the holster. Xu called back to his men: "Bring the woman out so Mr. Shealy can see she is unharmed."

His heart racing, Clark stared at the helicopter as one man jumped from the backseat and helped a blindfolded Jessica onto the ground. Her head was shaved and her hands tied behind her back, but she walked with no apparent difficulty, escorted toward the Navigator by another hooded figure. She wore jeans, sandals, and a cotton pullover. She seemed calm, almost serene, as if she had already reconciled herself to whatever might happen.

His heart ached just from seeing her. It took every ounce of restraint not to drop everything and run to her.

"Jess, are you okay?" he called out.

At the sound of his voice, she lifted her head, the lips showing surprise and expectation. "Clark?"

"Hang in there, babe."

She nodded, holding her head a little higher. A guard led her by the arm.

Xu motioned toward Jessica, then turned back to Clark. "Unharmed, Mr. Shealy, as I promised. You let the professor get on the helicopter, and she stays that way."

Clark hated what he had to do next. It felt like his emotions might detonate, blowing his heart into a thousand pieces. This was for Jessica, he reminded himself. But the thought of giving Kumari over repulsed him, especially in these circumstances where the bomb threat would soon be neutralized and Kumari would be at their mercy. It left a putrid aftertaste as he considered his options, realizing again that he had no choice.

But it was Kumari who made the next move.

Without saying a word, the old man turned away from Clark and shuffled slowly toward the helicopter, carrying his computer in front of him. He walked past Jessica and her armed guard, past the gunman at the side of the Navigator, and eventually stopped beside the helicopter.

He glanced back at Clark and nodded, as if to say it was okay, and then allowed a hooded guard to help him into the black beast, the professor still clutching his laptop.

When Xu saw this, he took a few steps backward, his eyes now fixed on Clark. "Let her go!" Xu shouted over his shoulder.

They untied Jessica's hands and removed the blindfold. She squinted in the light. She quickly surveyed the entire scene, drinking in the danger, then started walking toward Clark, tentatively at first and then faster, almost a jog. She swung wide of Xu and ran to Clark's side, where he squeezed her with his right arm, fighting back the tears. She hugged him and stood at his side, facing Xu.

"I will not be going near Professor Kumari until that detonation device is disarmed," Xu said, looking them both over. "If you detonate that bomb or do something equally stupid like go to the authorities, I will personally hunt you down and make you pay. That's my promise to you. If you allow Kumari to ascend out of cell tower range without incident, you'll never hear from me again."

Xu stared at them for a moment before he turned and shouted some instructions to the man standing next to the Lincoln. The man brought the car around. Xu turned to Clark one last time.

"You and your wife will be free to go a few minutes after I leave. I am a man of my word, Mr. Shealy. Keep that in mind as you make some crucial decisions in these next few moments."

If this whole affair hadn't been so tragic, Clark might have laughed in Xu's face. A masked kidnapper bragging about his integrity. A killer who said he should be trusted.

But there was nothing funny about the unfeeling eyes that stared out from the ski mask. Or the fact that Professor Kumari would soon be at this man's mercy.

"I always keep my promises, Mr. Shealy."

27

CLARK DIDN'T WAIT for permission. A few moments after Xu left in the Lincoln, Clark and Jessica jumped into the Durango and raced out of the gravel pit, leaving the helicopter and Xu's guards behind. Clark hunched over as he drove, every nerve on end, his eyes peeled for any sign of the Lincoln. He half expected a shot from the marksman stationed on top of the rock pile to end his life. But would Xu's men really do that—knowing it might also result in death for Kumari?

"Stay low!" he said to Jessica, gently pushing her head down in the passenger seat.

Clark didn't dare breathe until he had put at least a mile between the Durango and the rendezvous spot. Still no sign of the Lincoln. He handed his Glock to Jessica, now upright in her seat. She checked the chamber and twisted around to keep a lookout behind them. A quick glance at her confirmed the telltale signs of her ordeal. Sunken eyes, bloodshot in the sunlight. The pasty whiteness of her stubbled head, contrasting against her summer tan. But there were no noticeable bruises, and she still handled herself with a sense of pride and an unspoken desire to fight back, unbowed from her captivity. Maybe she had not been sexually assaulted.

Either way, just the sight of her next to him sparked a small flicker of hope.

Clark was going so fast, the SUV was literally shaking, like it might blow apart if he didn't ease up on the accelerator. He actually hoped the cops would see him flying down the road and pull him over. If not, he would head straight to the North Vegas police headquarters, the building he had noticed when he dropped Johnny Chin off at the hospital earlier in the day. He would call the feds en route.

Three minutes later Clark lost his cell phone connection with Kumari. He swore and stared at the small screen in dismay.

"What's that mean?" Jessica asked.

"Trouble." Clark redialed Kumari's number and waited for an answer. After five rings, a message kicked in. Racing down the interstate, one hand on the wheel, he hit Redial.

Clark felt his throat clench this time, his stomach twisting with the pressure. "If he doesn't answer in fifteen seconds, I'm supposed to detonate the bomb." For the second time, Clark heard Kumari's voice mail begin.

"Maybe he's out of range already," Jessica suggested. "Maybe he's in the helicopter, high enough to lose coverage."

Clark glanced at the GPS tracking device attached to his console and shook his head. "Kumari's still at the blasting pit." He pointed at the GPS screen and redialed yet again. "If the helicopter had taken off, we would have seen more movement of the signal."

Kumari's phone kicked Clark into voice mail a third time. It had been at least thirty seconds. Could he really do this?

"Maybe he's trying to wipe everybody out before the helicopter takes off," Clark said. He redialed one last time, his finger now trembling on his phone. The trigger device—the Nokia—sat untouched in the panel between Clark and Jessica.

He waited for an answer, hoping against hope. *Please ... please ... pick up!* This time, Clark ended the call as soon as the voice mail started. He felt crushed. Defeated. As if he had just been ordered to pull the switch on the electric chair for an innocent man.

He reminded himself that this was *Kumari's* plan. Kumari was the one pulling his own trigger. Clark wasn't supposed to have any discretion in the matter. But when they put the plan together, Clark hadn't realized how difficult it would be to send this man to eternity.

With a shaking hand, Clark picked up the Nokia and flipped it open.

Maybe Kumari was trying to save himself from being tortured.

Maybe he had been separated from the laptop computer and detonating the bomb would kill the triad members and not Kumari. But Clark knew the reality was far more grim. His mind played it out in full-color video. Clark pushing the speed dial, the bomb detonating, Kumari and everyone else being blasted into tiny fragments that would rain down on the desert sand, covering the area with the cremated remains of a good and decent man. Sure, the blast would exact a rough form of justice. But Xu would escape. And it would also destroy any chance of a fairy-tale ending—the "best-case scenario" as Kumari had described it—a scenario where the authorities used the tiny GPS device to track Kumari and rescue him alive.

Clark couldn't do it. In the moment of truth, his hand froze on the phone, the Durango barreling down the interstate, Jessica staring in shell-shocked silence. He couldn't make himself push the button. Could not. It was one thing to make bold and heartless plans; it was another to kill an innocent man.

"God help him," Clark said. He closed the Nokia and put it down. He wanted to cry. "I can't do it, Jess. I just can't."

She reached over and put a hand on his leg. "It's okay," she said, her words soft and reassuring. "Maybe you're not supposed to."

In response, as if her words had soared to the very halls of heaven and ricocheted as an order to the triads, the tiny dot on the GPS device began to move. At first it wiggled and then it started heading north, away from the city, covering ground faster than any automobile could travel. "He's probably out of cell phone range now, anyway," Jessica said.

The decision, Clark knew, had just been taken out of his hands.

He checked the mirrors again. Nobody was gaining on them; that much was certain. But instead of feeling relief, the knot in his stomach only tightened.

How much pain has my cowardice caused my friend? he wondered.

"It's okay," Jessica said. "It's okay."

As Clark worked his own cell phone, trying to contact the U.S. attorney's office and the FBI after hours, he kept one eye on the GPS device. It tracked Kumari about thirty miles north of Apex and eventually came to rest somewhere in the middle of the desert. A mob hideout, Clark assumed. He realized now why they hadn't seen the Lincoln since they left the blasting area. Xu had probably headed straight to the hideout in order to torture the algorithm out of Kumari.

He would send someone else to finish the job with Clark and Jessica.

28

TWENTY MINUTES LATER, twelve blocks from the North Vegas police station, Clark heard the distant whir of blades, like the return of a demon whispering threats from the sky. "Did you hear that?" Clark asked Jessica.

"No."

Clark laid on the horn at the next busy intersection, slowing down only slightly for a red light. Tires squealed and angry drivers found their own horns.

"You're going to get us killed!" Jess yelled.

"Check for helicopters," Clark shot back, breathless. He had already hit the button to roll down Jessica's window.

She stuck her head out, twisting in her seat.

"Hang on!" Clark swerved around a slow driver, jerking Jessica and banging her head against the window frame. She swore at him, and it almost made him smile. *She's back.*

She pulled her head inside, her face pale. "They're coming."

"Fasten your seat belt!" Clark yelled.

As Jessica fumbled with her belt, Clark approached another intersection. The light was red ... of course. This time, the oncoming traffic didn't stop. He laid on the horn again, waited for the smallest opening, and shot the Durango through.

"How far away are they?" he asked.

"I don't know. Half a mile?"

Jessica still had the Glock in her right hand, and she knew how to use it—but what good would it do? A person couldn't shoot helicopters out of the sky with a 9mm Glock.

Traffic snarled and the helicopter closed in, the engine noise and roar of the blades growing ever closer. *Thwack, thwack, thwack.* Through Jessica's open window, it seemed like the bird was directly overhead.

Clark pulled partially onto the sidewalk and shot around some vehicles blocking his way.

"They're on top of us, Clark!"

As soon as the words left Jessica's mouth, a hailstorm of bullets rained on the front windshield. Jessica instinctively curled away from the glass, and Clark lurched back in his seat. The shattered glass, though riddled with bullet holes, held in place. "Give me the gun!" Clark shouted. They were firing large rounds from the helicopter, semiautomatics.

Instead of giving him the gun, Jess pulled her shoulder restraint behind her back, grabbed the hand grip on the door frame, and stuck her head out the side window, gun in her right hand.

"What are you doing?" Clark yanked the steering wheel hard to the right, jerking Jess back inside. Bullets bounced off the pavement beside him as the heavy Durango squealed around a corner, sliding onto a side street, narrowly missing another vehicle.

How did they find us?

Clark caught a glimpse of the copter's underbelly out his own side window as the pilot regrouped and swooped in for another run. Clark drove like a man possessed, erratically swerving left and right. He caught a glimpse of the gunman on the passenger side of the helicopter, sighting them in. The next second, Clark lost him again as the helicopter moved directly overhead. *Pang! Pang!* The bullets ripped into the roof of the Durango.

In a last desperate act, Clark pulled the wheel hard to the left, sending the Durango into an out-of-control spin, bouncing Jessica's shoulder against the passenger door. The wheels hit the curb, and the vehicle rolled, wiping out a mailbox, skidding across a front lawn. Clark's head banged against something, and his world turned fuzzy, spinning wildly. Abruptly, the spinning stopped and the Durango jerked to a halt, lodged partially on its roof, pinned against the front stoop of somebody's house.

Clark's door was crushed, wedged against the ground. Jessica's side of the Durango stuck up at a forty-five-degree angle, making his wife an easy target.

If she was still alive.

Dazed, Clark realized that the copter was circling back again. The smoky residue from his air bag made it seem like the car was on fire. He thought about the gas tank—exposed to the assassins' bullets.

Quickly, he took a mental inventory. His left shoulder blazed with pain, and he tasted blood in his mouth, but otherwise he seemed to be okay. He could move both legs and hands. But that was not his immediate concern. The helicopter had descended to treetop level, a black widow ready to devour the fly caught in its web. Clark heard Jessica groan.

"Can you move?" he asked.

"Not really."

"Crawl toward me, Jess. Get away from that window!"

He could hear the blades beating the air above them.

"I can't!" She frantically worked on her seat belt but couldn't get it loose . . . and he couldn't reach her.

They had come so far—how could he lose her now?

His eyes searched for the Glock, but everything was out of sorts, like some giant had picked up the Durango and shaken all of its contents loose. Shots rang out. He heard Jess scream, and his heart stopped. There! A black object! He reached for it. Grabbed it. More shots. He saw Jess frenetically pulling on the belt, trying to slide away from the window.

"Clark!" she screamed. She turned to him with pleading eyes, not willing to look at the barrel of death pointing down from the helicopter. She couldn't squirm loose. She quit trying. Taking Clark in, her face turned from panic to calm. He would never forget that look.

He flipped the phone open and pressed 2. Held it. Waited for an interminable second. *God, if this doesn't work . . .*

The fury of the explosion rocked the sky.

29

EVENTS BLED TOGETHER in the aftermath of the explosion. The shoulder pain numbed Clark, distorting his sense of time and place. His head throbbed and felt like it might explode. Some bystanders came running to the car. They knocked the shards of glass out of the windshield and cut Jessica's seat belt loose. Jess had blood streaming down her face from a cut on her forehead. When Clark saw her move and realized she couldn't put any pressure on her left leg, he was pretty certain it was broken.

Clark could hear sirens in the distance as the Good Samaritans helped pull Clark from the car. He couldn't use his left arm at all. "Agh." Clark winced as a helper pulled on his left shoulder. "Easy."

"Lucky you're not dead, buddy," a man said. Clark realized how right he was.

They helped Clark and Jessica to a spot on a neighbor's lawn, a safe distance from the car, while tending to their cuts. Clark thought he heard one of the women say she was a nurse, but for some reason he didn't really care anymore. He felt his body shutting down, the cumulative stress and searing pain taking its toll. It was as if he had gone into another dimension; events swirling around him were now taking place at the end of a long tunnel back to reality.

"I think he's going into shock," he heard someone say.

Helicopter debris littered the area while curious neighbors and motorists streamed to the accident site. For Clark, the scene became surreal. Sirens, questions, his wife's bloodied face, and the residue from the air bags all blurred together like a Monet painting, colors and hues with no distinct boundaries.

On the edge of consciousness, Clark fought against the growing sense that he wasn't part of this scene anymore. He tried working his way back to reality by sheer force of will. But the pain seared through his shoulder, pounded in his head, and overwhelmed his resistance. The Monet colors faded into a maddening collage, the pain in his shoulder dulled, and the last thing he remembered was a uniformed police officer asking him what happened. . . .

◁ ▷

Clark briefly emerged from the fog during the ambulance ride, floating in and out as Jessica answered questions from a Vegas cop sitting between Jessica's gurney and Clark's. Clark tried to contribute with his own fragmented thoughts, urging the officer to get the feds involved, but was interrupted by both the paramedic—"Take it easy, Mr. Shealy"—and the officer—"Mr. Shealy, you have the right to remain silent. Anything you say can and will be used against you . . ." The rest of the Miranda warning was lost in a tirade from Jessica, protesting how ridiculous this all was.

"We're the victims," she insisted. "Can't you see that?"

"I'm sorry, ma'am, but your husband has three separate warrants for his arrest on eleven different charges." The officer consulted a list. "Kidnapping, assault and battery, assault with intent to maim, assault with a deadly weapon, grand theft auto . . ." It was enough to send a guy back into shock, rendering him unconscious.

And it did.

◁ ▷

Later, it took nearly thirty frustrating minutes of answering questions from the locals before Clark talked to his first federal law enforcement official. The cops had separated him and Jessica. Clark's doctor had pumped just enough Darvocet into him to dull the pain without causing Clark to lose his sense of time and place. The doc had immobilized Clark's left arm and then, at Clark's request, deferred X-rays until the questioning was over.

"Looks like a broken collarbone to me," the doctor said, rushing off to the next emergency room patient.

Struggling to remain coherent, Clark fumbled with his answers and eventually turned cynical on the agents as they treated him like the accused felon he was. They couldn't seem to get past the fact that he had attempted to rescue Jessica alone, without help from the authorities.

Even in his drug-induced stupor, their bureaucratic questions made him realize he had made the right decision after all. Jessica was safe and being treated for her injuries. Preliminary reports indicated a broken ankle, a possible bone chip in her shoulder, the usual whiplash stuff, and the possibility of a closed-head injury. Basically, she would have a killer lawsuit against her own husband based on reckless driving.

Considering where she had been that morning, Clark should have been turning emotional cartwheels. Instead, he felt an impending sense of doom as he sat in his private, curtained-off section of the emergency room, answering questions and fretting over what was happening to Professor Kumari. Every minute of delay lessened the already-slim chances that his new friend could be rescued alive.

Relief came in the form of an FBI agent who introduced himself as Sam Parcelli, the first person who seemed more focused on catching the mob than grilling Clark. He was a middle-aged agent with leathery, pockmarked skin that probably resulted from a bad complexion early in life. Even in a sports coat and tie, he looked bony, with sunken eyes, long spindly fingers, and an Ironman Triathlon watch. He slouched next to Clark's bed, his mouth turned down in a been-there-done-that scowl, and took notes on his PDA even as the tape recorder spun away on Clark's bedside table.

"Your wife told me all about the kidnapping," he said, scrolling down on his PDA. "So you can skip that part. I've already got a few of my men looking for the GPS tracker in the wreckage from your vehicle. Right now, my top priority is locating Kumari."

"Thank God," Clark said.

"We'll deal with your multiple felonies later," Parcelli added.

"Right. Maybe you could actually help me with those if I cooperate?"

Parcelli stopped poking at the PDA and focused his narrow brown eyes on Clark. If he felt any sympathy, he was a master at hiding it. "Most of those are state offenses. Not my jurisdiction. But let me put it this way . . ."

As Parcelli stared, the room seemed to shrink. The tough-guy local cops had not scared Clark, but Parcelli was a different story—so matter-of-fact. He seemed like a man who didn't make threats and didn't play games. "An innocent man's life is in danger, Mr. Shealy. You might be the only hope he has. If you don't cooperate, I *won't* help you. That much I *can* guarantee."

Clark cleared his throat, took a swig of water through the straw sticking out of his plastic cup, and began spilling his guts. He told Parcelli everything—quickly, in chronological order. And Parcelli had the good sense to keep the interruptions to a minimum.

Actually, Clark decided not quite *everything* was relevant. He failed to mention, for example, that Kumari had e-mailed him the algorithm or that Kumari's trusted friend would be calling later that same year with the key. Clark also couldn't resist putting his own spin on a few events where it might be his word against somebody else's. But even in his own sanitized version, his list of indiscretions was lengthy—it was hard to spin the exploded kneecap of Johnny Chin or the collapsed nose of Dennis Hargrove.

It might have been partially due to the medication, but for some reason Parcelli made Clark extremely nervous, necessitating frequent pauses to suck water through the straw. Relief flooded Clark's body like a narcotic—or maybe it was the Darvocet—when Parcelli's cell phone rang and it became clear that his men had recovered the GPS tracking device.

"It looks like Kumari hasn't moved from that spot you described," Parcelli said after he finished the phone call. "My men are already heading there. We'll pick up this interview later. Is there anything else we need to know before we try to extricate Kumari?"

Clark pretended to be thinking hard, scrunching his face for effect. "Don't think so. Good luck."

Parcelli stared for a beat too long, unnerving Clark. Then he handed Clark a card. "If you think of anything—anything at all—give me a call."

30

THAT NIGHT, Clark and Jessica moved into a semiprivate room. Guards stood watch at the door. The treating physician detained Clark and Jessica for observation overnight because of possible closed-head injuries. Clark's diagnosis might have been affected by knowing that he would be transported to a local city jail if he left the hospital anytime soon. Consequently, he suffered intermittent short-term memory loss. With a number of criminal investigations pending, he never knew when that might come in handy.

The good news was that Jessica had not been sexually assaulted. Though her captors all wore masks around her, the man she identified as Huang Xu had actually been somewhat of a protector, insisting that only he and one of his men could touch Jessica.

That one exception, a stocky Chinese man with a viselike grip, seemed to know every pain-inducing pressure point on Jessica's body. He would dig his fingers into one such spot on the side of her neck, and she would nearly collapse from the pain, shrieking in agony as she begged him to let her go. If she tried to resist their demands, like getting her head shaved, or if Xu wanted her to scream during a phone call, he would simply nod, and this man would begin the painful torture. Jessica thought she saw a tattoo on the left side of the man's neck once when his ski mask slid up a little, though she couldn't swear to it.

There was also a time, Jessica said, when Huang Xu was not around and one of the other men decided to burn her with cigarette butts. Clark suspected there might have been other such incidents as well, but Jessica didn't want to talk about them, and Clark had the good sense not to push. Over time, perhaps, they would rehash the entire painful ordeal. Maybe he would ask about the photo Huang Xu sent him, maybe not. Clark knew just enough about hostage situations to realize that he might never know the full extent of what Jessica had endured.

They would both need counseling, and they would both need time—lots of time. But together, they would heal. Jessica was strong. A survivor. And perhaps, one step at a time, they could both rebuild some semblance of confidence and hope in their shattered world.

It was after 2:00 a.m. when Agent Parcelli reappeared in Clark's room. Clark pretended to be asleep, figuring he could also use grogginess to his advantage if necessary. But when Parcelli turned and quietly headed for the door, Clark knew his jig was up.

"I'm awake," Clark confessed.

Parcelli walked over next to the bed and stood there in the shadows, his face impossible to read. From the angle, Clark noticed a jutting chin that hadn't seemed quite so prominent before, covered with the sprouting stubble of a man who badly needed a shave and probably a warm shower.

"You feeling any better?" Parcelli asked.

Clark nodded. "Darvocet. Percodan. I'm lobbying for OxyContin."

Parcelli forced a thin smile. "Don't make me add narcotics to your list of indiscretions."

Clark tried to smile back but suspected he didn't succeed. The relief at rescuing Jessica had been short-lived, washed away by revelations about her mistreatment. Plus, Clark had maimed two men and killed several others. Kumari's fate still hung in the balance. Clark didn't feel much like celebrating.

He let the quiet hum of hospital machines form the question he couldn't bring his own lips to ask. They both knew why Parcelli had come back.

"Your friend didn't make it," Parcelli said at last. He sounded apologetic, his all-business tone replaced by a more sympathetic one. "We sent our best SWAT team in, but things turned chaotic. One of the triad members executed Kumari—a bullet to the head—before we could get to him. Three of their men are dead; four others wounded but expected to survive."

Clark felt his throat constrict, his heart sickened by the news even as he struggled to digest it. "Huang Xu?"

"He wasn't there. Somehow, he must have known we were coming."

For the next few minutes, Parcelli briefed Clark on other aspects of the investigation. They hadn't found Kumari's computer yet and thought it might have been pulverized in the helicopter explosion. Even so, they worried that the mob might have accessed the algorithm before the explosion.

"I think he would have erased it from that computer," Clark offered. "And the ones in his apartment as well. Kumari was no dummy."

That assessment prompted a long and piercing look from Parcelli, as if he knew something he wasn't saying. Clark decided it might be time for a quick change of subject.

"Did you figure out how the explosive device ended up on the helicopter?" he asked.

Parcelli said he was working two different theories on that one. It might have been that Kumari's laptop was on the helicopter. Perhaps his hard drive was protected by a code that Kumari wouldn't reveal even under extreme interrogation. Maybe the helicopter crew was supposed to finish off Clark and Jessica and then take the computer to an expert someplace.

On the other hand, Parcelli said, he tended to favor the explanation that Kumari intentionally and secretly dropped the explosive device out of his laptop's battery compartment before he got off the helicopter.

"Maybe Kumari heard them say they were going back for you and Jessica," Parcelli offered. "Later, Huang Xu might have taken the computer when he left the triad's hideout—before our agents arrived."

Knowing Kumari, just from the short time they had spent together, Clark favored this second theory. But there was another possible factor, in Clark's opinion, one he wasn't about to suggest to a no-nonsense FBI agent.

Maybe the explosion was an answer to a desperate prayer.

Clark closed his eyes and wished it were all simply a nightmare. "Was he tortured?" Clark asked.

Parcelli hesitated. His silence became Clark's answer.

"What did they do to him?" Clark asked. "How bad?"

Parcelli shifted from one foot to the other. "I really can't say."

The machines hummed, and neither man spoke for a few minutes. "I'll be back first thing in the morning," Parcelli eventually said. "The doc says he's got some pretty strong painkillers in you right now. We'll need a coherent and detailed statement. Three other triad members were apprehended on the interstate, about thirty miles from the hide-out. Two of them are suspects in Ms. Shealy's kidnapping. We'll need both of you as witnesses—voice identifications, descriptions of size and build, distinguishing marks that weren't covered by the masks, eye color—all those things will be critical for us to make our case."

"What about all my felonies?"

"First things first. You help us bring down the triad. Then we'll talk about the felonies."

"It was bad, wasn't it?" Clark persisted.

Parcelli nodded slowly. "Scalding water," he said.

When the agent left, Clark was grateful for the solitude. He heard his wife's rhythmic breathing on the other side of the curtain. It should have brought him tremendous comfort, having her back, but there were so many shattered pieces that could never be made right.

Jessica was alive because Clark had traded Kumari's life for hers. A good and decent man had been murdered. He was tortured because Clark didn't have the courage to trigger the detonation device as soon as he left the blasting area, even though Kumari sent the signal almost immediately. Clark could never forgive himself for that.

And then there was the matter of the algorithm—a secret at once so magnificent and so terrible that it seemed to reside at the very axis between ultimate good and evil. Soon, it would belong to him. Like the crosshairs of a target emblazoned on the base of his skull.

31

ON JUDGMENT DAY, Huang Xu rose early, stretched, performed his exercises, and centered himself. As a teenager, training under the watchful eye of the triad's Hung Kwan, he had mastered the martial arts, mind and body. He learned, among other things, how to enter an alternate state of perception, what Westerners called self-hypnosis. Xu had excelled, earning a place with the chosen seven, selected for leadership and education by Li Gwah himself.

He had been sent to America for a Western education.

In college, Xu continued his mastery of pain tolerance, disassociating mind from body, and put into practice the Buddhist principle of nonattachment. He held little regard for the things that motivated American college students, including the college women who found his disciplined body, long dark hair, sideburns, close-cropped beard, and mysterious ways magnetic. To defeat lust, Xu contemplated the loathsomeness of the body.

"Examine the body as a corpse," Li Gwah had taught him, "and see the process of decay that has already begun. Contemplate the various aspects of the body—the lungs, the spleen, the fat, the feces, and the liver. What is the body but a skin bag filled with bones, organs, and fluids?"

Xu attended medical school at Gwah's insistence but developed little respect for the American system of medicine. Drugs, surgery, rehabilitation—all the things held dear by his instructors had little to do with the real causes of disease. At age twenty-five, Xu helped perform clinical studies using self-hypnosis to reduce anesthesia and accelerate postoperative healing. The next year, he left the practice of medicine, concluding that the capitalist health-care system was more concerned with profit than holistic wellness.

"You have learned well," Li Gwah told him.

That same year, Xu began serving full-time in the Manchurian Triad.

His education continued under the tutelage of Gwah, the Shan Chu of the triad, a man who combined spiritual insight with political zealotry. It gave Xu, who had lost both parents in the aftermath of the Tiananmen Square crackdown, purpose and a cause worthy of his devotion—a new China undergirded by a revival of the old spiritualism. Nationalistic, but enlightened in the ways of Buddha. China, assuming her proper place at the top of the world's superpowers. China, resisting the dominance of Western cultural imperialism.

Xu believed fanatically in the triad's goals, rising quickly through its ranks, forging alliances and making enemies as each task required. Exposure to the West brought with it free thinking. But it was tempered by the memory of his parents' deaths. And a vision of the glory of China restored.

Which was one more reason why the events of the past few days had caused him so much frustration. The Abacus Algorithm had been developed by an *Indian* professor. That country, China's ancient rival, was experiencing its own economic revival. It competed with China for the attention of the West and, because of China's family-planning policies, would soon pass China as the world's most populous country. India, where the majority of people still worshiped millions of Hindu gods, had possession of one of the most powerful secrets in the world. If used skillfully, this simple formula could impact commerce, expose the secrets of other nations, and make the Indian subcontinent the hub for mathematical innovation. If used clumsily, the algorithm would throw the Internet into chaos. That much power did not belong in the hands of an *Indian* mathematician.

Like his mentor, Huang Xu followed the teachings of Buddha. But his was an imminently practical faith, which is to say, he molded the religion to fit comfortably with his agenda. He had no time for moral platitudes or hyperspiritualism. He spoke little of the Eightfold Path to righteousness and all but ignored the stringent moral code that had constricted the Buddha. He focused instead on individual enlightenment, inward peace, and mastering his emotions. He developed his own moral code, using the Buddha's teachings of nonattachment to fortify a cold-blooded approach toward reaching his goals. This strain of Buddhism, his own creation, he followed with total devotion. *Emotions* counted for nothing. *Regular people* counted for nothing.

The triad counted for everything. As did the man who ran it.

Xu remained steadfast in his desire to please the Master of the Mountain, the Shan Chu. It was not a blind loyalty, for Gwah had been forced out of China and lived a life of luxury in the United States that mocked his ascetic teachings. But the man had passion, vision, and a prophetic voice. His vices made him human.

At thirty-five, Xu's loyalty and tenacity had been rewarded with a position of power, heading the triad's operations in the United States. More important, Gwah had hinted on more than one occasion that someday Xu might be the Chosen One. His meteoric rise had brought with it jealousy and distrust. Today, as Xu faced Li Gwah to account for the debacle over the algorithm, Xu's colleagues would be gloating.

They, too, had learned the principle of nonattachment.

◁▷

Xu bowed slightly at the waist, and Li Gwah returned the gesture. Except for the shaved head, the older man looked every inch the CEO of a major U.S. corporation, not the leader of a Chinese organized-crime ring. He wore a custom-designed suit from Hong Kong, expensive Italian loafers, a Swiss Blancpain watch, and cologne by Calvin Klein. His couture set the tone for almost the entire organization, except for former golden boy Huang Xu, who arrived in a pair of linen slacks and a button-down, untucked shirt. He meant no disrespect, but he had learned to be his own man in an organization that valued conformity in the extreme.

Gwah's office, like the man, was a cross between Eastern religion and Western capitalism. Minimalist. A tabletop desk with a glass top and black legs. A few twenty-first-century swivel chairs, also black.

A glass coffee table. There was no computer—Gwah didn't use one. Same for a fax machine or smartphone. Gwah's only concession to modern technology was a simple cell phone.

Xu had been summoned here a few times before and knew better than to take a seat. A couple of Gwah's staff lieutenants stood off to the side.

Gwah picked up a folder and handed it to Xu. "Look at these, please." Xu braced himself. Calm. Focused. Centered.

The folder contained a few newspaper articles and pictures. He had expected something about the algorithm, but these articles had to do with misdeeds by the Chinese government. Xu had seen these allegations before.

"Falun Gong practitioners in our country say the government is harvesting organs from live Falun Gong prisoners," Gwah stated casually. "They remove kidneys, livers, and corneas from the prisoners before they kill them. They throw the prisoners into incinerators to destroy the evidence. A kidney is sold for a hundred thousand American." Gwah stopped, waiting for Xu's reaction.

Xu stood stoically, puzzled at why Gwah was bringing this up now. Xu knew Falun Gong to be a nonviolent, quasi-spiritual movement that combined tai chi–like exercises with bits of philosophy from a number of Eastern sects. After a nonviolent protest at the main Chinese government compound in 1999, adherents of the religion were branded an "evil cult" by the government, jailed, and persecuted. But the Manchurian Triad had never been allies with the Falun Gong. Xu had never seen their persecution as an issue that merited *his* concern.

"Our government denies this reprehensible conduct, but the statistics suggest the allegations are true," Gwah continued. He showed Xu a chart demonstrating a dramatic increase in organ transplants from Chinese donors. "What do you think?"

"Despicable," Xu said. He had learned to be a man of few words around Gwah. Today, he would be especially careful.

Gwah seemed to appreciate the succinct response. "What does the civilized world do about this atrocity—this 'despicable' conduct as you say? They turn their heads and pretend it does not exist. Why do they turn their heads? Because Falun Gong practitioners are the victims, and they would have died in prison anyway."

Xu could not see where this was going. What did this have to do with his failure to obtain the Abacus Algorithm? Gwah had always been unpredictable in an effort to keep his charges off-balance. But this came out of nowhere.

"If, however, this same thing happened to Christians in China, the world would take notice. They would demand investigations. They would scream about human rights violations. They would stop propping up a failed Communist regime. It might even open the door for a return to a Chinese dynasty. Do you agree?"

A light glowed faintly—dim, creating shadows in his mind, but still illuminating a few thoughts, a few connections. Xu understood part of Gwah's thinking now, but the part still lurking in the dark corners concerned Xu most. "Yes," Xu said tentatively, "I agree."

"Good. It will be our next initiative. We will place blame on the government and increase our profits. I need someone to oversee it. Someone I can trust."

In that instant, the point became clear, every dark corner illuminated. The great Li Gwah would never even mention Xu's contemptible performance in the fiasco with Clark Shealy. Gwah knew that Huang Xu would be prepared for that discussion. Xu would take his verbal tongue-lashing, offer an apology, and redeem himself with the next assignment. Gwah wasn't about to let him off that easy.

Xu's mind returned to his teenage years. The matter of pain. He could not graduate from his tutelage with Gwah until he could stand in front of his mentor, allow the jujitsu master to inflict pain at Xu's most sensitive areas, and never flinch. Xu was prepared for equal amounts of emotional pain now—and a humiliating lecture. He would handle it with the same resiliency he had mastered for physical pain. But to simply ignore the issue and pretend it didn't exist? To use it as leverage against Xu, without giving him a chance to defend himself?

"You have an American medical school education," Gwah continued. "You have learned the intricacies of surgery. I need you to return to China and make this your mission."

This whole line of discussion caught Xu entirely off guard. He was not prepared for *this*—torture as a job. Dismembering live human beings for profit. Was this what the Manchurian Triad had come to? In the past few years, he had felt himself losing touch with his mentor, but never had he expected something this barbaric. The very thought of it ran contrary to every fiber of his being. Was this the glory of China? The way of the Buddha?

"I cannot," Xu said. "It is not the right way."

Even as he heard the words, he could hardly believe he had said them. Gwah had the unfettered power to decree executions of triad members. Insubordination to the Shan Chu was treason of the highest order.

Gwah stood there for a moment, his eyes narrowed. "Are you sure, my son?" His voice was soft, but the words carried the ominous tone of a threat. "Killing fifty thousand people to rescue two billion is surely not wrong."

"With respect, Shan Chu, it is if there is any other way." Xu bowed deeply. "Dismembering humans for profit makes us no different from the government we seek to displace."

Gwah took a step forward, his disappointment evident in every wrinkle on his face, every frowning muscle. Xu steeled himself for abandonment or perhaps living with a death sentence on his head. The Shan Chu had that kind of power.

Instead, Xu was reminded once again that he could seldom discern his mentor's intent. "You are right, of course. We cannot do this," Li Gwah said. He paused, giving time for Xu's relief to sink in. "But if we cannot, why did you torture Professor Kumari? Why order your men to execute him rather than allow him to be rescued?"

"The greater good demanded it, Shan Chu. As you have pointed out, the government of our homeland dismembers thousands and sells their parts as if they are somehow less than human. Yet this one man held the key to power—the coming of a day when China would be ruled by the sons of enlightenment, not the sons of Marx. Because, Shan Chu, the salvation of two billion sometimes requires the sacrifice of one."

"You have spoken wisdom, my son. You have refused to do what should not be done. You are willing to do what should. You have proven your discretion—your capacity to lead."

Xu could hardly believe his ears. He was ready to accept his blame, to shoulder his responsibility. He had been prepared to fall on his sword. Instead, the Shan Chu had affirmed Xu's leadership. At the lowest point in Xu's career, Gwah had lifted him up. *This* Huang Xu would not forget. Xu would do anything for the man who believed so strongly in him.

"Sometimes the salvation of two billion requires the sacrifice of more than one. Sometimes it is a few."

"Yes, Shan Chu."

"The last page in the folder I have entrusted to you records the names of several persons associated with the church Professor Kumari attended. It is said that Kumari's pastor, a man named Abhay Prasad, has knowledge of the Abacus Algorithm. This time, you must not fail to disgorge this man's secrets. His weakness, the thing he loves more than anything else, is his church. The members."

The eyes of Li Gwah bored deeply into Xu's, searching for any sign of weakness. "If you harvest the body parts of his small band of followers, Huang Xu, and Prasad alone has the power to stop the harvest by telling you what he knows, he will talk. These acts of atrocity can then be laid at the feet of the BJP and the Indian government. The world will condemn this persecution of Christians and we will possess the algorithm at an opportune time. You must not fail me again. This algorithm will be your legacy."

Xu considered this. He tried hard to swallow his repulsion at what he had been asked to do. *The body is nothing but a skin bag filled with bones, organs, and fluids. "I have killed you all before. I was chopped up by all of you in previous lives,"* the Buddha said. *"We have all killed each other as enemies. So why should we be attached to each other?"*

The greater good for two billion people. Xu knew that a chance at restoration in the Manchurian Triad was rare and never easy. If he truly wanted to redeem his role as head of American operations, there was only one way.

"I understand," Huang Xu said.

PART II

THE LAW
STUDENTS

Good men must not obey the laws too well.

RALPH WALDO EMERSON

32

JAMIE BROCK WATCHED every deliberate step Professor Walter Snead took on his way to the front of the classroom. The man was sixty-one going on eighty—a walking billboard that the life of a trial lawyer would take its toll. A year and a half ago, he had closed the doors on his prominent personal injury and criminal defense practice in Los Angeles to join the ranks of Southeastern Law School's distinguished faculty. He said he made the move for quality-of-life reasons. The rumor mill posited a number of far more interesting scenarios. *Nobody* claimed it was because he loved law students.

Snead had Matlock's slicked-back gray hair but none of the television lawyer's good nature or charm. Plus, he outweighed Andy Griffith by at least fifty pounds, causing the loose skin under his chin to jiggle a little as he limped and scowled, limped and scowled, making his way down the steps to his lectern.

He was rumored to have been a chain-smoker until the day he rustled up enough clients to sue big tobacco for billions. The way Snead told it, he quit cold turkey, though close associates whispered about the daily smell of smoke on his clothes. Snead had a dark complexion, decorated with dark brown liver spots, and a gloomy mood to match.

Eventually, he settled in at the podium and opened his seating chart. Though she was a third-year student and tried to convince herself she was beyond caring, Jamie's palms moistened from force of habit. Snead was old-school, famed for his use of the Socratic method.

He would call on a maximum of one or two students per class period, grilling them with questions about cases they had read. In Jamie's opinion, it was an enormous waste of time, an intellectual fencing match in which the teacher had every advantage.

The problem, from Jamie's perspective, was that nobody learned anything about the law that way. And she wasn't alone in her feelings.

But Snead, universally despised by students because of his Snead-centric view of life, obviously disagreed. He was one of a handful of upper-level professors who tenaciously clung to the method pioneered by a Greek philosopher more than twenty-four hundred years ago. Come to Snead's class unprepared and risk embarrassment. Come prepared to the hilt and things were only incrementally better. The man was stubborn and cynical. He loved berating students.

Snead glanced over the seating chart, surveyed the class, and studied the seating chart some more. It was the same routine every day—a former trial lawyer's sense of the dramatic. "Mr. Haywood," the professor said in his raspy smoker's voice, "what was the issue in the case of *Novak v. Commonwealth of Virginia*?"

Snead fixed his bloodshot eyes on the middle of Jamie's row, a seat occupied by an eloquent African American student named Isaiah Haywood. Tradition required Isaiah to rise and state the issue in dispute. Next, Isaiah would be asked to state the facts of the case and answer a series of impossible questions about the opinion. It was a tradition the students had followed, with minor variations, in every Socratic-method class since the very first day of school. Snead adhered to the ritual with an obsessive fervor—barking at any students who began to mumble their answers before rising to their feet.

Isaiah Haywood did not stand.

A silent tension spread across the room, stretching the air so taut it was almost hard to breathe. How did Professor Snead know about *The Plan*? How could he possibly have known it was *Isaiah's* plan?

There has to be a law student snitch.

From his seat, Isaiah stared back at Snead—two boxers in prefight intimidation mode. "I'll pass," Isaiah said.

"Was the case too difficult for you, Mr. Haywood?"

"No."

"Is the law somehow below you? Is it unworthy of your lofty thoughts and magnificent reasoning?"

"Hardly."

"Then why don't you humor me, *rise to your feet*, and state the issue in *Novak v. Virginia*."

"I think I'll pass."

Snead's jaw tightened, an anger born of betrayal. He shook his head and made a show of scribbling something next to Isaiah's name. He turned to the young woman seated next to Isaiah—a psychological ploy designed to punish a law student for the sins of her neighbor. "Ms. Wagner?" Snead's voice carried up the rows and hovered around the head of the small blonde staring at her fat textbook—the words like the blade of a guillotine. "The issue in *Novak v. Commonwealth of Virginia*, if you please."

"I'll pass."

This brought another snarl from Snead, another vigorous scribble on his chart.

"Mr. Hernandez?" Snead said, working his way toward Jamie's end of the row.

"Pass."

"Ms. Valencia?"

"Pass."

"Ms. White?"

"I'm sorry, Professor. I pass."

White was only three seats down from Jamie—the plan working precisely the way Isaiah had diagrammed it. It was a move in retaliation for Tuesday's criminal procedure class when Snead called on an African American student in the second row named Davon Jones. Davon had not prepared for class and caused a collective gasp when he admitted as much. Snead, intent on making an example of the young man, required Davon to stand and read—word for word—the entire statement of facts from the case in question. After Davon mumbled through that process, Snead started drilling him with questions.

Unfamiliar with the case, Davon would volunteer a feeble answer that would draw a sharp retort from Snead. "No! No, no, no! A first-year student would know better."

After fifteen of the most painful minutes in Jamie's law school career, Snead finally put the class out of its collective misery. "It's obvious to me, Mr. Jones, that you are so woefully unprepared, we are wasting everyone's time." Snead closed his textbook and folded his seating chart. "Perhaps by Thursday you could do us the favor of reading the cases."

Without further ado, Snead tucked his criminal procedure textbook under his arm and limped disgustedly out of the room. Instead of the usual hum of conversation that accompanied the end of class, the students packed in stunned silence. Jamie felt at once embarrassed for Davon and angry at a professor who treated second- and third-years like children.

That day, Isaiah Haywood broke the silence, saying what everyone else was feeling.

"That guy's a pompous jerk," Isaiah said, loud enough for the entire class to hear. "We ought to be embarrassed for letting him humiliate us like this."

A few students ignored Isaiah and continued packing their computers and books. Most stopped to listen.

"Don't worry about it," Davon said without turning to look at Isaiah. He spoke with his head down, focused on the books he was placing in his backpack. "I should have been prepared."

But Isaiah wasn't buying it. "You've got your reasons. You're a human being. You deserve to be treated like one."

Davon shrugged and mumbled something that Jamie couldn't hear four rows back.

"We study these civil rights cases, we worship the opinions of Thurgood Marshall, and then we let the man treat a brother this way?" Isaiah asked.

Great, Jamie thought, *now it's a race issue.*

"Not me," Isaiah said. He raised his voice as a trickle of students started leaving the room. "I think it's time we initiate the Rosa Parks plan."

Isaiah proposed that everybody whom Snead called on the next time the class met should pass. A sit-down strike of sorts. This would force Snead to either teach the class without the Socratic method or cancel class for the second time that week. If he chose the latter, Isaiah and a few others would petition the administration and write an article for the student paper.

"Let's make the teachers teach," Isaiah exhorted. "The Socratic method is junk."

Though nobody took a vote, Isaiah spent the next two days lobbying students to abide by the plan. He talked Davon into skipping class so that he wouldn't have to pass for the second time in a row. But somehow, Snead must have caught wind of the plan because he called on Isaiah first. And now, working his way down the row, he was only two seats away from calling on Jamie.

She had read the case. Though she didn't appreciate Snead's style of teaching, neither did she like the Rosa Parks plan. She couldn't really put a finger on why. Part of it was the fact that she was a lone wolf and didn't like peer pressure—the Law Student Union, as she derogatorily referred to it. Guys like Isaiah would poke fun at students who tried too hard, so that the cool thing in law school was to get good grades without looking like you were even trying.

What was wrong with giving 100 percent? The whole thing was childish. Jamie was tired of it.

"Ms. Gallagher-Stargill?"

The woman sitting two seats down, who carried a chip the size of a redwood on her shoulder, made her announcement with glee. "Ms. Gallagher-Stargill passes, Professor Snead."

Snead stared for an extra second or two before he made another notation on his chart. "Mr. Farnsworth," he said without looking up.

The student sitting next to Jamie, a nineteen-year-old whiz kid named Wellington Farnsworth, jumped to attention. Wellington's classmates called him "Casper," a tribute to Wellington's doughy white complexion; soft, pudgy build; and squeaky adolescent voice. Wellington had accepted the nickname with characteristic good nature.

"Yes, sir," Wellington said, looking straight ahead so he could ignore the icy stares from fellow students.

"What is the issue in *Novak v. Commonwealth of Virginia?*"

"The issue, Professor Snead, is whether the confession of a sixteen-year-old boy should be thrown out because the police lied to him about the evidence."

The hissing started almost immediately. It was the law students' way of venting. A time-honored method of showing displeasure at Southeastern Law School.

Snead wrapped his knuckles on the podium. "Let's show a little respect." He glared around the classroom, but the students knew the individual sources of the hissing would go undetected. That's why the ritual was so popular—no one could tell where it was coming from.

"Did the court permit the prosecutors to use deception?"

"Yes. In particular, the court held that a lie on the part of an interrogating police officer does not necessarily mean that the resulting confession is untrue or involuntary. The court more or less applied a totality-of-the-circumstances test."

There was more hissing as Professor Snead followed up. "Do you agree?"

"No, sir. I disagree. It seems to me, Professor, that police and prosecutors ought to be held to at least the same standards as criminal defendants. If a defendant lies during a police investigation, he can be charged with obstruction of justice. Why should the police be able to lie and get away with it?"

Jamie almost raised her hand to speak against such lunacy—and probably would have on any other day. Jamie knew that Wellington was smart. *U.S. News & World Report* ranked Southeastern among the top twenty law schools in the country. Only one out of fifty applicants was accepted. And Wellington, now a second-year student, had been admitted at age eighteen. But he was only book smart. And his child-prodigy brain apparently had a hard time wrapping itself around the realities of the criminal justice system.

In Jamie's world, the prosecutors wore white hats and all other lawyers wore black. Jamie believed in law and order for very personal reasons. Novak, the defendant in this case, was an animal who had slaughtered two neighbors: a seven-year-old boy and a nine-year-old boy. According to the facts in the court's opinion, Novak nearly decapitated the seven-year-old. Why should the courts do backflips to protect defendants like him? What about the victims?

Jamie would dedicate her career to avenging the victims. She had promised that much on her mother's grave.

Snead apparently wasn't buying it either, creating one of those rare occasions where Jamie actually agreed with her professor. He snorted at the answer. "What about wiretaps, Mr. Farnsworth? Or confidential inside informants? Or undercover police officers? Aren't half the investigative tools available to police based on some kind of misdirection or deception?"

Wellington Farnsworth could not have looked more uncomfortable. By answering, he had alienated his classmates. Now Professor Snead had turned on him as well. A bead of sweat broke out on Wellington's lip as he shifted around a little, his round baby face wearing the expression of a man who had just been exposed on *Cheaters*. "There's no doubt that a lot of investigative tools *are* based on deception, Professor. But the question is whether they *should* be. I would assert that some of these programs blur the lines between investigative techniques and criminal activities, between police officers and criminals."

Snead smiled condescendingly. "So you're saying, Mr. Wellington, that there's no difference between the police officers in this case, who used deception to obtain a confession, and the sixteen-year-old defendant, who stabbed two of his neighbors to death?"

"I'm not saying that. It just seems to me that we outlaw fraud and deception in every transaction in our society except for the most important ones—transactions where citizens are being interrogated and accused of crimes."

This time the hissing turned into groans of disapproval. For Jamie, it took everything she had not to join them.

◁▷

Jamie followed Wellington into the second-floor hallway after class. She saw Isaiah, hands flying in animated conversation with his friends. He stopped midsentence as Wellington walked past.

"Impressive," Isaiah said, loud enough for Wellington to hear. "Book-award material." It was a reference, Jamie knew, to the award the law school gave for the top grade in each class. It was rumored that Wellington already had seven.

To his credit, Wellington ignored the comment and kept walking toward the stairwell.

"One guy takes the whole class down," Isaiah said.

Wellington shrugged, never looking back.

Isaiah shook his head. "Suck-up."

That did it. Jamie stopped walking and turned toward Isaiah. "Why don't you leave him alone?"

The surrounding students grew quiet; the flow of students shuffling toward the stairwell slowed considerably.

Isaiah tilted his head back, analyzing Jamie as if she were a lab specimen. "Another defender of Snead and his revered Socratic method?" Isaiah scoffed. "Let's be good sheep in there. Don't bleat too loud at the slaughter."

"You're a real jerk sometimes," Jamie countered, shaking her head. She turned and walked away.

She usually got along fine with Isaiah, but she had seen a different side of him today. Mean-spirited. Arrogant. Okay, so maybe she had seen him arrogant a time or two before. Still, his comments had been way over-the-top this morning.

At least he had the good sense to keep his mouth shut as she stalked away and took the stairs.

33

JAMIE SHOWED UP at the legal aid clinic fifteen minutes late for her 1:00 p.m. shift. It was the first time all semester she had not been on time, and she had her reasons. Primary among them was the self-absorbed Isaiah Haywood, whose shift, along with a few others', was supposed to end at one. Surely he would be gone by now.

She climbed the steps of the legal aid clinic, a converted brick house located in the run-down Techwood area of Atlanta, a stone's throw from Georgia Tech. She twisted the large doorknob and yanked hard on the door, a habit she had developed because the door tended to swell and stick after a hard rain.

She stepped into the entry hall with its worn wooden floors and took a left into the former dining room that now served as an office. It had two metal desks with cracked pleather high-back chairs, a few plastic chairs for clients, and expanding folders full of client files that occupied every square inch of shelf space on the interior wall and a good portion of the floor. There was an old desktop unit and monitor on each of the desks, but the students all brought their own laptops. Jamie had never even seen the desktops turned on.

One of the desks was occupied by a third-year student named Lars Schrader, who shared the Friday afternoon shift with Jamie. Lars was a blond Swede who practically lived in the gym and had the grades to prove it. He gave Jamie his patented "Whazup?" and she muttered some lame excuse for being late. When she didn't see Isaiah still hanging around, she felt her neck muscles relax. She didn't need another confrontation.

She had been second-guessing her decision to call him out yesterday in the hallway, alternating between increased anger at the way Isaiah had acted and a nagging feeling that she should have just kept her nose out of it. She wanted to put the whole affair behind her, but that wasn't going to be easy. She, Isaiah, and Wellington had become the talk of the school. Along with Professor Snead, of course, whose name was always on the tips of the chatty students' tongues, generally preceded by a curse word.

The phone interrupted her thoughts, and Lars let it ring four times. Both he and Jamie knew the phone call would probably mean another client file, and they both already had enough to keep them busy through graduation. Snead, as a relatively new faculty member, had been assigned oversight of the legal aid clinic. Jamie couldn't imagine that there was another legal aid clinic in the entire country whose faculty sponsor had less enthusiasm for the job.

"I'll get it," Lars announced loudly, shooting Jamie a perturbed look. He talked to the client for a few minutes about some kind of landlord-tenant problem while Jamie settled in and fired up her laptop. She checked the legal aid calendar. Her first appointment wasn't until two. She pulled out her Uniform Commercial Code book and hunkered down for forty-five minutes of studying.

Lars hit the Mute button and turned to Jamie. "It's an eviction case," he said. "Your specialty. Should I transfer the call?"

Jamie already had five eviction files and, by her estimation, at least ten more active cases than Lars. "You ought to learn how to handle them too," she said.

"Why? I'm going to be a personal-injury lawyer. I'll never handle another eviction case in my life. Besides, she should pay her rent if she wants to stay in the apartment."

"Maybe she can't pay her rent," Isaiah Haywood said. He had slipped into the room and leaned against the entry door. Jamie stiffened, then buried her nose in her book. But Isaiah was undeterred. "Maybe she's a single working mom with three little kids. Maybe her employer just outsourced her job. Maybe her mother just got diagnosed with cancer and doesn't have medical insurance."

Lars took the phone off mute. "Somebody will be right with you," he said. Without waiting for an answer, he hit Mute again. "Maybe she's a single young female who hasn't worked a day in her life and still receives an allowance from Dad at age twenty-one," Lars said, checking his notes. "Maybe she can't pay the rent because all of her hard-earned allowance money goes up her nose every Friday night."

"Everybody's entitled to a defense," Isaiah retorted.

"Good; you take her case," Lars grunted.

"Everybody's entitled to a defense," Isaiah said. "But not everybody's entitled to a defense from *me*. Only the lucky ones."

Jamie rolled her eyes and resisted the urge to take the bait.

Lars cussed and picked up the phone, making no effort to sound interested as he garnered more details about the case. Isaiah pulled a plastic chair in front of Jamie's desk.

"Are we cool?" he asked. Jamie could tell that the charm was in full throttle—concern pooling deep in the brown eyes, a serious tone in his voice. This was Isaiah Haywood, the former University of Georgia starting cornerback. Class cutup. Ladies' man. Defender of society's underdogs in every case they ever dissected in law school.

By halfway through his first semester, Isaiah had already hit on almost every decent-looking girl in his class, including Jamie. "Might as well start at the top," he told her, though she knew he had already flirted with at least three of her classmates. She gracefully rebuffed him, but they later became friends. Jamie, the would-be prosecutor. Isaiah, the heir apparent to Johnnie Cochran.

"We're cool," Jamie replied. "But I still think you owe Farnsworth an apology."

Isaiah scrunched his face as only he could do. "You can't be serious. Maybe I overreacted a little, but *an apology*?" Isaiah shifted in his seat, dramatizing how uncomfortable he was just thinking about it. "I mean, if Casper wants to listen to his own drummer, that's cool. But he should have told me he was going to do that *before* class, and I would have called the whole thing off. Once he lets the rest of us hang out there like that, dangling in the wind, just so he can get another book award—"

"That's not fair and you know it," Jamie interrupted. Isaiah gave her a wounded look, but she wasn't buying it. "Maybe he felt a sense of responsibility. And you, more than anyone, ought to appreciate a person who takes a stand against the crowd."

"The man scares me," Isaiah said.

"Wellington?"

"Yeah. That mentality. Abide by the rules. Placate the system. Defend the status quo. Card-carrying member of the Republican Taliban."

It was a diversionary tactic, Jamie knew. Isaiah could argue end-lessly about political issues. Two years ago, during con law class, a debate between Isaiah and Jamie on the issue of capital punishment had established her reputation as a budding prosecutor. And a person not to be messed with.

Isaiah had waxed eloquent about the discriminatory nature of the procedures and the mechanics of death. "Modern-day lynchings," he called them, citing statistics about the disproportionate number of black men on death row. "All we've done is trade a rope for a needle."

The class was quiet as Jamie raised her hand to respond. Slowly, in hushed tones, she told the story of her own mother's murder. The night she came home as a sixteen-year-old girl to find her mother dead, her father bleeding from a gunshot wound to the abdomen. She painted the scene in graphic detail, then quietly ticked off a list of the intruder's prior convictions. "Don't tell me that man deserves to live," she said. The class sat in stunned silence. Not even Isaiah challenged her statement.

After class, he sought her out. "I'm against the death penalty because I think it's discriminatory," he said. "But I'm sorry if I sounded insensitive toward the victims."

She had not seen that side of her classmate before. "We're okay," she said. "Just don't change the law until we put this scum away."

They shook on it—a touching of closed fists that was as good as a notarized contract. He walked away with her respect.

Which was why she wanted to at least be honest with him now. "I would have done the same thing Wellington did," she said. "Snead just didn't get that far."

This seemed to rock Isaiah back. The king of quick comebacks actually took a minute to process it. "Serious?"

Jamie nodded.

"Yeah, but you're hot. Any woman with legs like yours is entitled to hang the rest of us out to dry." Isaiah smiled, flashing the pearly whites that had melted the hearts of so many female members of the Bulldog Nation. He had apparently decided the Wellington issue wasn't worth losing a friendship over.

With anyone else Jamie might have been appalled at such sexist comments. But two years ago she had learned that Isaiah would be Isaiah no matter what. "Sounds chauvinistic to me," she said.

"Not really. I would have been just as mad if an ugly *female* student dissed my plan. I discriminate based on ugliness, not whether somebody is a man or a woman."

"Mature."

"But the two of us. Are we okay?"

"We're okay."

"Great. Then let's make it my place tonight. We could hang out in Buckhead for a while first, just so everybody knows we signed a truce."

"Not that okay."

34

JAMIE'S 2:00 P.M. APPOINTMENT, a gentleman named David Hoffman, came strolling in nearly twenty minutes late and settled on one of the plastic seats in front of Jamie's desk. Despite Jamie's hints, he offered no apologies or excuses for his tardiness.

She handed him a clipboard with a long form designed to see if he qualified for legal aid. The rest of the world had digitized, but legal aid still believed in hard copies with real signatures. Jamie had to help half the clients fill it out.

Hoffman frowned at the paperwork. The man was slender, perhaps late thirties, with thin blond hair, piercing blue eyes, and a ruggedly handsome face that looked like it had seen a barroom brawl or two. He had a small crook at the bridge of his nose and a slight scar above the right eye.

His demeanor was not what Jamie had come to expect from her legal aid clients. Nor did he dress the part. Jeans, yes. But the polo shirt betrayed a more prosperous lifestyle. Plus, how many of her clients carried the latest version of a BlackBerry on their hip?

He smiled at her—dimples and all. Quite a flirt for a guy wearing a wedding ring. "Do I really need to fill this out?" he asked.

"I'm afraid so."

"You don't have, like, a short version? An EZ form?"

"No."

He sighed, apparently surprised that the dimples hadn't worked their magic. He spent another few seconds surveying the form. "What's the right answer?"

"Excuse me?"

"How much can I say that I make and still have you guys represent me for free?"

Jamie frowned at him. She had enough legitimate clients—folks who truly needed her help. The last thing she needed was a scam artist. "Why don't you just answer the questions honestly, and we'll take it from there?"

"By the book," he said. "Good to see you people do things the right way around here. I need a lawyer who handles things by the book."

Finally, David Hoffman stopped talking and started filling out the form.

◁ ▷

Hoffman claimed only twelve thousand dollars in income the previous year, safely within the legal aid qualifications, and Jamie asked if he could bring his tax returns to their next meeting. Legal aid wasn't supposed to be used by middle-class Americans trying to save money on legal bills.

At Hoffman's request, they moved across the hall to the conference room. His legal matter was apparently too confidential for the prying ears of Lars Schrader. Jamie moved some boxes from the seats to the floor and pushed papers and files away from a small part of the conference room table.

She opened Hoffman's new file—a manila folder containing Hoffman's form and little else—and jotted a few headers on a legal pad.

"Now, Mr. Hoffman, what kind of legal problem do you have?"

Hoffman pulled a few folded pieces of paper from his back pocket and handed them to Jamie. She read the summons carefully and decided that she might not need those income tax returns after all.

The summons required Hoffman to attend Fulton County Court the following Friday to answer charges of impersonating a police officer and breach of the peace. Class 5 felonies—far more interesting than the typical misdemeanor diet of legal aid students. Under the rules of the clinic, Jamie could handle Class 5 felonies only if she had the approval of the clinic's supervisor—Professor Snead. As for Snead,

Jamie knew he wouldn't care. He would sign off on anything; he just didn't want to be bothered with actually having to appear in court.

"These are pretty serious charges," Jamie said, feeling like a real lawyer. "What happened?"

Hoffman was a good storyteller, and he seemed to relish this tale. He was in the repo business, he explained, and got into some trouble with a car owner about two weeks ago. Seems that Hoffman was preparing to tow away a practically new Buick Lucerne when the owner, a sixty-three-year-old man with a history of two bypass surgeries, spotted Hoffman and came running out of the house, cursing loudly.

Hoffman tried to tell the irate man that he just wanted to peaceably repo the vehicle, but the man danced around, calling Hoffman names and threatening lawsuits. Hoffman admitted that he might have flashed a fake deputy sheriff's ID, but the old man still wouldn't calm down. Eventually, Hoffman got the car hooked up to his wrecker, at which point the man climbed on the hood of his car and refused to get off.

"What did you do?" Jamie asked.

"I drove away."

"And what happened?"

"The old geezer slid off the front of his car and grabbed his heart after he hit the ground. Last time I saw him he was in the back of an ambulance."

As always, Jamie had a hard time listening to these types of stories and not judging her clients. Especially cases like this one, where the client really had no legitimate defense.

"Where did you get the fake ID?" Jamie asked.

Hoffman made a face. "Is that really relevant?"

He had a point. "I guess not. But so far, I haven't heard a good defense."

"I'm repossessing the guy's car under authority from the bank. How can that be a crime?"

"Did he ask you to stop?"

"Yes, but—"

"Under the law, you're only entitled to repossess a car if you can do so without a breach of the peace. If the owner tells you to stop, you have to stop."

"I didn't breach the peace," Hoffman protested. "*He* was cursing at *me*. I just did my job and tried to get out of there."

"Was he sitting on his car when you tried to get out of there?"

"Yes."

"And did you know that?"

"Yes. Probably."

"And did you intentionally pull away in an abrupt manner in order to knock him off the car?"

"Whose side are you on, anyway?" Hoffman asked.

It's a fair question, Jamie thought.

35

JAMIE SHIFTED in her seat in the packed courtroom at Fulton County Court, Criminal Division. She recrossed her legs—right over left, trying to get comfortable on the hard wooden benches. David Hoffman's preliminary hearing was scheduled toward the end of the day's docket; first, she had been forced to sit through several other routine cases, including the painful exercise of watching Isaiah Haywood defend a man facing his second possession charge.

Haywood, resplendent in a shimmering gray pin-striped suit, cuff-linked shirt, and pink tie, pulled out all the stops in his lengthy cross-examination of the arresting officer. As Isaiah grilled the man on his disciplinary record, the judge stifled a few yawns, looked conspicuously at his watch, and reminded Isaiah that it was a crowded docket.

When it came time for closing arguments, Isaiah alienated the judge again, insisting that he needed more than the three minutes the judge had allotted. *Not a good strategy,* Jamie thought, *in a case where the judge will render a verdict without the jury.*

"All right," a frustrated Judge Chalmers said. "Five minutes. No more."

"Judge, this man is facing a serious criminal charge. With respect, I think due process requires that I be given more than five minutes. I can understand that, for the court, it might get tedious hearing these same cases day after day. But for my client, this is his life."

But Judge Chalmers held firm. After arguing with Isaiah for at least five minutes about the length of time for the closing argument, the judge held to his five-minute limitation and "not a second more."

"Note my objection," Isaiah fumed.

"So noted."

David Hoffman, sitting next to Jamie, leaned closer. "If anything happens to you, I want him as my lawyer."

"No, you don't."

The next ten minutes proved her point. The prosecutor waived her closing—"We'll rest on our evidence"—while Isaiah launched into a passionate argument attacking the credibility of the undercover police officer. The court ruled immediately.

"Under normal circumstances, I might have considered releasing your client on time served and twelve months probation," Judge Chalmers said. "But, Mr. Haywood, since you seem so intent on preserving everything for appeal, perhaps I had better stay within the sentencing guidelines and not be quite so lenient. Mr. Radford—" the court turned to the defendant, who rose to his feet at the prompting of Isaiah—"I hereby find you guilty of possession of .5 grams of cocaine, a Class 5 felony, and I hereby sentence you to one year in jail with all but six months suspended under the usual stipulations."

The judge turned to the clerk, who was busy making a note of the verdict. "The defendant is to begin serving immediately and should be credited for his time already served."

"Request that the sentence be suspended pending our appeal," Isaiah said.

"Denied."

"Request that the defendant be allowed out on bond pending appeal."

"Denied."

Isaiah stood there, motionless, probably stunned. *But not half as stunned as his client,* Jamie thought.

"Anything else, Mr. Haywood?"

"Not until the retrial," Isaiah said.

"Have a nice day, Mr. Haywood."

The clerk called another case.

"I think we're up after this one," Jamie said.

But Hoffman wasn't looking at her. He had seen something behind them that had apparently troubled him. He stiffened and turned to Jamie.

"Does everybody have to go through the same metal detector we did?" he asked.

"Yeah. Why?"

"Don't look now," Hoffman whispered, his eyes straight ahead, "but I'm pretty sure I saw a guy with a gun tucked into his waistband, just under his shirt. He's in the third-to-last row on the other side of the courtroom."

Jamie tensed, her mind racing to the Fulton Courthouse shootings that had taken place several years earlier. Security had tightened considerably since then, but there were probably still a hundred ways to smuggle weapons into the courtroom.

"Are you sure?"

"Not really. He's sitting on the end, toward the aisle. Asian American guy. Funny right ear. Tattoos on his neck and forearms."

Jamie started to turn, but Hoffman put a firm hand on her arm. "Don't look," he said. "I think he noticed me scoping him out. Don't draw any more attention right now."

Suddenly Jamie's case didn't seem that significant. "Can you just go up and casually mention something to the bailiff?" Hoffman asked. "Maybe he could walk back there and talk to the guy and see."

Considering the alternatives, it seemed like a reasonable plan to Jamie. Attorneys would occasionally walk past the wooden rail that separated the spectator section from the well of the courtroom and whisper discreet questions to the clerk or bailiff while cases were being heard. If the man in the back of the courtroom was armed, it could be no accident. He might be a jilted husband who had gotten a raw deal in a divorce or a psychotic criminal defendant or who knew what else. *The point is—you don't sneak a gun into court unless you intend to use it.*

"Excuse me," Jamie said as she slipped past Hoffman and a few others in her row. She walked discreetly to the front of the courtroom and past the counsel tables while the other lawyers were settling in for their next case. She approached the bailiff, an older man with a good-size paunch, leaning against a side wall. She glanced back, casually surveying the courtroom, finding the man whom Hoffman had described.

He was staring at her.

She took a step sideways and put her back to the man, explaining to the bailiff what Hoffman claimed he had seen. The bailiff nodded and asked Jamie to return to her seat. As she did, he followed her into the spectator section and walked back to talk with the man Jamie had identified. Before Jamie sat down, Hoffman slid out of the same row.

"I'll be right back," he whispered as he passed Jamie.

A bathroom call, she figured. *Or maybe Hoffman wants to "coincidentally" walk by the gentleman as the bailiff discovers the gun.*

Jamie climbed into her seat and turned to look. The bailiff was leaning down and talking to the man, who appeared to be protesting his innocence. Hoffman walked by, without even glancing at the man, and left the courtroom. The man eventually lifted his shirt, and the bailiff appeared satisfied.

On the way back to the front of the courtroom, the bailiff stopped at Jamie's row. "He's clean," the bailiff said. "But thanks for bringing it to my attention."

"Sorry," Jamie whispered.

"No problem."

Satisfied, Jamie busied herself with some schoolwork, half-listening to the case at the front of the courtroom.

She started getting concerned about ten minutes later, when Hoffman had still not returned and the case being tried was wrapping up. Jamie packed her coursework into her soft leather briefcase and flashed a nervous look toward the back door. She noticed that the Asian American man accused by Hoffman was no longer sitting in the courtroom.

"Closing arguments?" Judge Chalmers asked the litigants.

"The prosecution rests on its evidence."

Jamie felt her muscles tighten. She wasn't the nervous type, but the prospect of standing in front of Chalmers without her client wasn't doing much for her appetite.

"Defense?" Chalmers asked.

"I do think there's an important point of law for the court to consider," the young female lawyer said drily. She picked up a case from her counsel table and started rambling on about its holding.

Take your time.

"Excuse me," Jamie said. She slid past the two young men on the outside of her row one more time. She walked out the back door and into the hallway, looking left and right, then walked around the corner to the men's bathroom.

Hoffman had disappeared.

She stopped the first guy who emerged from the bathroom, a wiry middle-aged guy with dark, leathery skin and bulging eyes. "Excuse me," she said. He stopped and eyed her curiously. "Was there a guy in there in his late thirties, blond hair, medium build, tall—about six-three?"

"No, ma'am." It felt strange being called *ma'am* by a guy old enough to be her dad. Maybe it was her lawyer uniform.

"Are you sure?"

He smirked. "You mean, did I check in the stalls?"

Jamie shifted her weight. This was ridiculous. "Yeah, I guess so."

"I don't make it a practice to check out the stalls every time I take a leak," he said, enjoying himself way too much. "But unless he's standing on the toilet, he ain't in there."

"Thanks." She checked her watch. Glanced both ways. *What's wrong with Hoffman?* She was tempted to go in the bathroom and check herself but decided to take the weasel's word for it. Maybe Hoffman had somehow slipped back into the courtroom.

After one more check around the hallways, Jamie reentered the courtroom and stationed herself along the rear wall. Hoffman still had not returned.

Three minutes later, with her client still AWOL, Jamie heard Chalmers call her case. She walked to the front of the courtroom and explained the situation, asking for a brief continuance. "Perhaps you could drop us down one or two cases," she suggested.

Out of the corner of her eye, Jamie noticed the prosecutor dip her head as if she couldn't bear to watch the court's reaction. The bailiff gave Jamie a look of pity. But Jamie held her chin high. It was, after all, a reasonable request. And it wasn't even remotely her fault.

"Is there anything else you would like the court to do in order to accommodate your schedule?" Chalmers said, deriding her with his eyes. "Perhaps we could provide you with a cup of Starbucks as you wait."

Jamie felt the anger rising but, like a good trial attorney, beat it back. Why did some judges believe it was their duty to be so condescending? "It's not an unreasonable request, Your Honor. I'm sure there's some sort of emergency or Mr. Hoffman would have returned immediately."

"No doubt." Chalmers leaned forward and frowned. "Is this your first time in my court—" he checked his docket sheet—"Ms. Brock?"

"No, Your Honor, I've been here a couple of times before."

"Then you should know the procedure. If your client doesn't show for a preliminary hearing, you have two choices: stipulate to probable cause and allow the case to be set for trial—which, by the way, I would highly recommend—or insist on the formality of the preliminary hearing, and I'll continue the case but in the meantime issue a bench warrant so we can hold your client in jail until the hearing is held."

Granted, Jamie was new to defending felons. But this whole proceeding, and especially Chalmer's judgmental attitude, struck her as being disrespectful of the notion of justice. That, more than anything else, offended her.

"Does that mean my request is denied?" Jamie asked.

Chalmers lowered his chin, deepened his frown, and at the same time gave her a bewildered look over the top of his glasses. It was, Jamie thought, the type of look Chalmers probably gave his dog right after he discovered a yellow puddle on the kitchen floor, just before he kicked the poor little mutt.

If the judge even had a dog.

"It means," Chalmers said slowly, "that you have two choices. Choice A: you waive the preliminary hearing on behalf of your client. We go directly to trial and everybody's happy. Choice B: you play it stubborn. I issue a bench warrant. Your client gets arrested. And Ms.

Simms, the prosecuting attorney assigned to handle the case, gives me a date about thirty days out for the preliminary hearing. Nobody's happy, except a few of the boys at jail who are always excited about new company.

"Now—" Chalmers gazed around the courtroom, mugging for the crowd—"what will it be? Choice A—everybody's happy?" He gave Jamie an exaggerated smile. "Or choice B—nobody's happy except a few of the nastier boys in our county jail?"

"Choice A," Jamie said without smiling back.

"Excellent choice," Chalmers said, generating a few snickers from the spectators. He turned to his clerk. "Call the next case. And have Ms. Brock sign the waiver of probable cause hearing on behalf of her client."

Jamie glared at Chalmers for a moment before approaching the clerk. She would wring Hoffman's neck when she found him. Then she would figure out a way to win his case. Chalmers's attitude had really started the competitive juices flowing.

36

SATURDAY, MARCH 29

BY 9:00 A.M., Jamie was in her gray Toyota 4Runner, her three-year-old black Lab panting in the passenger seat, heading toward their favorite spot on the planet. It was a perfect spring day, one of a handful that Jamie could expect each year in Atlanta before the serious heat arrived. The forecast called for a cloudless sky with temperatures topping out in the upper seventies. A light, muggy breeze meandered in from the southwest, but it wasn't strong enough to kick up any serious waves on Lake Lanier.

"You ready for a paddle, Snowball?" she asked. The black Lab's enormous tail thumped against the passenger door, his long tongue lapping up the cool air from the AC vent. He nudged closer to Jamie's lap, the excitement dancing in his eyes.

He snuck a Shaquille O'Neal–size paw on the middle console. When Jamie glared at him, Snowball diverted his gaze, feigning interest in the front windshield.

"Stay in Snowball's seat," Jamie encouraged. He withdrew his paw, but the tail didn't slow. "Lie down."

Snowball compromised, sitting erect as his head swiveled, taking in the sights and smells of the field trip. Jamie rewarded him by reaching over and scratching his chest.

As she relaxed, her mind wandered to David Hoffman. She had called him five times without success. Cell phone. Home phone. She had left three messages.

It was the strangest thing. She had actually grown to like the man based on the few minutes they had spent together this week. He seemed to be one of those guys who operated on the shadowy edge of the law, seeing what he could get away with. But he was also a charmer, and to be honest, she was impressed by the audacity of a guy who tried to repo somebody's car with the owner sitting on the hood.

A car cut her off and she hit the brakes hard, sending Snowball sprawling into the dash. Somehow, her clumsy companion scrambled back to his lookout perch. She reached over and rubbed his head.

"You okay?" she asked.

His brown eyes were smiling, tongue hanging out the side of his mouth. He was with his master, on his way to the lake, with his Frisbee in the backseat.

Life didn't get any better than this.

After two broken hearts, Jamie had traded in college boyfriends for a hyper black Lab puppy, swearing off men until she completed law school. It was one of the best deals she had ever made.

◁▷

In a prior life, before the demands of law school consumed her, Jamie Brock, future prosecuting attorney, had been Jamie Brock, Olympic hopeful. She had always been a fair athlete, but her Lone Ranger mentality kept her from enjoying most traditional team sports. She discovered a love for kayaking as a high school sophomore stalking a senior boy who was a dedicated member of the Lanier Canoe and Kayak Club. Using her dad's money and connections, Jamie bought her own kayak and started training competitively. As a teenager, the same wiry build that caused boys to pass over her in favor of classmates with better curves served her well in the world of kayaking.

By her sophomore year in college, Jamie was on the national developmental team for the five-hundred-meter K1 races. Plus, in the eyes of college boys, the athletic build and flat abs were in, while her rounded counterparts became a little too rounded after packing on the freshman fifteen. But during the summer before her senior year, Jamie picked the wrong day for a bad race, coming up one place shy during the Olympic trials, missing a spot even as an alternate. She cried herself to sleep and put her boat in storage. It would be more than a year before she brought it out to paddle just for the fun of it.

But that was all ancient history now. It seemed like another life—Jamie as world-class kayaker and man-eating college student. She felt as if she had passed directly into middle age and now found herself packing up Snowball for a leisurely Saturday paddle on the lake, believing that two-legged males were highly overrated.

Jamie pulled into the gravel parking lot adjacent to the boathouse, checked to make sure there were no cars coming or going, and turned Snowball loose. He darted left and right across the lot, zigzagging to the lawn next to the boathouse, stopping to slobber on familiar club members he greeted along the way and anyone else who happened to be there.

"Snowball!" the regulars would exclaim, pretending to be happy to see him. Some would reach down to stroke his head for a few seconds before he would dart off in search of the next victim. The lake sparkled in the sunshine, canoes and kayaks dotting the sprint lanes marked by the orange buoys. Coaches stood on the dock, stopwatches in their hands, squinting at the paddlers. One dad recorded the whole thing with a video camera.

Jamie called out to Snowball and showed him the orange Frisbee she had carried from the 4Runner. She hurled it toward a grassy area away from the dock, and Snowball broke stride.

Like a panther, he raced across a dirt patch and flew through the grass, eye on the Frisbee as the wind changed its trajectory. As it began its descent, Snowball timed his leap perfectly, a ten out of ten on the scale of Frisbee catching, and jogged back to Jamie to collect his praise.

"Good boy, Snowball."

He dropped the Frisbee at her feet and sat ramrod straight, waiting for the next throw. She rubbed his head, scratched his ears, and told him what a great Frisbee player he was. He gave her that yeah-yeah-yeah-just-throw-the-stupid-Frisbee look, but Snowball wasn't fooling her. He lived for Jamie's praise.

They repeated the drill—fling, run, jump, retrieve, praise—until Snowball finally plopped down in the grass, exhausted.

"My turn," Jamie said. She stripped down to a pair of black spandex shorts, a sports bra, and shades, then gathered her kayak and paddle from the boathouse. Snowball followed her and stretched out on the dock, sunning himself and collecting his breath while she put the boat in the water. He would need a second wind. If he held true to form, he would jump in and swim out to Jamie just before she started her third or fourth run, requiring her to paddle back to the dock with him swimming at her side.

The first time he had done it, Jamie had decided she couldn't interrupt her practice for him. She sprinted off on her next timed five-hundred-meter paddle, and he tried coming after her. When she had eventually turned around, she saw his blocky black head chugging along barely above the water, panting like a freight train, looking like he might go under at any moment.

She would get him back to the dock and demand that he stay there while she paddled away. After she'd completed two or three more sprints, Snowball would be back in the water again. Obedience was not his forte. But his loyalty and enthusiasm made it nearly impossible for Jamie to stay mad at him.

"You stay," she said as she paddled away.

He rested his chin on his big paws and looked at her with pleading eyes. The water was calling his name.

37

JAMIE DID A FEW TIME TRIALS and offered some coaching tips to the younger members. It was her first time on the water all spring and it felt great to get back at it. She skimmed across the water, propelled by smooth, quick strokes that kept the kayak gliding evenly. She rotated her entire torso with each stroke, using her abs as much as her legs, shoulders, and arms. She made the strokes look effortless, the proficient result of hours of practice under the watchful eyes of world-class trainers. Even though she had not been training, she still had more speed than most of the competitive racers.

But she also tired easily. And after a few runs, she spent her time giving advice to a sixteen-year-old girl who reminded Jamie a lot of herself at that age. Thirty minutes later, she realized that Snowball had not yet ventured into the water to swim out and greet her.

She paddled toward the dock and searched the banks as she approached. But Snowball wasn't on the dock or on the shore area or swimming anywhere near the kayaking course.

She pulled her kayak out of the water and started asking around. A few paddlers recalled seeing him, but not during the last fifteen minutes or so. Jamie left her boat on the dock and started calling for him. She felt a tingle of fear but didn't let herself slide into a full-blown panic. It was not like Snowball to leave the dock area, yet there were a thousand innocent explanations. Her gut, however, was telling her something different. It was a gnawing feeling, originating from that special bond between owner and pet, that something was seriously wrong.

After a few minutes of walking around the boathouse and parking lot, calling Snowball's name, adrenaline and fear started taking over. Other paddlers joined in the hunt, and within ten minutes Jamie counted nearly twenty fellow members of the Lanier Canoe and Kayak Club combing the premises.

As Jamie felt the knot tighten in the pit of her stomach, they expanded the search. A few members started paddling along the shoreline away from the dock and calling Snowball's name. Others jumped into their vehicles and drove around in ever-broadening loops, calling for Snowball out their open windows.

The search party peaked out after about an hour and a half, then started dwindling as paddlers had to leave. They assured Jamie that Snowball would be okay, and more than a few shared *Incredible Journey* stories about lost pets that found their way home. Labs had an unbelievable homing instinct, people told her.

At half past one, a few of the female paddlers took off for a local strip mall and returned with materials to make more than fifty missing dog posters. It wasn't until nearly three hours later, as Jamie drove from one part of the massive lake to the next, tacking her posters to trees and stop signs, that she allowed herself to truly consider the possibilities.

Snowball loved everyone. If some stranger had coaxed Snowball into his or her truck or car, the dog would have bounded happily along, amazed at his luck in finding such an attentive new friend. Snowball was a purebred and might be worth a fair amount of money to somebody who had a female black Lab. Or maybe some guy just wanted an awesome new hunting dog, already trained and ready to go.

Whoever had Snowball would love him. And Snowball would love them, despite their moral and ethical shortcomings. That dog was so loyal, he would probably do anything to win approval, even if his master was abusive.

The thought of it—some thug kicking Snowball around while the poor dog wondered what he had done wrong—angered Jamie. It strengthened her resolve to stay out looking for him all night if she had to.

It also made her cry. As she tacked up the last poster, tears of anger and frustration welled in her eyes. "Snowball!" she cried out, her voice hoarse with emotion. He was just a dog—she knew that. But she wondered if life could ever be the same without him.

38

JAMIE EVENTUALLY MADE her way back to the boat dock, changed out of her paddling clothes, and continued her vigil under the late afternoon sun. The breeze from the lake carried a slight chill, accentuating her sense of loneliness and despair. A few stray paddlers came by for a late workout, and Jamie asked them to keep an eye out for her dog. Mostly she sat alone on the dock, occasionally calling Snowball's name, convinced that she should sit tight at the last place they had been together.

It was nearly five thirty when her cell phone rang with an unidentified local number.

"Are you looking for a black Lab?" a man's voice asked.

Jamie's heart leaped, then pounded against her rib cage. "Yes. Did you find him?"

The caller hesitated, and in that brief moment of silence, a thousand scenarios shuffled through Jamie's mind. Snowball was fine, cavorting around the lake with a female canine hottie he just couldn't resist. Snowball was dead, hit by a truck, the bloody corpse splattered on the road. Snowball was frantic, sniffing his way back to Jamie after escaping his captors.

"We found him down by the lake," the man said. "We tied him up so he wouldn't run away."

Thank God. "He's okay?"

"Sure. He is fine."

Relief flooded Jamie's body. She felt herself go weak. "Thank you so much! You have no idea what this means to me."

"I have a dog," the man said. "I know."

For the first time Jamie noticed the slightest hint of a foreign accent. "Where is he?"

"It may be easier if we brought him to you or, maybe, if you prefer, we meet someplace," the man replied. He asked where Jamie was located. Since this man was on the other side of the lake, they agreed to meet at a spot halfway between. He gave Jamie directions to a campground area.

"I don't mind driving to where you are," Jamie said. "It's really no problem." She wondered how Snowball ended up on the opposite side of Lake Lanier. The perimeter of the lake must be at least thirty miles.

"No, is no problem for us, either. We can meet at the campground. We will be driving a white Trailblazer SUV with tinted windows."

"Okay. I'll be there in about ten minutes max. Is this your cell number—the one you called from?"

"Yes."

"Great. Can I ask your name?"

"Dmitri. And you are Jamie, right?"

For a moment, the fact that he knew her name startled her. Then she remembered the posters. And Snowball's name tag and owner information.

"That's right." She was already heading for her 4Runner. "See you in a few minutes, Dmitri. And thanks again."

"It is no problem."

◁▷

When she arrived at the KOA campground, the Trailblazer was already there. Through the front windshield, Jamie could see two men sitting in the front seat, and she thought she noticed the silhouettes of two others in the back as well, though it was hard to tell. The driver was a middle-aged guy, balding with just a stubble of hair on top, a dark complexion, and five o'clock shadow. The passenger was younger—a close-cropped blond with darting, ice blue eyes. Both men appeared thin. The passenger smiled and hopped out of the SUV. He was tall, maybe six-three or six-four, with a pensive air and a small earring in his left ear.

Jamie got out of her car as well, waiting anxiously for Snowball to come bounding out the back door of the Trailblazer. The passenger walked toward Jamie and extended a hand. "You must be Jamie."

She shook it and glanced around him at the Trailblazer. "Are you Dmitri?"

"Yes."

Something was not right. This wasn't the way to return a healthy dog. "Is Snowball in the backseat?"

In answer, the man reached to his lower back and pulled a gun from his waistband. He jammed it into Jamie's side. "Get back in your car," he growled. The pleasantness was gone, along with the stilted Eastern European accent.

Her mind racing, Jamie did as she was told. Dmitri hopped in the backseat and placed the cold steel of the barrel at the base of Jamie's neck. "Follow my directions and nobody gets hurt," he said.

"What do you want?"

He jammed the gun into her neck. "No questions. Just drive."

Trembling, Jamie did as she was told, turning where Dmitri said to turn, glancing in her rearview mirror as the Trailblazer followed. A few miles from the campground, Dmitri guided her down an abandoned dirt road and into a remote clearing that seemed miles away from the nearest house. Jamie tried not to panic, knowing she would need her wits about her for any chance of escape.

Like a lawyer, she analyzed the cold, hard facts, assuming the worst. Four men. A vulnerable young woman. A remote location where her screams couldn't be heard.

They had probably seen her posters and decided to use the dog to lure her to this spot. She was certain they would try to rape her. She would not go down without a fight.

"Stop here," Dmitri said.

She stopped the car.

"Turn it off."

She obeyed. Though she knew that every order she followed made her more vulnerable, she also knew that she must choose carefully her point of resistance. Right now, the man had a gun pointed at the back of her head.

"Don't move."

From the backseat, Dmitri placed a gag cloth in Jamie's mouth and pulled it tight, tying it behind her head, cutting into the corner of her lips. As he did so, he gently pulled her short, dark hair out of the way, giving her the creeps as his fingers brushed lightly against her skin.

"Lean forward and place your hands behind your back."

Jamie slowly leaned into the wheel, her mind in hyperdrive. *Is this the time? I can't let him tie me up like this! But if I try to turn on him now* . . . She placed her hands behind her and felt Dmitri slap a pair of plastic handcuffs on her wrists. He tightened them.

Next, they dragged her out of the car—Dmitri and his shorter companion, a sinister-looking man who leered at Jamie as if he couldn't wait to take his turn. They stood her against the hood of her 4Runner, facing the Trailblazer.

The back door of the vehicle cracked open, and Snowball came flying out! He crash-landed on the ground and plunged headlong toward Jamie, flying at her, forgetting everything she had taught him about not jumping on people. They had muzzled him, but he had no leash to slow him down. At the last second, Jamie turned sideways, bearing the brunt of the big dog's loving blow with her hip. He nuzzled her, rubbing up against her, wagging his tail, then hopped around in nervous excitement, probably wondering why she didn't reach down and give him a hug.

Seeing him brought tears to her eyes.

Jamie bent down, hands cuffed behind her back, and let Snowball maul her. It felt so good, even the scratches on her legs and arms. She rubbed her face against his head.

She stood and tried to grunt some commands through the gag—*Attack, Snowball! Attack!* But it came out indistinguishable, and Snowball only cocked his head and looked at her with curious concern. *Attack!* Jamie tried to scream. She made a little kicking motion toward the shorter man, the American.

He laughed.

But Snowball sensed something was wrong. He pawed in the dirt and pine needles near Jamie's feet, then turned and faced the men, standing his guard—straight back, his eyes darting warily from one man to the other. He sensed Jamie's helplessness and let out a low, muzzled growl. She loved that dog.

"Smart dog," Dmitri said. "Like I said, I like dogs."

Jamie stared him down, her fierce eyes drilling through him. She *would not* let them see weakness.

Dmitri stepped closer, less than an arm's length away. Snowball stood his ground, a low growl emanating from the back of his throat. Jamie knew that if Dmitri touched her, Snowball would attack. Muzzled or not, he would do everything within his power.

"Dogs are great, but accidents happen," Dmitri said softly, leaning even closer. Jamie could see the dirty pores on his face, the sweat beading on his forehead. She could smell the stale breath. He pointed his gun at Snowball's head.

No!

Jamie leaped at him, head down, trying to split open his face. But Dmitri was quick and sidestepped her attack. He smiled, aimed the gun at a lunging Snowball, and pulled the trigger.

39

THE GUN MERELY CLICKED, and Dmitri laughed, simultaneously landing a vicious kick squarely against Snowball's ribs, sending the dog sprawling to the ground. Without a whimper, Snowball was up again, jumping at Dmitri, who kicked the dog a second time. Jamie went after Dmitri too, but another man grabbed her from behind and threw her against the vehicle.

Somehow, in a blur, Dmitri ended up in her face, his body pinning hers against the SUV. He was stronger and quicker than she had anticipated. His buddy was dragging Snowball away by the collar.

"You've got a client named David Hoffman," Dmitri snarled. He was like a dog himself, baring his teeth. "He's got something that belongs to me. Something *very* important. More important, even, than that dog is to you." He paused for a second. Jamie leaned back as far as possible against the vehicle, but Dmitri was so close she could hardly bring him into focus.

"If you hear from him, it is *imperative* that you contact me. I must talk with him. This time we are just giving you a warning. A silly little game. If you hear from Hoffman and don't get in touch with me immediately . . . I will use real bullets next time and your puppy dies." Dmitri smiled—dull white teeth, the bottom ones crowded, Jamie noticed, as she tried to fight back the fear and blaze every detail into her memory.

"Of course," Dmitri continued, the smile gone, "this should be our little secret. If you tell anybody—*anybody at all*—there will be consequences. Do you understand?"

Jamie stared him down. Not even the satisfaction of a nod, though she trembled on the inside.

"Do you understand?"

She did not flinch.

Dmitri nodded and took a half step back. "We'll see how tough you are when you start losing the things you love."

He took a piece of paper out of his pocket, pulled down the collar of Jamie's T-shirt, then stuffed the paper in her sports bra as she twisted away. "Keep this number close to your heart, Jamie," he said. "Call it if Hoffman contacts you. Leave us a message letting us know where he is. Don't try to play games with us."

Dmitri grabbed Jamie's shoulder and twisted her around, cutting the cuffs off. When she faced him again, he had the gun aimed at her forehead as he backed away. Dmitri turned to his unnamed companion. "Let him go," he said. Snowball circled in front of Dmitri, positioning himself between Jamie and her assailant.

After the men climbed into their TrailBlazer and drove away, Jamie dropped to her knees. She had the gag out of her mouth in a matter of seconds and threw her arms around her dog. She removed his muzzle, and Snowball took full advantage, his long tongue slobbering everywhere as he sensed that the danger had passed. He couldn't get close enough as she rubbed him and told him everything would be all right. When she touched his ribs, he whimpered a little. She couldn't tell if the ribs were broken, but Snowball seemed to be moving around okay.

Then Jamie's emotional dam burst. The whole thing had been so sudden, so unexpected, so incredibly bizarre. As the emotions came flooding out, Jamie trembled and hugged her dog, tears soaking into Snowball's warm and wiry fur. She kept saying over and over, "You're a good boy, Snowball. You're a good boy. Mommy's proud of you."

Eventually she stood and wiped her cheeks. She and Snowball climbed into the 4Runner, and Jamie immediately picked up her cell phone. She dialed 911. "My name is Jamie Brock, and I'd like to report an assault and battery," she said.

◁▷

Jamie spent a frustrating two hours at the Fulton County police precinct, recounting her story, examining photos of Russian felons, and helping a sketch artist put together a composite. On the good side, they allowed her to take Snowball into the interview room, where he tried clumsily to make new friends before settling down. And they took her complaint seriously—it was, after all, kidnapping, assault, and battery. The young detective who asked most of the questions, a handsome, patient, and soft-spoken man named Drew Jacobsen, treated her with dignity and compassion.

On the bad side, the whole experience brought back flashes of the night her mother had been murdered. The sterile police environment—radios squawking, the endless questions, the secretive looks exchanged between officers, and worst of all, the sense of futility that came from sitting in an interview room answering questions and filling out forms while the perpetrators roamed free.

But Jamie believed in the system. Hers was not the kind of naive belief that many have—she knew its warts and imperfections due to human frailty—but she had seen the system work. Her mother's killer was on death row, exhausting one appeal after another. Some day, the system would exact its ultimate revenge.

In the second hour of questioning, exhaustion settled in on Jamie. It was a bone weariness, the result of adrenaline turbocharging her body for hours and then leaving her system as precipitously as it came, the emotional fatigue from a roller coaster of grief, desperation, fear, and anger. As the evening wore on, she could hardly concentrate on the composite of Dmitri.

"I think the nose was a little longer, a little thinner." She waited patiently, Snowball lying at her feet, as the sketch artist made his changes. *Too much,* she thought.

"Better?" the sketch artist asked.

She made a not-really face. "I don't know," she said. "Maybe not quite that thin."

And so it went. "The chin—a little too blocky. . . . No, I think the eyes were a lighter blue, eerie, almost like an albino. . . . Yes, that's it. But something's still wrong with the face structure . . . cheekbones, I don't know."

After three-quarters of an hour, Jamie gave up. According to Detective Jacobsen, they needed to get the composites out as soon as possible; every minute was critical. And when she closed her eyes, Jamie was no longer sure if she was seeing the man who had abducted her or the features she and the sketch artist had been toying with for the past forty-five minutes.

"That's him," she finally announced.

"Are you sure?"

Jamie would soon be a lawyer. She had seen her own father grilled on the stand by the defense lawyer for her mother's killer. Jamie knew the weaknesses of eyewitness testimony better than most. She knew that every word she uttered would be twisted by a defense attorney later, particularly if she expressed any doubt.

"I'm sure," she said.

As Jamie left the station, Drew Jacobsen said he would be in touch if anything major broke. He told her again, for the third time, to contact him if she heard anything from David Hoffman. The investigators had considered having Jamie call the phone number Dmitri had given her so the police could set up a sting operation. But for now, Jacobsen explained, they had decided against it. They didn't want to increase the risk of danger to Jamie. In the meantime, they were running traces on the number.

Jamie thanked Jacobsen and said she hoped to hear from him soon. She meant it, too. The man had won Jamie's unqualified admiration when he took Snowball outside during Jamie's stint with the sketch artist—right now, any friend of Snowball's was a friend of Jamie's. Plus, he had these amazing brown eyes and a square jaw that made Jamie feel safer just being around him. And one other thing, though technically it didn't matter since she was on a celibacy pledge until she graduated—the man wasn't wearing a ring.

Jamie knew that the safety she felt at the precinct would evaporate when she walked out the front door. The television cops could send someone to watch your condo night and day, but in reality the police worked under the constraints of city and county budgets. And they had hundreds of unsolved cases all vying for their attention. Jamie trusted Drew Jacobsen, and she didn't regret coming here.

Still, as she left, even with Snowball sticking close to her side, Jamie felt very much alone.

After she pulled away from the precinct, Jamie zigzagged through side streets and pulled enough U-turns to convince herself that she wasn't being followed. She worked her way to I-85 north and headed out of town, merging onto I-985 and making it about sixty miles before she nearly dozed off. She suddenly realized that she couldn't even remember going past the last two exits. She found a hotel that allowed dogs, a grubby little place that smelled like smoke even in the nonsmoking rooms. She checked the chain lock twice before lying down on the bed with the lights on.

Snowball didn't waste any time joining her on the bed, scratching and circling for a minute before he found the perfect spot and plopped down. He curled up in the crook of Jamie's legs, right where she could reach down and rub his ears.

Within ten minutes, with the television blaring and the lights shining bright, both dog and master were sound asleep.

40

THE NEXT MORNING, Jamie slept until nearly nine. She would have slept longer, but Snowball just couldn't take it anymore, rooting around on the bed, trotting around in little circles on the floor, and then finally sitting by the door and staring intently as if his bladder might burst at any moment. Jamie took him outside to do his business, then drove to a nearby convenience store for toothpaste, a toothbrush, deodorant, and a brush. She returned to the hotel and spent about five minutes getting ready. She herded Snowball into the 4Runner and headed north. They could stop for breakfast at a QT and still be at her brother's house before he got home from church.

As she entered the mountains of northern Georgia, the altitude and breathtaking scenery helped her forget the images from yesterday's trauma, turning her thoughts to Chris and his family. Sometimes it was hard to believe that she and Chris sprouted from the same pool of DNA. Sure, there were physical similarities. Chris was three years older and had the same sculpted facial features as Jamie—prominent cheekbones, dark brown eyes, straight white teeth, and matching dimples when he smiled. The girls in high school and college had swooned over Jamie's older brother. And, she had to admit, her more feminine version of the same face had not fared half-bad with the boys in college.

But the skin-deep similarities of the Brock siblings only accentuated their personality differences. Chris was an extrovert; Jamie brooded. Chris was a small-church pastor; Jamie wanted to be a prosecutor. Chris had already married and fathered two lovely children. Right now, the only men Jamie had time for in her life were the legends of the law—Judge Learned Hand, Benjamin Cardozo, and John Wigmore, the author of a famous evidence treatise. They didn't exactly make great bedfellows.

And most important of all, Chris had forgiven their mother's killer. Jamie wanted to see him get the needle—she needed revenge.

Like all siblings, they had a few things in common. A once-revered father who had suffered a stroke and now barely recognized either of them. Fond memories of a loving mother. Intolerance for the arrogant UGA fans who dominated the state. Adoration for Chris's two children. And a love for Snowball.

Snowball showed the feeling was mutual when Chris and his family pulled into the driveway of their house at a few minutes before one o'clock and found Jamie and her dog camped out on the front porch. There was supposed to be a key hidden under the mat, but somebody had apparently used it and forgotten to put it back.

Snowball bolted straight for Chris and would have flattened the preacher but for Jamie's call, reminding Snowball of his obedience school training. Private Snowball heeded his boot camp lessons, stopped short of his uncle, and waited for Chris to bend over and rub his head in approval. The dog's tail swung wildly back and forth, nearly knocking over Chris's two little girls, who tried to give him hugs. The girls giggled as Snowball wagged and nuzzled and drooled.

An hour later, after joining Chris and the family for hamburgers cooked on the grill, Jamie started making excuses to leave. She loved her brother, but he was an old maid when it came to worrying about her. Instead of the truth, she fed him a line about leaving town for a few days. She wondered if he would mind taking care of Snowball. Feeling a self-imposed double shot of guilt—one for misleading her brother, the other for abandoning her dog—Jamie bent down and hugged Snowball's neck.

"It's for your own good," she whispered, and Snowball wagged his tail.

"He'll be fine," Chris promised.

Jamie stood. Getting too sentimental might make everyone suspicious.

"I know. I'm just going to miss the big lug."

Snowball wandered away from Jamie, nonchalantly approaching the kitchen table, where the family had finished their feast a few minutes earlier. He noticed one of the kids' paper plates, a leftover piece of hamburger calling his name. He peeked over his shoulder to make sure Jamie was engaged in conversation, jumped up and snitched the burger from the plate, swallowed it in one bite, then grabbed the plate itself.

Table manners had not been his strength in obedience school.

"Snowball!" Jamie yelled, freezing him in his tracks.

But when Chris lunged for him, Snowball took off. "You little thief," Chris said, giving chase. He glanced back at Jamie. "Now's a good time to go—he won't even notice."

Snowball darted back and forth, the paper plate hanging from his mouth, the girls and Chris giving chase.

"Hurry back," Chris shouted to Jamie.

She smiled, thanked him, and headed for the front door. She would be halfway to the 4Runner before Snowball even knew she was gone.

◁▷

On the way home, Jamie stopped at a gun shop in Gainesville and purchased her first handgun. Until today, she had always supported a waiting period for handgun purchases. But with Dmitri and his gang issuing their threats, she suddenly appreciated the wisdom of the instant background check.

This gun was, according to the clerk, exactly what a young, single woman would need for protection. A .45 caliber, the clerk explained, large enough to stop any attacker with a single bullet. The gun itself had a flat profile—small and sleek. It was single action, according to the clerk, and Jamie nodded as if she had been looking for a single-action, .45-caliber gun all along. "Kimber makes excellent guns," the clerk bragged, and Jamie nodded some more. When she wrapped her hand around the grip, her finger extended comfortably to the trigger.

"Think you can handle the recoil?" the clerk asked. "It has a pretty good kick."

That was when Jamie knew this gun was for her.

She passed on the concealed-carry vest the clerk tried to sell her. She would make sure the safety was on and stuff it in her backpack. Not exactly legal, but getting a permit to carry a concealed handgun would take several days, not to mention the fact that her court petition would tip her hand to the men who had accosted her.

On the way down I-985 from Gainesville, Jamie called Drew Jacobsen. The detective took about five minutes to bring her up to speed on the investigation. He hadn't made much progress, in Jamie's opinion, but it was nice to hear his voice anyway.

She told him that she had dropped Snowball off with a family member and then, somewhat embarrassed, mentioned that she had purchased a gun.

"A pistol?" he asked.

"Yeah. It's a Kimber .45," Jamie said, hoping she sounded semi-intelligent with her new gun lingo. "A Pro Carry II."

"A .45?" Jacobsen hesitated as if he wanted to say something more but decided against it. Instead he asked, "You planning on carrying it concealed?"

"I was thinking about it."

"You know you'll need a permit."

"Of course."

"That can take several days."

"So I've heard."

Jacobsen hesitated again, and this time Jamie knew why. He was on thin ice here. "Of course, I'm a big supporter of the permit laws in most circumstances, and I would never counsel anyone to ignore them. But in certain hypothetical cases, I could see where the application process itself might tip off the very people a young lady might be trying to protect herself from."

"So you're saying I shouldn't get a permit," Jamie stated, just to get a reaction.

"I'm just talking hypothetically," Jacobsen said.

"Sure. And hypothetically speaking, I was going to carry it in my backpack."

"Do you even know how to use the thing? Have you ever had lessons?"

"I've never fired a gun in my life."

"Well, in my capacity here on the force, I couldn't actually give lessons. It just so happens, however, that I'm heading to a shooting range tomorrow on my day off. Might be a good place for you to get a little target practice."

"Amazing," Jamie said. "I was thinking about going to that same shooting range. Can you tell me where it is?"

Jacobsen laughed and gave her directions. They agreed on a time. "In the meantime," he said, "please be careful. That piece is nothing to play around with."

Jamie liked the fact that he sounded concerned. "I'll keep that in mind," she said.

◁▷

Jamie arrived at her condo a few minutes after six. As in the *Law & Order* episodes, she went room to room, pointing the gun in front of her, checking every closet. Nobody was there, but it felt invigorating doing it.

Until she noticed Snowball's food and water bowls. Suddenly the house seemed very empty.

She turned on the television. She locked the dead bolt. She called her brother to check on her dog.

She slept that night with the bathroom light on and the bathroom door cracked open, the light spilling softly into her bedroom. She kept the loaded gun on the nightstand. Three times she woke up and reached over to touch it. Each time, after feeling the cold steel, she slipped back into a fitful sleep.

41

"CAN WE TALK?" The pretty brunette with earnest brown eyes touched Isaiah's arm.

A law student? He didn't think so. She looked to be midthirties. He couldn't recall seeing her around the law school before. If he had, he would have noticed.

"Sure."

She had short-cropped hair, stylishly spiked. A killer body.

"Can we go someplace private?"

"Thought you'd never ask."

She didn't smile. "I'm serious."

Isaiah shrugged. Law students passed on both sides of the corridor. "Private like the library or private as in my place at ten?"

"The library will do fine."

"I was afraid of that."

She followed him down the hallway, mysteriously quiet. He held out his hand to shake. "Isaiah Haywood," he said.

"I know," she said, shaking his hand.

Interesting. They kept walking, Isaiah nodding at a few friends passing in the other direction. "A lot of people might take that as a cue to share their name."

She let silence be her answer. He noticed her movements out of the corner of his eye—lithe, fluid. Definitely an athlete.

"Beach volleyball?" he asked.

"What?"

"You're an athlete. I can tell. I'm guessing beach volleyball."

"No."

He opened the door for her as they entered the library. She had a sleeveless blouse on—strong shoulders, but not bulky. A body-fat ratio that would barely move the needle. "Gymnast?"

"Nope."

"There're usually some empty tables back and to the right." He paused a beat to formulate his next guess. "Cheerleading?"

She gave him a half smile. "Hardly."

"What do you mean by that? Cheerleaders are incredible athletes these days."

"Yeah. So are poker players."

"What's that I detect?" Isaiah gave her a teasing smile. "A sense of humor?"

She shook her head and frowned, the makings of a grin forming on her lips. "Actually, I'm a diver."

He stopped and looked her over. "My favorite sport," he said.

She brushed some hair in place with her left hand. A wedding ring. *Could she be more obvious?*

Isaiah found a private spot at a table isolated among the stacks in a far corner. She sat opposite him and leaned forward.

"My name is Stacie Hoffman," she said, her voice soft and secretive. "I need to hire you as my lawyer. Actually, you'd be representing my husband and me. I need to know this will all be confidential and absolutely secret."

Her eyes pinned him back. A hint of eye shadow, nice lashes, beguiling . . . if it weren't for the ring. "The only problem with representing you is that I'm still a law student," Isaiah offered. "There's the small matter of graduating from law school, followed by a trivial little thing called a bar exam, and then a nasty little law that makes it illegal to practice without a license."

"Don't you work in the legal aid clinic?"

"Yes."

"Don't you represent clients there?"

"Yeah, but that's done under a third-year practice rule. Technically, we're being supervised by one of our professors, even though he's never actually there."

"All right, I'm hiring you as my legal aid lawyer."

Isaiah shifted in his seat, torn between liking the spunk of this woman and feeling like she might be playing him. Real clients paid real cash. One of the things that got old fast in law school was having friends and family members, and friends of family members, all hit you up for free legal advice. At first it was flattering. But by his third year, Isaiah had had more than his fill. Plus, this woman was married.

"There are forms to fill out. We can't just represent clients who walk up to us in the hallway. Besides . . ."

Stacie put a hand on his arm. "Just hear me out." Her gaze sizzled with intensity. "Please."

"No promises."

"I know."

He shrugged and slouched a little lower in his seat. *What could it hurt?*

"You don't want to take notes?"

Isaiah tapped his skull. "Steel trap, baby."

Her look said she was not impressed. "My husband is being represented by your colleague, a law student named Jamie Brock. We can't go directly to Jamie because we think they might be watching her. My husband saw you argue a case in court the other day and thought maybe you would help us."

"Who is 'they'?"

Stacie lowered her voice. "The triads. Chinese mafia."

Isaiah gave her a skeptical nod. *I see.* The crazy thing was that she actually looked sane.

"My husband attended court with Jamie Friday on a Class 5 felony—impersonating a police officer. But before his case was called, David—that's my husband—saw a member of the mafia he recognized from several years ago. They're trying to kill us, Isaiah. David set up a diversion and bolted from the courtroom. He ditched the guy and then circled back and picked up his car. We've been in hiding all weekend."

As she talked, Isaiah tried to assess her credibility. She was educated and compelling, not the kind who might typically imagine false mafia figures. Though she occasionally glanced around the library, she didn't appear to be overly paranoid. It was hard not to take her seriously.

"So what do you want me to do? Why not just go to the cops?"

Stacie leaned forward a little more, and the movement had a kind of magnetism to it. Isaiah found himself sitting up a little straighter, drawn by the captivating pull of a nice-looking woman who needed him. Even if she was married.

"David and I are part of the federal witness protection program. We testified against some leaders of the Chinese mafia four years ago in Nevada. But now they've done something the federal agents said would never happen—they've found us here in Atlanta. We need you to approach an FBI agent we think we can trust and let him know our identities have been compromised. We need to start over with new identities."

Snead had briefly touched on the witness protection program about a month ago in crim pro class. Isaiah didn't remember much from that discussion, but he thought he recalled some basics. "Isn't the U.S. Marshals Service supposed to supervise the witness protection program?"

"Yes. But somebody in that office compromised our location, Isaiah. Or somehow it leaked out. Until we find out how—we want to deal only with this one FBI agent. No marshals."

"Why don't you just go to him yourself?"

"We don't even want the FBI to know where we are unless we know for sure that this guy's willing to help us. We're a little spooked right now, Isaiah. And we're not willing to trust these federal bureaucrats until we can get a new protection deal in place—one that severely restricts the number of people who know about our new identities. We need an intermediary to negotiate that deal so that David and I can stay in hiding until it's in place."

The whole thing sounded intriguing to Isaiah, but it had a serious downside. "So you want me to talk to this FBI agent so the mob can put *me* on their hit list."

"They won't even know you're representing us. That's why we didn't approach Jamie. Like I said, she's probably being followed."

Suddenly Isaiah found himself whispering. "Why not go to a real lawyer? Why me?"

"We need someone who hasn't been compromised by the system. Someone young and idealistic. We've been burned by lawyers in the past." Stacie reached into her purse and pulled out a white legal envelope. She handed it across the table. "My husband is a little unorthodox, but he's a pretty good judge of character. And we're not asking you to do this for free."

Isaiah's instincts told him not to grab it. Stacie laid it on the table, and Isaiah stared at it for a second before sliding it back toward her.

"It's a retainer," she protested.

"Legal aid clients don't pay."

Stacie frowned, and the brown eyes turned soft . . . pleading. "Look, I don't want you to get in trouble for us. And if you can't take the money, I understand. But we both know this is not a legal aid case, Isaiah. We're not really asking you to practice law; we just need you to serve as a go-between with this FBI agent. David and I really struggled with whether we should even ask you to get involved in something like this. If you choose to help us, paying for your services is the least we can do."

She nudged the envelope back toward the middle of the table, and this time Isaiah picked it up. He slit open the end and peered inside. Cash. A stack of hundreds.

"How much?"

"Two thousand for starters. If we get the new identities and a new start, we'll pay another twenty."

Isaiah wondered where they got that kind of money, especially in cash, but he was going to be a lawyer soon. That was one question real lawyers never asked.

He still thought he should reject the money. On the other hand, this case—and Stacie in particular—had already drawn him in. How often did a young lawyer have a chance to do something this meaningful? David Hoffman was right about one thing: this case fit Isaiah's personality, his passion. The Hoffmans needed somebody to take on the system. Somebody who wasn't afraid to color at the edges of the box, maybe even a little outside it.

Plus, though this was definitely a secondary point, he had more than fifty thousand in student loans. He gently riffled the bills with his thumb. They seemed real.

"One more thing," she said. "You can't tell your instructor. Nobody but you and Jamie can know about this. David doesn't trust your professor."

"How does your husband know Professor Snead?"

"He knows a lot of things."

"That's a reply straight out of a James Bond movie." Isaiah lowered his voice and did an imitation. "'He knows a lot of things.'" Then he gave her his best serious-lawyer look. "Problem is—that doesn't tell me anything. If you want me to be your lawyer, I've got to know what you know."

Stacie didn't shrink back. If anything, she got more intense, her eyes becoming lasers. "That's where you're wrong, Isaiah. This is not a game. We're dealing with the mob here—the Manchurian Triad. The *less* you know, the better. This is dangerous. And if you're not up to it, we'll get somebody who is."

"Now you've done it."

"What?"

"Threatened my manhood." He leaned forward and raised his hushed voice an octave. "If you're not man enough, we'll get somebody who is." He waited for a smile, a flicker in her eyes, a slight loosening of her tense neck muscles.

She sat stone-faced. Not even a courtesy grin. This woman had a serious humor deficiency. But then, she had the mob after her. A damsel in distress. A good-looking damsel. Plus, she had money.

"What's the agent's name?" he asked.

"Sam Parcelli."

42

THE SHOOTING RANGE was not at all what Jamie expected. It felt sterile, hollow, and loud. She wore bulky safety glasses and large earmuffs, her hair pulled up inside a baseball cap. There were six shooting lanes about fifty yards long with paper targets at the end. All but two of the lanes were occupied. Bullet casings lay scattered on the floor.

She didn't feel the intoxicating allure of firearms that she had seen in the eyes of some men she had known. Nor did her new friend, Detective Jacobsen, wrap his arms around her and gingerly show her how to hold her new weapon of destruction. Which was fine with Jamie. She wasn't the type to be treated like she might break at any minute.

To his credit, Jacobsen kept the contact to a minimum. When he first inspected the gun, he shook his head a little as if maybe Jamie had more guts than brains. "Nice piece," he said, turning the gun over in his hand. "It'll have a little kick."

"So I've heard."

He walked her through a whirlwind gun-safety course. The Kimber had a narrower grip than Jamie expected, and it fit comfortably in her hand. Plus, she had to admit, she felt powerful holding the thing. And a little more secure.

Jacobsen was right. The gun recoiled against her when she fired it, causing her to jerk the shot upward. He showed her how to sight the gun in, the proper grip, and the best stance for accuracy—a shooter's crouch, arms straight out in front, both hands on the grip. They started at ten yards, then twenty, and eventually thirty-five. Though Jamie was a natural athlete, her would-be assailant really didn't have much to worry about if he stayed at least thirty-five yards away.

Two hours passed quickly. When she left, Jamie was no expert, but neither did the gun feel like a complete stranger in her hands. She thanked Drew Jacobsen profusely.

"I hope you never have to use it outside a shooting range," he said.

The thought of it made her shudder.

When Jamie climbed into her 4Runner and picked up her phone, she noticed three calls from Isaiah Haywood. She called him back without checking his messages.

"We've got to talk," he said.

His serious tone made Jamie realize how much her world had changed in three short days. Isaiah undoubtedly wanted to talk about a new strategy for crim pro class. Just last week, the biggest issue in her life had been whether to pass if called on by Professor Snead. Now she was being stalked by professional criminals and learning how to kill a person, if necessary.

"What about?" she asked.

"I can't say over the phone."

She didn't have time for this. "Look, Isaiah, if you're calling about crim pro class, I'm actually pretty busy right now—"

"It's about David Hoffman," Isaiah interrupted.

Her blood went cold. She lowered her voice. "What about him?"

"We've got to meet," Isaiah insisted. "I really don't want to talk about this on a cell phone."

Now he really had her worried. If Isaiah knew something about Hoffman, it could trigger all kinds of chaos. Jacobsen would want to know. Dmitri might come back after her. This was not good—she just wanted Hoffman out of her life.

"Where do you want to meet?"

"Someplace a young, hip African American would never be noticed," he said.

She reeled off the names of a few Buckhead bars, but Isaiah rejected them.

"I was thinking the Waffle House just off exit 6 on Route 400 North," Isaiah said.

It made Jamie smile. At least Isaiah hadn't lost his confident cynicism. "In this traffic, it'll take me forty-five minutes to get there," she said.

"No problem," Isaiah said. "I'll get a table. You can't miss me. I'll be the only black guy there without an apron on."

43

AT THE RESTAURANT, Jamie argued that they needed to bring Snead into the loop immediately. Isaiah, halfway through a plate of sticky blueberry pancakes, disagreed. "Snead won't let us take the case," he argued. "Plus, he's an A1 jerk." He forked another small mountain of pancakes into his mouth—Jamie's chance to respond.

"We can't do this without him. We're not even lawyers yet."

"I've been thinking about that," Isaiah said, sliding the pancakes into a cheek. "Stacie Hoffman's right. I'm not really acting like a lawyer. More like a messenger boy. Besides—" he paused, chewing and swallowing—"if the feds go for it, they'll know we're not lawyers. It won't be like we're scamming anybody."

"That doesn't make it right." Jamie had a bad feeling about this, and she had learned to trust her budding legal instincts. She was already skirting the edge of the law—the concealed handgun sitting in her backpack. Why complicate matters?

"Maybe this is why they came to me," Isaiah continued, slicing off another pile of pancakes dripping with syrup. "They can't afford to play this one by the rules."

They argued about it for a few more minutes, and then Isaiah lowered his voice and checked around as if the FBI might have surveillance cameras inside the Waffle House. "I've done some research on Snead," he confided. "Why do you think a dude who's making a couple million a year filing tort cases in L.A. would give that up and move to the A-T-L to teach?"

"I don't know. Quality of life, maybe."

"Or maybe," Isaiah said, emphasizing the point with his fork, "there are four criminal cases presently on appeal that Snead handled at the trial level where an appellate lawyer is claiming ineffective assistance of counsel."

Jamie's prosecutorial mind-set kicked in. "That happens all the time. Felons don't have anything else to argue, so they attack their own lawyers."

"And two of his previous cases actually got reversed on that basis," Isaiah countered. He waited for Jamie's reaction, but she gave him nothing but a poker face. "His track record as a criminal defense lawyer is abysmal. I couldn't find a single case he won. And now he's teaching crim pro."

"And you're doing all this research because . . . ?"

Isaiah's syrupy smile lit up the booth and half of the Waffle House with it. "Next time he calls on me in class, he'd better be ready to man up."

Eventually, the two agreed to disagree about telling Snead. Jamie couldn't go with Isaiah to meet Parcelli anyway, so it would be Isaiah's call.

Jamie filled Isaiah in about the men who had assaulted her at Lake Lanier. He listened intently and shoveled the rest of the pancakes down. He chased them with a swig of milk.

As Jamie finished the story, his forehead creased with concentration. He rubbed the short stubble on top of his head. "Did you say the dude's name was Dmitri?"

"Yes."

"That's Russian."

"Last time I checked."

"Did he look Russian?"

"I guess so. I mean, what does a Russian look like? He was a white guy with blond hair who faked an Eastern European accent when I first talked to him."

"Definitely not Chinese."

"No, Isaiah. Definitely not Chinese."

"But Stacie said the Chinese mob was after her. The triads."

"Good point." Jamie took a drink of water. She would have to call Detective Jacobsen with this new twist. "Maybe Hoffman testified against both—the Russian mob and the Chinese mob. Maybe we're getting caught in the middle of a mob war."

Isaiah's face seemed to brighten at the prospect. "That's what I'm talkin' about," he said. "Real lawyering. Mobsters everywhere. A beautiful woman as my partner."

"This isn't a game, Isaiah. And you're stuck with me, not a beautiful woman."

"And modest, too!" He wiped his mouth, the playfulness disappearing as he did so. "You need somebody to stay at your condo with you?"

Jamie shook her head. "I've got a friend."

"Male or female?"

"None of your business."

"What's his name?"

"What part of 'none of your business' don't you understand?"

"Well, I'm just sayin'—seems to me we're partners here. And I want to make sure my girl—"

Jamie plopped her backpack on the table, cutting him off. She unzipped the small compartment on the bottom of the back, revealing the sleek polished metal of her gun. Isaiah's eyes went wide.

"His name is Kimber," Jamie said. It was melodramatic, she knew, but it got Isaiah's attention.

"My partner's packin'!" Isaiah's lips curled into the proud smile of a dad watching his daughter's first steps. Just then, their waitress reappeared at the linoleum table, a heavyset woman, midforties, food stains dotting her white uniform. She had her hair pulled back in a clip and long fake nails polished red.

"Is that a Kimber?" she asked Jamie.

44

CRIM PRO TURNED unusually quiet as Professor Snead limped his way to the front of the classroom, removed his seating chart, and surveyed the room. His eyes locked on Isaiah Haywood's empty seat, and then his stubby finger scrolled down the list of names.

"Mr. Haywood," he called out.

The class waited a few seconds. Snead called the name again.

"He had an interview in Washington, D.C., today," Jamie said. Even as she spoke, she wrestled with her own definition of the word *interview*. Questions and answers. She supposed it could cover this.

"With what firm?" Snead asked.

"The federal government," Jamie responded.

"I see." Snead licked his lips. Made a mark on the chart. "If I recall correctly, I asked each of you at the start of the semester to make every effort to work your job interviews around my class schedule. Am I getting senile, or do some of you remember that?"

A few students lowered their heads. Others looked disapprovingly at Snead for taking shots at Isaiah in his absence. A hissing noise emanated from behind Jamie.

"Ms. Brock, do you recall that?"

"I think so, sir."

"Good. Maybe I'm not as senile as I thought."

His finger returned to the seating chart. When his head popped up again, he was looking directly at Jamie. She peered back at him over the raised monitor of her laptop, her fingers suspended above the keys. It was the first time all semester she had not done the reading.

"Ms. Brock," he called out, "why don't you tell us the issue in *Commonwealth v. Gary*?"

"I'm sorry, Professor." Her throat tightened. Never in three years of law school had she uttered these words. "I'm not prepared."

Snead scowled at her, the gray eyebrows lowered in condemnation, displeasure written on every wrinkle of his face. He let Jamie's remark just hang out there, conspicuous as a neon sign on a desert highway.

Finally he turned to Jamie's immediate right. "Mr. Shaeffer, did you inconvenience yourself and read the case?"

"I did."

"Perhaps you could help Ms. Brock out."

◁ ▷

This guy needs to loosen up, Isaiah thought. He was sitting across from Agent Samuel Parcelli at the Great American Bagel Bakery just outside the metal detectors in Terminal B of Reagan National Airport. They both nursed strong coffees. Parcelli was strictly no-nonsense, with tanned skin, a marathoner's build, and the eyes and nose of a hawk. Everything about him said he had been around the block a few times.

When he set up the meeting over the phone, Isaiah said he represented David and Stacie Hoffman. Today, he tried to look the part. His imported beige suit, only slightly wrinkled from the plane ride, was Johnnie Cochranesque. When Parcelli asked for a card, Isaiah reached into his suit coat pocket and mumbled a lame excuse. He'd left his briefcase in Atlanta and this was a new suit. Parcelli handed Isaiah his own business card—government-issued, light brown. Boring.

For the first few minutes, Isaiah tried to find some common ground—airplane complaints, this coffee's terrible, nice weather, March Madness—but Parcelli wasn't interested. Isaiah slid forward and put his forearms on the table, leaning into it. He told Parcelli that the mob had found the Hoffmans, that Isaiah's clients suspected a leak in the marshals' office.

"They trust you, Mr. Parcelli. They'll help you catch this member of the Manchurian Triad who spotted David Hoffman if you'll agree to do two things. One, set them up with new identities. And two, personally oversee the process yourself—involving only those members of the marshals' office that you handpick and trust."

Parcelli didn't move a muscle, not so much as a twitch. Isaiah wanted to check to see if the guy was still breathing.

The agent took a deliberate sip of coffee. "I can't do that," he said to Isaiah.

"Why not?"

"Before I answer that, you need to answer one of my questions. How do I even know you actually represent the Hoffmans?"

"As opposed to what?" Isaiah said, trying to sound insulted. "That I'm some triad member trying to get information about their whereabouts? So I decide to sit down with an FBI agent and ask a few questions?"

Parcelli waited again before responding. The whole pace of this conversation was driving Isaiah crazy. "You're not licensed in Georgia," Parcelli eventually said.

Darn. The man had done some checking. "I didn't say I was."

"What state are you licensed in?"

Isaiah quickly ran through his options. Every lie would lead to another, a dead-end option that might lead to charges against him for misleading a government agent. For lack of a better alternative, he turned to the truth. Or at least the first cousin of the truth. "I'm a law student, representing the Hoffmans through our legal aid clinic."

He expected this might bring a lecture or a condescending smile. Instead, Mount Rushmore didn't react. "I knew that," Parcelli eventually said. "Professor Walter Snead is your supervising attorney. Jamie Brock is your classmate."

Unreal. Parcelli's command of these facts surprised Isaiah. Maybe all the stories about Big Brother spying on its citizens were true. "If you know all that, you know I really do represent the Hoffmans."

"I know you're not licensed to practice law," Parcelli said.

Isaiah shrugged as if he couldn't be bothered by such technicalities. "Are you willing to help us or not?" he asked.

Parcelli sighed. "I'd like to. Your clients risked their lives to help us put away some very dangerous men. But I've got a couple of serious problems, Isaiah."

Parcelli opened another creamer and poured it in his coffee. "You were right—this stuff's way too strong." He stirred until the color turned a lighter shade of brown. "Four years ago, the Manchurian Triad captured Jessica Shealy, your client, and held her hostage. They called Clark Shealy, now known as David Hoffman, who was a bounty hunter, and offered to free his wife if Clark could find and produce an Indian mathematician who had developed a very valuable algorithm. Shealy found him and traded the man for his wife. Later, the Shealys testified against the mob and became part of the witness protection program, signing a memorandum of understanding specifying what their duties were. I'm sure you've reviewed that document . . ."

Isaiah nodded but made a mental note: *Ask for a copy of the memorandum of understanding.*

"It requires complete candor and disclosure of all relevant and material facts. Unfortunately, Mr. and Mrs. Shealy never told us that the mathematician, a man named Professor Moses Kumari, entrusted Shealy with the algorithm before he died."

It was news to Isaiah as well, and he made another note: *Be more thorough on client interviews.*

"You know how we found out that your client has a copy?" Parcelli asked.

"Why don't you tell me," Isaiah said as if he had a choice.

"Because Mr. Hoffman recently sent a message through a mob hit man named Johnny Chin, presently serving a life term in California, that Hoffman was ready to sell the algorithm to the mob." Parcelli waited a beat for that piece of information to sink in. "Since he's the one who contacted the mob first, it seems a little strange for him to blame his present troubles on the marshals' office." Parcelli raised an eyebrow, punctuating that last point.

Isaiah hoped his own expression wasn't revealing how much this information caught him off guard. And shocked him. "What's the nature of this algorithm?" he asked.

"You might want to ask your clients that question," Agent Parcelli suggested. "My only point is this: your clients brought this little dilemma on themselves. Until they're ready to tell us everything they know—including giving us a copy of the algorithm—they shouldn't expect any further protection from the federal government."

This suddenly felt like a movie scene—intrigue, a double cross, a secret algorithm. But in the movies, the debonair defense lawyer always had a clever comeback.

"I'll talk to them about it," Isaiah said, feeling like the clueless law student he was.

45

JAMIE ARRIVED at the law school ten minutes early for her six thirty meeting with Isaiah. She had reserved one of the small study rooms in the library for privacy. She waited for Isaiah in the marble-floored main lobby of the stately redbrick building that served as the home for Southeastern Law School.

For three days now, Jamie's life had been a living hell. She carried a loaded Kimber in her backpack, checked her rearview mirror constantly, called Chris several times a day to check on Snowball, double-checked locks before going to sleep, and then hardly slept at all. She was not the nervous type. But she had been attacked. And the cops weren't making much progress. Even now, she scanned the law school lobby for any signs of trouble.

Thick Persian rugs were scattered around the lobby with over-stuffed leather furniture placed in a square on each one. Some first-year study sessions occupied three of the groupings, so Jamie took a seat on the fourth. She removed her federal tax book from her backpack and opened it to Wednesday's assignment. Reading tax cases was like driving through Atlanta during rush hour—boring, frustrating, and an incubator for new curse words.

She couldn't help overhearing the obnoxious study group a few feet away, first-years trying to impress each other with their knowledge of tort law, as if being the top dog in a study session would somehow guarantee success on the exam. Jamie had given up on study groups after her first semester and watched her grades quickly improve. Other students swore by them.

"Not if the plaintiff had the last clear chance to avoid the injury," one particularly loud student said. "He can't recover a dime if he was the one who had the last clear chance but didn't stop in time."

"I don't think that's right," a softer voice said. "I think it only applies to defendants."

"You're wrong—check the case," the first student bellowed. She said it with such confidence and acidity that her friend shrank back into the couch. "Why do you think they call it 'last clear chance'? It applies to whichever person had the last chance to avoid the accident."

Jamie knew it was none of her business, but she had this thing about justice and getting stuff right. She ambled over as the group moved on to the next point. "Actually," she said, standing just behind one of the chairs, "last clear chance only applies to defendants. It's a doctrine used to take the sting out of contributory negligence."

The first-years fell quiet as Jamie continued. "In some states, if the defendant is negligent but the plaintiff is also contributorily negligent, even in the slightest degree, the plaintiff's negligence completely bars her from recovering anything. To make that doctrine a little less harsh, the law says that the plaintiff might still be able to recover if the defendant had the last clear chance to avoid the accident."

"Thanks," said the soft-spoken student whom Jamie had bailed out.

"Yeah. That helps a lot," the other said. "Though Sullivan said it wasn't really used that much. I doubt it will be on the test."

Her good deed complete, Jamie slipped back to her own Persian rug and returned to the drudgeries of tax law. But she couldn't keep her mind on the intricacies of the Internal Revenue Code. Instead, she thought about her gun.

Even though she carried it around with the safety on, she worried about it constantly. What if it discharged accidentally? What if she thought somebody was going to assault her and shot in self-defense, only to find out later it was a mistake? What if she tried to shoot an assailant and ended up hitting a friend?

The talk of last clear chance gave her an idea.

Maybe she should remove the cartridge from the chamber. According to Jacobsen, her gun held seven additional rounds in the attached magazine. It was a single-action trigger, and Jamie already knew she could pull it quickly. An empty chamber might be an additional fail-safe, and it might give her a chance to bluff somebody by actually pulling the trigger once *before* the bullets started flying. It would give her target a last clear chance to stop. And how likely was it that she would end up in a situation where she could squeeze off only one shot?

She decided that she would empty the chamber later. She checked her watch: 6:45. She called Isaiah's cell for the second time. Voice mail. She was on pins and needles, anxious to hear how his meeting with Parcelli went. It had been Isaiah's idea to meet in person. He didn't trust cell phones or the Internet. But if he didn't show up soon, she might just use her first bullet on him.

She turned her attention back to her federal tax book. What could she think about next?

At seven, with Isaiah still a no-show, Jamie found herself on the fence between anger and worry. If something had happened to him, she would feel terrible. If not, she might make something happen. She called his cell one more time and left another message.

She packed up her books and decided to check around the library. Maybe he had slipped by her. After ten minutes of searching, she came back to the lobby and discovered her seat was taken. She walked out in front of the building to wait for Isaiah there.

That's when she saw him.

The founders of the law school had had enough foresight to buy a large piece of property that was part of an old rail yard in downtown Atlanta scheduled for redevelopment. When the redevelopment took place, and the area became Atlanta's newest hot spot to live, the law school found itself in one of the city's most desirable locations with sufficient acreage to surround the building with trees, a walking path complete with marble park benches, a huge asphalt parking lot, and a large grassy quad area directly in front of the school. That large and flat piece of grass saw constant use—school picnics, students lying in the sun to study, ultimate Frisbee, and on nights like tonight, pickup football games.

Isaiah faded back to pass, smiling as he evaded a rusher and darted left, the ball held casually out to his side in a way that would give any coach a heart attack. He had stripped down to a pair of baggy khaki shorts and sneakers, and his upper body gleamed with sweat. He stopped suddenly and heaved the ball three-quarters of the length of the quad in a perfect spiral—outdistancing his receiver by at least five yards.

"I thought you were faster than that!" Isaiah yelled.

"Reggie Bush ain't that fast."

Jamie folded her arms across her chest. She felt the heat of anger coloring her face. She couldn't believe how rude this guy was.

He spotted her as his ragamuffin team was huddling up.

"Jamie!" He acted surprised.

She scowled at her watch. She scowled at Isaiah. She scowled at his teammates, just for good measure.

"You wanna play?" asked a clueless second-year who didn't understand scowl language.

"No thanks. Isaiah and I were supposed to be meeting together forty minutes ago."

"Gotta run, guys," Isaiah said.

"Next score wins," somebody suggested.

But Jamie's ice-cold stare ended that idea.

Isaiah toweled off with his shirt as they entered the building. "I was waiting out front for you," he said. He pulled his torn T-shirt on over his head. "Figured I'd see you when you arrived."

"What time did you get there?"

"You know, six thirty or so."

"Or so?"

That pretty much quelled the conversation until they got inside the small study room. With Isaiah still glistening with sweat, the cramped quarters smelled like a locker room. Jamie gave him a few seconds to apologize but quickly realized it was a lost cause. She knew that she should probably drop it, but she had always believed if you had something eating at you, it's best to get it out in the open.

"We were supposed to meet at six thirty," she said. Even to her, it sounded pretty chiding.

"I was here at six thirty . . . African American time."

She gave him a skeptical look. "What's that supposed to mean?"

"I'm a victim of the way I was raised." Even Isaiah couldn't fight off a smirk with this lame excuse. "When our church was supposed to start at eleven, it would start at eleven thirty. We called it African American time."

"Yeah, but courts don't run on African American time."

"Au contraire," Isaiah said. "Perhaps you didn't attend the panel presentation featuring accomplished trial lawyers earlier in the semester. Our dear Professor Snead made an excellent point about showing up late."

"You're quoting Snead?"

"Just because he can't teach doesn't mean he couldn't try cases."

Jamie sighed. "I thought you said he lost most of his criminal cases."

"Yeah, but he won big verdicts in his tort cases," Isaiah said. "And that's where the money is. Anyway, on this panel, Snead the accomplished trial lawyer—as opposed to Snead the pitiful law school professor—said he always arrived in court a few minutes late. He said that only one person could be in charge of the courtroom—either one of the lawyers or the judge. By arriving late, he showed the judge that he wasn't going to abide by the court's picayune rules on things as trivial as starting time."

"And you bought that?"

"I arrived late in Snead's class for three straight weeks afterward."

"Maybe someday you can be just like him."

Isaiah wiped some sweat off his brow with the sleeve of his T-shirt. "You're good," he said. "You ought to be a prosecutor."

Having avoided an apology, Isaiah told Jamie about his meeting with Parcelli. "This dude was clinical, Jamie, like a robot." He told her that Parcelli claimed the Hoffmans violated their memorandum of understanding by trying to sell Professor Kumari's algorithm to the mob. Parcelli wasn't willing to even talk about new identities or additional protection unless Hoffman gave up the algorithm.

Jamie wanted to take the problem to Snead. "We're just students, Isaiah. You shouldn't have even met with Parcelli in the first place. We don't even know if Hoffman has this algorithm. And if he does, why did he offer it to the mob?"

But Isaiah reminded her that the clients didn't want Snead involved. "We should at least get the entire story from Stacie Hoffman first," he argued. "Our first duty is to our clients. If the Hoffmans have the algorithm, maybe they'll trade it for protection. Maybe the Hoffmans didn't contact Johnny Chin like Parcelli claimed. Maybe somebody in the federal government set them up." Isaiah paused and leaned forward. "I've been giving this a lot of thought, Jamie. Before we decide what to do, I owe it to my client to meet with her and find out the entire story."

"I thought she wasn't actually a client," Jamie said.

"Whatever she is, I still owe it to her to meet with her first."

"And then we'll go to Snead," Jamie said.

"We'll see," Isaiah said with a wink.

"And then we'll go to Snead," Jamie repeated, more firmly than before.

The next day, after Stacie confirmed that she and her husband had the algorithm but still refused to give it to the government, Isaiah himself called Snead and scheduled the appointment for first thing Thursday morning.

46

SNEAD'S OFFICE WAS the disastrous result of trying to cram all the paraphernalia from a trial lawyer's plush corner office into the smaller, cubicle-size space of a law school professor. The monuments to Snead's ego that seemed a natural part of a spacious office overlooking downtown Los Angeles felt claustrophobic here. The walls were cluttered with diplomas, pictures of Snead with important friends, bar admission certificates for a half-dozen states, an artist's sketch of Snead arguing in front of the U.S. Supreme Court, a framed cover story from *Lawyers Weekly* naming Snead as one of the highest paid lawyers in 2001, and the obligatory handwritten letter from a client singing Snead's praises. It made Jamie wonder what her own wall might look like at the end of her legal career.

The office was also cluttered with piles of paper that had fanned out like snowdrifts across the floor and desk, shelves full of law books, and scattered trinkets and memorabilia from Snead's trials. Blue books from past exams were everywhere. The place smelled like a combination of cigarette smoke and air freshener, the way hotel rooms smell right after they've been sprayed, topped off by a generous whiff of men's cologne.

The meeting got off to a rocky start when Isaiah showed up fifteen minutes late. From there, it went downhill.

"You did what?" Snead snapped when Isaiah told him about the meeting with Parcelli. "If I told the state bar about that, they probably wouldn't even let you sit for the exam this summer."

Isaiah ignored the dig as he and Jamie tag-teamed the story, a strategy they had planned in advance. By the time they finished, Snead had already turned two shades darker and snapped a pencil that he had been fingering as the students talked.

Jamie cleared her throat and prepared to offer a solution. "We think we should file suit for specific performance of the memorandum of understanding," she explained. "That agreement specifies that the government will provide the Hoffmans with new identities if the Hoffmans' true identities are discovered through no fault of their own. We should petition the court to enforce that promise by providing a court-approved supervisor to ensure that only a limited and highly selective number of people in the marshals' office are involved this time."

"If the Hoffmans breached the memorandum of understanding, they can't ask for specific performance," Snead growled. "It's blackletter law, Ms. Brock."

"According to what Stacie Hoffman told us, there is no breach of the agreement," Isaiah interjected. "Her husband didn't receive the algorithm until forty-eight hours after Kumari died. By then, the Hoffmans had already given the police taped statements, taken a lie detector test, and signed the memorandum of understanding. The statements they made about not having the algorithm were truthful at the time. Later on, during their grand jury and trial testimony, nobody asked them if they possessed the algorithm. From the government's perspective, the less said about the algorithm at that point, the better."

Snead did a quick little head shake, and the jowls jiggled. Up close, Jamie was struck by the dark and baggy circles under the man's reddened eyes—the toll of a life under constant pressure. "Even if you can prove that the Hoffmans didn't lie about the algorithm, you're still not out of the woods," Snead lectured. "How can you say the Hoffmans aren't at fault when the entire reason they were discovered was because they tried to sell the algorithm on the black market?"

Jamie prepared to answer, but Isaiah jumped in again. "Because they *didn't* try to sell it, Walter." She saw Snead bristle at the use of his first name, but Isaiah just kept talking. "Stacie swears they didn't contact Johnny Chin. Maybe there's a mob informant inside the marshals' office who gave the mob Hoffman's location and then sent the letter, hoping the feds would blame Hoffman for revealing his own location. Maybe Chin heard that the mob had found Hoffman, and so Chin comes up with this brilliant idea of writing himself a letter that appears to be from Hoffman. Chin gives the letter to the authorities, hoping they'll knock some time off his prison sentence and also believe that Hoffman caused his own downfall."

"Pretty far-fetched," Snead growled. He turned to Jamie. "Who do you think sent that letter?"

Isaiah nudged her foot, but she ignored him. "I honestly don't know, Professor. I want to believe the Hoffmans didn't send it, but these other scenarios that Isaiah threw out leave a lot of questions. Why would a mob informant write such a letter? Why not just tell the mob where Hoffman is living and be done with it? And how would Johnny Chin know that the Hoffmans had the algorithm?"

"Why are we working so hard to talk ourselves out of this?" Isaiah interjected. "Right now, David Hoffman is a client of the legal aid clinic. It's our job to defend him and his wife, not second-guess what they're telling us. You've called it the red-faced test, Professor. Make every argument possible in favor of your client unless you turn red from embarrassment while making it. And in case you hadn't noticed, that test can take me a long way."

Snead thought about this for a moment, looking past the students, over their shoulders, as if trying to discern what to do by looking at his own picture on the office wall. What would Walter Snead, Supreme Court advocate, do?

Eventually he turned back to Isaiah. "I'm impressed with your *passion* for this client," he said. His voice was a low rumble emanating from a cigarette-damaged voice box. "Something I wish you had more of in my class. And I'm impressed with Ms. Brock's candor. . . ."

Jamie winced at the backhanded dig intended for Isaiah.

"But I can't let you risk your careers on a case like this. We're not dealing with a hypothetical moot court case here. This client has the feds frustrated with him and the mob after him. Ms. Brock has already been threatened. You both have promising legal careers. I won't allow you to jeopardize them this way."

Snead pushed back from his desk a little—a sign the meeting was over. "Ms. Brock, prepare a motion for state court withdrawing from the representation of Mr. Hoffman."

Out of the corner of her eye, Jamie could see the storm clouds on Isaiah's face.

"Good day," Snead said.

The students stood. "That letter," Isaiah said, pointing to the hand-written note framed on Snead's wall, "is that from one of your first tobacco clients?"

"Yes." Snead gave it the look of a proud papa. "She lost her husband to cancer at age thirty-eight. She was left alone to raise twins—three-year-olds—and a baby. We didn't bring him back, but we got the widow 5.8 million."

"I wonder how many people tried to talk you out of that one," Isaiah said. "Nobody beat big tobacco back then."

Snead hesitated for a moment, taking in the point. "That didn't involve the mob, Mr. Haywood. This case is different."

◁▷

In the hallway outside the office, Isaiah sarcastically thanked Jamie for her help. "I thought you wanted to take this case, too," he said.

"I did. But not if I had to mislead my own supervising attorney in order to get permission. Everything I said in there, Snead would have eventually figured out. I didn't want him pulling the plug on this thing just before we went to court or something. It's better to put everything on the table now."

Isaiah frowned, shook his head, and walked away. His silence hurt Jamie more than any argument would have. Still, she felt she had done the right thing.

Ten minutes later, the same woman who couldn't tell a lie to her law school professor was doing a pretty good job misleading her brother. "I'm into kind of a complicated situation with the condo right now," she said. "I'm getting it all straightened out and should be able to have a pet again soon. Could you possibly keep Snowball for a few more days?"

"No problem," Chris said.

It wasn't a total lie. She *was* having some complicated problems. What bothered her most was the feeling that she couldn't tell the good guys from the bad guys in this endeavor. Jamie viewed the law in simple terms. Black-and-white. Crime and punishment. But in the witness protection program, especially with a client who seemed like a con artist, all the world could be painted in shades of gray.

Why should she put her life on the line for that?

47

SNEAD WAS IN ANOTHER foul mood for Thursday's class—as berating and hostile as Jamie had ever seen him. As class began, Jamie thought that either she or Isaiah would be first on the chopping block since they had both passed when called on in class the last two weeks. Despite her chaotic life, this time Jamie was ready.

But Snead ignored them both, even when Jamie twice raised her hand to help out the stumbling student who had been chosen. It was as if Jamie didn't exist. It dawned on her that Snead might not call on her for the rest of the semester, thereby ensuring that she could never make up for the bad class participation grade she had earned on Tuesday.

When class ended, Jamie could feel the hypercharged tension seeping from the room like air out of a punctured tire. Jamie's own neck and back muscles began to relax. How could a teacher she didn't even respect have that much effect on her? Most of the students quickly packed their books and computers, anxious to leave this class behind, but a few of the usual brownnosing suspects made their way to the front so they could ask Snead a few impressive questions.

"Ms. Brock and Mr. Haywood!" Snead's voiced boomed over the bustling classroom. "I would like to speak with you for a moment before you leave."

Jamie looked at Isaiah, who gave her an I-don't-know shrug. They both sauntered down to the front of the classroom and waited patiently as the other students asked Snead their questions and acted interested in his answers. Well, at least Jamie waited patiently. Isaiah made a big show of looking at his watch and, after a few minutes, asked Jamie if she knew when they might be done because he had another class to study for.

Not to be rushed, Snead waited until he had answered every question and then waited a while longer as the other students left the classroom. By then, Isaiah was a bundle of nerves and energy, shifting from one foot to the other, checking his watch, even text-messaging a few of his friends.

"Thank you for waiting," Snead said in his normal monotone drone. The students nodded. "I've decided that your idea of petitioning the court for injunctive relief in the Hoffman case might have some merit. I will act as your supervising attorney. As our clients are in danger and time is therefore of the essence, I will expect you to have a motion for preliminary injunction ready to file tomorrow. We should ask that a hearing be scheduled for Monday. Mr. Haywood, I will leave it to you to obtain the clients' permission."

Jamie couldn't believe what she was hearing! This same man, just hours earlier, had pooh-poohed this idea. Now here he was—not only acquiescing to the case, but affirmatively directing it.

What happened?

"There is, however, one condition." Snead looked directly at Isaiah. "I want Mr. Farnsworth to work the case with you."

"Wellington Farnsworth?" Isaiah was incredulous.

"Do you know another Mr. Farnsworth?" Snead asked.

"Why do we need *him*?"

Snead placed his books under his arm and started toward the steps. He stopped and turned long enough to get the final word. "Mr. Farnsworth is the best writer I have in any of my classes this year. He has matriculated at Southeastern for two years and received only one B, the rest As. He graduated from Old Dominion with a perfect 4.0 as a math major. If the nature of this algorithm becomes an issue— for example, the government claims that national security is at risk, a student like Mr. Farnsworth could prove invaluable. Of course, since he is not yet a third-year, I would expect the two of you to handle all courtroom proceedings."

Snead turned and started limping up the steps. "Good day."

Isaiah and Jamie returned to their seats and packed up their backpacks. Neither spoke until Snead left the room.

"What was that all about?" Jamie asked.

"I don't know," Isaiah answered. "But the law firm of Haywood and Brock is open for business."

"I think you mean Brock, Haywood, and Farnsworth."

Isaiah snorted. "Snead said that Farnsworth had to be on the team. He didn't say we actually had to give him anything to do."

◁▷

Later that afternoon, in another small library conference room, Jamie met with Isaiah and Wellington to lay out a game plan for their case. Wellington showed up in blue dress shorts, sandals, and a button-down Hawaiian shirt that should have been a size or two bigger. He had on thick reading glasses and hadn't bothered to comb his blond hair all day, as far as Jamie could tell.

Isaiah took it upon himself to dish out assignments. "I'll handle the witnesses. Jamie, you can handle the legal arguments and closing statement. Wellington, why don't you draft the complaint and motion for preliminary injunction?"

With only twenty-four hours to get the initial pleadings filed, Isaiah had apparently reconsidered whether Wellington should be given any assignments, at least insofar as grunt work was concerned. Maybe his new plan was to make Wellington work all night.

Jamie was ready to argue—after all, why should Isaiah examine all the witnesses?—but Wellington spoke first. "That sounds good," he said. He started making notes about the types of pleadings Isaiah wanted, basically doing everything short of saluting.

"Looks like the boys have got this all figured out," Jamie said.

"I just thought—" Isaiah started.

"No. It's fine. Really." Jamie waited, seeing if Isaiah would read the tone in her voice.

No chance. He and Wellington started discussing what they needed in the pleadings. It soon became obvious that the case also demanded a supporting memorandum of law. When Wellington broke the uncomfortable silence by volunteering to write that as well, Jamie felt sorry for the kid.

"I'll help on the memorandum," she said. "That's too much work for one person to do in just one night."

"Thanks," Wellington said, glancing up from his notes. "I've already done a little research on what we need to prove." He checked the screen on his laptop. "We'll need an affidavit from our clients. To get the court-supervised injunction, we'll have to prove a likelihood of success on the merits and that irreparable harm would occur if the government were not required to relocate the Hoffmans and give them new identities. Plus, according to Section 9-21.990 of the Federal Witness Security Act, we have to prove that the Hoffmans are in jeopardy through no fault on their part."

"Impressive," Jamie said, drawing a shy and fleeting smile from Wellington. The kid had a round and smooth baby face. And he was only what? Nineteen? He looked like he shaved only once a week.

They discussed some of the procedural issues they were up against. The first problem would be getting a hearing as soon as possible, hopefully Monday. The second problem was that Stacie and David Hoffman had agreed that Isaiah and the team, including Snead, could proceed with the case only if the Hoffmans didn't have to appear in court. They couldn't risk showing their faces. The third problem was making sure the case stayed confidential.

"Confidentiality should be no problem," Wellington said. "We can file all our pleadings under seal to be opened and viewed only by the judge. We can ask for a closed hearing on Monday as well."

For every procedural question Isaiah and Jamie surfaced, Wellington seemed to have the answer. He had a soft-spoken and disarming way of talking that was beginning to put even Isaiah at ease.

"How do you know so much about this stuff?" Isaiah asked. "You're only a second-year."

Wellington's face went from pasty white to a shade of light pink. "I got the book award in civil procedure," he said quietly. "And last summer, I clerked for the U.S. attorney's office."

"You clerked for the U.S. attorney's office?" Isaiah gaped as if the opposing quarterback had just thrown an interception right into Isaiah's hands. "You're the man, Casper."

"They needed someone to help on some patent cases that involved a lot of mathematical formulas. I was one of fourteen clerks from around the nation working on various specialties in the patent office. They called us the Geek Squad."

That comment, and the unassuming way Wellington said it, made Isaiah smile broadly.

"The Geek Squad," he repeated, shaking his head. "We've got our own charter member of the Geek Squad."

48

"THE LADY IN BLACK." Those were Isaiah's first words when he laid eyes on Jamie in Federal Courtroom 4 in downtown Atlanta on Monday morning. She was wearing a black skirt and jacket, a white blouse, heels, and understated silver earrings with a matching necklace. She had pulled her dark hair away from her face. She wanted her appearance to be classy and conservative. Isaiah certainly approved. "I hope we get a male judge," he said.

Jamie ignored him.

But an undeterred Isaiah, who had shockingly arrived ten minutes before court, didn't know when to let something go. He revised her nickname to "The Black Widow" and Jamie was afraid the moniker might stick. It seemed that every law school class had at least one designated person in charge of nicknames, and Isaiah was that person for the 3Ls. Much to her delight, Jamie had avoided a nickname until now, probably because she came across as serious and intense. But when Isaiah tried it out as they waited, it rolled off his tongue.

"The Black Widow and Casper," he said. "What a team."

"So what's your nickname?" Jamie challenged.

Isaiah spread his hands. "Don't need one."

"How 'bout GQ?" Jamie suggested, though she knew it was lame as soon as it left her mouth.

Isaiah wore a shimmering black suit with a thin, red windowpane pattern—a five-button job that hung low on his body. He wore cuff links, a brilliant red tie, and a pocket handkerchief to match. For Isaiah, he had gone light on the bling—just a small, gleaming gold earring in his left ear. He would have looked great as an ESPN announcer, but he apparently hadn't read the same studies Jamie read on dressing for *courtroom* success.

And then there was Wellington. He had on a beige sports coat, baggy khaki pants, a frayed white shirt, and a yellow tie with a faded stain. In planning the seating chart, Isaiah had relegated Wellington to the front row of the spectator section, claiming they couldn't have too many lawyers at the defense table.

A few minutes later, two confident men wearing standard dark blue suits entered the courtroom. "The one on the right is Agent Parcelli," Isaiah whispered. Introductions were made all the way around. The U.S. attorney assigned to the case was short and gregarious, midfifties if Jamie had to guess, with an easy smile and a reassuring way about him. He had a full head of short blond hair gelled neatly into place. Wrinkle lines radiated from the corners of his eyes—the downside to a constant smile and sunny disposition. He introduced himself as Allan Carzak, *the* United States Attorney for the Northern District of Georgia. The big gun, in other words—no assistant sent to do this job.

After shaking hands with the law students, Carzak greeted everyone in the courtroom by first name—the clerk, the federal marshal, the court reporter: "How was your weekend, Marsha? Fred, how's that golf game? Amanda, is your daughter still playing softball?"

By nine o'clock, all the players were in place except two. The federal judge selected at random to hear the case had not yet appeared. According to the clerk, that judge would be Christina Torriano, the court's youngest female member. Wellington, who had a small manila folder of research on each of the eight potential judges, said Torriano was sharp, ran a tightly controlled courtroom, and had a good-size chip on her shoulder. "A Bush appointee," he added.

The other missing player was Professor Walter Snead. And none of the students had his cell phone number . . . if he even carried one.

To Jamie's horror, the judge arrived first. She was short and well-fed, with dark, curly, shoulder-length hair. The marshal called the session to order, and Torriano surveyed her courtroom. "This hearing is closed to the public and will remain so until further notice. All pleadings in this case shall be filed under seal, and the file itself will remain in my chambers.

"Are Counsel ready to proceed?"

"Yes, Your Honor," Carzak said.

Isaiah stood at the defense table. "Ready, Your Honor."

Torriano stared at him. "Where are your clients, Counsel?"

"They will not be appearing today, Your Honor. They were concerned that word of this hearing might leak out and that by appearing they might be endangering their lives. They're in hiding right now."

"You expect to obtain a preliminary injunction without your clients even showing up?"

"Yes, Your Honor."

"Good luck." Her tone indicated he would definitely need it.

"Thank you, Your Honor," Isaiah said.

The judge then turned her attention to Wellington and raised her eyebrows. "Are you Professor Snead?"

He stood. "Oh no, ma'am." His voice trembled a little. "I'm a second-year student helping with research. Professor Snead isn't here yet."

"He's not here?" If tones were objects, Torriano's would have been a stiletto.

"Not yet, Your Honor," Isaiah said when it became obvious that no words were coming out of Wellington's mouth. "We expect him any second."

Carzak stood and tried to help. "There was an accident on the connector this morning, Your Honor. Traffic's worse than usual."

"Yet somehow, magically, everyone else managed to make it on time." Her Honor turned toward Jamie and Isaiah again, her drawn face reflecting her annoyance. "This is no example for you to follow," she said. "Court will stand adjourned until your professor graces us with his presence."

She banged the gavel, the lawyers stood, and she exited the courtroom.

Ten minutes later, Snead came limping down the middle aisle of the courtroom, leaning heavily on a cane. He shook hands with Carzak before hobbling over to the defense counsel table. While waiting, Jamie had become so mad at the man she could have spit on him, but now, seeing him with the cane, she regretted the fact she had jumped to conclusions.

As Snead settled into his seat at the end of counsel table, right next to Jamie, she decided not to bring it up. Snead had always limped. Maybe he was dealing with a chronic thing that had suddenly taken a turn for the worse.

"What's with the cane?" Isaiah whispered, speaking past Jamie to the professor.

Snead looked at the cane, propped against the table, as if he were just as surprised as Isaiah to see it there. "Oh, this," he said. "I always take it with me to court."

◁ ▷

Five minutes later, Judge Torriano called court to session, delivered a blistering rebuke to Snead for being late, then asked if the professor had anything to say. Jamie expected Snead to stand and mumble some vague apology.

He did stand. He leaned on his cane. "I thought full professors were entitled to an extra fifteen minutes," he quipped. "That's the way it is at Southeastern."

"Well, that's not the way it is in *my* courtroom," Torriano snapped. "You would do well to make sure you are on time for all future proceedings."

"I'll keep that in mind, Your Honor."

The judge stared at Snead for a long second, making it obvious that this was not the response she wanted. She gave him another few beats to apologize. Then she let it pass.

"Call your first witness," she said to Isaiah.

49

JAMIE WAS STRUCK by the supersized majesty of federal court. She had represented legal aid clients in the stuffy and crowded confines of state court—small rooms with hard wooden benches filled to overflowing. But here, in the United States District Court for the Northern District of Georgia, they were surrounded by outlandishly high ceilings, hardwood trim, thick rugs, and heavy satin drapes. The lawyers and court personnel were swallowed up by the immensity of the place—everything about it said that Jamie had just hit the big time.

Except that her client was nowhere to be found, and the judge was scowling at them.

Isaiah explained to Judge Torriano that he would be relying on the affidavits of Stacie and David Hoffman filed with the motion for preliminary injunction. For his first witness, he would like to call Agent Samuel Parcelli to the stand as a hostile witness.

"Objection!" Carzak said cheerfully. "I can't cross-examine the Hoffmans' affidavits, and I object to them coming into evidence." He said it with a tone of condescension that made Jamie fume. "As for Parcelli, I can't stop them from calling him as a witness, but he's not necessarily a hostile witness as that term is used in a court of law."

Wellington had researched these points over the weekend, and Isaiah immediately started citing the list of cases Wellington had uncovered. The affidavit could be considered as evidence at a preliminary injunction hearing because the matter would be decided by a judge, not a jury. The court could give it whatever weight she saw fit. Furthermore, Parcelli was employed by the government, the very party that the Hoffmans accused of violating the contract. If anybody qualified as a hostile witness, Parcelli did.

Isaiah and Carzak went back and forth for a few minutes before Torriano banged her gavel and ruled in favor of Isaiah on both points. Jamie's exultation was short-lived, however, when Professor Snead leaned over and whispered, "That's a bad omen. If the court rules in our favor on evidentiary issues, it's a sure sign she's going to rule against us on the overall case. That way, on appeal, we won't have any evidentiary rulings to complain about."

Talk about perverse logic, Jamie thought. But in a way, it made sense.

Parcelli took the stand and fostered the impression of a serious and dedicated, if somewhat brooding, federal agent. He testified in succinct and no-nonsense sound bites, never giving Isaiah any more information than absolutely necessary. Isaiah held his own, stalking the courtroom and firing one question after another without the aid of notes. He got Parcelli to admit that the Hoffmans had testified truthfully both in front of the grand jury and at trial. That their testimony had helped put four members of the Chinese mafia behind bars. And that the memorandum of understanding required the Hoffmans to testify truthfully but did not require them to turn over the particulars of any algorithms they might later come to acquire.

"Assuming Mr. Hoffman even has such an algorithm, Mr. Parcelli, you wouldn't know for sure *when* he obtained it, would you?"

"He must have acquired it before Professor Kumari died. Yet the very day that Kumari died, we took a recorded statement from Mr. Hoffman where he claimed he did not possess the algorithm or any copies of it. He said he didn't really even know what it was."

Isaiah stopped pacing and turned toward the witness. "How do you know that Hoffman obtained the algorithm *before* Kumari died, as opposed to *after*?"

Parcelli grunted his frustration, as if this law student couldn't have asked a dumber question. "Professor Kumari and Mr. Hoffman spent hours together before Hoffman turned Kumari over to the Chinese mafia so they could torture the professor in their attempt to obtain the algorithm. The only person who knew the algorithm at that point was Kumari. I think it's pretty obvious."

"You can't say for certain that Kumari didn't tell someone else about the algorithm before he came to America, can you?"

"Not for certain."

"In fact, wouldn't it make sense for a man like Kumari to let somebody else in on his secret just in case something happened to him?"

"Objection, calls for speculation."

"Sustained."

Isaiah nodded in Carzak's direction, the way you might pat an opposing player after a good tackle. "In any event, if Kumari did tell somebody else about the algorithm, that person could have conveyed the information to Mr. Hoffman a good while after Kumari was killed. Isn't that possible?"

"Highly unlikely. But anything's possible."

"Or Kumari could have buried the information someplace and told only Hoffman about its location. So Hoffman wouldn't have technically had the algorithm when you asked him about it. Isn't that possible?"

"Unlikely."

"But possible?"

"Yes, I suppose."

"And finally, Kumari could have sent the information to Hoffman by some delayed technique—by a time-triggered e-mail, or the U.S. mail; we all know how slow that is, or—"

"That's enough, Mr. Haywood," Judge Torriano interjected. "The court gets the point."

Professor Snead, like a color commentator, leaned over to whisper in Jamie's ear. "Cutting us off—that's a very good sign."

◁▷

It took Carzak about ten minutes to undo the damage that Isaiah had inflicted during his hour of questioning. Carzak first established that Parcelli actually liked the Hoffmans and certainly didn't want anything to happen to them. But, Parcelli testified, in his experience, successful witness protection depends first and foremost on the witness. If the witness tries to scam the government, as Parcelli feared the Hoffmans had done, or if the witness reestablishes contact with the criminals who were after him or her, not much could be done to help.

"Did you personally help investigate the circumstances surrounding the computer-generated letter that Mr. Johnny Chin received, purportedly from Clark Shealy, a man also known as David Hoffman, offering to sell the algorithm to the Chinese mafia?"

"Yes, I did."

"Did you find any indication whatsoever that such letter came from a source other than Hoffman himself—for example, the marshals' office of the United States government?"

"No. There is no such evidence."

Without providing further details, Carzak directed Parcelli's attention to the witness protection program in general. There are over seventy-five hundred witnesses and about ten thousand family members who have been part of the program, Parcelli said. The feds, including the marshals' office that the Hoffmans were accusing of leaking information in this case, had *never* lost a single witness *unless* that witness contacted his former associates, as Hoffman had done with Johnny Chin.

Parcelli then testified about his conversation in Washington, D.C., with Isaiah Haywood. Even though Hoffman had tried to sell the algorithm to the mob, the government was willing to overlook that conduct, relocate the Hoffmans, and provide them with new identities, subject to only one condition: the Hoffmans *must* turn over the algorithm to the government. Obtaining that algorithm was, Parcelli said, a matter of national security.

"What would happen if Mr. Hoffman sold that algorithm to a member of an organized-crime ring?" Carzak asked.

"Among other things, that crime ring could access sensitive financial secrets and quite possibly cripple the entire Internet," Parcelli said.

"Come on," Carzak said. "That sounds a little melodramatic."

"That's not the half of it," Parcelli answered. He had the look of impending doom as he turned solemnly to the judge. "Even though this is a closed proceeding, I'm not authorized to say anything more."

50

WHEN ISAIAH RESTED HIS CASE, Carzak surprised everyone by calling Johnny Chin to the stand.

"Where is the witness now?" Judge Torriano asked.

"The marshals have him in a holding cell."

"Very well, then."

A few minutes later, Jamie watched Chin limp down the aisle of federal court, wearing an orange jumpsuit, handcuffs, and ankle chains, escorted on each side by a federal marshal.

Chin climbed into the stand looking sullen, casting angry looks at everyone in the courtroom, including Allan Carzak. His eyes were sunken and his skin drawn, as if death couldn't wait for the coroner's pronouncement before beginning its facial reconstructive work.

"Good morning," Carzak said.

Chin did not respond.

Like a smiling dentist rooting out wisdom teeth, Carzak pried information from Chin question by question. First, Carzak laid a solid foundation, having the witness describe how a bounty hunter named Clark Shealy had apprehended Chin when Chin was working for the Chinese mafia. Then Carzak took Chin through a careful series of yes or no questions.

Yes, Clark Shealy contacted Chin while Chin served time in San Jacinto. Yes, Shealy asked Chin to contact the Chinese mafia, the triads, about buying an algorithm Shealy had obtained from a man named Professor Moses Kumari. No, Chin had not contacted the mafia, going instead straight to the Department of Justice with the information.

Carzak ended the testimony by introducing a computer-generated letter into evidence. "Is this the letter you received from Mr. Shealy?" Carzak asked.

Chin barely glanced at it. "Yes."

"When did you receive this letter?"

"Sometime near the end of February."

Carzak looked at Isaiah. "Is Counsel willing to stipulate that this letter arrived on February 26, or do we need to introduce the affidavit from the custodian of San Jacinto who logs in the mail?"

"I don't stipulate to anything," Isaiah said. "And the affidavit is inadmissible hearsay."

"What?" Torriano said. Anger flashed in her eyes before she apparently recalled her obligation to maintain neutrality. "I mean, objection overruled. You can't argue that your affidavit comes in as evidence but the one introduced by the government does not."

"I just did," Isaiah mumbled.

"And stand up when you address the court," Torriano barked.

Isaiah stood. "We object, Your Honor."

"That's better. Objection overruled."

"I could have achieved that result sitting down," Isaiah said.

Jamie's stomach flipped. Just what she needed. Carzak the Magnificent trying a flawless case for the government, and Isaiah going into his smart-mouth routine.

"What?" Torriano asked, her neck muscles tight.

"Nothing, Your Honor."

"I have no further questions, Judge," Carzak said.

Isaiah shot up from his seat. Wellington had provided Isaiah with some research on Chin as well, cataloging all the charges the government filed against Chin during its prosecution of the Manchurian Triad. "Murder one, assault with a deadly weapon, conspiracy to commit murder, three violations of the RICO Act, four counts of wire fraud, and one count of extortion—is that everything, Mr. Chin?"

"Close enough."

"You've killed men for money, but you want this court to take your word about a letter you allegedly received from my client?" Isaiah was practically shouting.

"You don't have to take my word," Chin said. "The letter is right there."

"Which could have been typed by anybody on any computer," Isaiah responded. "Including one of your mob buddies on the outside."

"Is that a question?" Chin asked.

"Isn't that possible?" Isaiah spit back.

"Anything's possible."

"That's what Mr. Parcelli says, too. Wonder who wrote these scripts."

"Objection!"

"Sustained."

Isaiah didn't even slow down. "I notice that one of your conspiracy convictions was for your part in plotting a revenge killing. Is that true?"

"I'm an innocent man, sir." Chin smirked as he said it—a man serving three life sentences with nothing to lose. "A victim of the system."

"Speaking of your expertise in exacting revenge, I also noticed you walk with a limp. Did my client have anything to do with that?"

"Your boy shot out my kneecap and tried to pull out my teeth," Chin snorted.

"And you hate him for it, don't you?"

Watching Isaiah, Jamie found herself on the edge of her seat. He loved aggression, loved the stage. He had the gift. She wondered if she would ever be this good.

"I hate his guts, Counselor. I hate his lawyer's guts. I hate the system for protecting a man who tortures and maims. But does that mean I fabricated this letter? Afraid not. My methods are much more direct."

"You wanted the government to cut you a deal. You figured you could kill two birds with one stone."

Carzak came to his feet again. "Judge, I'm trying to be patient. But that's a speech, not a question. As Mr. Haywood knows, the government didn't give Mr. Chin anything in exchange for his cooperation. Not one day off his sentence."

Isaiah stepped toward the witness. "But you thought they would, didn't you, Mr. Chin? You thought they would."

"Counsel!" Torriano barked. "Move away from that witness. This is not *Boston Legal*; this is federal court." She glowered as Isaiah took a baby step or two away, never losing eye contact with the witness. "Mr. Carzak's objection is sustained."

After a few seconds of attempted intimidation, Isaiah stalked back to his place behind counsel table. "No further questions," he said, and his tone conveyed the rest of the sentence—*for this piece of trash*. He plunked himself in his seat and placed his chin in his hand, the picture of disgust.

Jamie leaned toward him. "You made your points," she said.

"I suck," Isaiah responded.

51

"NO PRESSURE," SNEAD SAID just before Jamie rose to deliver the closing argument, "but it's all on you."

Wellington leaned forward, sticking his nose between Jamie and Snead. "Can we get a quick recess?" he asked. "I just thought of something."

"It doesn't work that way," Snead grunted.

But Jamie, who had been impressed with Wellington's work, thought the kid was at least entitled to a minute of their time. Ignoring Snead, she stood. "May I have a minute to confer with Co-counsel, Your Honor?" Jamie asked respectfully.

Judge Torriano studied Jamie for a moment, possibly remembering what it felt like as a young woman trying her first case in federal court. The hard eyes melted a fraction; iron became lead. "We've been going all morning," Torriano announced. "Let's take a five-minute break."

The Southeastern team huddled as soon as the judge left the bench. The storm brewing in Snead's eyes was all the warning Jamie needed not to cross him again. But Wellington didn't seem to notice.

"What did Stacie Hoffman tell you about the algorithm?" Wellington asked Isaiah.

"Not much. She said her husband obtained a copy but not until after he gave his sworn statement to the police."

"Did she say what the algorithm might be used for?"

"No. She just said this Indian guy supposedly developed a formula that would crack a lot of Internet security codes. She didn't go into any detail."

"Did she say anything about prime numbers?"

"No."

"Are you sure?"

As Isaiah thought about it, Jamie considered the irony of what she was watching. Last week, the two were sworn enemies. Now . . . partners, one step away from friends.

"Yes, Wellington. I'm sure." Isaiah sounded edgy.

Okay, maybe associates *was more accurate,* Jamie thought. *Partnership might come with time.*

"We'll need to call Parcelli back to the stand," Wellington insisted. "There are a few questions you've got to ask him about that formula."

Isaiah gave Wellington a look, a twisted face that conveyed his feelings better than words would have—*Are you crazy?* But he was obviously starting to trust Wellington. His work on this case had been exquisite, his pleadings a thing of beauty. Why doubt him now? Besides, what did they have to lose?

"I say we give it a try," Jamie said.

"I agree," Snead said, still frowning.

"A cracker conspiracy," Isaiah said.

52

"PLAINTIFF RECALLS AGENT PARCELLI," Isaiah said. Though he tried to sound confident, Jamie could tell his heart wasn't quite in it.

"For what purpose?" Allan Carzak asked pleasantly. All of his sugar was starting to sicken Jamie.

"To ask him some questions about the type of algorithm in question."

"That information is protected by national security concerns," Carzak countered.

"I agree," Torriano said before Isaiah could even warm up his arguing muscles. "Plus, that line of inquiry is irrelevant. If your client has the algorithm, he doesn't need this witness to describe it. If your client doesn't have the algorithm, testimony about its nature is irrelevant."

What? Jamie felt like she had just witnessed a masterful case of doublespeak that would take her a month to unravel.

Wellington, not surprisingly, had processed it instantly. He was leaning forward again, tapping Jamie on the shoulder, like that annoying kid in junior high who kept borrowing your pencil. "Put me on the stand," he whispered.

"Huh?"

"Put me on the stand. Qualify me as an expert in mathematical formulas. Ask me these three questions." He shoved a piece of paper containing some handwritten notes into Jamie's hands. She showed it to Snead as Isaiah argued about the court's ruling.

Snead looked as confused as Jamie. He shrugged. Jamie slid down and tugged on Isaiah's arm. "One minute, Your Honor," he said.

Jamie told him the plan.

"You'd better know what you're doing," he whispered. Then to the judge: "The plaintiff calls Wellington Farnsworth as a rebuttal witness."

"This is getting ridiculous," Carzak mumbled.

But Torriano had no choice. A plaintiff was entitled to call a rebuttal witness. "Make it quick," she snapped.

While Wellington stumbled his way to the witness stand, Isaiah leaned down and whispered to Jamie. "Why don't you take a shot at this one? I missed that evidence class where we covered the qualifications of experts."

◁▷

Jamie began by asking questions about Wellington's undergraduate degree in applied mathematics, his experience in the patent office, and a thesis he had written as an undergrad about differential equations. She did everything but ask him about his grade in high school algebra. Carzak shook his head in amazement, and even Snead, Jamie's own supervising attorney, had his hand over his mouth to hide a smirk.

"I'd like to present Mr. Farnsworth as an expert in the field of applied mathematics," Jamie said at last.

Carzak stood with his arms spread wide. "Judge, you know he doesn't meet the new standards for experts. For example, he's never worked in the field of applied mathematics, he's never published a single scholarly article, he's never—"

"Actually," Wellington interrupted, "I've published two. In the *SIAM Journal on Applied Mathematics*, I wrote a report titled 'Applied Cryptography: Protocols, Source Codes, and Standards,' and the journal *Numerical Algorithms* published one of my papers titled 'Linearizations of Matrix Polynomials.'"

Normally, Jamie would have stifled a yawn just hearing the titles. But today, in the combat of the courtroom, they took on an intriguing, almost-magical mystique. *This guy is seriously smart.*

"I also served as a panelist at the Workshop on Analytic Algorithms and Combinatorics sponsored by the Society for Industrial and

Applied Mathematics. Other panelists included professors from Johns Hopkins, Carnegie Mellon, Harvard, and—" Wellington's tone dropped to a hushed reverence while Carzak tried to recover his panache—"Dr. Gilles Schaeffer from the École Polytechnique in France."

As Wellington finished his answer, Judge Torriano leaned forward, her chin propped on her fists. She seemed enamored with the whiz kid already.

"Any other questions, Mr. Carzak?" she asked.

"Judge, he still doesn't meet the relevancy standards in *Daubert*—"

"Yes, yes, I know," Her Honor said. "But those standards are primarily a safeguard in jury cases so that jurors don't get swindled by junk science. This court will not grant Mr. Farnsworth's testimony any more weight than it is due. But I'd at least like to hear what the young man has to say."

Carzak sat down, and Jamie heard Snead, sitting behind her, whisper his assessment to Isaiah. "It's over," he said. "When a judge lets you qualify a law student as an expert, she's guaranteed to rule against you."

Jamie glanced at Wellington's list of questions. "Mr. Farnsworth," she began, though it felt weird to call him by his last name, "can you think of any kind of algorithm that would be so powerful and crucial that it would shut down the Internet if it fell into the wrong hands?"

"Objection," Carzak said, but a curious Judge Torriano overruled him.

"Most Internet security is based on public-key encryption," Wellington responded. He slid forward in his seat as he warmed to the subject. "Public-key encryption is dependent upon certain one-way mathematical formulas, and the effectiveness of these formulas is in turn based on the unique characteristics of prime numbers. While it is relatively easy to multiply prime numbers together, it is nearly impossible to rapidly factor a large number into its prime components."

As Jamie watched the judge's eyes begin to glaze over, she immediately appreciated the genius of Wellington's next question. "What does any of that have to do with this case?" she asked.

"If Mr. Hoffman possessed an algorithm valuable enough that the mob would kill for it, I can only assume it was a formula for rapidly factoring numbers into their prime components. Such a formula, if it existed, could serve as a key to unlock most asymmetric encryption codes on the Internet. The owner would be able to steal bank accounts, access proprietary documents, and tap into financial institutions. The existence of such an algorithm would fit the description that Mr. Parcelli gave in his testimony—it could threaten national security and shut down the Internet."

Suddenly a lot more hung in the balance than the safety of two government witnesses. Jamie turned to the final question.

"If somebody had possession of such an algorithm, why would they try to sell it to the Chinese mafia? Wouldn't legitimate Internet security companies pay millions, even billions, for such a formula?"

Carzak was on his feet. "Objection, Judge." For once, his ever-present smile was gone—Mr. Rogers on a bad day in the neighborhood. "That calls for pure speculation."

"I agree," Torriano ruled. "Save that one for your closing argument."

Jamie nodded. It occurred to her that Wellington probably knew the question was objectionable when he wrote it. Most likely, he had intended it as a road map for Jamie's closing. She made a mental note.

53

CARZAK STOOD at his counsel table, not even bothering to approach the podium. "Do you work at the legal aid clinic at Southeastern?" he asked.

Wellington looked dumbfounded by the question. "No, sir."

"But you are aware that the legal aid clinic has certain guidelines in terms of accepting clients, is that right?"

Jamie couldn't figure out where Carzak was going. But her training from trial advocacy kicked in. When in doubt . . . "Objection, Your Honor. Relevance."

"If Your Honor allows me a little leeway, I'll link it up in my closing argument," Carzak promised.

"Proceed."

Carzak nodded his thanks to the judge and turned back to Wellington. "Mr. Farnsworth, is it your understanding that a person's income must be at or below the poverty level to qualify as a client for the legal aid clinic?"

"I think that's correct."

"And they have to fill out forms stating their income. Right?"

Jamie objected again, but Torriano overruled her again.

"Yes," Wellington said.

"And Mr. Hoffman originally came to be represented by this team of lawyers—" Carzak arched his hand toward the opposing counsel's table—"because he was a client of the Southeastern legal aid clinic, is that right?"

"That's my understanding," Wellington said.

Carzak grinned and took his seat. "That's all I have," he said.

A perplexed Wellington Farnsworth stepped down from the stand.

"What was that all about?" Jamie asked Isaiah.

◁ ▷

Jamie gave her closing argument first. She thought she would be nervous, the judge staring at her with the sole power to protect the Hoffmans or allow the government to abandon them. But once Jamie got started, the competitive instincts chased away the nerves. A belief in the justice of her cause brought out the passion.

She told the story of David and Stacie Hoffman like the proud parent of an honor roll student. They didn't fit the profile for government witnesses. These were not former mobsters who had turned on their partners in crime, but decent people trying to earn a living, their lives forever changed by mafia intrusion. Jamie explained what Stacie had shared with Isaiah over the weekend, elaborating on the facts Wellington had put in the affidavits—the kidnapping of Stacie and the heroic rescue by David. Jamie described the nightmare they had lived ever since—leaving family members and friends, risking their lives to testify against the Manchurian Triad, moving across the country to start over. It was, she said, an American tragedy with no happy ending.

And now, rubbing salt in their wounds, somebody had revealed their location to the Manchurian Triad and set them up by sending a computer-generated letter to Johnny Chin. Did a leak from the marshals' office cause this tragic turn of events? Or did somebody from the mob find the Hoffmans independently and then use Johnny Chin to make it look like the Hoffmans had caused this problem themselves? Jamie admitted that she didn't know the answer to that question. But there was one thing she did know: David and Stacie Hoffman did not write that letter to Johnny Chin or otherwise reveal their location to the mob.

If the Hoffmans possessed this valuable algorithm, why would they wait four years and then try to sell it to the mob? They could get millions, maybe even a billion, selling it to a legitimate company that wouldn't try to kill them for it. Did the government's case make any sense at all?

No, Jamie concluded, surprised at the strength of her own emotions.

The Hoffmans had risked their lives to serve the Department of Justice. And now, after using the Hoffmans as witnesses and after asking every court who heard their testimony to believe in the Hoffmans, the government wanted to abandon them, throw them away, and have this court believe the word of a hired mafia killer.

Not in my country, Jamie said. That's not my government.

She took her seat, scowling at the injustice of it all.

"Wow," Isaiah whispered. "You blew them away. This one's in the bag."

"I agree," Snead whispered cautiously, "unless the government can pull a rabbit out of its hat."

But Allan Carzak did not look like a beaten man as he took his place behind the podium.

◁▷

"It all makes sense now," Carzak claimed, talking to the judge like he would an old college friend. "I'm sitting there listening to Mr. Farnsworth's testimony—" Carzak turned and motioned toward Wellington—"who, by the way, is very smart. You ought to consider a career in the Department of Justice when you get out of school, young man."

Wellington blushed, and Jamie felt like she was watching a time-share salesman.

"I'm thinking: the kid's got a point. And Ms. Brock argued it so eloquently in her closing. Why would Hoffman go to a mob hit man if he had this incredibly valuable algorithm that could bring a billion dollars from legitimate businessmen? Why would he wait four years? And why wouldn't he turn over a copy of that algorithm to the government now if he really wanted protection?"

Carzak held his hand in the air, hesitating, looking to Jamie like the magician he was—everything in place but the white handkerchief. "That's when it hit me. Hoffman doesn't have the algorithm! It's been obvious, right there in plain sight the whole time. He fell on hard times four years after he testified. You heard it yourself from Mr. Farnsworth. I mean, the man was so poor, he qualified for legal aid! So he says to himself, 'I played with fire once before and didn't get burned. Maybe I can do it again.'"

Carzak was talking with both hands now, selling his own theory so passionately that he almost had Jamie believing him. "He calls on his one sure contact with the Manchurian Triad—Johnny Chin—intending to scam the mob out of millions for an algorithm that he doesn't even have. That's why he contacted the mob. He intended to scam the mob out of a couple of million and then get the government to provide him with a new identity.

"The only problem with that strategy, Judge, is that Johnny Chin didn't go to the mob and act as a middleman. He came to us! And now, by contacting a former mafia connection, Mr. Hoffman has violated the terms of his memorandum of understanding. You don't have to take my word for that. You don't even have to rely just on the word of Mr. Chin, because Ms. Brock is right about him as well—he's a witness with a very checkered past. But in this case, his testimony is corroborated by the most powerful corroborating evidence of all—the testimony of our own common sense. Only one answer explains why Hoffman still refuses to give the algorithm to the federal government, even in exchange for a new identity—he doesn't have it!"

Carzak smiled, shaking his head. "And to think I almost missed it. Right there under our noses, Judge, all along. Hoffman gambled away his government protection, a contractual right—his birthright, so to speak, for a bowl of stew. It was a million-dollar gamble, but it was a gamble Mr. Hoffman lost. And unfortunately for him, this court is required to leave him with the consequences of that gamble."

Carzak returned to his seat, still acting a little dumbfounded that he hadn't seen it all along. "I almost missed it," he mumbled again.

"Brilliant," Professor Snead groaned, just loud enough for Jamie and Isaiah to hear.

Isaiah leaned back in his seat as if he wasn't impressed. But out of the side of his mouth, he whispered his admiration to Jamie, "Of all the lawyers in the world . . . on my first big case, I draw David Copperfield."

"Carzak the Magnificent," Jamie sneered. And she knew that she had finally proposed a nickname that just might stick.

54

AT 2:00 P.M., the Southeastern Nightmare Team, as Isaiah had started calling their disparate group, gathered in Snead's small office at the law school. Judge Torriano had ended that morning's hearing by saying that she needed a few hours to research some issues before she ruled. She said she would have her clerk set up a conference call at two and the court would announce her ruling.

Jamie was not optimistic. Though she still held out a slight glimmer of hope, she knew that Carzak's argument had swayed the judge. To be honest, it had swayed Jamie, and she was opposing counsel. Carzak's theory was the only scenario that really made sense.

The three students all ignored the uncomfortable chairs, preferring to stand as they waited for the phone call. There wasn't much banter as they nervously watched the clock and Snead immersed himself in some papers on his desk. His only comment didn't do much to lift Jamie's spirits. "If she begins by telling us what a great job you all did—we're toast. Judges always compliment the losing side just before hammering them."

When the phone call came, though they were expecting it, Jamie and Wellington jumped. Snead answered the call in his typical gruff tone, placing the clerk on the speakerphone.

The clerk took roll and then put Judge Torriano on the line. "I want to begin," she said, "by telling all three students at Southeastern what a marvelous job they did on this case." Isaiah murmured a curse as Torriano continued. "If all the lawyers who entered my court were as prepared and eloquent as you three, it would be a pleasure to be a judge. Professor Snead, you should be very proud of them."

Torriano paused, but Snead didn't say a word.

"But after considering all the evidence and the arguments of counsel, the court feels compelled to rule in favor of the government and deny the motion for a preliminary injunction . . ."

The rest of the court's comments barely registered with Jamie. It was like the ruling ignited an explosion of pent-up emotions that Jamie didn't even know she had stored. Like a grand finale, all the events of the past several days fired their emotional impulses at once—her abduction, the danger to Snowball, buying a gun, her first major case, the disappointment of losing—paralyzing her mind with emotive intensity. Though she hadn't really expected to win, the reality of losing still hit hard. She heard Judge Torriano say something about a scheduling order for the case. She digested the looks of disappointment on the faces of her associates. But when the call ended, Jamie was just beginning to come out of the post-fireworks fog.

"Wellington, you work on the appeal," Snead said. "Isaiah, I'm assuming that you're going to contact the clients?"

"Sure."

"I'll call some longtime friends at DOJ and see if I can work some political angles," Snead concluded.

Jamie was the only one without a post-ruling assignment, accentuating her feeling of helplessness and defeat.

On her way to the car, she tried to look at the bright side, to give herself a little pep talk. They really had tried a good case. She had survived her first major hearing in federal court and confirmed that she was actually pretty decent at this courtroom stuff. She just wasn't cut out to be a good loser.

But that was okay. She was going to be a prosecutor. She would only file cases she believed in, cases where the evidence was strong. There was a reason that most prosecutors won 90 percent of their cases.

She wasn't feeling totally better as she approached her car, but she wasn't suicidal either. It had been a long weekend with virtually no sleep followed by an even longer Monday. She would take off a few hours early and drive north to her brother's house.

She missed Snowball terribly. One of the greatest things about dogs was the way they treated you like a rock star every time you entered the room. It didn't matter if you'd won the lottery, gotten yourself fired, or swindled some defenseless widow. To your dog, you walked on water without getting your ankles wet.

The minute Jamie would set foot in her condo, Snowball would come flying—tail wagging, feet skidding. *Jamie! Jamie! My hero!* Right now, Jamie could use a little hero worship.

Instead, she was confronted with a note, folded in half and left underneath the driver's side windshield wiper on her 4Runner. It was a cut-and-paste job, each letter in a different font and from a different magazine.

It read: *You really should have called.*

PART III

THE CODE

Where there is mystery,
it is generally suspected there must also be evil.

LORD BYRON

55

JAMIE CALLED HER BROTHER IMMEDIATELY. "How's Snowball?" she asked, barely breathing.

"He's been great," Chris said. There was a pause. "Well, he's been a little ornery. Okay, so maybe you owe us for two pairs of sandals he chewed on and a flower vase he knocked over with his tail. But the girls love him. They've been begging to get our own dog all week."

Jamie didn't know what to say. She was so relieved that Snowball was okay it caught her off guard. Speechless.

"Jamie?"

"Yeah. Sorry. I got distracted. So, I mean, Snowball's okay physically? He hasn't been sick or anything?"

"As far as I can tell, he's doing great," Chris said. "A little diarrhea when you first left, but otherwise, he's adjusted fine. He sleeps in our bedroom, by the way."

Jamie's heart took a sudden plunge when she heard some background noise—the sound of a car radio. "Where are you right now?"

"I'm in the carpool lane at school—picking up the girls."

Jamie tried not to panic, but she couldn't ignore the siren in her head. "Is Amanda home with Snowball?"

"No, she had some errands to run. Is that a problem?"

"Listen, Chris, this might sound crazy. But can you get your neighbors to check on him right away? Maybe even take Snowball into their house until you guys get home? I'll explain when I arrive tonight."

"Um, sure. I'll try." Jamie heard the familiar concern in her brother's voice. Other law students had mothers. Jamie had Chris. "Is everything all right?" he asked.

"I'll explain when I get there."

◁▷

When Chris called back forty-five minutes later, Jamie could tell right away from his tone that something was wrong. "Snowball's not looking good," he said. "I'm taking him to the vet."

Jamie was already on I-85 but had not even made it to the city's perimeter. The traffic was bumper-to-bumper, and now she felt an increased urgency . . . and nausea. "What do you mean, 'not looking good'?"

"He's sick, Jamie. Food poisoning or something."

The air left her lungs. This couldn't be happening. "Get him to the vet right away, Chris. Please hurry."

The next two calls were both made by Jamie. She had Chris describe Snowball's symptoms in detail. Drooling, vomiting, convulsions. Eventually Snowball grew lethargic, but he somehow made it to the vet. The dog had a stubborn streak and an iron will; Jamie knew that much. He might need every ounce of it to survive.

On the next call, Jamie spoke directly with the vet. He had pumped Snowball's stomach right away but hadn't noticed much improvement. He was an old country doc who had seen every kind of dog poison case imaginable—mushrooms, toads, paint thinner, rat poison. It was amazing what dogs could survive.

But Snowball had this guy worried. The dog's breathing was short and shallow. His heart rate, frighteningly fast. Honestly, the doc didn't know if Snowball was going to pull through or not. Traffic had thinned out a little, and Jamie was weaving in and out, tailgating when necessary. She knew if she could just see Snowball again, somehow he would find the strength to live.

"Do whatever it takes to save him," Jamie ordered. "I'll worry about the costs later." She laid on the horn and bullied some cars into making room. She was still two and a half hours away.

"We're already doing everything we can," the vet said. "I've got two golden Labs of my own."

◁▷

The next phone call was made by Chris.

"I'm sorry, Jamie," he said softly. "We lost him."

56

THEY STOOD IN THE BACKYARD by a big hole that Chris had dug by hand. It was a shaded patch of earth next to a large Georgia pine, a grave befitting the most majestic of dogs. Chris had laid Snowball carefully in the hole, flat on his side, his legs fully extended—the way Snowball often slept at night, utterly exhausted from another day of rambunctious adventure. They held hands—Jamie, Chris, Amanda, and the two girls, Lola, age six, and Sophie, age four.

Jamie had cried for Snowball for more than an hour on the way to Chris's house. Sobbed for him, really. Sobbed for herself. At the very least, she wished with all her heart she could have seen him one last time.

When she arrived at the house, she put on a stoic front for the little girls, even forced a smile, though surely her red and puffy eyes gave her away. She pulled Chris aside in the kitchen and told him everything. Chris had already talked to a Rabun County deputy sheriff, who had been dispatched after Jamie called Drew Jacobsen. Chris resisted the opportunity to lecture his kid sister about honesty or about putting his own family at risk or any number of things. Instead, he just gave her a hug and assured her it would be okay.

Snowball was just a dog, she kept telling herself. But it was a lie. He was so much more than just a dog. The feeling of senseless loss reminded her too much of her mother's funeral. She had lost a certain innocence with her mother's death—the belief that things happen for a purpose, that the world was generally just, that bad things don't happen to good people. She felt those same emotions again, along with the familiar swell of anger and the bitter taste of revenge yet to be exacted.

At the graveside, she tried to push those emotions aside as she pursed her lips and bowed her head while Lola led them in prayer. It was the cute prayer of a child, unashamed to pray for a dog, trusting enough to believe she would see him again.

They turned to Chris, who decided to try a eulogy. "There are good dogs, and there are great dogs," he said, embracing the task. "Rin Tin Tin. Lassie. Shadow on *Homeward Bound*. But in all of dogdom, there has never been a dog quite like this one."

Chris had his head down, but he ventured a peek at Jamie, as if making sure his lame attempt at humor wasn't causing more grief. "He was the all-time Frisbee champion of the universe, a world-class barker, and one of the smartest canines God ever created."

Jamie shook her head and gave Chris the look that said he was being an idiot but it was okay: she loved him for it. "Excuse me," she said. "I thought I was at the funeral for Snowball."

Chris smiled. Amanda smiled. The girls looked confused.

"He was a great dog," Chris said seriously. "And you couldn't help but love him."

He was all that, Jamie knew, and a lot more. Everyone at the graveside now looked at her. "In truth, he wasn't the smartest dog," Jamie said. "Or the most obedient. And you'd better make sure your shoes were out of reach." Jamie glanced at Amanda, a well-known cat lover and dog tolerator. Even her eyes were wet. "But he sure was loyal. And he was the best friend anybody could ever ask for."

Jamie wanted to say more, but she felt the tears coming on. She choked on her words, felt herself losing control.

"Is Snowball in heaven?" Sophie asked.

"You bet, honey," Chris said, bending down to brush back Sophie's hair. "Probably playing Frisbee."

They stood there for another minute or two, and it suddenly hit Jamie hard—the realization she would never see him again. "Can I have a minute alone?" she asked.

As the family filed inside, Jamie crouched beside the grave. She rubbed his ears again, the way she had a thousand times before. She ran her fingers down his back, gently calling his name. She had seen him lying like this so many nights, but always before with that barrel chest gently breathing in and out. She bent in and kissed him, whispered her thanks for a million moments of happiness, and positioned his Frisbee between his paws.

As a final tribute, she reached down and undid the Velcro straps on her own Chacos, her favorite water sandals. They were frayed around the edges where Snowball had nipped at them as a puppy and gnawed on them as an adolescent. She had told him *No!* too many times to count, thrown away two other pairs of shoes he had demolished, and finally discovered a bitter apple spray that she squirted in Snowball's mouth if he tried to take another bite at her Chacos. But here, at his graveside, she regretted every feeling of frustration, every time she had snapped at Snowball or lost her patience. She took off the sandals and placed them gently in the grave. His Frisbee. Her sandals. What more could a black Lab want? She stared for one long, last minute at her sweet companion, then stood and picked up the shovel.

"You *were* a great dog," she said. "The best ever."

57

AT A MOVIE THEATER IN BUCKHEAD, a few miles from the law school campus, Isaiah Haywood settled into a seat at the end of the top row, middle section. Right where they had planned. They had chosen the seven o'clock showing of a horror flick that bombed the weekend before, and predictably, only a few others settled into the theater seats before the previews rolled.

A few minutes after the opening credits, a woman arrived and walked deliberately up the steps toward him, surveying the sparse audience as she did so. She wore baggy jeans, a long-sleeved black sweater, and sneakers. Isaiah did a double take.

Stacie had been a close-cropped brunette; this woman had curly auburn hair. She wore glasses and carried a large handbag. She took a seat next to Isaiah. When the screen brightened, he could make out the attractive silhouette of Stacie's eyes and thin nose. The determined jaw. "I almost didn't recognize you," Isaiah said.

The woman turned and looked him over. "And you are?"

He hesitated, her unsmiling face creating a sliver of doubt. But the theater *was* nearly empty. And this woman *did* sit down right next to him. "Your male escort," he said.

"You hesitated," she shot back. She helped herself to some popcorn. "That's the best I can hope for."

"Maybe you should try being a blonde," Isaiah suggested.

"Been there."

Isaiah let a few seconds pass while a loud scene played itself out. He leaned toward her. "Sorry about the ruling," he said. He had already given Stacie the gist of it over the phone. They had agreed to meet here to discuss the next steps.

"You tried. I'm not surprised at the court's decision."

The movie sound track turned quiet and foreboding, creating a mood for the grotesque figures on the screen. It seemed a fitting backdrop.

"The U.S. attorney argued that you guys don't really have the algorithm. That you were just trying to scam the Chinese mafia out of some money. He said if you really had the algorithm, you would have sold it to some legitimate Internet security companies."

"We've got the algorithm," Stacie said. It was still a whisper, but it was an emphatic one.

Isaiah waited a moment for further explanation. None came.

"Why didn't you sell it to someone safe? Why go to the mafia?"

"We didn't."

Isaiah again waited for more detail but none came. "That's it—we didn't?"

"It's complicated, Isaiah. And there are things I can't say. But I *can* tell you that I've changed in these last four years. There's no way I would let David risk our lives just to scam the triads out of money."

Isaiah felt frustration gnawing its way to the surface. He had risked a lot for the Hoffmans—he deserved more than a trust-me speech. In a different setting, he might have been more forceful. But whispering in a movie theater had its limits.

"The government says they're willing to be proven wrong," he whispered. "Snead has talked with the U.S. attorney. If we give the feds a copy of the algorithm, they'll give you continued protection and a new identity. They've given us twenty-four hours to consider it—"

"No way."

"Stacie, you need to at least think this over. What good is this algorithm if you don't live long enough to cash in?"

"It's not about the money, Isaiah." She was whispering louder now, intensity riding on every syllable. "The man who created this algorithm died protecting it. Don't you understand why we wanted *you* to work this case for us? This is the same government that traces its own citizens' phone calls without a warrant. The government that makes innocent citizens like David and me testify against the mob and then acts like they're doing us a favor when they make us hide for the rest of our lives. Do you really want them to have the most powerful decryption tool ever discovered? One that allows them to decipher secret messages sent over the Internet? Do you really want to be the one to destroy the right to privacy as we know it?"

Isaiah didn't really know what to say. He shared Stacie's distrust of authority, but this sounded a little like the rant of an anarchist. A conspiracy theorist. New world order, and all that other nonsense.

"Isaiah, that algorithm is the only thing keeping us alive. It's our insurance policy. Once we give that up, we're expendable."

As they talked, a middle-aged man cradling a tub of popcorn and a soda entered the theater from the left—twenty minutes after the movie had started. He surveyed the theater before taking the aisle seat on the last row of the front section. *Nobody sits in the front section when there are plenty of elevated seats left in the back.*

"How do you think the triads located us again in the first place?" Stacie asked.

Isaiah took another drink of soda to give himself a few seconds to think. It sounded like a trick question. "I don't know," he admitted. "Your theory about a leak in the marshals' office makes sense." What Isaiah *didn't* say, because this wasn't the time to pick a fight, was that Carzak's theory made even more sense.

"The feds are using us as bait, Isaiah. Their raid on the triad's hiding place four years ago was a fiasco. The government managed to keep a lid on it with regard to publicity, so it never became another Ruby Ridge, but it's one of their greatest internal embarrassments ever. The triad's U.S. leader, Huang Xu, and several of his top lieutenants escaped. Professor Kumari was killed. Now they're using us to lure Xu back out in the open."

Isaiah watched the images flash across the screen—contrived horror, otherworldly. But the lady next to him, if she was telling the truth, was trapped in her own horror show. A government sworn to protect her, using her as bait. The triads hunting her down.

"David and I have given this a lot of thought," Stacie continued. "Maybe the feds thought that Xu ended up with the algorithm. One way to find out would be for them to send a letter to Johnny Chin saying that we wanted to sell it. They leak our location to Xu and then they watch. If he kills us, it means he already has the algorithm and wants to dispose of any competitors. If he tries to kidnap us, it means he doesn't have the algorithm and wants to torture it out of us."

Isaiah's head was spinning. "If you really believe that, why did we even file this lawsuit? What makes you think the government wouldn't leak your new identity as well?"

"That's why we wanted court oversight, Isaiah. As long as this witness protection program operates in the shadows, David and I have to rely on the good faith of the U.S. attorney and the U.S. marshals. But with Parcelli hand-selecting the persons who would be involved in our case and the court appointing a trustee to oversee our protection, there would be little chance of another leak."

They talked for a few minutes about appealing the court's ruling. Isaiah thought they might have a good chance, but Stacie was ready to let it drop. She thanked Isaiah for trying. It was time for her and David to take matters into their own hands, she said. She would rather have done this with the government's help, but she was prepared to do it without them.

As they talked, Isaiah watched the man in the front section of the theater. At one point, the man turned and glanced around. Maybe it was just the movie, but Isaiah was getting the creeps.

"What do you think of that guy down there?" Isaiah asked.

"Front section?"

"Yeah."

"You leave first," Stacie said. "I'll follow in a few minutes. Call me on my cell in ten minutes so we can check on each other."

Isaiah insisted that Stacie leave first. The man in the front didn't even seem to notice when she did so. Isaiah followed a few minutes later and called Stacie from his car.

"You okay?" he asked.

"I'm fine," she said. "And I don't think I'm being followed. But next time, let's go see a comedy."

Isaiah checked his mirrors again. *Next time?*

58

AFTER HANGING UP WITH STACIE, Isaiah called Snead at home. The professor answered on the third ring, his gruff voice saying, "Walter Snead," as if he were still answering the phone in his private law firm. *Somebody needs to get a life,* Isaiah thought.

"It's Isaiah. You asked me to report in after meeting with Stacie Hoffman at the movies."

"Yes. Well, what's the verdict, Mr. Haywood?"

"Two thumbs down," Isaiah said. He couldn't resist, though he knew Snead wouldn't laugh. "Too much demon possession and blood, though the vampires are hotties."

Snead didn't respond.

"Sorry. As for the legal case, the client does not want to appeal."

"I'm not surprised," Snead said. "Do they want to take the government's deal?"

"No. They really believe the government has already outed them once and is using them as bait. They think the algorithm serves as sort of an insurance policy. They want to keep the algorithm and still get new identities."

Snead sighed into the phone, as if he were talking to a renegade adolescent. "Did you tell them that particular deal's not on the table?"

"Yes."

"And?"

"It's the only deal they're willing to consider."

"I see," Snead said, though Isaiah was pretty sure he didn't. "Let me ask you a question, Mr. Haywood. And I want your gut-level, honest response."

"Okay."

"Do you believe them? Do you think the government is leaking information and using Mr. Hoffman as bait?"

Isaiah pondered this for a moment. "Honestly, I don't know."

"I've been thinking," Snead said. "Maybe we should up the ante and find out." He couldn't have surprised Isaiah more if he had just announced his engagement to Jessica Simpson. "Instead of suing for specific performance of the memorandum of understanding, a case in which the government has nothing to lose, we could file for damages under the Federal Tort Claims Act." Snead's gruff voice grew excited by the genius of his own idea. "We could take depositions and issue sub-poenas—get to the bottom of this thing. We could sue for nine or ten million based on fraud and intentional infliction of emotional distress."

Only Snead would think that a good tort suit could solve all of our problems, Isaiah mused. "It'd be an even stronger case if the Hoffmans ended up dead," he said sarcastically.

But Snead missed the tone of voice, intoxicated as he was with trial lawyer greed. "Yes, but it's still pretty strong. The Hoffmans are in fear for their lives. I've tried some asbestos cases where we recovered for fear of cancer even though the patient had no manifestations. Fear-of-AIDS cases for bad blood transfusions. There's precedence out there..." Snead trailed off as if he had been talking to himself all along.

"I'll call Wellington immediately," Snead said, changing direction. "I'll get him started on the research and the pleadings. They gave us twenty-four hours to respond. We'll give them a shot across the bow."

"I'm sure Wellington's got nothing better to do," Isaiah said.

◁▷

Allan Carzak was eating a late dinner at one of his favorite Italian restaurants, regaling some friends with courtroom stories while his wife rolled her eyes. His cell phone rang, the ringtone from *Mission: Impossible,* and he checked the caller ID. Sam Parcelli, FBI, still on the job late at night.

The Hoffman case was the first time he had worked with Sam, but the man was living up to his reputation. Intense, tenacious, uncompromising. Sam never gave it a rest. He had called Carzak several times late at night or on the weekends—the clock and calendar apparently of no consequence.

Carzak answered and asked Parcelli to hang on for a minute. "I'll be right back," Carzak said to his dinner companions, then left the restaurant so he could hear Parcelli better.

"Somebody killed that young female lawyer's dog tonight; what's her name? Hang on . . ."

"Jamie Brock," Carzak said.

"Yeah, Jamie Brock. She left the dog with her brother in north Georgia. Somebody poisoned it, left her a note. 'You should have called.'"

Carzak thought about this for a second, scrunched his forehead. "Any leads?"

"We're assuming it's the same guys who assaulted her the other day. We've got sketches out and we're working with the locals, but so far we've come up dry."

"How would the triad know about the hearing?" Carzak asked.

He waited while Parcelli collected his thoughts. The FBI agent was always precise and calculating—in what he said, in how he investigated cases, and especially during phone calls with U.S. attorneys. "That's an open question. Lots of possibilities. We're running some background checks on everyone who was in that courtroom today as well as Judge Torriano's law clerks. We'll look at the court staff in the clerk's office who had access to the initial pleadings. Somebody could have tapped into the clerk's computers, followed one of the law students or the professor around . . . Who knows? There're a thousand ways these guys could have found out. Sealed proceedings are still a sieve; you know that."

Carzak couldn't argue with him. How many times had sealed negotiations or the amounts of confidential settlements or the testimony from secret proceedings found their way into the press? Virtually every high-profile grand jury hearing Carzak had handled, for starters.

"We need to take exclusive jurisdiction of this investigation," Carzak said. He had shifted into problem-solving mode. "Witness tampering, obstruction of justice—we've got three or four grounds for running off the locals."

"We've already done that. It's our case."

There was defensiveness in the agent's voice—one of the weaknesses Carzak had already discovered. With other agents, Carzak had managed to build trust quickly; they were on the same side, after all. Often, Carzak and the agents became friends. But with Parcelli, there was an invisible wall. Because of the importance of the case, Parcelli was reporting directly to the FBI's deputy director. He chafed at any direction from Allan Carzak.

But that wouldn't stop Carzak from doing his job.

"Sam . . ." Carzak paused. He had learned the value of letting a person's name hang out there for a second—it made your point better than cursing or screaming ever could. "This is getting complicated. We can't let anything happen to this girl. I'll put the marshals' office on her 24-7 if that's what it takes." The insinuation was subtle, but pointed nonetheless. If the FBI couldn't do the job, Carzak would deploy the U.S. Marshals Service.

"We've got it covered," Parcelli said quickly.

"Let's hope so."

◁▷

The drive from her brother's house in Rabun County to her home in Atlanta was one that Jamie relished during the daylight hours. The north Georgia roads would wind their way to the peak of a Georgia mountain, where a curtain would part on a panoramic view of God's creation—rolling mountains, the rich greens of pines and oaks, meandering streams gurgling their way down the hillsides. It was here that kayak companies and white-water rafting outfitters dotted the waterways—giving tourists the rides of their lives on frothing rivers with Indian names.

Jamie could navigate the Class IV rapids just fine but preferred the glassy surface of Lake Lanier on a calm summer morning. She thrived on mastering the technical aspects of flat-water kayaking. Form, efficiency of stroke, stamina, and speed were enough to worry about.

White-water kayakers had to yield themselves to the river, riding the unpredictable current the same way a person would ride a wild stallion. Jamie did not love what she could not control.

At night, the spectacular drive became a harrowing descent. The roads seemed to narrow, the slopes steepened, and the ever-present fog cut visibility to a minimum. Most drivers would clench the steering wheel a little tighter and concentrate on the next bend in the road. Jamie pulled out her cell phone and dialed Drew Jacobsen's number. She was tired, drained from the emotions of the day. It was late. She needed to talk with somebody.

Rationalizations, she knew.

It was the third time that day she had called. The first time was shortly after she discovered the note on her windshield, as soon as she had gotten off the phone with Chris. The second time was after Snowball died and Jamie had regained her composure. Drew told her that he would call the Rabun County sheriff's office and the FBI, who showed up forty-five minutes after Jamie arrived at Chris's house. On the way home, as she prepared to call Drew a third time, she wondered if she was wearing out her welcome.

If she was, she couldn't tell from the tone of his voice. His concern warmed her. But her emotions, she reminded herself, were on overdrive following Snowball's death. She couldn't trust herself right now; she knew that much.

Drew explained that the feds had asserted their jurisdiction and he had been instructed to stand down. He asked Jamie if the feds had contacted her yet about round-the-clock security.

They had sent a few agents out to her brother's house to interview her, Jamie said. They were going to meet her at the condo when she arrived home and check it out. She didn't think they would be watching her 24-7.

"Sounds like you need your own private protection," Drew suggested.

Jamie started to decline. She was going to be a prosecutor someday; she would have to get used to death threats. But for some reason, she let the thought linger for a moment.

Long enough, it turned out, for Drew to think she was worried about cost. "I know a guy who's very good. And very cheap. He's got a full-time job with the department, but he moonlights under the right circumstances."

He paused for a beat. "I think he's available."

"Drew, I don't need you to do this. I'll be fine."

But Drew insisted, and after an appropriate amount of protesting, Jamie conceded. In truth, Snowball's death and her own abduction had her pretty well stressed-out.

"What time are you getting to your condo?" Drew asked.

"I told the agents I would meet them there at midnight. I don't know how long they'll take to check things out."

"I'll be there by one," Drew said.

◁▷

That night, Jamie's emotions stewed together in a toxic mix that poisoned any possibility of sleep. *Anger and hatred.* The scums who killed an innocent dog just to make a point. She fantasized about a shoot-out, the Kimber taking them down. *Confusion.* Who were her stalkers? Did they belong to the triads that Hoffman testified against? Or was this the Russian mafia? How did they know where Snowball was? *Fear.* Was she next? When? How could she protect herself?

But mostly, *loneliness.* As a puppy, Snowball had slept in a crate. The adolescent Snowball earned his own soft mattress on the floor, right next to Jamie's bed. But then he began the assault. Every few nights he would try his luck, jumping up on the foot of the bed, waiting to see if Jamie ran him off. In less than a month, he had established new turf.

She drew the line when he tried to worm his way up to the pillows. And she woke up more than once to find he had crowded her over to the very edge of the bed, or forced her, in a half-asleep state, to curl into a tiny ball so he could sprawl across the bottom of the bed.

And now, tonight, when she was on the verge of dozing off, she could almost feel him nuzzle against the crook in her legs or flop a paw over her foot or make those guttural noises that signified a deep and contented sleep. But then she would open her eyes and see the emptiness at the foot of the bed, and the pain would stab at her heart.

At three o'clock, she threw on a pair of jeans, a sweatshirt, a ball cap, and sandals and walked outside to the street in front of her house. She spotted Jacobsen's car, right where he said it would be, and climbed into the passenger seat.

"The first night's always the hardest," he said.

59

THE RAIN SEEMED TO BE coming in massive horizontal waves and Allan Carzak couldn't stay dry even under his umbrella. He loved thunderstorms at night—a display of heavenly fireworks and divine percussion, lighting up the midnight sky. At night, thunderstorms were romantic. But when he had a lunch appointment on the other side of town, they were nothing more than a pain in the rear.

The bottoms of his pant legs were soaked and his shoes squished as he stepped off the elevator at the U.S. attorney's office after returning from lunch. With a slew of things on his to-do list, the last thing he needed was Professor Walter Snead, clutching a dripping-wet golf umbrella and soggy leather satchel, waiting in the reception area.

It was all Carzak could do to force a smile and shake Snead's hand.

"I only need five minutes of your time," Snead said. "It's a courtesy call about a lawsuit I'm filing."

Carzak checked his watch. "Five minutes?"

Snead nodded. "At the most."

Snead followed Carzak back to his office. Melanie, Carzak's assistant, politely asked if Snead wanted anything to drink.

"Coffee. Black."

The men took seats at a small round table in the corner. A few minutes later, Melanie reappeared with Snead's coffee.

When she left, Snead unzipped his briefcase and placed a manila folder on the table. Slid it toward Carzak. Took a drink of his coffee. "This is your copy of a lawsuit I'm filing this afternoon," he said.

"Federal Tort Claims Act. It accuses the U.S. Attorney's Office, the U.S. Marshals Service, and the FBI of fraud and gross negligence in violation of their respective duties to protect David and Stacie Hoffman pursuant to the memorandum of understanding."

Snead slurped some more coffee as Carzak scoffed at the manila folder, deciding not to touch it. "How is this any different from the lawsuit you just lost? Your request for injunctive relief was premised on a claim that the government violated the terms of the memorandum of understanding. The court didn't see it that way."

Snead let a smirk pull at the corners of his lips. Carzak, as was his custom, sat facing the pane-glass wall formed by the floor-to-ceiling windows of his eighteenth-floor office. The long fingers of water dripping down the window silhouetted Snead and, combined with the round face and hanging jowls of the old man, reminded Carzak of the Davy Jones character in *Pirates of the Caribbean*. It fit, Carzak thought, because Snead used lawsuits like tentacles, entangling defendants in complex federal litigation until they capitulated.

Plus, Snead had a charter membership in that modern-day band of buccaneers who called themselves "plaintiffs' lawyers."

"My first lawsuit was to make you honor the agreement from this day forward," Snead said sanctimoniously. "It assumed that thus far you've been playing by the rules. But this lawsuit takes a different approach, seeking damages for fraud and gross negligence based on a violation of your duties as defined by the witness protection agreement." Snead actually poked the table with his fingers here, accentuating his point. "They're running for their lives because the marshals' office leaked their location . . . and we intend to prove it."

Snead let the accusation hang melodramatically in the air for a few seconds and then leaned forward, close enough for Carzak to catch a whiff of the man's soggy wool suit mixed with tobacco and coffee breath. "I'm gonna raise Cain *myself* this time. No law students and quick preliminary injunction hearings. *I'll* take depositions, issue interrogatories, subpoena documents. *I'll* raise enough reasonable suspicion in this baby—" Snead tapped the folder containing the lawsuit—"that the court will have to let me pry open the lid on this whole nasty witness protection program. And we both know that won't be pretty."

Carzak opened the folder and pretended to study the lawsuit. He had learned a long time ago that you didn't argue with bombastic lawyers like Snead—it was a waste of breath. You let them blow off their steam . . . then you annihilated them in court. Carzak was already formulating his collateral estoppel defense, an argument that the court had ruled on this issue in the first lawsuit and shouldn't be asked to do so again.

But in the meantime, he needed to appease Snead a little, giving his own team time to react. "I'll look into it from our end," Carzak promised. "I can tell you this much: if I find the marshals or FBI played fast and loose with the protection of one of our witnesses, I'll set up the firing squad and provide the bullets myself."

This seemed to set Snead back a little. The big man was aching for a fight, not an ally. But he recovered quickly, his face sagging into a disapproving scowl. "I appreciate your willingness to guard my clients' safety and constitutional rights," he growled. "But as the Romans were fond of saying, 'Sed quis custodiet ipsos custodes.'"

Impressive, Carzak thought. *Davy Jones speaks Latin.* It was the oft-quoted phrase "Who guards the guards?" But truly smart people didn't need to prove their worth by speaking foreign languages.

"I don't know about all that," Carzak said, "but like I said, I'll help you get to the bottom of it."

◁▷

Carzak escorted Snead out of the office and asked his assistant to get Sam Parcelli on the phone.

"Line one," the ever-efficient Melanie said a few minutes later. Carzak put in his earpiece so he would be free to pace. Melanie closed the office door.

"Walter Snead just paid me a visit," Carzak said. He was walking haphazardly around the office, playing with a rubber band. "Brought me a courtesy copy of a lawsuit that alleges we blew Hoffman's cover. He's asking for . . . let's see—" he picked up the folder and flipped through the pages of the complaint—"ten million dollars, give or take."

"Maybe we could split the difference; settle for five," Parcelli said.

"Funny."

"Relax," Parcelli said, drawing the word out in a condescending tone. "A wise lawyer once told me that truth is only what can be proven in the courtroom."

Carzak hated it when agents quoted him, using his own words as ammo against him. "Snead has a reputation in these things. He's relentless. We need to be squeaky clean."

"I'm on it," Parcelli said. "And it's funny you should mention Snead's reputation."

Parcelli pulled in a breath, and Carzak heard the rustling of papers. "Our California office has a file on Snead. They were about six months away from possible indictments when Snead quit practicing law and started teaching. They had traced lots of cash from legal settlements into an undesignated account. Snead would withdraw cash from the undesignated account in chunks slightly less than ten thousand. Never paid a dime of taxes on the money."

"He was a tax cheat?" Carzak stopped pacing. Parcelli had his attention.

"Better yet. They think it was walking-around money for bribing judges. There've been rumors of corruption swirling around a few state court judges for years. That's what started the probe in the first place."

Carzak thought for a moment about the possibilities. "Any hint of mob involvement?"

"Not yet. But it wouldn't surprise me."

"Okay," Carzak said, "let me summarize. We've got a dirty attorney suing us for ten million, a member of the witness protection program who has dropped off the face of the earth while trying to sell a dangerous encryption formula to the Chinese mob, an innocent young law student who had her dog killed by stalkers, and the deputy director of the FBI personally involved in this fiasco probably wondering how we could let things get so fouled up."

"That about nails it," Parcelli said.

"I think I need a drink."

Carzak finished the phone call and walked over to the breathtaking view of Atlanta available from the wall of windows on the north side of his office. On a clear day, he could see the Georgia Dome, Philips Arena, the CNN Center, the clogged interstate connector making its way through the downtown district. In fact, on a clear day he could see all the way past Georgia Tech to the new construction around the Atlantic Station area. But today, with the wind blowing the rain in horizontal sheets and streaking the window with a web of interconnected rivulets, the entire city took on a gloomy and foreboding haze.

Just thinking about his job—U.S. attorney for the northern district of Georgia—used to give Carzak a pinch-me feeling. The smart and extroverted country boy from rural Georgia had made good. Even after he grew comfortable in the job, it still gave him a sense of power. He won at least 90 percent of his cases as a U.S. attorney; he had the full investigative power of the United States of America at his disposal. Trying a case was always a rush, but especially when he started his opening statements this way: "Ladies and gentlemen of the jury, my name is Allan Carzak, and I represent the people of the United States of America. . . ."

But this afternoon, he felt none of that majesty and empowerment. Instead, he felt helpless. This case, perhaps the most important one he had handled in the last ten years, was spinning madly out of control. If the triad somehow obtained Kumari's algorithm, it would define Carzak's career. *Isn't he the guy who let that dude in the witness protection program cut a deal with the mob and jeopardize the security of the entire World Wide Web?*

When Parcelli called back ten minutes later, Carzak was still scrolling through doomsday scenarios in his head.

"I've got an idea," Parcelli said. "But you'd better sit down before I tell you."

"Okay," Carzak said. He started pacing again.

"And don't say no until you hear me out. . . ."

60

BY TUESDAY NIGHT, Jamie had grown somewhat accustomed to living under the protection of the federal marshals. They made it clear they couldn't watch her 24-7, but they were definitely making their presence known.

Monday night, she had given them her class schedule. They followed her to school on Tuesday, conducting a walk-through as she attended classes, their telltale earpieces and dark blue blazers giving them away. She supposed that was the whole point. They followed her to lunch, these bulky blue shadows. They used a spare key to check out her condo before she arrived home, met her at the door, and told her that someone would periodically make passes through the neighborhood.

"What's the president doing for protection while you guys keep an eye on me?" she asked, trying to lighten things up a little.

"That's the Secret Service, ma'am. We're with the marshals' office."

It was a joke, buddy.

Yet despite all the efforts of the U.S. marshals' office, Jamie didn't really feel secure until 11:00 p.m. rolled around and her new, unpaid security consultant parked in front of the condo and called her cell.

"Reporting for duty," Drew Jacobsen said. "I'll expect coffee at one and ice cream at three thirty."

"How do I fire you?" Jamie asked. "You're getting too expensive."

"You can't. That's the whole point."

She took a deep breath, and the rationalizations started. *It's nothing personal. I would do this for anybody guarding me, except for maybe the*

*federal marshals, but then again, they're not staying out there all night. And
if I do feel the least bit of attraction for the man, which I'm not admitting
I do, then it certainly has nothing to do with the fact that we have been
thrown together in the middle of this high-pressure, life-threatening situation. It would be deeper and more substantial than that.*

All of this, and a dozen more thoughts, cascaded through Jamie's
hyperactive brain at the very moment her mouth said, "Why don't you
just come up and keep watch from inside? It would be more comfortable than sitting in the car."

Drew started by listing a dozen reasons that wouldn't be a good
idea, including the fact that he might be able to spot any suspicious
drive-bys better from his vantage point on the street. But then, to
Jamie's surprise, he switched gears. "However, if it's not too late, I
did want to talk to you about a few things I've found." He sounded
formal, official.

"I'll start the coffee," Jamie said.

They sat at Jamie's dining room table. She had moved her law
books and half-finished course outlines to a corner. She closed her
laptop and pushed it aside as well.

Drew took the room in, his eyes landing on some bookshelf pictures of Jamie in her kayak. "You a kayaker?" he asked.

"I used to race a little."

He looked at her, probably thinking that she must have been slow
since her shoulders and arms didn't look like a Russian weight lifter's.
Everybody expected kayakers to be bulky. But the opposite was true.

"I'll bet you were fast," he said, surprising her.

"I did all right."

"'All right' as in 'Olympics' all right? Or 'all right' as in 'I could usually make it down the course without tipping over'?"

"I missed the Olympics. But not by much."

"Impressive."

He actually *looked* impressed. And he also looked . . . well, he looked
good for an unmarried police detective. *Very* good. He had thick black
hair that he wore longer than most cops, with unruly bangs that accentuated piercing dark eyes. He had a bit of a Latino look, despite the

Anglo name, with sharp facial angles that contrasted markedly with his soft-spoken personality. Jamie bet that when it was necessary, Drew could play a convincing bad cop. But when he smiled, with the perfect white teeth and a small dimple that formed on his right cheek, lesser women would have melted.

Not Jamie Brock. Not yet, anyway.

Drew placed a folder on the table. He pulled out some handwritten notes. "Your man Walter Snead is quite a civil trial lawyer—" he looked up, apparently wanting to gauge Jamie's reaction—"and a pushover when it comes to criminal defense."

Jamie shrugged. "Meaning what?"

"I have a friend in the L.A. area who owed me a favor. I had him run a report on Snead. He cross-referenced newspaper articles and checked case files at the courthouse. He limited his search to the last five years and only those cases filed in L.A. County. Here's what he found. . . ."

Drew pointed at some math in the middle of the page. "Eighty percent of his personal-injury cases settled out of court—nothing unusual about that. But this statistic caught my attention: most of his large personal-injury settlements—thirteen out of nineteen to be exact—had the same three judges assigned to them. That's three judges out of a pool of fourteen. Pretty amazing, huh?"

Jamie nodded. It was statistically suspicious, but it was not impossible.

Drew drank some coffee, and Jamie could tell the man was working hard not to sound overly enthusiastic. "Here's where it gets really interesting. Of the thirteen cases assigned to those three judges, Snead received favorable rulings on important pretrial motions in eight of them."

Drew raised an eyebrow, and Jamie couldn't deny the sinister implications of that statistic. Trial judges didn't like to make important pretrial rulings. They'd rather leave the issues hanging out there, like swords of Damocles, the uncertainty of them forcing the parties to settle.

"Were any of those rulings appealed?" Jamie asked.

"Not those. It's my understanding that you would have to try the entire case before you could appeal them. But you would know more about that than I do."

Jamie flipped a wrist. "That's basically right."

"In three other cases that didn't settle, the opposing attorney challenged the pretrial rulings, went to trial and lost, but then got the case reversed on appeal. Just goes to show how messed up the rulings were in the first place."

Jamie tried hard to make sense of all this. She tried to think of innocent explanations. "Maybe it's the old boys' club. Maybe these are college buddies, frat brothers."

"Judge Elaine Estrada might not appreciate those insinuations," Drew said. He gave Jamie a sinister little "gotcha" smile. Even that smile was cute, she had to admit.

"Plus, there's the matter of the criminal cases. These same three judges heard a fair number of Snead's criminal cases, and guess what?"

"He happened to win based on miraculously effective pretrial motions?"

"No. Just the opposite. He lost every time he had a case in front of them. Every . . . single . . . time."

Jamie remembered her conversation with Isaiah from the week before—the same abysmal assessment of Snead's criminal defense record. But it didn't make sense. Why fix only the civil cases? Before she could say anything stupid, something else Isaiah said dawned on her. *Because the civil cases are where the money is. Contingency fees. Snead gets one-third of any amount in settlement.*

"So you're saying he sells out his clients in the criminal cases in order to collect big fees in the civil cases?"

Drew held up his palms. "I'm not saying anything. I'm just giving you the stats." He took another drink of coffee. "But if you want my *opinion* on the matter . . ."

"Do I have a choice?"

"Maybe there's a highly structured corruption ring that reaches into the highest echelons of the Los Angeles bar. Maybe Snead is just one part. Maybe he makes money on the civil cases and provides kickbacks to the three dirty judges. Maybe there's some mob money involved—there usually is when we're talking high-level corruption."

"Maybe he's just one heckuva civil lawyer and a pitiful criminal lawyer."

Drew gave her a lopsided half smile. "And maybe he's a Boy Scout leader on the side."

Drew pulled out another piece of paper and turned serious again. "We also turned up a few things on your buddy Isaiah Haywood." Jamie tried not to show her shock. "Between college and law school he got busted for possession with intent to distribute. Cocaine. Fulton County. Somebody pulled some strings, and the next thing you know he's got a suspended sentence. He stays clean for six months, and the judge wipes out the charges."

Jamie stared at her cup for a moment. Isaiah had always come across as ready to party . . . but she was still pretty disappointed in him. *You think you know somebody . . .*

Drew must have read the consternation on her face. "I'm not saying that either of these guys had anything to do with the mob finding out about the hearing. I just thought you might want to know."

Jamie leaned back and stretched, suddenly very tired. It was incomprehensible that Isaiah, or even Professor Snead, could have anything to do with her abduction. Or Snowball's poisoning.

"It's hard to know whom to trust," Jamie said.

"I've got some advice for you. . . ." Drew Jacobsen's brown eyes turned intense, and the muscles on his face pulled tight. "Until this is over, don't trust anybody."

61

JAMIE STRUGGLED THROUGH her UCC class on Wednesday after lunch, unable to concentrate with everything else going on. The blue suits from the U.S. marshals' office had made an earlier appearance at school and promised to meet Jamie at her condo that night. Fortunately, her UCC professor disdained the Socratic method and Jamie was in no danger of being called on as her mind drifted.

After class, she exchanged a few comments with friends as she packed up her computer, her thick textbook, and her colored highlighters and pens. As always, the Kimber rode all by itself in the zipper compartment on the bottom of her backpack. She had unzipped that area on the right side a few inches, precisely at the spot where the handle of the Kimber rested. Even with the backpack straps over both shoulders, she could reach around with her left hand and quickly unzip enough of the pocket so she could pull the gun out with her right hand in a matter of seconds. She had practiced for nearly half an hour last night before Drew Jacobsen came over. A good sequence took no more than two seconds. Jamie Brock, quick draw. Welcome to the wild, wild West.

Jamie's UCC class was on the second floor, and Jamie, of course, never used elevators for such a short distance. Today, by the time she hit the stairwells—large, hollow, windowless caverns with plastic grips on the steps—the crowd of students leaving the second floor had already slowed to a trickle. Jamie descended the steps, lost in thought over her slumping classroom performance, David Hoffman's dangerous case, and Drew Jacobsen's interest in her as a person, not just a victim. At least that's how she evaluated it.

Her mind elsewhere, she never would have registered alarm if the man in front of her had not slowed down ever so slightly—a pace too leisurely for any full-blooded Southeastern student. She casually reached around to her backpack with her left hand. Somehow, feeling the outline of the Kimber's handle made her feel better. It didn't register until it was too late that the man in front of her wasn't carrying a backpack at all.

It happened so quickly, so unexpectedly, that Jamie had a hard time processing everything. With a dull thud, the noise of the ventilation system stopping, a power outage plunged the stairwell into darkness. It was totally black. Only later would Jamie realize that somebody must have removed the exit lights earlier in the day. Jamie stopped abruptly on the steps, instinctively reaching out for the handrail with her right hand.

The few students in the stairwell started murmuring, and then it hit her—a sharp elbow in the solar plexus, a blow with such force that it jolted her back, knocking the wind out of her. She couldn't breathe, couldn't scream. Her thoughts jumbled as she tried to recover, holding tight to the handrail with her right hand while simultaneously reaching back again with her left, finding the zipper on her backpack . . .

She felt a whirlwind of motion behind her, so fast it seemed the man was inhuman. He clamped his hand over her mouth and put her in some kind of martial arts headlock, twisting her neck.

She scrambled to free herself, adrenaline fueling her body. But this attacker was so strong, so quick—he had her neck wrenched at a weird angle, and it seemed to affect every nerve up and down her spine. She was virtually off her feet, the pressure intense on the side of her neck, the carotid artery . . .

She had her right hand on the gun now, but she was losing consciousness fast. Her mind played tricks, floating away. She pulled the Kimber out, no longer thinking, just reacting. She stuck the gun in his ribs, felt herself descending into a whirlpool of darkness, pulled the trigger once, twice . . .

His grip didn't loosen!

Is this what death feels like? Defiant to the end, she twisted one last time in rage and fear. And then the darkness won.

62

SOMETIME LATER, Jamie began the process of fading back in. Exactly how much later, she had no idea. It was not a smooth passage, more like fits and starts, reality merging with apparitions, and it was hard to tell which was more frightening. She felt the road rumbling beneath her, saw Snowball's neck being twisted around, his head snapping off like a twig; she felt the handcuffs, saw the ghoulish face, the nose flattened by the stretched nylon of a stocking, the insides of the man exploding as she pulled the trigger a third time.

She closed her eyes and tried to control the thoughts inside her head, sifting the realities from the nightmares. What did she remember? Where was she? What was happening to her? What was *real*?

The horror of it all and the precariousness of her situation helped bring her thoughts in line. This time, when she opened her eyes, the phantoms had vanished, replaced by a single cold, stark reality: Jamie was a hostage.

She was in the back of an enclosed truck, some kind of Ryder or U-Haul moving truck, lying on her back, hands cuffed in front of her. It was dark, but enough light bled in that she could make out some silhouettes. She assumed that meant it was still daylight outside.

She was bound to some kind of gurney—wide canvas straps pulled snug around her torso and legs. She was fully clothed, still wearing the jeans and formfitting cotton top she had worn to class earlier that day. Or was it yesterday?

She was not gagged.

The ride was smooth. The gurney itself was anchored somehow

to the floor of the truck. Next to her stood a man with a gun, his face squashed flat and indistinguishable by a nylon stocking. He held on to a strap on the side of the truck to keep his balance. As far as she could tell, he was the only other person in the back of the truck with her.

The stocking on the man's head frightened her even more than the gun. It not only distorted his facial features, but it also spoke of something more sinister. Rapists wore stocking masks like this. Men who tortured. They were animals, not human beings. It made the hair on the back of her neck stand on end. It terrified her.

She felt vulnerable. Naked. The man just stood there and stared. Speechless.

She tried to think rationally and put the pieces together. Her very survival, she knew, might well depend on clearheaded thinking and her ability to develop a relationship with her captors. She knew the standard advice for hostages. *Give them what they want. Try to develop some kind of bond with them.*

But the thought of giving this man what he wanted gave Jamie the creeps. What if he wanted information about Hoffman? She couldn't help him even if she wanted to. But what would they put her through before they would believe her?

Jamie strained to remember faces in the stairwell. There must have been at least two men—one in front of her and one behind. The man behind had been lightning quick, like some kind of martial arts expert.

She remembered pulling the trigger on her Kimber . . . not once but twice. After Snowball died, Jamie had ditched the last-clear-chance theory and pulled the blank out of the chamber. Two shots to the gut—who could survive that?

But she didn't remember hearing the echoes of a gunshot. She didn't remember feeling the recoil. The man behind her had never released his grip.

Which led to her next line of thinking. *Who had access to my gun?*

As she ran down the list of possibilities, the man standing beside her spoke. He startled Jamie, jerking her back to the present. "We're not going to hurt you," he said.

For some reason, that statement frightened Jamie most of all.

◁▷

When the federal agents first told Wellington Farnsworth about the kidnapping, his stomach went into such turmoil, he wondered if he'd ever eat again. He asked a slew of questions about Jamie, said a prayer for her safety, and then realized that he was undoubtedly in danger too. He was nineteen years old, barely old enough to be out of high school, and now a possible target for the mob?

At least his name wasn't on any of the pleadings filed in federal court. Since he was a second year, the only names on the pleadings, in addition to Walter Snead's, were Jamie's and Isaiah's. On the other hand, he had been sitting in court with them all day Monday and had even taken the stand to testify against the government.

He was at grave risk. There could be no rationalizing around that.

Wellington considered the irony. He had always avoided every unnecessary risk life tried to throw at him. Cell phones while driving—80 percent of crashes involve distractions within three seconds of the crash. Roller coasters—according to a German study, the adrenaline rush can speed up the heart, triggering an irregular heartbeat. He almost rode one once but decided not to when the ride operators couldn't produce a defibrillator. Using pens at restaurants to sign credit card receipts—a television investigative report once found that such pens contained more germs than bathroom door handles.

And now this! What were the odds of surviving a mob hit list? This was precisely why he wanted to practice patent law. Scientists, for the most part, were harmless. His nearest brush with crime would be the technology component of home security alarms.

His first inclination was to call home. But he was a law student now. The federal agents had said he couldn't talk to anybody about this except Isaiah and Professor Snead. They had emphasized that *anybody* meant *anybody*. They promised to provide him protection. As if that had done Jamie any good.

After fretting about his own safety for a few minutes, Wellington started feeling guilty. At least he was still safe. Jamie was the one who needed his thoughts and prayers right now.

He decided to start by doing what he did best. Analyze. Research. Eliminate variables. He assumed that Jamie's kidnappers had captured her to get access to Hoffman and ultimately the algorithm. If that was the case, somebody must have told the kidnappers that Jamie was still in contact with Hoffman, that she was part of a team representing him in federal court. The field of possible suspects was relatively small.

When he had drafted the second federal court lawsuit seeking millions in damages, Wellington was told that the only line of communication with the Hoffmans was a connection between Isaiah Haywood and Stacie Hoffman. Accordingly, Wellington had assumed they would have Isaiah run the new lawsuit past Stacie for approval. But when he talked to Snead about obtaining authorization from the client, Snead had answered Wellington cryptically. "I've already taken care of that," he'd said.

In the back of his mind, Wellington logged away three possibilities. First, Snead had already asked Isaiah to get authorization. Second, Snead never obtained his own client's approval to file a multimillion-dollar lawsuit. That seemed unlikely. Or third, Snead had his own channel of communication going with the Hoffmans.

At the time, it didn't seem to matter which of these possibilities was true. Snead said he had taken care of it, and Wellington took the professor at his word. But now, Wellington was curious.

He sent a text message to Isaiah and learned that Isaiah had never obtained authorization from Stacie Hoffman. Next, he logged on to Westlaw and started searching cases filed by Snead in the California state court system. He first examined the cases that resulted in reported opinions since they were all in one database. No luck. Next, he started reviewing cases filed by Snead that never made it to trial. It was tedious work since there was no statewide electronic database, but Wellington stayed at it, county by county, city by city.

By late afternoon, Wellington's persistence paid off. He sent another set of text messages to Isaiah explaining his findings. Isaiah, in turn, called Snead and insisted on an emergency meeting. He and Wellington agreed to meet together beforehand.

◁▷

David Hoffman received the gut-wrenching news in a phone call from Snead. *This changes everything.*

He sent a text message to Stacie, following the prearranged protocol. Cryptic messages. No specifics: **meet me at 6 instead of 8.**

The reply came immediately: **ok. problem?**

His one-word response: **yes.**

63

WELLINGTON NIBBLED at a fingernail as he waited for Isaiah in one of the overstuffed chairs in the law school lobby. His leg bounced with nervous energy. By the time Isaiah showed up, five minutes and thirty seconds late, Wellington was wound so tight he could barely think straight. They would be meeting with Snead in less than ten minutes.

"'S'up," Isaiah said.

Wellington stood and awkwardly shook Isaiah's hand. Wellington could never quite figure out how to do the "brother's" handshake. "Sorry," he said.

As the two students sat down, Wellington glanced around to make sure nobody else was within earshot. He slid forward on the bulky leather furniture and handed Isaiah a stack of papers he had printed out. "Here's what I was talking about," he said. He waited in silence as Isaiah reviewed the documents.

"Does Snead know you have these?" Isaiah asked.

Wellington shook his head.

"Let me confront him," Isaiah said. "Play off my cue."

"Okay," Wellington said. His heart was saying, *Gladly*.

◁▷

The two students made it to Snead's office on time, but as soon as Isaiah started talking, Snead held up a palm. He led them into the hallway and explained his fear that the office might be bugged, a prospect that sent Wellington's heart racing and mind reeling.

Snead led the students to the teachers' lounge, a place where

Wellington had never before set foot. He had imagined that the place might have a certain mystique to it—the stomping grounds of some of the most brilliant minds in legal academia—but in reality the room was rather boring. It was the size of a large classroom, stocked with vending machines, a microwave, a sink, and an oversize refrigerator. There were a few couches along the outside edges, and several square, restaurant-style tables in the middle. The professors obviously didn't believe in picking up after themselves, littering the place with old newspapers, magazines, and dirty dishes.

The law students and Snead cleared one of the tables and took a seat. It was after 5:00 p.m., so the lounge was otherwise empty. If Wellington had had his preferences, he would have kept the meeting in Snead's office so he could be separated from the intimidating professor by the large oak desk. But he wasn't in charge of logistics, so he simply slid his chair back a little from the table and crossed his legs.

"I hope you gentlemen are being careful," Snead said. "We don't know for certain that Ms. Brock's disappearance is a kidnapping, but there's no sense taking any chances."

"Trust me, Professor," Wellington said, glad for something they could agree on. "We're being careful."

"We're actually here on a related matter," Isaiah began. He apparently didn't believe much in pleasantries. "We want to know why you never told us that you previously represented David Hoffman while you were in private practice."

Wellington watched closely as Snead blanched and then recovered quickly. He had been a trial lawyer for years and had lots of practice at getting ambushed.

"What are you talking about?" Snead growled, his face instantly changing from concerned professor to combatant.

"Do you deny it?" Isaiah prodded.

"I'm not admitting or denying anything," Snead huffed. "If you have a point to make, Mr. Haywood, it would do you well to make it. If not, this meeting is a waste of everyone's time."

Isaiah plopped some documents on the table. "All right, Prof, here's my point. You represented David Hoffman in California yet chose to keep that a secret." He slid the documents toward Snead, who made a point of ignoring them. "Wellington found these through Westlaw."

Leave my name out of it, Wellington wanted to say.

"One of these is a breach-of-contract case—Hoffman, who was then known as Clark Shealy, suing because he didn't get paid on a bond. And here's one of your rare forays into representing a defendant instead of a plaintiff in a civil case—Shealy being sued for violating some guy's constitutional rights with an unlawful arrest."

Snead's face gave nothing away. "Are you suggesting some impropriety because I happened to represent a law-abiding bail-bond enforcement agent?"

"Did you tell the federal agents investigating Jamie's kidnapping about this?"

"I don't divulge my prior representations of clients. That's protected information."

"Not when it's publicly available," Wellington interjected. He surprised even himself with the comment, but Snead's claim was so spurious that he couldn't just let it slide.

Snead shot Wellington a withering shut-up look.

"It's also irrelevant," Snead said, the color rising in his face.

Isaiah gave an incredulous snort. "Clark Shealy, your former client, moves to Atlanta with a new identity under the witness protection program. He just happens to stumble into the legal aid clinic where you just happen to be the supervising attorney. He is represented by Jamie Brock. Stacie Hoffman runs this ruse of communicating through me, pretending she doesn't trust you. And then, after all of this subterfuge, Jamie Brock is kidnapped, and you have the temerity to say it's irrelevant?"

Isaiah pulled out his cell phone as Wellington watched the disintegration of the roles between student and teacher. Isaiah had become the interrogator, Snead the indignant defendant. Wellington found himself siding with Isaiah, though he might end up having a nervous breakdown before the meeting was over.

Snead sighed. He looked from one student to the other, and the anger seemed to drain from his face. "Put the phone away," he said calmly. "You're entitled to know."

For the next several minutes, Snead did a passable job at confessing. He had been Shealy's lawyer for a few years in California. They had played cards together. Might have done a little gambling together, truth be known. He had given Shealy some behind-the-scenes advice on his witness protection deal, though Shealy had also hired a seasoned criminal defense lawyer to negotiate the fine points. Shortly after Snead started teaching at Southeastern, about a year and a half ago, Shealy had reinitiated contact under his new name and identity.

At this point in the story, Snead abruptly stopped and refused to go forward without promises of confidentiality from both students. "I'm about to divulge some serious client confidences," Snead promised. "I'm hiring you both to help me on this case and therefore need your pledge to keep confidential what I'm about to tell you. If you can't make that promise, I can't share this little saga with you."

Reluctantly Wellington agreed. Curiosity, and the forceful personality of a law school professor, could be strong motivators. Even more reluctantly, Isaiah agreed.

Snead folded his hands and continued—a grandfather regaling the grandchildren with fables and fairy tales. Since the students already knew about Hoffman's prior run-in with the mob, Snead skipped right to the juicy part.

"Before Professor Kumari died, he put in motion some kind of e-mail process that would send Shealy the secret algorithm within forty-eight hours unless Kumari preempted it. Kumari made Shealy promise that he would sell the algorithm to legitimate digital-encryption companies and send the profits to the church in India so that they could use it to help educate the Dalits. Kumari himself was a Dalit who had managed to rise to prominence despite the caste system. Kumari told Shealy that he could keep a 10 percent commission. And because Kumari ended up sacrificing his own life in exchange for Mrs. Shealy's, Clark wanted to fulfill that promise." Snead paused and shifted in his seat. He looked like he could use a cigarette.

"There was one problem," Snead continued. "The algorithm sent to Shealy was itself encoded. Shealy was supposed to receive the key from one of Kumari's friends, but the key never came. That's why, about a year and a half ago, the man you know as David Hoffman asked me to help broker a deal with a handful of authentic Internet security companies. But I couldn't get that deal done because Hoffman wasn't willing to show them even the encoded algorithm until they paid his asking price. Those companies weren't about to pay until they could be assured that they could decode the algorithm and it would work."

Snead lowered his voice to a conspiratorial level. "After those talks broke down, Hoffman said he would keep working on decoding the formula and would contact me when he had solved it. The next time he popped up was when he strolled into our legal aid clinic on that repossession lawsuit. Far as I know, he still doesn't have the algorithm decoded."

Isaiah looked skeptical. "I still don't understand why you kept your prior representation of Hoffman a secret."

"The client asked me to," Snead responded. "He had his reasons, which must remain confidential. And I chose to abide by his wishes."

64

THE NIGHT BEFORE, just prior to telling his wife good-bye, David Hoffman had slipped a note to Stacie with the designated spot for tonight's meeting. Every night it was someplace different. They limited meetings to an hour or less. No shows of affection. They arrived at different times and left at different times. They had precise procedures to follow prior to the meeting to ensure they weren't being followed.

They lived at different addresses and, technically, in different cities. Since the day David had spotted the triad member in Fulton County court a few weeks earlier, he and Stacie had lived separate lives, meeting only when they knew they hadn't been followed.

Despite these precautions, David worried that they weren't being careful enough. Stacie continued to work at the same day job she had landed nearly eighteen months ago when she and David decided to sell the encrypted algorithm. David had called in a few favors from his prior life, resulting in a new ID for Stacie's job application, complete with a clean Social Security number and Georgia driver's license. She was Tricia Martsen at work and Stacie Hoffman the rest of the time.

For strategic reasons, Stacie couldn't change jobs. But for the sake of caution, she had applied for and received a transfer of location immediately after David had been spotted in court.

Stacie was quick to point out that her change in appearance made her less vulnerable than David. When they entered the witness protection program, David had steadfastly refused plastic surgery. "You can't improve on perfection," he had said. But the real reason was deeper. The feds had already confiscated his identity, but he would at least keep his own face—flaws and all—thank you very much.

Making the best of the situation, Stacie embraced it as part of the benefit of the bargain—a government-funded chance to fix a few facial features that she found less than perfect. Rhinoplasty to narrow the bridge of her nose, collagen injections for her lips, and a slight lift of the eyelids to make the eyes look bigger. She had turned plenty of heads before, in David's opinion, and he worried that with the plastic surgery she might attract too much attention.

But all of that took place before their trip to India. Before they had gone to visit Kumari's church in search of the key to the algorithm. When they arrived, they learned that his pastor and some other church members had been kidnapped and brutally tortured, their houses burned to the ground.

While there, Stacie fell in love with the remaining church members who rebuilt the building and especially with the Dalit children who clung to Stacie at the Christian school. That week in Mangalore had changed Stacie in ways David had never anticipated. She came back determined to decode and sell the algorithm so they could keep David's pledge to Professor Kumari. And to do so, she was now content to hide those near-perfect features behind thick black glasses, a pale complexion, and a stringy auburn wig.

Tonight, they were scheduled to meet at the Holiday Inn Express near the Gwinnett Place Mall in Duluth, Georgia, about forty minutes northeast of the city. Some nights they met at a restaurant, others a coffee shop or a mall or a theme park. But, to David's great chagrin, even on nights like tonight, when the meeting took place in a hotel, there was no chance of being intimate with his own wife.

He arrived a few minutes early, walked through the hotel lobby as if he were a guest, and found a seat in a white plastic lounge chair next to the small rectangular indoor pool. There were three young kids doing cannonballs, even though the sign said No Jumping.

Stacie walked through the doors just as the mom came and herded the kids out of the pool. Stacie found a seat next to David and greeted him with the formal handshake of a business associate.

"What's with the emergency meeting?" she asked.

David sighed. This wasn't going to be easy. "Jamie Brock, one of the law students helping on our case, was kidnapped earlier today. Walter called."

"Kidnapped?"

"She was last seen at the law school about five hours ago. She was under federal protection, but they think some triad members staged a power outage at the law school and nabbed her in one of the dark stairwells."

David watched the concern flash in Stacie's eyes. This would undoubtedly rekindle the raw emotions of her own experience. "I haven't heard anything on the news," she said.

"According to Walter, the feds are trying to keep it under wraps. They talked to Walter and a few law students and swore them all to secrecy. The feds think the mob is trying to use Jamie to get at us. They asked Walter if the triad had contacted him or me."

"How could they contact you?"

"They can't. They didn't. And they haven't contacted Walter yet, either."

Stacie thought about this for a minute and David gave her time to process the implications. In the last few hours, he had considered these developments from every possible angle. He knew it was time for Plan B, though he also knew that Stacie would vehemently resist the idea. She had never liked that plan—a high-risk attempt to nail the triad's leaders and gain protection in the process. Too little margin for error. Too much depended on their ability to dupe some very smart and ruthless men.

But what choice did they have? Walter Snead had talked them into staying in the area while he tried to negotiate a protection deal with the government that didn't require turning over the algorithm. They had concocted Plan B as an emergency measure if his efforts failed. That's where they were now. His efforts had proved futile. And Jamie Brock's life was on the line.

"I hate this algorithm," Stacie said.

David knew what she meant. The algorithm was knowledge. Knowledge was power. And power always came with a price. "We didn't ask for this, Stacie. But we can't just run away."

"There's got to be a better way than Plan B," Stacie said, reading David's mind. "Plan B plays right into their hands. They're trying to smoke us out." She sighed, and David could tell she was fighting back tears. "I'm so tired of all the double-crossing and deception."

David leaned forward, elbows on his knees. He blew out a deep breath and looked straight ahead as he talked, not wanting to read the look on Stacie's face. It was time to mention something he had never talked about before, not even with Stacie.

"Four years ago, hon, when I was frantic to rescue you, I said a couple of desperate prayers. You know, 'God, I'll do anything you want if you just get Jessica out of this alive.' No qualifications. And I meant it. I would have done *anything* just to wrap my arms around you one more time. But after your rescue, I really didn't think much about it again until I got the call from Snead today."

David turned and looked at Stacie in time to see her eyes moisten. "When Snead called, I thought about how Professor Kumari risked his life for us—for people he didn't even know. And I had this strange feeling—not really a voice or anything, but just a feeling—that maybe God was somehow saying this is the thing he wants me to do now. Take a risk for Jamie Brock the same way Kumari did for us."

"I know we can't just leave Jamie hanging out there," Stacie said. "But I wish there was some other way." She hesitated as if unsure whether she should admit what really worried her. "I don't want to lose *you.*"

"You won't," David said immediately, trying to muster a little false bravado. "This plan is foolproof. I mean, look who designed it."

Unsmiling, she took his hand and gave him a look that said she would see this through to the bitter end. David might talk a good game on the surface, but in reality he drew his strength from her. She had always been the rock in their relationship. And after her spiritual rebirth in India, even more so. Once she prayed about something and committed, all the demons in hell couldn't stop her.

"Are you scared?" she asked.

"Terrified."

"Me too."

He brushed her cheek with his index finger. The tears pooled in her eyes as she fought to hold them back. He leaned in to gently kiss her on the forehead.

"Can we get a room?" she asked, looking down. "We need to spend some time together."

He nodded and worked hard to hold his own emotions in check. This was not supposed to be the way it all went down.

65

JAMIE KNEW HOW to focus on the task at hand. Olympic caliber—that's what the newspapers articles had called her. You didn't become Olympic caliber without intense mental focus, an iron will, and the ability to endure pain.

She would need all three.

She rode in silence, staring at the ceiling, forcing herself to concentrate on the psychology of the hostage situation rather than how she got here in the first place. She didn't know how long they had been driving or how far they still had to go. The back of the truck was like an oven—her skin filmy with sweat, her mouth parched as the desert. She felt weak all over.

Had they drugged her?

She needed to get her bearings, and she had to know how far she could push the one man guarding her. She wanted to ride along in silence, but she wouldn't exactly be bonding with her captors that way.

"I'm thirsty," she said.

"You'll have to wait." He spoke without an accent—a flat, monotone voice. He was obviously trying to convey a total lack of emotion.

"How long?"

"A few more hours."

"How long have we been going already?"

"I can't say."

"I don't think I can wait a few more hours."

This time her captor didn't respond. He just stared at her through his stocking cap, freaking her out.

"Where are we going?"

Silence.

"What do you want from me?"

"You'll find out soon enough."

"If it's the algorithm, I don't have it."

Again, he didn't respond, and she took that as a good sign. He wasn't arguing. He didn't seem to be getting angry. She would push a little more. She wanted to see outside the truck. She needed to know where they were taking her. Was it day or evening? How many others were involved?

Even as she planned, doubts and anxieties attacked her, eating at her self-confidence like termites. She had no weapons. They had firepower and training, outnumbering her at least two to one. Not to mention the thick canvas straps holding her down.

"I have to pee," she said, swallowing her pride. It wasn't true, but if they stopped the truck and let her out, she could at least pick up some useful information.

"Hold it."

"You're kidding, right?"

His refusal to answer gave Jamie a strange sense of empowerment. She was having the last word, not him. He was probably low man on the totem pole, and his intimidation factor had gone down a notch or two. Even the creepy effect that came from the way the nylon stocking mashed in his face was a little less terrifying.

"I'm not kidding about this," she said. "I've really got to go."

This time he moved. He walked deliberately toward her and stood over her for a moment, swaying with the motion of the truck. The way he looked at her, leered at her, even with the stocking shielding his eyes, made her skin crawl. She shuddered and turned her head to the side.

He reached down and grabbed her chin with a gloved hand, turning her head toward him. He squeezed with strong fingers. Hovering over her, he let his eyes rove up and down her body. Then he locked back onto her eyes, destroying her sense of empowerment, the tiny victories she had just awarded herself.

"Shut up," he said, "or I've got ways to shut you up."

He stayed frozen there for a long second, his nylon mask nearly touching her face. He smelled of sweat and stale food.

After a few seconds, he let her go and walked slowly back to his spot near the side of the truck. He grabbed a handle and kept his eyes glued on her. He was volatile. Insecure. Maybe predatory. Now she knew he meant business.

She tried to calm her racing heart and summon another dose of courage. It would be easier to just cower in silence, but she couldn't allow herself to do that. This time, she would be more careful.

"Look," she said, "I'm not trying to make you angry. I'm just telling you—I've really got to go."

"Shut up."

The fear mixed with anger and frustration. She felt vulnerable and violated, but also just plain mad. What kind of coward treated another human being this way? If she had half a chance—her Kimber, a knife, a fistfight, *anything*! She would claw his eyes out if she could get her fingers loose and within reach.

That's when it hit her. It was probably a delusional thought, birthed by terror and desperation. But at the moment it seemed like she had no other choice. She asked to go. He refused. She told him she *really* needed to go. He refused.

What if she just did it? What if she peed right here in the back of the truck, right now? The thought disgusted her, but wouldn't it disgust him more? The temperature had to be nearly ninety degrees. How bad would it smell in an hour? What kind of stench would there be in two hours? If he had any real thoughts of violating her, wouldn't this be a guaranteed way to keep him at bay? Even Mr. Nylon Head would be grossed out by this.

Maybe next time he would believe her.

She thought about swimming pools and waterfalls and ocean waves. Tall glasses of water on the rocks and Lake Lanier. She thought about car trips as a child, being ready to burst at the seams, her father telling her to hold it until the next exit. She thought about the advice her brother gave when Jamie, as a young girl, was swimming in their subdivision's pool and had to go: *"Why take time to go to the bathroom when we're swimming in all this water?"* She thought about the hard rain that had fallen on Tuesday.

She banished every thought of her present situation, her fear and anger and the battle of wills she so desperately needed to win. She replaced those visions with thoughts of water and water and more water—*anything* to make her go.

Three minutes later, it worked.

◁ ▷

The caller wanted to remain anonymous. Huang Xu could deal with that. On the first call, Xu verified that the caller had insider information. Following that call, Xu authorized the wired funds, precisely as the caller had instructed. The receiving account was owned by a shell corporation in the Caymans that was a wholly owned subsidiary of another shell company that was a partnership composed of six other shells.

But Xu's men had already traced the supposedly impenetrable corporate maze back to its ultimate owner. If the caller didn't deliver, he would pay in blood.

"He's reserved a room tomorrow night at the Staybridge Suites on North Point Parkway in Alpharetta," the caller said. "He's using the alias of Brian Mackey."

"The money's in the bank," Xu replied.

"Now," the caller said, "let's talk about releasing Jamie Brock."

66

AT A FEW MINUTES after midnight, lying awake in the king-size bed, David glanced at the clock's digital readout. Stacie had fallen asleep, but David couldn't keep the images from flashing through his mind. Even now, as he stared at the ceiling, listening to his wife's rhythmic breathing, he could see it all so clearly.

There was the supernaturally calm face of Professor Moses Kumari, as he turned and looked at David just before climbing into the triad's helicopter. The bravest man David had ever met. On nights like this, David was still haunted by the professor's voice on his cell phone away message, the message David had heard several times after speeding away from the gravel pit. David's failure to detonate the Semtex explosives, and the torture that Kumari had had to bear as a result, still sent spindles of guilt down David's spine.

A year later, he was standing with Stacie in Mangalore, India, on the site where Professor Kumari's church had been burned to the ground and rebuilt. It felt like they had stepped back in time to the New Testament. The church members described miracles of healings, hundreds of conversions, and leaders being jailed on trumped-up charges. They lived simply and sacrificed so that Dalit children could have two new school uniforms and an English education.

Their new pastor, a man named Udit Guptara, had been a former member of the BJP, the radical Hindu political party, and had helped terrorize local churches before he became a convert. He told stories of how he would beat pastors, burn their houses, and file anticonversion charges against them. But when his wife became deathly ill, a local pastor came to his home and asked if he could pray for her. Guptara said he allowed the man in the house on one condition: "If she dies, you die with her."

When she recovered, Guptara converted to Christianity and became a pastor for the same religion he had once despised. It all seemed to strain credibility to David, but the other church members had nodded along as Guptara told his story, eyewitnesses to the miraculous.

During one of the last days of their visit, David and Stacie had pulled Guptara aside to tell him the real reason they came. The pastor knew they were friends of Professor Kumari, and they had initially told him they wanted to help the Dalit children that the professor cared so deeply about. But after watching Guptara for a week, and being unable to track down any of Professor Kumari's family members, they decided to confide in the pastor. After swearing Guptara to confidentiality, they told him everything.

"I'm afraid," David said, "that the persecution of the church and Pastor Prasad may have been the work of the Manchurian Triad, not radical Hindu groups." David paused to let that sink in. He had not only caused Kumari to suffer, but he may have caused a dozen or more church leaders to suffer and die as well. "But we need to know whether there is anybody else Kumari might have trusted with this algorithm key besides Pastor Prasad. It could be worth millions of dollars for schools just like yours."

Guptara rocked back and forth for a moment, deep in thought. "Kumari was a brave man, a godly man," the pastor said. "But I'm sorry. I do not know of a surviving church member who was entrusted with such a secret."

He must have read the look of disappointment on David's and Stacie's faces because he quickly shifted gears. "But perhaps God brought you here for a different purpose than you realize." He paused, looking from David to Stacie. "Professor Kumari demonstrated in the most radical way what our Lord did for each of us. Kumari traded his life for yours, Stacie, when you were in captivity. He took your place with the triads so that you might be freed, and you and David might be reunited. He suffered for you, just as Christ suffered and died for us.

"Perhaps you came here to find a key to a code worth millions of dollars. But perhaps God wanted you to find something more precious . . . more costly."

"Perhaps," David said in a tone that made it clear he was more interested in finding the code than being preached at.

But Stacie didn't say a word.

Later that night, as a courtesy, David and Stacie went to a church service where they sat surrounded by wide-eyed Dalit children whom Stacie had befriended that week, all crowding in too close for David's liking. Every time he would glance at one of them, they would look at him with a huge smile, an appreciation that this important man from America would esteem them worthy to be touched and would look them in the eye. And then the kids would snuggle a little closer, putting a hand on David's arm or leg.

David couldn't wait to get back to America.

But when the service was drawing to a close, and Pastor Guptara, after an interminably long message, started calling people forward for repentance, Stacie reached over and took David's hand. She nodded toward the front. "Come with me," she whispered.

Are you crazy? David wanted to ask. They were both emotional. Tired. The whole trip had been disorienting. But David hadn't totally lost his sense of pride and independence. Besides, God wouldn't be interested in someone like him. "I'm okay," David had said, his voice low. "You go."

And she did. Like a pied piper, with about a half-dozen kids following behind her.

After the service, Pastor Guptara baptized new converts outside in a hole in the ground that looked to David like a freshly dug grave lined with plastic. The children crowded around when Stacie stepped into the baptism waters fully clothed.

It was all surreal to David, as he and other church members stood behind the children who ringed the edge. The water was a muddy brown and David couldn't help but wonder when they had last changed it. The pastor stood next to Stacie, one hand on her back, the other holding her hands in front of her, and asked if she had put her faith in Christ. She nodded and he dunked her under.

When she came up, the children cheered and Stacie smiled and David somehow knew that this was more than just an emotional moment. She shook her hair out of her face, and the members pulled her from the tank and started giving her hugs.

"Is there anybody else?" Pastor Guptara asked when he had finished baptizing the last convert. To David, it felt like every head swiveled and looked directly at him.

"Think that about wraps it up," he said.

67

IT HAD BEEN EASY to resist Guptara's invitation three years ago. But now, the night before the greatest danger he had ever faced, David's sense of self-sufficiency was slipping away.

If he had been inclined to foxhole conversions, David certainly would have made the jump a long time ago. He had seen his share of foxholes. But the nagging sensation tugging at him now was something more than that. He believed that God had answered his desperate prayer and bailed him out four years ago, saving his wife from her kidnappers in the process. But David had never come through on his end of the bargain.

And now, a single thought dogged him: *Can a man con God?*

David knew the answer. He also knew that within the next forty-eight hours, he would undoubtedly be saying a few more desperate prayers. Jamie was already in the triad's grasp. Soon, he and Stacie would be putting their lives on the line. How could he expect God to help if David didn't at least try to make things right?

He pulled down the covers and slid out of his side of the bed. Stacie grunted and rolled partway over but didn't wake up. He walked over to the hotel desk and turned on the lamp, watching his wife for a reaction. She pulled the sheets tighter around her neck and kept sleeping.

David padded softly to the closet and removed the small metal box from the bottom of his gym bag. He opened the lock, pulled out a thick, worn Bible, and carried it back to the desk.

He had kept this Bible with him every day of his life for the past three years, poring over the underlined portions and margin notes. It was a New Living Translation, with Hindi and English translations side by side. David opened it to the New Testament and tried to remember the verses that Guptara had been preaching on the last night of David's visit.

Like almost everything else in his life right now, this Bible had its own mysterious background. It had been brought to him and Stacie in the middle of the night at their run-down hotel room in Mangalore by an eighty-eight-year-old widow from Kumari's church. She had waited until the night before they returned to the States, the night Stacie was baptized, to deliver her gift.

"It was Pastor Prasad's Bible," the woman explained. "He came to me a few nights before the persecution started. He somehow knew there might be trouble coming. He said if anything happened to him, I should keep this Bible hidden because it contained the key to a very important project that Professor Kumari had been working on. He told me to give the Bible to any Americans who came looking for it, but only if they were true friends of Professor Kumari and seemed to be honest."

The older woman had gently handed the Bible to Stacie. "After tonight, I knew that you were ready," the woman said.

Nearly every day for the next three years, David and Stacie had studied the Bible and Pastor Prasad's margin notes, trying to decipher the key to the algorithm. They had pursued one idea after another, and even consulted secretly with a few encryption experts, explaining vaguely that the Bible contained a hidden decipher key. Nobody could figure out what it was.

But tonight, none of those concerns mattered. David read the familiar margin notes not to discern a hidden key, but to understand what the pastor had been thinking. He turned to the book of Romans because he still remembered bits and pieces of what Guptara had said during that last night in India. David remembered thinking that it sounded too good to be true, like one of his con jobs. Confess and believe, Guptara had said. But who really believed that a simple prayer could wipe out years of sin? Apparently Stacie had. And David had watched her closely since that night. Something radical had happened to her, something she had never been able to shake.

It was hard to argue with a transformed life.

He was deep in thought when he felt a hand on his shoulder and nearly jumped out of the chair.

"Sorry," Stacie said.

He put a hand on top of hers. "It's all right."

"You aren't going to solve that tonight, David. Come back to bed. We both need our sleep."

He hesitated before responding. A part of him—the independent streak—wanted to work through this on his own. "That night you were baptized in India—what part of the Bible was the pastor preaching from?"

If Stacie was shocked to hear the question, she didn't let it show. She reached over his shoulder and flipped to Romans 10:9-10. She read the verses out loud. "'If you confess with your mouth that Jesus is Lord, and believe in your heart that God has raised him from the dead, you will be saved. For it is by believing in your heart that you are made right with God, and it is by confessing with your mouth that you are saved.'"

Stacie pulled a chair around and they talked about what those verses meant. David asked a lot of questions, and Stacie did her best to answer. After several minutes of discussion, and a long pause in the questions, she said softly, "It's time to surrender."

"You really think God can accept me?" David asked. "I'm a con man. I can't even count how many lies I've told, how many people I've ripped off, not to mention the gunshot wounds and torture."

"That's why they call it grace."

He thought about this for a long time. He'd been around church some as a boy and had heard about the thief on the cross. Pastor Guptara in India had compared himself to the apostle Paul, one day beating up Christians, the next day becoming one of them. And now Stacie told David about Matthew, a tax collector and fellow con artist, whom Jesus called as one of his disciples.

Maybe Stacie had a point. It seemed that Jesus wasn't very fussy about how you came.

Without another word, David began praying. He surprised himself with how rapidly and naturally the words came. He felt Stacie take a hand off his in order to brush away some tears. He asked for forgiveness and mercy, confessing his sins in broad categories so it wouldn't take all night. He asked for strength and wisdom and courage for the task ahead. And because he didn't want to take any chances, at the end of his prayer he opened his eyes and prayed the words on the page in front of him.

"I confess that Jesus is Lord and believe in my heart that God raised him from the dead," he said. "Amen."

Stacie chuckled at that last part, but he no longer cared. He felt a wave of forgiveness and freedom—and another emotion that he had never expected. For the first time in three years, he felt like he and Stacie were truly one again.

She leaned over and hugged his neck, whispering her own prayer of thanks.

When she was finished, he closed the Bible.

"Let's go to bed," she said. "Tomorrow could be a very long day."

68

AFTER SEVERAL MORE unsuccessful attempts to engage her captor in conversation, Jamie gave up. She rode in silence for the next few hours—planning, wondering, feeling gross and powerless. She imagined a hundred different scenarios once they arrived at their location. She tried to prepare herself for anything.

The temperature had dropped several degrees, and she had grown used to the stench of her own urine. She assumed it was now late at night. Eventually the steady hum of the interstate gave way to the stops, starts, and turns of local roads. Jamie felt the anticipation tense her tired muscles. She had actually grown used to the drone of the highway and convinced herself that Stocking Man wasn't going to molest her during the trip. But now that the trip was ending, who knew what horrors lay ahead?

The truck slowed and came to a complete stop, and the engine shut off. The resulting silence had its own eerie psychological message. She felt alone. Deserted. Miles from help.

The man stepped toward her, this time holding a gun with two metal prongs on the end directly in her line of vision a foot away from her face. "This is a stun gun," he said as Jamie stared at the prongs. He pulled the trigger, and a bolt of electricity jumped from one prong to the other, hissing like the tongue of a snake. Jamie flinched and jerked away as much as she could, terror sparking through her body.

"I'm going to untie you," the man said. "I won't use this unless you make me. But I won't hesitate to use it if you try anything."

"Okay," she managed.

The man reached over and released the bottom strap first, the one tight around her calves. Next, he released the strap around her hips. As he fumbled with the top strap, Jamie heard noises outside the back door. It sounded like somebody might be removing some kind of padlock.

Her captor removed the top strap, and Jamie sat up slowly on the gurney, eyeing him to make sure it was okay. Though her hands were still cuffed together in her lap, it felt good to no longer have the straps biting into her, tying her down to the gurney.

"Thanks," she said. Her captor nodded.

The man received a call on his cell phone. "Yes. Everything is fine. Open the door."

Her captor held the cell phone to his ear with his right hand, the stun gun in his left. Should she lunge at him now? The doors started to creak open. Soon she would have another kidnapper to deal with. But still she hesitated. *The handcuffs. The stun gun.*

As she sat there, every muscle poised to strike, torn between the danger of action and the consequences of inaction, she heard two gunshots rip through the silence of the night. There was shouting. Chaos. Another pop, more like a ping, the sound of a bullet hitting the back door. The man inside the truck grabbed Jamie and yanked her to her feet, his arm locked around her throat, the barrel of a gun against her head. She heard something clatter on the floor. *The stun gun? The cell phone?*

In the next instant, the back doors, which someone had started to open, swung closed. And then, just as abruptly as the shots had started, the night turned silent again, magnifying the sound of Jamie's captor panting in her ear. Jamie could literally smell the fear.

He yelled something in Russian, and Jamie picked up two names. *Dmitri. Sergei.*

Her captor waited, his breath coming in staccato bursts. But there was no answer from the outside, nothing but eerie silence.

He shoved Jamie toward the back door of the truck. "Move!"

A few feet from the door he stopped her and wrapped his left arm tighter around her neck. "Who's out there?" he yelled, this time in English.

The answering silence could only mean that her captor's accomplices had been killed or captured. Jamie felt a sudden flicker of hope, her heart hammering against her rib cage, adrenaline shooting through every fiber of her body. But in her next conscious thought, that hope crashed into grim reality. She was still a human shield, facing a door that would open to almost-certain gunfire. Even friendly fire might kill her.

If her captor didn't do it first. He inched closer to the door, pressing the gun more tightly to her temple.

"Answer me!" he yelled, holding Jamie squarely in front of him.

He waited another couple of beats, swung a leg around her, and kicked open the door. First one side, then the other.

Jamie flinched, ready for the firing squad.

69

NOTHING HAPPENED. No shots were fired. Nobody came rushing at them. The night was dark, silent, and ghostly.

With the back doors open, Jamie's captor dragged her closer to the edge of the truck bed. She could see that they were in a parking lot, with distant streetlights barely denting the darkness of the overcast night. A vehicle, some kind of SUV, was parked directly behind the truck, about forty feet away. There were no signs of life anywhere.

Jamie's captor glanced past her shoulder—looked left, then right. He pointed his gun toward the darkness, swinging it in an arc around the area.

Suddenly it was day—blinding lights coming at them from every direction. Headlights from the SUV. Spotlights from both sides of the vehicle. Jamie reacted instinctively, taking advantage of the sudden distraction. She stomped on her captor's foot, pulled at the arm around her neck, and thrust herself downward to escape his grip. In the same instant, even before she slid free, she heard the sound of gunshots, loud blasts from all around her, blowing her captor backward into the truck. There was yelling. Arms grabbed her from the floor and pulled her to safety.

Radios started squawking. Men who looked like SWAT team members scrambled into the truck, checking her fallen captor. They helped Jamie to a patch of grass next to an unmarked car, letting her lean against its side. An officer knelt beside her. "Are you okay?" he asked.

Jamie nodded. Speechless. She tried to fight back the shock.

"Are you sure? Do you need an ambulance? Did they hurt you?"

She knew what he was really asking. *Were you raped?* "No, I'm okay." She closed her eyes and tilted her head back, sucking in a long, deep breath. It was her first full breath, she realized, since her lungs had been placed under the viselike pressure of captivity several hours ago.

"Do you want some water?" someone asked. "Would you be more comfortable inside the car?"

She heard another voice, a few feet away, asking one of the men attending to her how long it might be before she could answer questions. They were all just disembodied shadows standing around her, silhouetted against the spotlights still shining at the back of the truck.

"Can we give her a little room for a few minutes?" a different man asked. The voice sounded familiar.

At first, Jamie thought her mind was playing tricks on her. After what she'd just been through, shock and hallucination would be a normal reaction. But when she opened her eyes, the face was there as well. If this was an illusion, her mind had quite a memory for details.

He squatted in front of her. She reached out and touched his shoulder.

"Drew?"

He nodded, brushing her hair away from her face.

◁▷

After several paramedics checked Jamie out, the federal agents whisked her away from the site of the shoot-out and interrogated her about the day's events. She would have to spend the rest of the night in a local hotel, so Drew headed to the nearest twenty-four-hour Walmart with a very detailed shopping list. Size-four jeans. Ladies' underwear, size small. Toothbrush. Toothpaste. Deodorant. T-shirt, women's small. Pajamas, size small. To his credit, Drew didn't ask any questions. Jamie would probably never be able to look at him again without blushing.

The conversation with the federal agents was pretty much one-sided—they provided the questions; Jamie provided the few answers she could. She vowed that when she became a prosecutor, she would treat her victims with a little more compassion. She had to keep reminding herself that none of this was her fault.

She did learn that her kidnappers were working with the same Chinese triad that had been pursuing the Hoffmans. The triad had apparently been trying to keep the feds off-balance by contracting with a few Eastern European thugs, the same ones who had first threatened Jamie at Lake Lanier and then kidnapped her. Her captors had taken Jamie to a marina in Jacksonville, Florida, where the triad had a large yacht waiting.

They were probably planning on using Jamie to force Hoffman out of hiding. After the shoot-out, the feds had staked out the area and searched every boat at the dock. They had found the triad's yacht and gained some incriminating information but were disappointed that no additional accomplices showed up. The FBI agents continued to work leads from the cell phones and other evidence they had confiscated. They would let Jamie know of any additional apprehensions.

In the meantime, they said, it was absolutely critical that Jamie *not* contact anybody to tell them she was safe. The FBI wanted other triad members to think that the triad still had Jamie in custody. The agents were apparently setting up some kind of trap that might require them to keep Jamie hidden for a day or two.

The FBI had secured a nearby Hilton where Jamie would stay for the rest of the night and possibly the next day. Drew Jacobsen would stay in an adjoining room, and the bureau's agents would patrol the premises.

When Jamie asked if she had a choice in the matter, the agent in charge gave her a disapproving look. "Of course," he said. "You're not under arrest or in custody. You can do whatever you want. But it's our job to protect you and apprehend the other members of the triad, and I would recommend letting us do our job."

"I think that's how we got here in the first place," Jamie said.

Eventually, however, she acquiesced. Jacobsen returned from his shopping trip as the questioning and evidence swabbing were winding down. They rode together in the backseat of an unmarked federal sedan to the hotel. Drew escorted Jamie to her room and asked for the fourth time whether she was really okay.

"I'm fine," she said with as much conviction as she could summon.

"If you need to talk—anytime—just knock on the adjoining door," Drew said.

"Okay," Jamie responded. In truth, she had a bunch of questions for her private security guardian angel, starting with the most obvious ones: What was *he* doing here? Wasn't this a federal case? How did they find her? But she knew every one of those questions could wait until morning. Other things couldn't.

She needed to get out of her soiled clothes. She needed a hot shower. She needed a soft bed.

She needed some time alone to think.

70

JAMIE DIDN'T REALLY even try to sleep. After what she had been through, sleep would only lead to nightmares, replaying distorted versions of the day's terrifying events. It seemed like every time she closed her eyes, she saw the man wearing the nylon stocking.

As the minutes marched by, she lay in bed with the television on and the bedside lamp burning, so many questions floating around in her mind. And so much pain. These last few days had rekindled bitter memories of her mother's death. The emotions she thought she had conquered came back with a force so great it was almost like losing her mom all over again. Losing Snowball, being held hostage, nearly getting shot—these things tormented her, like wolves fighting over a fresh kill, overwhelming Jamie's best efforts to maintain control.

A few weeks ago she was a third-year law student itching to get out in the "real world" so she could start prosecuting criminals. Her main concern had been whether to answer questions if called on in crim pro. Now, she was being hunted by the mob. Kidnapped. Threatened.

Life seemed so fragile.

At 3:30 a.m., Jamie rose from her bed and padded over to the door that separated her room from Drew's. She hesitated for a moment, recalled his words—*"if you need to talk"*—and knocked softly on the adjoining door. She waited, heard no sound coming from the other room, and knocked again. This time she heard a faint "Just a minute," and a few seconds later Drew opened the door.

He was wearing a pair of jeans and no shirt, his thick, dark hair matted. The man certainly kept himself in shape. He leaned against the doorjamb looking sleepy and squinting at the light.

"I'm sorry," Jamie said. "It's just that I couldn't sleep. And you said..."

"No, really, it's fine." He waved off her apology. "Let me get a shirt on, and maybe we can get some coffee or something."

She suddenly felt like an idiot for waking him up. "Are you sure? I mean, it can wait until later."

He smiled, the sleepy eyes coming to life. "Let's see, you knock on my door at 3:30 a.m. to tell me it can wait? I don't think so."

For some unspoken reason, it didn't seem right staying in one of the hotel rooms, so the two friends made their way down to the lobby. Drew talked one of the FBI agents into making a coffee run, and soon Drew and Jamie were sitting on an overstuffed lobby couch, their feet propped on a coffee table, discussing the previous day's events. Jamie, still wearing the pajamas Drew had bought earlier, kicked her sandals off. Drew was wearing his jeans, sneakers, and a T-shirt.

"Nice pajamas," Drew said. "They look even better on you than they did on the mannequin."

"They don't put pajamas on mannequins."

"Reality should never stand in the way of a good pick-up line."

They talked for a few minutes about everything and nothing. Drew asked how she was doing without Snowball. Jamie asked whether Drew ever had any dogs. He did—a greyhound he had rescued from the kennel. So they swapped dog stories for a while. When the coffee came, Jamie decided it was time to ask about a few of the things that had been keeping her up.

"How did you guys find me? And how did *you* end up down here?"

"I can go home if you want me to," Drew countered with a smirk.

"No, I'm really glad you're here," Jamie said emphatically. "But this is a federal case, and they don't usually bring local cops along for the ride."

"You don't have your watch on right now, do you?"

She looked down at her wrist and realized she had left it on the bedside table. "No. Why?"

"I'll show it to you later, but when you hired me for private security, I implanted a small chip inside your watch. It's like one of those

RFID chips they implant in a lot of retail products these days, or the ones they use to track the migration patterns of animals, only stronger." As he talked, Drew seemed to be watching Jamie to see what kind of impact this was having on her. In all honesty, she really wasn't sure how to feel about it. Thankful he had saved her life? Upset that she was being monitored without her knowledge?

"It's a passive, read-only tag, and the feds didn't even know I'd installed it," he continued. "That's why it took so long to rescue you. I was working at my desk job and didn't find out you'd been kidnapped until about seven o'clock. I helped them track you down but demanded to tag along . . . no pun intended."

Jamie took a sip of coffee. "You installed a tracking device in my watch and didn't tell me?" It felt a little weird.

"I should have told you. I know." Drew avoided Jamie's eyes and fiddled with his coffee cup. She felt guilty for jumping on his case.

"It's just that you were freaked out enough with everything going on and I didn't want to create more worry," Drew continued. "Plus, I wasn't 100 percent sure you'd let me do it. I know that doesn't justify it, Jamie. I'm just saying . . . it seemed like the right thing to do at the time. Now . . . I wish I'd told you about it."

"What other tags do you have on me?"

"None. I swear."

"Cameras in my apartment? And in my car?"

"No, but that's probably not a bad idea."

Jamie managed a weak smile, and it seemed to relax Drew a little. At least he was contrite about it and didn't try to make excuses. And it had ended up saving her life.

"Drew, I really am grateful you implanted that chip or code or whatever, especially the way things turned out. But you can't just track me like some wild animal and not even tell me about it. What about my privacy rights?"

He opened his palms in surrender. "I'm sorry, Jamie. I really am. I cared so much about your safety that I did something really stupid. From now on, what I know, you'll know."

She found it hard to stay mad at a guy who admitted his mistakes and in the process threw in a line about how much he cared. Especially when she felt so exhausted. Right now, she didn't need another fight. She needed an ally, someone she could trust. "Tell me about the way this whole thing came down," she said. "Start to finish. Every detail."

"Well, fortunately," Drew began, "this brilliant detective had implanted an RFID-type device in the watch of a beautiful young lawyer, although he admittedly should have obtained her permission first. . . ."

She nodded her encouragement. "You're off to a good start."

◁▷

Later, when they returned to their rooms, Drew lingered in front of Jamie's door. She turned to face him, told him thanks, and waited for a beat, frozen by an awkward mixture of fear and anticipation, wondering if he felt the same thing she did.

In response, he reached out and gently touched her arm, then took a step closer and brushed his lips against hers. She felt the electricity of that moment: two people meant for each other, her destiny starting to change. It was the perfect kiss, gentle and sensitive, from the perfect Southern gentleman. She wanted to lean in and kiss him back, to reward him for taking a chance with someone as emotionally tough and distant as she could be. But the past several hours had been traumatic, and her emotions were still on hyperdrive. It was not the right time to trust her heart.

"Thanks," she said again. Drew looked a little hurt as she turned and let herself in the room.

71

JAMIE SLEPT UNTIL NOON and spent the rest of the day cooped up in her hotel room. The feds were being remarkably tight-lipped about their plan but insisted that Jamie not be seen in public. She wanted to at least call Chris and a few of her friends from law school but the feds frowned on the idea. What if the triad had tapped into their phones? Besides, Chris wouldn't be worried. Only a few others like Wellington and Isaiah even knew about Jamie's kidnapping. The fewer variables, the better, the federal agents insisted.

Feeling helpless, Jamie tried to pass the time watching hotel movies. The minutes dragged by and she wondered if her life would ever return to normal again.

◁▷

At 8:30 p.m., David Hoffman checked the rearview mirror as he exited Route 400 and pulled onto Old Milton Parkway. He took mental note of the cars behind him, a habit he had fine-tuned in the last few weeks. After a few lights, he pulled into the right-turn lane and slowed, checking to make sure the other cars continued straight and passed him by. Remaining vigilant, Hoffman took a right onto North Point Parkway, then pulled into the first large office complex on his left. It was dark, but the parking lot was well lit and mostly deserted. He made sure that no cars followed him into the lot.

He waited five minutes before he pulled back onto North Point, turned right, crossed Old Milton Parkway, then took an immediate right into the parking lot of the Staybridge Suites.

After he registered, he parked behind the hotel in one of the few empty spaces and pulled out his access key for the back door. He had his Glock tucked inside a cowboy boot and a switchblade in his pocket. He walked quickly to the door, slid his key through the magnetic slot, and stepped inside.

His attacker seemed to come out of thin air, materializing inside the stairwell. Before Hoffman could react, the man dealt a crippling blow to Hoffman's larynx, caught him as he collapsed, and dragged him outside. Two others quickly joined the first assailant, cuffing Hoffman's arms behind his back as he struggled to draw a breath.

A Town Car screeched around the corner, and the back door popped open. The men threw Hoffman in the car. One of his assailants climbed into the backseat after Hoffman; the others ran to another vehicle. Hoffman, still fighting for air, feeling like his windpipe had collapsed, found himself pinned between two muscular men, one holding a gun to his head.

He recognized the man with the gun. The low forehead, the thick neck, the sideburn scar on the right side of his face, and a cobra tattoo on his neck. It was the man who had taken the place of Johnny Chin at Silvoso's clinic. The man Hoffman had seen in court.

As they pulled out of the parking lot and headed back toward the interstate, the passenger in the front seat turned around. A man, about David's age, with the rugged good looks of an Asian bad boy—stylish sideburns and short goatee, dark eyebrows, wide eyes, a demon-possessed smile.

The hair on Hoffman's arms stood up. He had met Huang Xu only once, at the blasting pit four years earlier, and Xu's face had been covered by a ski mask. But Hoffman had seen the FBI photos of the man who would haunt his nightmares, his visage burned forever into Hoffman's subconscious.

Xu seemed amused by his captive, like a mean-spirited kid ready to pull the wings off a captive fly. "You're good at dishing out torture, my friend. Tonight, we'll see how you fare on the receiving end."

After a few minutes of silence, the burly Asian next to Hoffman spoke. "Take off your clothes."

But Hoffman had regained his voice. "You're not my type," he replied.

"Umph!" Hoffman caught an elbow in the ribs from the man on the other side—a middle-aged balding man with a dark complexion. It doubled Hoffman over, knocking the wind out of him.

Hoffman grunted, trying to get some air back in his lungs. He gasped for a few moments as the car turned into the vacant parking lot of a boarded-up restaurant. The driver parked next to an old Dumpster behind the building.

"Take off your clothes," the man with the cobra tattoo repeated.

Without saying a word, Hoffman bent over and untied his shoes. He slipped them off, then the socks. The shirt came next. While Hoffman removed it, his backseat companions stepped out of the car. The cobra man went around to the trunk and grabbed another set of clothes—a pair of boxers, jeans, flip-flops, and a T-shirt. He threw them in the backseat.

"Put these on," he demanded.

The driver had a gun leveled at Hoffman over the front seat. Hoffman stripped completely down and put on the new set of clothes. They were guarding against listening devices, he knew. They threw his old clothes in the trash bin and had him stand outside the vehicle. Huang Xu waved a metal wand, the kind they use at airports, a few inches from Hoffman's body. It beeped just below Hoffman's stomach. Xu muttered something and moved the wand by the same spot a second time.

It beeped again, a nasty little noise that made Hoffman flinch. Xu's lips curled into a malicious smile.

He said something in Chinese that brought grins to the faces of the others. Hoffman felt like he might puke.

"You have a thing for GPS devices," Xu said. "This one must have been swallowed several hours ago because it appears to be lodged in the stomach or perhaps the upper intestines. But this time, Mr. Shealy, we came prepared. Knowing your penchant for such devices, we brought a police jammer in this vehicle."

The words were like a battering ram to the gut. Hoffman's first level of defense was splintered like the door to a medieval castle.

But it was the next sentence that put him in mortal terror.

"Just to be safe, perhaps we should also perform some minor surgery."

◁▷

When she lost the ability to trace David by the GPS device, Stacie Hoffman immediately called Isaiah Haywood. Sick with worry, she requested that Isaiah meet her at 11:00 p.m. at Centennial Olympic Park in downtown Atlanta, next to the springing-water fountains. Stacie knew she could talk Isaiah into helping, but she also threw in a twist that she had never once discussed with David.

"Can you ask Wellington Farnsworth to meet us there too?" she asked.

"Wellington?"

Stacie decided to act as if Isaiah had said yes. "You'd better drive separate cars," she said. "Things are getting a little dicey."

◁▷

Huang Xu didn't really expect to learn the location of the algorithm during phase one of the interrogation. More than anything else, it would be a test of Shealy's resilience. They would gain a few valuable pieces of information, nothing more. If they actually obtained the algorithm without taking things to the next phase, that would be a bonus.

They blindfolded Shealy and took him to the temporary Atlanta headquarters of the Manchurian Triad. After removing the blindfold, Xu demanded, in a calm and relaxed tone, that Shealy give them the Abacus Algorithm. Shealy responded with a demand of his own: "Prove to me you've released Jamie Brock. Then we'll talk."

Xu looked around at his men as if maybe he was missing something. "Did I say anything about negotiations?" he asked.

The men all shook their heads; they couldn't understand it either.

"I'll give you one more chance, Mr. Shealy," Xu said, stepping closer. "Where's the algorithm?"

Shealy spit, and Xu turned his men loose. They delivered kidney punches, a couple of blows to the face, and some body blows with enough force to crack a few of Shealy's ribs.

This time, when Xu addressed Shealy, his captive was curled in a fetal position on the floor.

"Where's the algorithm?"

The fear and pain had turned Shealy's eyes bloodshot, leery. The rabid eyes of a wounded animal.

"A SunTrust Bank in downtown Atlanta," Shealy gasped. "A safe-deposit box."

"I want it now. Tonight."

Shealy squirmed a little, gave Xu a furtive glance. "I can't get in there tonight. I swear."

Xu folded his hands together as if he was actually pondering this. In fact, he had already made up his mind to implement the next phase. Like a lie detector test, it would determine whether Shealy was bluffing.

Xu had learned that you could not generally beat the truth out of someone. The best truth serum came in that brief window of opportunity just before you subjected someone to truly unthinkable torment. Fear, not pain, was the best catalyst.

"I have a suggestion," Xu said. "Given that we have time, let's eliminate that GPS device that Mr. Shealy so inconveniently swallowed. That way, we will not need to carry a communications scrambler with us everywhere we go.

"Bring him back, gentlemen."

The triad members half carried, half dragged Shealy, coughing and spitting blood, into another room, where they strapped him to a padded examining table. Xu scrubbed his hands and pulled a bright fluorescent light into position, directly above Shealy.

"Cut off his shirt," Xu said.

"What are you doing?" Shealy gasped. The man was finally trembling, his face contorted with fear.

They ripped off his shirt, drawing gasps of pain from Shealy. Xu snapped on a pair of surgical gloves and picked up a scalpel. He leaned over Shealy while the man's bare chest rose and fell rapidly, hyperventilating.

"One last time," Xu said. "We want that algorithm tonight. Otherwise, I will remove the stomach and a portion of the upper intestines." He paused and watched the fear take root. "Did you know that I did some clinical work in self-hypnosis? It can be nearly as effective as anesthesia when it comes to blocking out pain. Which is a good thing, since we seem to be missing an anesthesiologist."

Shealy strained against the straps, his muscles flexing with fear-laced adrenaline. "I'm telling you the truth!" he cried.

72

WELLINGTON PARKED his Volkswagen Jetta, the car that boasted the government's highest side-impact rating, in an outdoor paved lot across the street from Atlanta's Olympic Park. It occurred to Wellington that he had no business being in downtown Atlanta at this time of night, much less involved in a clandestine meeting with somebody the mob was after.

Under his breath, he said a prayer for protection.

As he crossed the street, he noticed two African American men about a block away, loitering on the sidewalk in the direction he needed to go. He glanced at them and noticed, to his great consternation, that they were staring at him. Wellington focused on the ground as he walked, then snuck another darting glance at the men.

They were still staring.

Wellington picked up the pace a little, nothing noticeable he hoped, and rehearsed in his mind what he would do once they assaulted him. They could have his wallet and his watch. If they wanted, he would offer to accompany them to an ATM and take out the maximum amount of cash the machine would allow. He would not offer resistance. He had read somewhere that the odds of violence were substantially reduced by a compliant victim.

Surprisingly he passed by the men without incident, and his heartbeat returned to some semblance of normal. A few blocks later, he entered the park and felt a little safer. There were a few skateboarders and teenage hoodlums, but Wellington hoped the wide-open layout of the park, along with the soft overhead lights, would discourage random acts of violence. There was probably a study about the calm-ing effects of such lighting, but he couldn't remember if he had read it or not.

Wellington found a park bench near the springing-water foun-tains—streams of water that shot up in arcs from spots in the sidewalk, creating endless hours of wet fun for kids during the day. Wellington, who had arrived ten minutes early, began studying the order of the streams to see if he could detect a pattern.

"Are you Wellington Farnsworth?" a lady asked from behind the bench.

Wellington jumped to his feet and waited for his heart to fall back out of his throat. "Yes, ma'am," he said weakly.

"I'm Stacie Hoffman," she said, extending a hand. "Thanks for coming."

She was prettier than Wellington had imagined, though she tried to hide behind the unkempt auburn hair, a University of Georgia ball cap, and thick black glasses. She seemed frazzled and more than a little scared. Or maybe that was just him projecting. He shook hands, took a quick look around, and asked if she wanted to join him on the bench.

A few minutes later, Isaiah joined them. "Nice hat," he said. "Go Dawgs."

"Lost and found," Stacie replied. She suggested they take a walk while she explained her plan. "For some reason, I feel safer if we keep moving."

Wellington felt safer just having Isaiah with them. It wasn't only that the man was an athlete. Isaiah was street smart and confident. Relaxed. It allowed Wellington to hold his own head a little higher— *I'm with him, so I must be okay.*

But his new sense of security soon dissipated in the face of Stacie's tale. In fact, fear returned in double portion, causing Wellington's stomach to clench and flop and otherwise warn him that he had no business here. The triad had apparently captured David Hoffman, Stacie said. She couldn't reach him on his cell phone. To make mat-ters worse, a GPS device that David had ingested as an extra layer of security was no longer registering.

They walked a few steps in silence while Wellington considered the implications of a sophisticated and vicious enemy like the Manchurian Triad. Even if Wellington could help rescue David, would the triad members ever rest until they had their revenge? *Why is this my fight?* Wellington kept wondering.

After a pause, Stacie began laying out the plan that she and David had devised for a moment such as this. Unfortunately for Wellington, Stacie needed an accomplice or two. She didn't know where else to turn, she said. She was sorry that she had to ask them to get involved, but what choice did she have?

"Why not go to the feds?" Wellington suggested. Isaiah shot him a disapproving look, the same one he had used when Wellington ruined the boycott in crim pro class. But it would take more than a look to change Wellington's mind. "It's their job to handle stuff like this. They actually know what they're doing."

"What they're *doing*," Stacie began, the desperation evident in her tone, "is exploiting David and me, using us as bait. Who do you think helped the mob find us in the first place, Wellington?"

Wellington chose not to answer, conceding the point.

"And why would they do something like that—jeopardizing the life of a protected witness? Because this algorithm is so stinkin' important that the government will do anything and use anyone to get their hands on it."

"And if they get it," Isaiah added, "you might as well forget about the right to privacy. That will be just one more casualty in the government's self-justifying fight to keep us safe."

Wellington could tell that his defense of the government would fall on deaf ears with this crowd, so he bit his tongue. Soon, Stacie and Isaiah had worked out the details of a plan, including a role for Wellington, who would ride shotgun in Isaiah's car.

"I don't know," Wellington protested.

"About what?" a frustrated Isaiah said.

"About this whole plan."

If it had been a fair debate, Wellington might have won. But Isaiah made no pretenses of being fair. This was his turf, his time of night, and the third vote was cast by a fellow government-conspiracy theorist. Within ten minutes, Wellington had quit trying to convince Isaiah and started resorting to the phrase "Well, I've already told you what I think."

"I know what you think," Stacie finally said, exasperated. "But are you in or not?" She softened her tone, and Wellington's heart went out to her. "It's okay if you're not, Wellington. I really don't have any right to ask you to get involved. I just need to know."

For some reason, in that moment of weakness, Wellington's lips uttered words that his brain had not yet approved. "I guess I'm in," he said.

By now, they had wandered to the other side of the park. They used the time walking back to fine-tune the plan while Wellington fretted about what he had gotten himself into.

They stopped next to the same bench where they had first gathered.

"By tomorrow, it should all be over," Isaiah said.

The thought of the intervening twenty-four hours made Wellington's chest tighten. It was like he had gone to the movies, bought his popcorn, and then been swept onto the screen for an action movie . . . rated R for violence and gore. But in this real-life version, the bullets would kill and the good guys had no guarantees.

He looked from Isaiah to Stacie and then back again. "Do you mind if I lead us in a quick prayer?" he asked.

Isaiah shrugged, but Stacie appeared shocked.

"You don't have to join me," Wellington said quickly.

"No . . . no," Stacie said, recovering nicely. "I'd like to, Wellington. I think it's a great idea."

◁▷

Huang Xu held the scalpel suspended over Hoffman's stomach for a moment, then touched the skin below Hoffman's navel. Hoffman sucked in his stomach and closed his eyes, every muscle taut with apprehension, his cracked ribs burning with pain.

"I think I believe you," Huang Xu said. He laid the scalpel down, and Hoffman relaxed a bit, his chest still rising and falling with short, rapid breaths. As Xu peeled off the gloves, Hoffman opened his eyes.

"We have a jamming device the size of a quarter," Xu explained. "We will implant it in your neck. You may experience a little pain, but after what you were prepared to handle, it will seem like a pinprick."

He leaned over a little, closer to Hoffman's face. "You will have one chance to deliver the algorithm, Mr. Shealy. Just one."

"You'll kill me either way," Hoffman replied.

"Perhaps," Xu said. He walked away from the table and came back with a device that looked like a nail gun.

"Untie one hand so we can roll him on his side," Xu said to one of the men in the room. He turned back to Hoffman. "You may not know this, Mr. Shealy, but I'm a trained surgeon. And since we last met, you might say I completed a little internship in India. You know what I learned? How much more valuable organs are when they are harvested from a live person than when they are harvested from a corpse."

Xu lowered his voice, a smirk playing on his lips. "Would you care to guess one of the most valuable organs one can harvest?"

Hoffman said nothing, but he knew his trepidation was registering in his eyes.

"The cornea, Mr. Shealy. Two corneas will bring nearly two hundred thousand. Far better than the heart."

Hoffman jerked his head back in repulsion. His mind lingered on the word picture that Xu had so expertly drawn. "So yes, Mr. Shealy, you may have to die anyway. It would be unfortunate to have a person other than us who knows this algorithm.

"But I assure you, there are some things worse than a quick and painless death."

73

WELLINGTON HAD BEEPED his Jetta unlocked and had one hand on the door handle when he heard someone behind him call his name. He almost jumped out of his skin.

"Sorry," Stacie said. "I didn't mean to scare you."

"It's okay," Wellington said. He resisted the urge to grab his heart. "I'm just a little jumpy, that's all."

They stood there for a second, neither speaking. "Do you need a ride?" Wellington asked.

"Oh no. Thanks. I really followed you over here because . . ." Stacie stopped for a moment. "Actually, if you could give me a lift to my car in the parking garage by the CNN Center, I've got something I want to give you."

"Okay. Sure. Hop in."

Wellington jumped in first and made a clean sweep of the passenger seat—fast-food bags, books, a few stray coins, and pencils all got thrown in the back. As Stacie watched, he grabbed a pair of shoes and an old sweater from the floor and chucked them in the back as well. A few other items he just shoved under the seat. "I've been a little busy lately," he said. "Actually, it always looks this way."

"Don't worry about it."

On the way to the garage, Stacie gave directions and thanked him for his willingness to help. She directed him to the third level of the parking deck and had him pull next to her Honda Accord.

"Did you get the optional security package?" Wellington asked.

Stacie looked at him like he'd lost his mind. "What are you talking about?"

"On your car. You don't get side air bags without the optional security package."

"I don't think so."

"Then be careful. The side-impact rating for that car leaves a lot to be desired."

"I'll keep that in mind."

Stacie stepped out of Wellington's car and asked him to hang on for a minute. She popped the trunk on the Honda and fished around in the area where the spare tire should be located. A minute or two later, she closed the trunk and hopped back in Wellington's car with a locked metal box in her hands. She flipped through the combination quickly and removed the padlock.

With all this mystique, Wellington half expected a glowing light to appear from the box, emitted by the Hope Diamond or maybe the Holy Grail. Instead, the box contained only a single sheet of paper and a thick leather Bible.

Stacie waited for the overhead console light to go dark before she said anything. "Walter Snead told me that you figured out he had been our lawyer. He said you're probably the smartest student he's ever had. He also told me you were more or less a prodigy on solving ciphers and encryptions."

Wellington was glad it was dark in the car since he could feel himself blushing.

"Did he tell you about the encoded algorithm?" Stacie asked.

At that moment, it finally dawned on Wellington that he might actually be an arm's length away from the most important math formula in the world. What else would Stacie have in that box?

"Yeah," Wellington answered. "Professor Snead said that you were given an encoded algorithm, but the key from Professor Kumari's friend never arrived."

Stacie sighed. "Once we went into the witness protection program, we knew it would be impossible for Kumari's friend to find us. So we waited a year and then went to India looking for him. Kumari had told Clark, I mean David, that the person he trusted more than anyone would have the key. Since Kumari had wanted the algorithm sold to help the work of the Indian church among the Dalits, we figured his church associates might be a good place to start."

As Wellington listened, his leg got the nervous jitters. This could be one of the greatest mathematical breakthroughs of the twenty-first century, and he was sitting next to the person who owned it. Plus, he reminded himself as he quickly checked every mirror, people were willing to kill for the thing.

"What we found out was so sad. Kumari's pastor and other members of his church had been kidnapped and never heard from again. There were rumors that they had been tortured. We stayed for more than a week, making friends with church members and helping out in the Dalit school."

Stacie hesitated as if unsure about how much she should share. "On the last night we were there, I became a Christian and got baptized by the new pastor of Kumari's church."

"That's awesome," Wellington said, momentarily forgetting the danger lurking all around them.

"I thought you might feel that way," Stacie mused. She picked up the Bible, holding it with great care. "Later that same night, at our hotel, we got a visit from an older woman in the church. She told us that . . ."

Stacie stopped midsentence as if she'd heard something. She quickly placed the Bible back in the metal box, closed the lid, and turned to check behind her. "Did you hear anything?" she asked Wellington.

His heart was about ready to beat out of his chest, he was so scared. He had been hearing mysterious noises all night. "Maybe. Probably. But I might just be imagining it."

They both sat there for a moment, scarcely daring to breathe. One minute lapsed into two. Finally Stacie glanced around one more time and decided to continue. "Anyway, this lady came to us in the middle of the night and gave us this Bible." She pulled it out of the box again and handed it to Wellington. It was thick and well-worn, a version that had both English and Hindi side by side. The book felt weighty, its secrets costing people their lives.

Stacie explained how the Bible had been passed from Pastor Abhay

Prasad to this lady and then ultimately to her and David. It contained a very important key to a project that Kumari was working on, according to the woman. "We're certain she was referring to the key for the Abacus Algorithm," Stacie said. "That's what this other piece of paper is—the encrypted algorithm."

"Wow," Wellington said.

"The thing is—David and I have been trying to solve the code to this algorithm ever since we got our hands on this Bible. Walter told us we should have you look at it—that if anybody could solve it, you could. But, Wellington, this formula has caused so many people so much pain. And the thought of dragging one more person into it, before we even knew if you could really be trusted . . ."

Stacie turned in her seat so she was now facing Wellington. He noticed that she had removed her glasses. "But then, in the park, when you prayed for David . . . well, I know this sounds crazy, but it somehow confirmed that I could really trust you."

To Wellington, it didn't sound crazy at all. Overwhelming—yes. But not crazy. In Wellington's experience, God usually worked in strange and mysterious ways. Crazy was normal in the spiritual realm.

Stacie pulled the folded sheet of paper out of the box and handed it to Wellington. It was too dark to see what was written on it, and he wasn't about to turn on the light. He placed the paper carefully inside the front cover of the Bible.

"It's D-day," Stacie said. "I know I'm asking a lot. But if we had an algorithm that wasn't encrypted and actually worked, it would make things a lot easier—maybe even give us one more bargaining chip if we needed it. Bluffing gets old real fast."

Wellington couldn't believe she was entrusting this to him. He was being asked to decipher the most important algorithm in the world. In about ten hours!

"I'll see what I can do," he said. Even to his own ears, the response sounded so meager, so trite, for such an important task.

But Stacie didn't seem to be offended by it. "You can't let anybody know you have this," she said. "Not Isaiah. Not Snead. Not even David."

Wellington nodded. He was well aware of the sensitivity of this matter.

"Guard it with your life," she added.

He could have gone all night without hearing that.

74

WELLINGTON, WHO HAD never done drugs in his life, figured this was what being high must feel like. He barely made it back to his apartment without pulling over to the side of the road so he could study the encrypted algorithm right there. He probably would have, except the chances of an automobile accident increased dramatically when you did such foolish things. Something like one out of every ten accidents, as best he could remember.

He spread the paper out on his small kitchen table, the Bible on one side and his computer on the other, some mechanical pencils and legal pads there as well. He touched it with the sort of reverence one might reserve for the Dead Sea Scrolls. This was the Abacus Algorithm! Rapid factorization of numbers into prime integers! It would be a formula beautiful in its complexity, majestic in its exploitation of the unbendable rules that governed the distribution of primes. Wellington wished he could have met Professor Kumari himself. What kind of mind could distill such an algorithm?

Wellington understood, of course, that this was not the first algorithm developed to determine the prime factors of a given number. There were a number of other formulas, varying in complexity and sophistication, but they all had their limitations.

The elliptic curve method, for example, could find prime factors of a number if the primes were relatively small numbers—twenty to thirty digits or so—but not for the large primes required to break most computer encryption systems. The various "sieves" that had been developed provided some shortcuts and reduced the time required for a method called direct search factorization, which was nothing more than systematically testing every prime number to see if it could be a factor of the number in question. But using even the most sophisticated sieve could still take millions upon millions of computer hours to find the prime factors of a very large number.

From what he had heard about the Abacus Algorithm, it was so much more. This was a formula, not a sieve, a way to exponentially reduce the time it took to factor numbers. The key to every Internet lock.

But as he focused on the page in front of him, it just looked like so much gibber jabber. Sure, there were some mathematical concepts that Wellington might expect to see in such a formula, such as the concept of modality, binomial coefficients, and various congruence equations. But the encoding system used by Kumari had reduced the overall equation to gibberish. So many variables or numbers, or even mathematical functions, seemed to be represented by a set of five numbers, as if each set of five numbers, once the code was understood, would generate a single number or a single mathematical function or letter.

It was mind-boggling stuff. The more he stared at the formula, trying to make sense of the numbers, the more his head ached. Wellington reminded himself that he was dealing with an encryption technique designed by the same man who had solved a mathematical challenge that others considered impossible. And Wellington had only a few hours to decipher it.

It was not hard to figure out that Kumari had used a five-part encoding system—the formula was absolutely littered with five-number sets. Perhaps every fifth or sixth symbol in Kumari's formula was encoded this way. Thus, each sequence of numbers—for example, 24-50-42-1-3—had to mean something.

He began by noting the range of numbers represented in the various sequences. For example, the first number of the sequence always fell within a range from one to sixty-two. The second number ranged from three to one hundred forty-seven. The third number ranged from one to one hundred sixty-nine. But the ranges for the fourth and fifth numbers in the sequence were much smaller. The fourth number contained a range from one to twenty-eight while the fifth number only ranged from one to sixteen.

Those ranges were telling him something, but he couldn't quite put his finger on what.

The biggest key of all, however, was not the formula itself. Wellington picked up the leather Bible. An English-Hindi translation, NLT version.

Wellington leafed through the pages, focusing first on the margin notes and the verses underlined by the pastor. This guy scribbled lots of notes in his Bible, some in English, some in Hindi. Wellington thought about trying to download a program that might help him translate the Hindi notes but realized it would be nearly impossible for him to decipher. Besides, if the pastor knew the Bible would be passed on to an American, Wellington assumed he would not put the key in a language most Americans couldn't read.

Instead, Wellington focused on the English notes and the English verses the pastor had underlined. He went through the verses systematically, plugging in different iterations from his number sequences. What if he wrote down all the numbers in the verses the pastor had underlined, put them in order, then cross-referenced them against the code? For instance, maybe the first number to appear in the underlined verses corresponded to the number 1 in Kumari's encoded algorithm. He started that exercise but after a few minutes realized that many of these underlined verses probably went back several years, predating the algorithm and the code Kumari had put in place. Next, he focused on any numbers the pastor had written in the margins, applying different approaches to them.

For three hours, Wellington worked his what-ifs and plugged in trial symbols and numbers based on different assumptions regarding underlined verses and margin notes and the strange code Kumari had used. What if this? What if that? Eventually he quit focusing on the Bible and began focusing on the formula itself, applying every decryption trick he had ever learned. Not once did he leave his seat at the table—no breaks, no stretches, just one method after another.

Hours later, all he had to show for his efforts was a growing headache.

75

THE SUNTRUST BANK at the intersection of Fourteenth and Peachtree in downtown Atlanta didn't open until 10:00 a.m. Hoffman and his captors—Huang Xu and two other members of the Manchurian Triad—arrived five minutes early in a conspicuous black Lincoln Town Car. At Xu's direction, the driver cruised around the block twice, past the bank building itself, the Peachtree Plaza, and the Sheraton Hotel behind the bank complex.

Traffic on Peachtree Street, the main artery for Atlanta's financial district and the upscale businesses of Buckhead, moved at its usual ultraslow pace, the road jammed with cars and SUVs and lane-hogging delivery trucks. Pedestrian traffic was a steady trickle, not New York City by any means, but enough lawyers and bankers and investment gurus to give the area a self-important, urban feel.

"Park here," Xu said after the second lap. He pointed to a driveway that looped in front of the Peachtree Plaza, just beyond the entrance to an underground parking garage and adjacent to the bank building. Sitting in the circular drive, the occupants of the car would be able to watch the revolving front doors of the bank and be well positioned for an escape.

"You're coming with me," Huang Xu said, motioning to Hoffman.

Hoffman took a split second, closed his eyes, and offered a final silent prayer. He got out the back door and waited, like a loyal hunting dog, for Xu to alight from the front passenger seat. Underneath Hoffman's bulky shirt he had been wired for obedience. A number of electrodes—two hooked to his nipples, two to the soft tissue on his upper back near his armpits, two near his hips—were strategically positioned to provide a debilitating electrical surge whenever Xu pulled the trigger on the Taser gun he carried in the pocket of his suit coat. It was, Xu boasted, Taser's newest wireless long-range electric-shock weapon.

Earlier that morning, to show Hoffman the full extent of the range, Xu had the driver of the Town Car pull over in a deserted parking lot. Xu dragged Hoffman out of the car, removed his blindfold, and made him run—ten yards, twenty yards, thirty. The pain of trying to run with cracked ribs was excruciating, but nothing compared to what happened next.

Smiling, Xu pulled the trigger on the Taser, bringing Hoffman to his knees, disrupting his neuromuscular system, and sending his muscles into agonizing contractions as the current pulsed through him in two-second cycles for the longest twenty seconds of Hoffman's life.

A few minutes later, as Xu put the blindfold back on Hoffman, he drove home his point. "Today, my friend, you are an epileptic. Prone to sudden seizures. Lucky for you, I am a physician and will treat you during your convulsions. That's the little role-playing that will happen if you try anything stupid. Understand?"

Hoffman understood. With drool running down his chin and struggling to maintain his balance, Hoffman climbed back into the car. He felt dazed and nauseated for the next ten minutes.

And terrified much longer than that.

When they reached the SunTrust building, Xu followed Hoffman through the revolving doors and into the main lobby. A bank of elevators was located on their left, the open glass doors for the SunTrust lobby on their right, a food court and plaza directly ahead.

They walked into the lobby of the bank and took a seat on the other side of the desk from the customer assistant nearest the door. Xu sat with his back to one of the lobby security cameras, his hand shielding his face from another one. Hoffman sat gingerly, every movement causing sharp pain in his ribs. The nameplate on the lady's desk said she was Cynthia Lawson. Her face was round and pleasant as she gave Hoffman her best customer-service smile. "How can I help you?"

"I need to access my safe-deposit box," Hoffman said.

"Certainly."

Hoffman provided his box number and name while Ms. Lawson fished the keys and signature card out of a drawer. Hoffman noticed Xu glance around the bank lobby without ever lifting his head. There were three tellers at the counter, a few customers already forming a line, a branch manager sitting at a desk in a glassed-in corner office, which was partially obscured by open miniblinds, and one other customer assistant seated at a desk in the lobby and flipping through some papers. There was no visible security guard on the premises. One outside wall was all glass, giving the occupants a view of the Fourteenth Street sidewalks.

"Follow me, please," Ms. Lawson said.

She led them past the side of the bank teller stations and back into a small vault with a massive steel door at least two feet thick. The inside walls of the vault, which Hoffman estimated to be about twenty feet wide by forty feet long, were lined with various sizes of lockboxes, all numbered and shining like coats of armor at a medieval castle. But for the smaller size of the boxes, it reminded Hoffman of a mausoleum he had seen as a child. About a third of the room was actually another small, self-enclosed vault, containing rows of oversize safety boxes and a counter along the length of one wall.

Hoffman showed his driver's license and signed the entrance record card. It was only the second time Box 273 had been accessed. Cynthia Lawson wrote in her name, the client ID, the date, and the time of access.

"Okay," she said. "Do you have your key?"

Hoffman and Ms. Lawson both inserted their keys into Box 273, a three-by-ten-inch box located at eye level about a third of the way into the room. As Xu watched from behind, his right hand inside his suit coat, the door for Box 273 hinged open and Hoffman pulled out the small, metal rectangular box.

"Do you want to access it here or in a separate, private room?" the clerk asked.

Hoffman looked up at the ceiling-mounted security cameras. "Does the other room have cameras?" he asked.

"No, it doesn't."

"We'll use that one," Hoffman said.

He carried the lockbox in both hands, following Cynthia Lawson out of the vault and across the lobby. Huang Xu, his head low, trailed a step behind. Lawson unlocked the door to the small, rectangular room with reinforced block walls, no windows, and a Formica desk that extended across the length of the far wall. A solitary chair faced the desk and wall. A few pens and legal pads were placed neatly along the desk.

"Just call me when you're done," Lawson said, pointing to a small buzzer next to the door.

After the woman left, David Hoffman carefully placed the lockbox on the desk and removed the lid, exposing a single sheet of paper folded in half.

◁▷

Outside the bank, Wellington Farnsworth and Isaiah Haywood waited. They had arrived earlier in Isaiah's tricked-out Camaro, complete with spinners, tinted windows, and a Bose sound system that could rock an entire block. Wellington was too stressed to remember the vehicle's side-impact rating.

After riding with Isaiah to Fourteenth Street and pushing an imaginary brake on the passenger's side of the vehicle too many times to count, Wellington wished more than ever that he had checked on that rating. Once they arrived, Isaiah parked directly across the street from the SunTrust Bank and Peachtree Plaza, in the middle of a side alley next to a high-rise commercial building, ignoring the numerous No Parking signs posted on the alley.

Wellington looked at the signs and frowned.

"We can see the bank and that little driveway loop for the Peachtree Plaza next to the bank," Isaiah said defensively. "Don't sweat it. Nobody will tow the car with me in it."

What do you mean, me *in it? What about* us?

As if in answer to Wellington's thoughts, Isaiah began outlining his plan. "See that outdoor café over there, right next to the bank? I need you to go order a coffee or something and grab one of those seats. You'll be closer to the bank's front door in case we need somebody on foot or they have Hoffman in disguise so we can't recognize him from this distance."

Both Isaiah and Wellington had studied the pictures of Hoffman provided by Stacie. Still, Wellington didn't feel quite up to completing this new assignment.

"Why don't we stay together? Seems like it would be safer that way."

"For us, maybe," Isaiah said. "But this isn't about us anymore."

Though Wellington couldn't exactly figure out *when* it had stopped being about him, or even *why* it had stopped being about him for that matter, he obediently crossed the street (with the light) and picked up a diet soda and newspaper at the outdoor café.

As he waited, he tried to occupy his mind by focusing on the algorithm encryption, a challenge that had kept him up all night. After he had exhausted several possibilities related to the underlined biblical passages, Wellington had decided to ignore the Bible and try to solve the numbers as some type of substitution pattern. Maybe each number stood for a particular letter or possibly for a different number. When this concept failed to produce results, he assumed that certain combinations of numbers stood for single letters or single numbers. Or perhaps he was supposed to add the numbers in the five-number sequences, or divide them, or add the first and third and subtract the second and fourth.

It would have made him crazy had he been fully rested. Exhausted and stressed-out, he didn't stand a chance.

After twenty minutes of waiting, Wellington saw Hoffman and another man enter the building. Frantic, he called Isaiah immediately.

"I know," Isaiah said. "I saw them."

"I'd better come back over so we're ready to go," Wellington suggested.

"Just sit tight," Isaiah said. "Stacie should be calling any second."

◁▷

In the bank lobby, the second customer assistant, a woman named Tricia, transferred a call to Cynthia Lawson. "There's a problem with an overdrawn account," Tricia explained. "He sounds pretty upset. He asked for you by name."

◁▷

Leaning over the desk, Xu reached into the safe-deposit box and unfolded the paper. He spread it out before him and began studying its complex mathematical schemes. Hoffman wondered how much of the formula the mob leader really understood. Did he even realize it was encrypted?

"This thing better work," Xu said sharply.

They were interrupted by a brief knock on the door and a turning of the dead bolt. A customer assistant entered, closed the door, and stared at the men, a cell phone and keys in one hand, a bank document in the other. Her name tag identified her as Tricia Martsen.

Xu stood up and stiffened, stuffing the paper in his suit coat pocket.

"Excuse me, Mr. Hoffman," she said, holding out the document as she walked toward them. "But access to this safe-deposit box is supposed to require the signature of both you and Mrs. Hoffman."

"It's not a problem," David said quickly. "She asked me to come by and get something for us. If you want, you can give her a call."

"I really am sorry," Ms. Martsen said, stopping a few feet from the men. She smiled, but it wasn't convincing. "Procedures."

Xu stared at her for a second, intensity coiling every muscle. "We were just leaving," he said.

Xu started to go around her, but the startled assistant shuffled half a step to the side and held her ground. "You've already accessed the box," she sputtered. "We will need to at least call." She extended the cell phone . . .

And jammed the antenna hard into Xu's neck, her face turning dark with hatred.

The veiled Titan stun gun did its debilitating work, sending a hundred thousand volts through the body of the shocked triad leader. The auburn-haired assistant with the thick glasses pulled the gun back a few inches as Xu fell to his knees, moaning in pain, bracing himself with one arm against the wall of the room. But as David Hoffman stepped toward his wife, he saw Xu's posture stiffen, an almost-instantaneous, miraculous recovery. A steely look flashed across Xu's face, the eyes of a warrior.

Xu spun and rose, the speed of a black belt, his right hand knocking the stun gun from Stacie's fist. David had not hesitated. In the split second it took Xu to spin toward Stacie, David lunged, using his head as a battering ram, hoping to rearrange Xu's face to match Dennis Hargrove's, the Vegas bounty hunter. Xu deftly sidestepped David and flipped him like a rag doll to the floor. David landed hard on his side, the pain from the already-broken ribs nearly crippling him.

Sprawled on the floor, David heard a *thwack* behind him. He looked up just in time to see the results of a vicious blow Stacie had landed with the safe-deposit box, the corner slicing into the back of Xu's skull, spattering the wall and desk with drops of blood. David watched Xu's eyes roll back in his head as the force of the blow sent him crashing into the wall a second time. He slid to the floor and lay there motionless, his head tilted awkwardly to the side.

Before David could struggle to his feet, Stacie had dropped the safe-deposit box and recovered her stun gun, driving it once again into Xu's shoulder. He convulsed, his body jerking involuntarily, his eyes vacant. As David stared, she held it there for ten seconds . . . fifteen . . . twenty. Her face was contorted into an animalistic intensity.

David grabbed her around the shoulders, winced as the pain shot through his ribs again, and pulled her away from the fallen man. "It's okay," he said softly. "It's okay."

76

DAVID AND STACIE DRAGGED Xu into a corner of the small room so that his body would be behind the door if anybody looked in.

"He's breathing," David said.

"Thank God," Stacie murmured, mostly to herself. "I almost killed him."

"It's okay, babe," David said. He slowly raised the shirt he was wearing and pulled the electrodes off his body. Just lifting his arms made the pain slice through his broken ribs.

Stacie looked at the electrodes wide-eyed. "What're they?" she asked.

"My leash." He finished removing them and reached out to hold Stacie by the outside of both arms. "You okay?"

"Yeah."

She looked as bad as he'd ever seen her. The auburn wig had become skewed in the fray, her glasses knocked to the floor. She looked frightened and weary, the large brown eyes shooting around the room. He gently embraced her, but she soon pulled away. "I don't know how long Isaiah can keep Cynthia Lawson on the phone," Stacie said. "We need to return this box and get out of here."

"I didn't know Xu would actually come in with me," David said. "I thought he would send one of his men. I was worried he might recognize you."

"For a moment, I thought he did," Stacie said.

She opened the door, and David walked into the main bank lobby. He tried to stand as straight as possible, but the ribs wouldn't allow it. After closing the door to the private room, Stacie joined him.

"Anything else, Mr. Hoffman?" she asked.

"No. I think that about does it."

Slightly stooped, David walked out of the bank and took a right toward the atrium and food court. A few seconds later, after returning the lockbox, Stacie followed. They walked quickly across the food court and toward the side entrance for the Sheraton Hotel.

"It's almost over now," he said.

"I've heard that before."

◁▷

Wellington watched a third man climb out of the Town Car and walk past the outdoor café where he was sitting. The man was tall, six-three or six-four, and weighed at least two-fifty. He had a dark beard, short stubble on top, and a large earring in his left ear.

Wellington placed his newspaper on the table and dialed Isaiah as soon as the man was past. "Another one just went in the bank," he reported.

"I know that," Isaiah said. "I think you oughta go in there after him. See what's going on."

The ink from the paper had already stained Wellington's sweaty hands. The thought of following this thug into the bank nearly made him stain his pants.

"What if he recognizes me?"

"They don't even know who you are."

"Easy for you to say."

"C'mon, you big wuss. Just go see what's going on. You can keep the phone on and talk to me the whole time if you want."

Wellington took a deep breath, calming his nerves. "All right."

He rose from his seat and checked in both directions—for what, he didn't know—then walked with great trepidation toward the door of the bank building. Wellington entered the lobby just as the thug was walking out of the SunTrust doors. The man stopped and looked in all directions.

"Did you say a loaf of bread and a gallon of milk?" Wellington said into his cell phone.

"No, you *didn't* say that," Isaiah snorted. "Why don't you just tell him you're following him?"

Ignoring Isaiah, Wellington did a smooth left turn and pushed the button for an elevator. He counted to five and glanced over his shoulder. The man was heading toward the revolving door.

"Suspect leaving building," Wellington whispered into his cell phone.

Just then, the man turned and looked straight at Wellington, freezing the law student in his tracks.

77

WELLINGTON FREAKED and did the first thing that popped into his mind. When the elevator door opened, he jumped on.

"The guy spotted me," he said to Isaiah, but his phone was showing no coverage on the elevator.

He rode the elevator to the second floor and hopped off. As soon as the doors closed behind him, Wellington pushed the Down button and called Isaiah.

"Where are you?" Isaiah shouted. "Our man just left the building; he's heading toward his car."

"I'm coming," Wellington said. "Just a second." The elevator doors opened, and he jumped back on. He got off at the lobby and ran from the building, the closest thing to a sprint that Wellington Farnsworth had ever done.

◁▷

David and Stacie Hoffman walked into the Sheraton lobby and began searching for the hunched-over body of Walter Snead. Because of his ribs, David had trouble taking deep breaths. He quickly scanned the front desk area, the couch and seating areas, and the empty bar.

"I can't believe he's not here," David said.

Stacie had called Snead the night before and told him to meet them in the Sheraton lobby. He would rush them to Hartsfield airport for a flight out of Atlanta. Stacie had told Snead that she and David would likely have at least one triad member captured and possibly a location for where they were holding Jamie. She had given him no further details.

"What time did you tell him to meet us?" David asked.

"I told him to be here at 10:00 a.m.," Stacie said, her face tight with frustration. "I told him to wait all day if he had to." She pulled out her cell. "I'll call the feds myself."

"I'll check outside," David said. As he turned, two serious-looking men in blue blazers started walking his way. They had just appeared from a door that led to the parking garage. David's instincts told him to run.

"Mr. Hoffman," one of them called out.

Stacie's head whipped around. She glanced at the men and darted for the front door. David followed as best he could.

They burst through the front door and almost ran into three additional men: one dressed like a bellhop, one in shorts and a Hawaiian shirt, and a third man, dressed like an FBI agent, whom David had no problem recognizing.

Sam Parcelli flashed his badge.

"Huang Xu is in a private room for customers attached to the SunTrust Bank lobby right next door," Hoffman gasped, wincing from the pain in his rib cage. The two men whom Hoffman had seen inside now joined them. "Stacie should be getting a call any minute from one of our lawyers, a kid named Isaiah Haywood, who will be following a couple of triad members back to their headquarters. They had blindfolded me, so I don't know where it's located."

"A law student?" Parcelli scowled. "Whose idea was that?"

David and Stacie looked at each other, though neither fessed up. Parcelli nodded toward the two men in blue blazers. "Check out the bank," he said. "Clear the building first. Get Hutchinson and Romano to join you."

He turned back to Stacie and David. "You two are going with me."

"We were supposed to meet Snead here," David protested. "We've got other plans."

"Those plans have changed."

◁▷

"Slow down!" Wellington shouted.

"Are you kidding? They're almost out of sight!"

Isaiah sliced through traffic, swerving from one lane to the next on Peachtree. At a red light, he looked left and right, waited for a break in the cross traffic, then darted through.

"What are you doing?" Wellington asked.

"I should have left without you," Isaiah replied.

Unlike Isaiah, the driver of the Town Car was actually stopping at red lights, not wanting to draw attention to himself. Isaiah closed the gap by a block or so, then backed off. "Better not get too close," he said.

Praise God, Wellington thought.

Just then, Isaiah's cell rang.

"Do you want me to handle that?" Wellington asked.

But Isaiah had already picked it up. He answered and listened for a few seconds and mouthed "the feds" to Wellington. It was just like Stacie had outlined it.

Isaiah started giving a running commentary, street by street, into the phone. He followed at a distance as the Town Car pulled onto Interstate 85. "The FBI agents are just leaving the Sheraton," he whispered to Wellington.

Watch the road, pal, Wellington wanted to whisper back.

On I-85 the Town Car picked up speed, and the next major problem reared its ugly head. "Don't look now," Isaiah said, holding the phone away from his mouth, "but there's a cop car gaining on us."

"How far back are the feds?" Wellington asked.

Isaiah put the phone back to his ear. "Where are you guys now?" He listened. Then, "Okay, that's about two miles behind us."

"How fast are you going?" Wellington asked Isaiah.

Isaiah gave him a don't-bother-me look.

Wellington glanced in his side-view mirror. The police lights came on.

"He's trying to pull you over," Wellington said.

Isaiah snuck a peek in the rearview. "I don't see anything," he said. But then, into the phone, "The state police are trying to pull me over. What do you want me to do?"

The feds must have told Isaiah to keep driving. Maybe they were trying to get through to a dispatcher and explain the situation. But word didn't seem to be reaching the officer tailgating Isaiah and Wellington, lights flashing and siren blaring. The Town Car, a quarter of a mile ahead, slowed to the speed of traffic.

"If you don't pull over, the mob will know something's going on," Wellington said.

"I'd have never thought of that," Isaiah snorted. He put on his turn signal and worked his way to the right lane. "When I stop this car, I want you to get out," he told Wellington. "Get in front of the cop car. Delay them; tell them what's going on. Whatever."

"What are *you* going to do?" Wellington asked. This plan gave him a severe stomachache. Arguing with the authorities, particularly the state police, was not exactly his strength.

"I'm going to take off so we don't lose these guys."

"With all due respect," Wellington said, "this is a stupid plan."

But Isaiah was already skidding to a stop on the shoulder.

78

ON THE TRIP BACK from Jacksonville on Friday morning, Drew rode in the front of a black sedan driven by an FBI agent named Lester Aranson while Jamie slept in the back. About ten thirty, Drew woke her up to tell her the news that Lester had heard from the Atlanta office.

"The feds arrested Huang Xu at a bank in downtown Atlanta," Drew said. "They're following a few other triad members to a place believed to be their headquarters."

Jamie felt lighter at the news—the first real breakthrough in the last two weeks. She had a strong desire to be there, to actually see justice served, but she knew the feds probably wouldn't let her within ten miles of the triad headquarters. "How long before we get to Atlanta?" she asked.

"About four more hours," Drew said.

For better or worse, Jamie realized, it would probably all be over before she even returned to the city. The triad that had tried to shatter her life either would be brought to justice or would slip through the cracks one more time.

"I wish I could be there," Jamie said. The silence from the front seat confirmed her assumption that she could not. She closed her eyes and pretended to sleep. Instead, she prayed for justice.

◁▷

Wellington sheepishly got out of the Camaro and started walking toward the police car, his hands on top of his head. Immediately two officers jumped out and yelled at Wellington to get back in his car.

Motivated by thoughts of Jamie bound and gagged by the Manchurian Triad, Wellington took a few more steps. "I need to explain something highly important," he shouted.

"Not one more step!" one of the cops yelled, drawing his gun.

Wellington stopped, his knees nearly buckling.

"Back in the car!" the man yelled.

Wellington took a step back . . . two, and then Isaiah punched the gas. The tires spun and squealed, leaving behind some long, black skid marks and two shocked police officers. The driving cop jumped in the car, quickly backed up so he wouldn't run over Wellington, and took off after Isaiah. The other officer ran toward Wellington, grabbed him, and threw him toward a concrete barrier. He forced Wellington to stand spread-eagle and cuffed Wellington's hands behind his back.

Wellington interrupted the reading of his Miranda rights. "I understand all that," he said. "I waive it. But please listen to me."

"Save it," the cop said gruffly. "You and your buddy are in a lot of trouble."

But Wellington knew he couldn't back down. Not this time. "My friend and I were trying to keep within sight of a vehicle driven by members of a Chinese triad, the Chinese mob," he said, talking quickly. "Some FBI agents should be coming by any minute, trying to close the gap. But in the meantime, they asked us to keep these guys in sight. It's a long story as to why—but if you don't believe me, just call the FBI." Wellington looked over his shoulder, hoping to see a screeching federal sedan any minute.

The officer gave him a shove. Kicked Wellington's legs even farther apart. "Why don't you just turn around and shut up while I pat you down," he said.

He finished patting down Wellington's chest and waist and had started on the first leg when the sedan came speeding past. The feds had a blue light on the dashboard to alert traffic but were not using their siren.

"There they are!" Wellington cried. "That's the FBI car. At least call your partner. Call the feds. Something! It's a matter of life and death!"

The cop watched the sedan. He turned again to Wellington. "Don't move a muscle," he said. Then he reached for his radio to alert his partner.

◁▷

Isaiah had his own problems. He had put a little space between his Camaro and the state police car based on the element of surprise. But he could no longer see the Town Car that he was supposed to be following. Worse, he was fast approaching a major decision—stay on I-85 North or veer onto Route 400, another eight-lane divided highway that ran in a northerly direction west of the I-85 corridor.

He still had the FBI agent on the phone. "I lost visual contact," Isaiah said. "You want 400 or I-85?"

"Just a second," the agent said.

"Hurry up."

The state trooper was gaining on Isaiah, siren blaring. If the driver of the Town Car heard the siren, he would probably take the first exit and never be seen again. Isaiah decided to slow down a little. He couldn't risk pulling within sight of the Town Car right now, not with the police officer hot on his tail. Maybe Isaiah could make up the distance once the state trooper figured out what was going on.

"That state cop is behind me again with his siren blaring!" Isaiah said into the phone. This was getting ridiculous.

"We know. We've alerted their dispatcher."

"I'm taking 400," Isaiah said. "You guys can take 85." He swerved at the last minute toward the exit on his right. He was hoping to shake the trooper, but it didn't work. Isaiah slowed some more, and the trooper was now right on his bumper.

This was so frustrating! Isaiah felt like punching somebody. The mob was getting away while the good guys were stumbling over each other, worried about a traffic infraction.

At that moment, just when Isaiah was ready to do something drastic, though he wasn't quite sure what, the trooper turned off his siren. Isaiah rolled down his window, stuck his arm out, and gave the officer a thumbs-up.

Then he punched the accelerator. *Let's see what this baby's got.*

79

ISAIAH GUESSED RIGHT. He caught sight of the Town Car a few miles after the 400 turnoff as the vehicle rolled through the exact-change lane at the toll booth. The state trooper was still behind Isaiah but had killed his lights and siren. Isaiah decided to make up a little more time and go through the Cruise lane, though he had no Cruise Card on his windshield. For the first time that day, he allowed himself to enjoy the adrenaline rush—the rules of the road no longer applying to him.

"I've got them in sight again," he told the FBI agent. "I'm just going through the toll booth."

"We know," came the response. "We've established visual contact with you."

"I thought you were going I-85."

"There are multiple vehicles involved," the agent said. "Maintain visual until we catch you; then you can back off and slow down."

"Ten-four," Isaiah said. He smiled to himself. Sure, it sounded hokey and maybe a little disrespectful. But after everything he'd been through, a guy was entitled to have some fun.

◁▷

A few minutes later, Isaiah was following the FBI sedan at a distance. He wasn't about to miss the fireworks. The sedan took the Holcomb Bridge Road exit, a six-lane local highway heading northwest through a gauntlet of traffic lights. Isaiah followed. And he wasn't the only one. The state trooper passed Isaiah and tucked in several car lengths behind the federal sedan. Two other nondescript sedans passed Isaiah and fell into line as well. Two local police cars appeared out of nowhere, trailing Isaiah and the other state trooper by about half a mile. *It would be a good time to rob a bank someplace.*

Everyone turned left on Highway 9, including Isaiah, who set off a chorus of horns when he ran the light after it had turned red.

Isaiah followed the law enforcement entourage to a strip mall located on the fringe of the Roswell historic district. Six federal agents jumped into action, securing the parking lot and vacating the businesses—a Wings restaurant, a tanning salon, a dry-cleaning establishment.

One of the agents directed Isaiah to a spot by another federal car on the far side of the lot. "We're going to need a statement from you after this is over," he said.

"What's going on?" Isaiah asked.

"There's a wooden fence behind this strip mall," the agent explained. "On the other side of the fence is a large, historic brick house converted into an office, tucked back among those trees down there. It's where the Town Car is parked. We're securing all four sides, and then we'll move in."

"Is that where they're holding Jamie Brock?" Isaiah asked. It had been at the front of his mind the entire day, the reason he had agreed to help Stacie in such a high-risk assignment, the reason he was determined to not let the Town Car out of sight.

The agent looked dumbfounded at the question. "She's already been freed," he said.

Isaiah felt a rush of elation, the joy of winning a huge SEC football game times ten. "What? When?"

"I can't talk right now," the agent said over his shoulder as he hustled away and pulled out his radio. "Stay in this area, and I'll fill you in later."

Isaiah called Jamie's number, but she didn't answer. He left an elated message, all the while watching his tax dollars at work. He had never been much of an FBI fan before, but even a cynic like him had to be a little impressed at this operation.

Within minutes, the place was crawling with law enforcement officers. They quickly secured the strip mall, as well as the historic estate located across the street from the mob headquarters. Though Isaiah couldn't see it, he assumed they had done the same with the residential neighborhood that abutted the back of the brick house and the row of houses on the other side.

In the midst of the law enforcement officers scurrying around, another black sedan pulled into the parking lot, and Stacie Hoffman got out of the backseat. Isaiah jogged toward her and called her name. She looked haggard, but her face lit up as Isaiah approached. She gave him a quick hug.

"Thank you so much, Isaiah. I'll never forget this." She turned to the man next to her, who appeared to be in a fair amount of pain. "This is my husband, David," Stacie said.

Even before David could express his thanks, one of the agents handed the Hoffmans bulletproof vests. "Put these on quickly," he said, ignoring Isaiah. "We're taking you to that white van over there." He pointed to a vehicle parked about seventy-five feet from the house. "It'll be just outside the perimeter. With binoculars, you should be able to ID anybody who comes out.

"Keep your heads down. Let's go."

Before they hustled away, David turned to Isaiah and lowered his voice. "I knew we could trust you, Isaiah. We owe you our lives."

"No problem," Isaiah said. But he couldn't help feeling like a hero.

◁▷

Isaiah stood in the parking lot, mesmerized by the beehive of activity swirling around him. Local police stopped and rerouted traffic; officers pushed pedestrians a few blocks away. SWAT teams and officers in bulletproof vests swooped in and blockaded the driveway of the brick house with federal sedans and what looked like armored trucks. Agent in Charge Parcelli stood behind one of the vehicles with a portable mike and speaker. He ordered the triad members to toss out their weapons and come out with their hands on their heads.

There must have been fifty rifles trained on the building. It seemed to Isaiah like the entire National Guard had suddenly converged on Roswell, Georgia.

Isaiah didn't exactly have a front-row seat, but he was inside the taped-off area, squatting behind a federal sedan, about a hundred yards from the building. He could see the front door through a stand of pine trees. He was so engrossed watching the house that he didn't realize Wellington had arrived. He felt a tap on his arm.

"How'd you get here?" Isaiah asked.

"The state police brought me here," Wellington said. "I guess the feds called and said I might be needed for questioning."

"You did good, my man," Isaiah said. He could tell from the look on Casper's face that the kid had never felt so cool in his entire life. But that didn't mean he felt safe.

"Shouldn't we move back a little farther?" Wellington suggested.

80

THE FIRST FEW ACTUAL ARRESTS went like clockwork, as far as Isaiah could tell. Watching it all go down, the culmination of a case on which he had risked his own life, made Isaiah's body hum with intensity. A few minutes after Parcelli started making demands on his mike, six members of the Manchurian Triad marched out of the brick building, one at a time, hands on their heads.

These were mob members, Isaiah reminded himself. Men who would snuff out a human life without remorse. But today, they had no options. They calmly left the building, heads held high, eyes focused straight in front of them. Federal agents swarmed the gang members, hustling them away from the building, handcuffing them, throwing them in the back of squad cars.

After the initial round of arrests, Parcelli got back on his microphone. He warned that anybody else inside should leave the building immediately. The entire scene grew disturbingly quiet. Isaiah had his eyes glued on Parcelli, who appeared ready to give the order for the agents to swarm the building. That's when Isaiah heard the sound of breaking glass and saw smoke pouring out of an upstairs window.

He thought at first that someone had fired a smoke bomb or tear gas into the building. But then he heard someone shout, "Fire!" and a nearby police radio crackled with a confirmation that the fire had been started on the inside, blowing out a window. "They're burning evidence," somebody said.

Parcelli motioned forward, and dozens of agents stormed the building. Smoke still billowed from the upstairs window, but the fire didn't appear to be spreading. Sirens blared in the distance behind Isaiah, the sound of approaching fire trucks. Ever curious, Isaiah edged closer.

A few agents scrambled out of the building with another Chinese man handcuffed between them. A few seconds later, two more agents appeared with a man in custody, hands cuffed behind his back, and Isaiah had to shake his head to make sure he wasn't seeing things.

Walter Snead. Hunched over. Pulled along by two feds. He stumbled, but the agents had a tight grip on his arms and kept him upright, dragging him toward the vehicles until the professor gained his footing again. He was wearing dress pants, a white shirt, a yellow tie—it was Snead dressed for class in everything but his sports coat. The man's gray hair was disheveled, his face contorted in a trademark Snead scowl.

What was *he* doing here?

The men had pulled Snead about twenty feet from the building when Isaiah heard a pop that seemed to come from the second or third floor. Snead lurched forward, his body going limp, the agents keeping him from doing a face-plant on the concrete. A bright red spot appeared in the middle of his shoulder blades, spreading like a starburst on his back.

Isaiah ducked behind a car, watching the building through the glass windshield. Chaos erupted. He heard somebody yell, "Gun, upstairs right!" He heard other gunshots, tried to get his bearings, watching while trying to keep his body shielded, focused on the mob headquarters.

The explosion that rocked his world came from a totally unexpected direction.

81

THEY WERE STILL ABOUT two hours from Atlanta when Lester's phone rang again. Jamie kept her eyes closed but listened carefully. Lester kept his remarks vague and cryptic. After a few minutes of listening, he asked, "Where do you want me to bring her?" and Jamie knew she was headed in for more questioning. He signed off, and Drew started in with the questions.

"What's the word?"

"You might want to wake up Ms. Brock," Lester said.

Drew reached back and touched Jamie's knee. She pretended to wake up, stretch a little, open groggy eyes. "What's up?" she asked.

"Lester just got a call from the FBI team in Atlanta," Drew said.

Jamie sat up straighter. She checked out Lester's face in the rear-view mirror and could tell that something was terribly wrong. She braced herself for the news.

"We located the triad's headquarters," Lester said, his eyes on the road. "We made some clean initial arrests, six members of the triad's leadership including the granddaddy, a guy named Li Gwah. The AIC gave one additional warning and sent the SWAT team in."

Lester hesitated for a moment, and Jamie sensed an uncertainty as to how much he wanted to share. She waited him out, and eventually he continued. "There were three other men still in the building. They apprehended one without incident. The second was Walter Snead—"

"Professor Snead?" Jamie couldn't hide her shock. She couldn't begin to wrap her mind around this. What was *he* doing *there*?

"They apprehended Snead, but he claimed that he had been

kidnapped by the mob. Thing is, since he wasn't restrained in any way when they found him, the agents treated him like a suspect. They had him about twenty or thirty feet away from the building when one of the gang members shot him from an upstairs window. The agents now think that Snead might have been a victim after all and that this sniper was left behind to burn evidence and eliminate anybody who might be able to provide eyewitness testimony. Snead was DOA at the hospital."

Jamie felt her systems shutting down. Snead dead. It could have been her.

"It gets worse," Lester said, but Jamie couldn't imagine how.

"Before the agents could reach this gang member, he apparently detonated an explosive device that killed two other witnesses and a federal agent stationed with them in a van."

"Who?" Jamie asked. "Who were the witnesses?" She knew the answer, but she had to hear it anyway.

"David and Stacie Hoffman."

"How? How could that possibly happen?" The incompetence of the feds astonished Jamie. Angered her. How could the mob murder witnesses already in federal custody?

"Some members of the triad captured David Hoffman last night," Lester explained. "Hoffman obviously knew these men were after him, and somewhere in the process he had managed to ingest a GPS device so his movements could be tracked by his wife. His wife realized he had been captured but didn't report it to the FBI."

To Jamie, the last statement sounded defensive, the spin doctors at work.

"Anyway, the mob apparently implanted a device in Hoffman's neck that acted as a jammer, obfuscating any GPS signal. When Hoffman was freed, nobody realized that this chip might also be an explosive device, one that could be detonated by remote control. Apparently the last man in the headquarters, before he was apprehended, detonated the explosive device and took out the Hoffmans."

The car fell quiet as Jamie struggled to take it all in. Witnesses dead. Evidence destroyed. Things weren't supposed to end this way. She felt an overwhelming sadness, a melancholy. She had only been with

David Hoffman on a few occasions, but she had been struck by his zeal for life. She had believed passionately in his innocence. The system had failed him in so many ways.

"So four people are dead," Jamie said. "And none of them are members of the triad."

"That's correct," Lester admitted. "Depending on how you categorize Walter Snead. I think the jury might still be out on him."

"Hardly the FBI's finest moment," Jamie said. She knew it wasn't Lester's fault, but she just couldn't believe this could happen.

"The collateral casualties are tragic," Lester said, and Jamie resisted the urge to add, *No kidding*. "But on the other hand, this raid broke the back of the U.S. operations for one of China's most powerful triads. We apprehended their top leadership. Our agents were able to extinguish the house fire quickly and preserve most of the evidence. We'll have everything we need to put these men away for life."

"A rousing success," Jamie said.

Wisely, Lester picked up on the sarcastic tone and decided not to answer.

◁▷

Three hours after the explosion, Wellington still had not made sense of everything he had seen. For nearly an hour, locked in a sterile interview room in the federal building in downtown Atlanta, he answered every question that two somber FBI agents threw at him. They made him feel like a felon, not a hero who had helped them nail the mob.

He was already bone weary when Sam Parcelli walked into the room. Wellington recognized him from the hearing in federal court.

He took a seat directly opposite Wellington and stared vacantly for a few seconds. The man's eyes were sunken and bloodshot, with large dark circles underscoring them. He unnerved Wellington.

"I understand you're not willing to tell us about conversations you might have had with Ms. Hoffman," Parcelli said flatly.

"I think they might be covered by attorney-client privilege," Wellington said, his quavering voice trumpeting his uncertainty. "I just wanted to research the issue first."

"What year are you in law school, son?"

"I'm a 2L."

"Can 2Ls practice law?"

"No." Wellington rubbed his hands over his face. He forced himself to meet Parcelli's gaze. "But I was providing assistance to somebody who was practicing law. Therefore, I think the conversations might be covered."

Parcelli sighed, signaling his weariness at playing cat-and-mouse games over attorney-client privilege issues when four people were dead. "What are you hiding, Wellington?"

"Nothing. I've already told the other agents everything I know."

Parcelli studied Wellington some more, as if the mere act of staring might serve as some kind of truth serum. It almost did. "Isaiah's already talked to us," Parcelli said. "Told us all about the conversations you had with Ms. Hoffman. We're basically just checking to make sure both stories line up."

Wellington remembered the holding in *Novak v. Commonwealth*: law enforcement officers could lie when gathering evidence. "Okay. But I still need to do the research first."

Parcelli leaned forward. "Look, Wellington, I've got an agent dead. Three witnesses blown away. Your own law school professor is one of them. I don't have time for games here. You can either cooperate or look at obstruction-of-justice charges."

If Parcelli was trying to intimidate him, it was working like a charm. Wellington felt physically sick from the pressure, nearly overwhelmed by a desire to provide Parcelli what he wanted. But still, he had a duty.

"My duty to my client is not a game to me," Wellington said, his voice still shaky.

"Your dead client," Parcelli reminded him. He let the reality of that statement sink in for a minute. Then he pushed away from the table and took a deep breath.

"Do you have the algorithm, Wellington?"

"I can't say."

"Let me tell you what I already know," Parcelli said. "I know the algorithm is coded and doesn't make sense unless somebody can figure out the key. I know that of all the people working on the Hoffmans' case, you would be the most likely one to try to decode it. And I know that before the Hoffmans died, they had entered into a deal with the government to provide the encoded algorithm in exchange for one million dollars. I even have the account number of some bank in the Caymans that the Hoffmans were going to use to channel the money to a church in Mangalore, India. Did they tell you about that, Wellington?"

The young man sat there dumbfounded. Stacie had never said anything about a deal with the government. But the part about the Mangalore church seemed to authenticate Parcelli's story. Wellington could tell that Stacie had been impressed by the sincerity of the people she met there.

"She didn't tell me that," Wellington admitted.

"Well," Parcelli said, "the algorithm seems to have disappeared. If the Hoffmans had a copy with them, it was destroyed in the explosion." He stood, hovering for a moment over Wellington. "That formula sure has caused a lot of headaches for anyone who tried to hang on to it. A superstitious man might say it's cursed, what with all the deaths trailing in its wake. I'll tell you this much: if I had possession of it, I'd probably sell it to the government. Heck, I'd probably give it away. The sooner the better. That's what I'd do."

Parcelli slid a card across the table. "Let me know if you find out anything about who might have that algorithm. The government's still willing to pay fair market value. Still willing to put a million into that account the Hoffmans set up—" he waited a beat as if to make sure Wellington was listening—"or any other account. Keep that in mind, would you, son?"

"Yes, sir," Wellington said.

PART IV
THE DEAL

There are two tragedies in life: one is not to get
your heart's desire. The other is to get it.

GEORGE BERNARD SHAW

82

MOST OF SATURDAY, Jamie watched endless news coverage of the event. Since the feds were being incredibly tight-lipped, the coverage contained a lot of speculation and hearsay, as well as a few human-interest interviews with stunned neighbors. They were just living normal lives, they said, and were shocked to discover that organized criminals were operating in that same neighborhood. Jamie could certainly empathize.

It wasn't until Drew Jacobsen called on Saturday night that Jamie received any substantive information about the evidence found at the triad's headquarters. Though Drew didn't know all the details, he knew enough to be optimistic. "With the federal sentencing guidelines, they could all be lifers," he said. "The death penalty's not out of the question if they can make some of the murder-for-hire charges stick."

Jamie couldn't muster a fraction of Drew's enthusiasm for the outcome of the raid. An FBI agent, Snead, and the Hoffmans had died. Earlier, Snowball had been poisoned. Jamie felt like she had ingested poison as well. Her black-and-white view of the criminal justice system had been destroyed by the gray shadows of the witness protection program and the power-hungry prosecutors and law school professors who might or might not be corrupt.

In Jamie's opinion, it was no time to celebrate.

But Drew had different ideas. "I've been asked to interview with the FBI," he said, trying hard to contain his elation. "I tried to get in about five years ago but didn't get past first base. I guess some of the agents from this case recommended me."

"That's great," Jamie said.

They agreed on a time—7:00 p.m. on Sunday. And a place—Copeland's Cheesecake Bistro at Atlantic Station, about five blocks from the law school.

Jamie marked it on her calendar.

◁▷

SUNDAY, APRIL 13

If the size of the hastily arranged funeral was any indication, the Hoffmans had not trusted many people during their four years as government-protected witnesses in Atlanta. The pastor of a church Stacie had been attending used the occasion to preach a sermon rather than eulogize the dead. There was nearly a one-to-one ratio between the media attending the event and the mourners.

Jamie sat quietly through the Sunday afternoon service alongside Isaiah and Wellington. She wore a black silk dress and heels, prompting several comments from Isaiah about the Black Widow being back. To Jamie, the comments seemed ill-timed at the very least. Wellington was his normal subdued self, ill at ease in a sports coat and tie. It never ceased to amaze Jamie that this kid wanted to be a lawyer.

After the service, Wellington pulled Jamie aside in the parking lot. "Can I speak to you for a minute?" he asked, glancing around.

"Sure."

"Um. Not here. Can we go somewhere?"

Jamie had lived through enough of the cloak-and-dagger routine for two lifetimes, but she agreed to meet him at a local bookstore a few blocks away.

"Let's meet in the back of the store, at the coffee shop," Wellington suggested.

◁▷

Over two lattes, Wellington explained his problem. Speaking hypothetically, he wondered what might happen if he had received a copy of the encrypted Abacus Algorithm from Stacie Hoffman and needed legal advice about what to do with it. Could Jamie provide such advice under the protection of the attorney-client privilege?

Jamie assured Wellington that his hypothetical secrets were safe with her, and he launched into his story. U.S. Attorney Allan Carzak was planning to convene a federal grand jury next week and had subpoenaed Wellington to testify on Wednesday morning. Wellington knew what Carzak wanted. He would ask Wellington whether Stacie or David Hoffman had ever given Wellington a copy of the Abacus Algorithm. Carzak would probably demand a copy as evidence in the case against the Manchurian Triad members. If Wellington refused to answer the questions or provide the algorithm on the basis of attorney-client privilege, Carzak would probably have the judge compel Wellington's testimony. If Wellington still didn't comply, he would probably go to jail for contempt.

As Wellington unburdened himself, his tone got more intense, his face more flushed, and Jamie suspected that a full-blown panic attack was only moments away.

"The FBI agent in charge, Samuel Parcelli, told me that he made a deal with Stacie before she died. She supposedly agreed to sell the government the algorithm for a million dollars. He said the feds would cut the same deal with me and I could do what Stacie wanted—give the money to the church in Mangalore, India."

The first time Wellington took a breath, Jamie jumped in. "Do you think Stacie really agreed to that?"

"No way," Wellington said. "She thought the government had set her up. She couldn't stand the FBI. She believed they would use the algorithm to destroy everyone's privacy."

"How do you know her feelings about this issue so well?"

Wellington reddened even more. "Actually, I only met her once."

"So where are these strong feelings about privacy coming from?" Jamie asked.

Wellington looked down. "I don't know. Could be me, I guess." Then he quickly added, "But I really think she felt the same way."

"Do you have the algorithm?"

"Hypothetically?"

"No, Wellington, in reality. Do you have it?"

He sighed. "She gave it to me late Thursday night. It's encrypted, and she thought maybe I could decipher it."

"Did you?"

Wellington's face dropped, and he shook his head. It occurred to Jamie that the guy probably felt like a total failure. Wellington had never seemed very strong in the self-image department in the first place. He probably blamed himself in some way for how things had gone down.

"Does the government know for sure you've got it?" Jamie asked.

"I don't think so. I haven't admitted anything yet." He hesitated, apparently unsure of how much he should divulge. Jamie waited him out.

"Jamie, I've also got a separate . . . let's call it a document—that might help somebody figure out the key," Wellington continued. "I haven't discovered how it works yet, but that doesn't mean the government wouldn't be able to. If I got subpoenaed to testify, they'd probably ask if I know anything about the key to the encryption method as well."

Jamie gave Wellington her best reassuring smile. She had a plan, she told him. It wasn't foolproof, but it might get him out of testifying.

"That would be awesome," Wellington said. He looked close to tears. "This algorithm has already ruined enough lives."

83

DRESSING UP WAS NOT usually Jamie's thing, but for Sunday night she made an exception. She wore a black, sheer top with a V-neck and bell-shaped sleeves, a short skirt, gold pumps, a chunky gold necklace, and a thick gold bracelet. She purposely left her watch on the dresser. After half an hour using a flat iron on her hair, she was satisfied with the effect of her superstraight, slinky hairstyle. She topped it off with gold chandelier earrings with black accents.

The Black Widow was ready.

She arrived twenty minutes late, but Drew didn't seem to mind. "Wow!" he said. "You look great!"

Drew looked pretty good too—khaki slacks and a polo shirt, the thick dark hair framing that poster-boy face. He looked like the kind of man most women dreamed about. Jamie remembered how Drew had taken care of Snowball the first time she met him at the police station, how his sensitivity had touched her most of all.

"Thanks," Jamie said.

Though Drew had already put their name on the list, they were told the wait would still be another thirty minutes. After a few minutes of small talk, Jamie asked Drew if she could use his phone. "My battery's dead," she explained.

She dialed her brother's number in northern Georgia and before long had a nice little family squabble going. She made a face at Drew to show her embarrassment, put her hand over the phone, and told Drew she'd be right back, that she just needed a little privacy. She walked around the corner, ended the call, and accessed Drew's call history. She scribbled down the numbers, dates, and times, then meandered back to where Drew waited patiently.

Twenty minutes later, they followed a waiter through a maze of other patrons, winding their way to a small table in the back, next to a wall lined with mirrors. It wasn't exactly the intimate atmosphere Jamie had planned for this meeting. The ambient noise level seemed just below a dull roar, with the clanging of dishes, background music, and conversation buzz from other tables making it hard to talk at normal levels. Plus, the tables on each side were so close that Jamie could have reached out and held hands with her fellow diners.

Copeland's Cheesecake Bistro knew how to pack them in.

Jamie picked at her food and dodged Drew's "Are you okay?" questions until the waiter had cleared away the main course. She waited for one more "Are you *sure* you're okay?" inquiry before she started her cross-examination.

"I just can't stop thinking about the way the triads used that jamming device as an explosive," she said. "It's hard to imagine that an explosive small enough to be implanted in somebody's neck could do that much damage."

"It's those cop shows on TV," Drew replied, his soft brown eyes watching Jamie intently. "Most people think you've got to be strapped with tons of explosives to blow up a building. The truth is, it only took twelve ounces of Semtex inside a terrorist's cassette recorder to blast Pan Am flight 103 out of the sky over Lockerbie, Scotland."

"Still, it shows a level of sophistication," Jamie said. She hesitated, played with her water glass for a moment, then looked straight across the table. "Wonder why they didn't check me for GPS devices. Wonder why they didn't use a jammer on me."

She watched Drew carefully. The bedroom eyes—sexy, relaxed—glimmered slightly with apprehension.

"Good question," he said. "They probably assumed that since they nabbed you unexpectedly in the middle of the day, you wouldn't be wired."

He answered quickly, she noticed. *Too quickly?*

"Didn't they capture Hoffman unexpectedly too?"

This time Drew hesitated. His thirst apparently called, and he took a sip of Coke. "Yeah. But he knew they were after him."

"Another thing that's been bugging me is the kidnapping itself. It keeps coming back, replaying itself in my mind. I'd really forgotten all about it, probably suppressed it, until I tried to sleep that first night. Every time I closed my eyes, I was in that stairwell again.

"And the thing is, Drew, I distinctly remember pulling out my gun and firing two shots, right into the gut of the man who grabbed me from behind. But nothing happened."

This time Drew tried a quizzical look. "You probably had the safety on. When you're under that kind of pressure, if it's not habit, you don't usually remember things like not releasing the safety."

"I thought about that possibility. But I distinctly remember squeezing the trigger. It clicked back. Would it do that with the safety on?"

"No," Drew admitted, "probably not. But you don't always remember things right when you're under that kind of stress."

Jamie took a deep breath and leaned back in her chair. This was going exactly as she thought it would. Not the way she hoped, but definitely the way she expected.

"And so I called the Jacksonville coroner's office on Friday afternoon. At first, they just gave me the runaround. But I was very persistent. Told them I had been the victim in the kidnapping that resulted in three men being shot—one Russian guy and two others. Told them I worked for the district attorney's office in Gwinnett County, which isn't exactly true, but I did clerk there last summer. They finally told me what I knew they would say."

She leaned into this next part. She watched the blood slowly drain from Jacobsen's face. He was good at conducting interrogations, but not so good on the receiving end. "There were no autopsies, Drew. No bodies. No three men killed. How does that add up? I thought autopsies were mandatory whenever the cops shot and killed somebody."

In response, Drew just stared back. The bedroom eyes had run out of answers.

84

JAMIE WAITED HIM OUT, a technique she had learned in trial practice class. *Do not speak when the witness is struggling to find an answer.*

"What are you saying?" Drew eventually asked. He spoke softly, avoiding any hint of indignation.

"You know exactly what I'm saying." Jamie felt the anger crawling up her spine, stiffening her neck, reddening her face. "The mob didn't kidnap me; the feds did. It was all a big setup, and you went along with it. My own government knocks me out, ties me down in the back of some truck, and then puts me in fear for my life."

Jamie felt the tears stinging her eyes. Tears of anger. Frustration. She knew the importance of this algorithm, a national-security risk of enormous proportions, but what could possibly justify this? "My own government violates every constitutional right I have." She paused, boring into him. "And they use someone who pretends to be my friend. For what? So you could bring Hoffman out of hiding? So the federal government could get its precious algorithm and start spying on other people's lives, violating more constitutional rights?"

Drew had his hand out now, palm down, trying to get Jamie to settle down. He looked around, obviously concerned about the eavesdroppers. "Jamie," he said, his voice nearly a whisper, "it's not that way. Is that what you really think? Is that how you really feel?"

She laughed. Shook her head. "Like you really care how I feel."

"I'm sorry," he said.

"Sorry? That's it? A little remorse and it's all better? They killed my dog, Drew. Kidnapped me. And you're *sorry*?"

As her voice rose, Jamie's rant drew a sea of staring faces. Conversations at tables around her halted. Jamie didn't care.

Drew kept his voice low, his tone urgent. "Jamie, we didn't have anything to do with Snowball or the first time the mob came after you. That part was real. That's why we had to take action. This threat wasn't going away."

She pushed away from the table and stood, aware that she had drawn a crowd of onlookers. "Good luck in the FBI, Drew. You should fit right in."

She turned and stalked toward the door. Drew followed and quickly caught up with her, mumbling apologies, telling her she had it wrong. When she was outside, heading down the walkway toward the parking garage, he reached for her arm.

She shook it loose with a look of disdain. "Don't you *dare* touch me."

"Jamie, I know you're upset. You're entitled to be. But listen to me, just for a minute."

She crossed her arms, staring him down. *One minute. Clock's starting.*

"I did this for you, Jamie . . ."

You're off to a bad start, buster.

"I cared about you. Worried about your safety. These guys play for keeps. This wasn't about bringing Hoffman out of hiding. It was about getting you out of harm's way."

"Did it ever occur to you and your friends that you could just ask? That maybe I would have been fine with leaving the area for a few days? That maybe you didn't have to stage a kidnapping and put me in fear of rape—of *rape*, Drew, a woman's worst nightmare—before I might cooperate with you?"

With others milling about the sidewalk, Drew tried his softer tone again, always the cop, worried about who might overhear. "Okay, it was stupid. And yes, part of the motivation for the feds was getting Hoffman to play out his hand so they could get the algorithm. But that wasn't why I went along.

"Sure, maybe you would have gone away, Jamie, but for how long? A week? A month? A year? Don't you see—you would never have been out of danger until we busted these guys."

"If that was the plan, why didn't you just ask me to go along? Why not let me in on the scam? After all, it was *my* kidnapping."

Drew shook his head, his eyes pleading. "You would never have gone along. You would never have deceived your own client. The plan could only bring Hoffman into the open if he really thought the triad had captured you."

She gave him a rueful smile. "No, you're right, Drew. I would *never* have betrayed someone that close to me."

The comment rendered him speechless, as she knew it would. He took a deep breath and stared at the ground for a moment. "What are you going to do?" he asked gently.

"I haven't decided yet."

This time, when he looked back at her, he had the look of a defeated man. His handsome face reflected a deep sadness, a regret that he couldn't possibly find the words to express. For the first time since she pieced her theory together, Jamie felt a tinge of sympathy.

"If you want to pursue this," he said, "and file a lawsuit or disciplinary proceedings or whatever, I'll testify for you. Against myself, if I have to. I won't try to cover this up."

To this, Jamie didn't respond. She would take it under advisement. "You'd better go back in there and pay." She forced a thin smile. For now, she had finished venting. She was still furious of course, but what else was there to say?

Drew sighed deeply, brushed a hand through his hair, and focused somewhere past Jamie, at some distant spot on the sidewalk. "The day before the kidnapping, I found some pictures in an envelope on your car windshield. They were pictures of you—pumping gas, entering the law school, getting out of your car at home—and every one of them had your head in the center of thin red crosshairs."

Jamie could see the tears building in his eyes as Drew faced her squarely. "I care about you, Jamie. I took the pictures to the FBI. They came up with the plan."

His tears didn't melt her—she wasn't even sure they were real—but they softened her anger a little. The red flare of emotion had burned itself out, replaced by a smoldering frustration.

But her suspicions only grew. *"We didn't have anything to do with Snowball,"* Drew had said. *"That part was real."* Maybe they didn't. And maybe those pictures were authentic as well—placed on her windshield by the mob rather than the FBI. She wanted to believe him, but she couldn't just take his word for it. He had already lied more times than she could count.

Whom could she trust in cases like this? Drew said he cared about her; therefore, he lied to her. It was all so very sad.

"I need to be going," she said.

"Can I at least walk you to your car?"

"I'll be fine."

"Can I call you sometime?"

Jamie thought about her watch. The GPS chip that Drew had allegedly planted there. The lies, the hurt, the fear he had put her through.

"Maybe I'll call you," she said.

And they both knew it would never happen.

85

WELLINGTON COULDN'T get enough church on Sunday. He went to the morning service. Then after lunch, he drove across the suburbs to the Hoffmans' funeral. Yet he still felt the need to be in the pew on Sunday night. After all he had been through, and given all he was facing in the coming week, he needed as much inspiration as he could get.

It hit him halfway through the Sunday night service. The answer came precisely the way he knew it would—a flash of insight when he was barely thinking about it. It had been blindingly simple all along.

The pastor was preaching from Psalm 119, the longest chapter in the Bible. One hundred seventy-six verses, to be precise. Wellington was seated in the third pew from the front, the fourth seat from the aisle, participating in the second worship service of the day.

Each set of five numbers in the algorithm is not a code; they're place markers.

The first number in each set—what was the range? He couldn't remember exactly, but it was pretty small, something like one through fifty or sixty. The ranges for the second and third numbers in the series were larger, if Wellington remembered correctly, something like one through about a hundred and fifty. But the fourth and fifth numbers in the series were small again, even smaller than the first number. He was pretty sure that none of the fifth numbers were larger than twenty.

He didn't have the code with him; in fact, he had hidden his hard copy in the middle of one of his two-hundred-page class outlines and had camouflaged the electronic version so deep in one of his computer files that nobody would ever find it. But Wellington knew without even looking that his hunch would prove correct. The first number represented the book of the Bible. The second number, the chapter. The third number, the verse. The fourth number, the word in that verse. And the fifth number, the letter in that word. The system could be versatile, kicking out either letters or numbers, even spelling out mathematical functions. And the Bible he had been given was important, not because of what verses might be underlined or what the margin notes might say, but simply because the decoder would need to know which particular translation to use.

He was antsy now, anxious to get home, pull out the Bible Stacie had given him, and plug in the letters and numbers. He tuned out the preacher and started leafing through his Bible looking for the longest verse, the longest word. He found a verse, Esther 8:9, that contained sixty-five words. He found a word, the name Maher-shalal-hash-baz, that contained eighteen letters.

This was it! He was sure. He started counting the minutes until the service ended. After the final praise song, he left the building as if it had caught fire. He hustled home, breaking the speed limit by an unprecedented ten miles per hour. He pulled out the encrypted math formula, cross-referenced the numbers against the Bible, and felt the air rush from his emotional balloon. Something still didn't make sense. Sometimes, this method would generate meaningful results, illuminating part of the formula. But on other sets of numbers, it just generated more gobbledygook. Frustrated, he rechecked his work, paying careful attention to the parts of the formula that remained a mystery. After fifty minutes of frustrating agony—so close but not quite there—it hit him! The reason for the underlining. One last twist from the brilliant mind of Professor Kumari.

Wellington smiled to himself, content in the knowledge that within a few hours he would be able to unlock the key to history's most exquisite math algorithm. He downloaded the software program he needed and got right to work. Two and a half hours later, he filled in the last missing variable!

He spent the next hour factoring large numbers into their prime components, amazed at the efficiency and symmetry of the formula he had revealed. He tried to break the formula down into its component functions so he could determine why it worked. But it was far beyond even Wellington's gifted mathematical brain, on another level altogether. It was as if Wellington could only add and subtract, but Kumari could perform calculus. Wellington felt like an aspiring young artist who had just uncovered the *Mona Lisa* in his attic.

Kumari's mathematical feat in deriving this formula was, quite simply, awe inspiring.

Which made it that much harder for Wellington to do what he knew had to be done. There were some technological advances, he had concluded, so staggering in their implications that they went beyond man's present moral ability to handle them. Like splitting the atom. Or perhaps the manipulation of DNA. Granted, this mathematical formula didn't present the same kind of ethical issues, but it would present its holder with vast power over the secrets of the most important communication medium in the world.

If the government had the formula, they could use it to violate the closely guarded secrets of its citizens. And if the formula fell into the hands of a criminal enterprise, or even a power-hungry individual who was not a criminal, the repercussions would be even worse. No message sent and no business conducted over the Internet would be safe. There were six billion people in the world. And Wellington was the only one who knew the key to this algorithm. God had entrusted him, and nobody else, with this incredible secret. The sensation was like he'd been given a supernatural gift, Superman discovering he could fly.

Wellington felt so inadequate, so overwhelmed. He realized that this was a typical response when God gave a person a monumental calling. It was the awe of the Virgin Mary when she was told she would bear the Christ child, the trepidation of the apostle Paul when he was commissioned to take the gospel to the Gentiles, the wonder of David the shepherd boy when he was chosen to be king. Or how about Gideon, a lowly farmer whom God called to lead the Israelites against the fierce warriors of Midian?

This would be Wellington's legacy, like it or not. The way Wellington saw it, God had taken this powerful algorithm out of the hands of the mobsters and government officials and given it to him—Wellington, a second-year law student. And Wellington's job was to keep it under wraps until the world was ready for it, until Internet encryption technology had moved beyond reliance on prime factorization. Or until such time as using the formula would do more good than harm.

After all, when David was just a shepherd boy, Samuel the priest told David he would be king, but David had to keep it a secret until the appointed time. If David could keep that kind of thing a secret, Wellington could certainly keep his mouth shut about an algorithm.

But there was still one major problem. When Wellington thought about the grand jury subpoena, his palms started sweating. He couldn't lie, not under oath. There was a verse in Proverbs someplace that promised a false witness would not go unpunished. His only recourse would be to stare down the authority of the federal government and refuse to say anything. The very thought of such a confrontation made him sick to his stomach.

He didn't mind keeping the world's biggest secret, but how would he ever survive if Carzak convinced a judge to hold Wellington in contempt? Comparing himself to biblical characters was one thing. Facing jail in real life was quite another.

86

THEY ATE LUNCH AT THE STOCKYARDS. Medium-rare T-bone steak for him, salmon for her. They cruised the Fort Worth malls. Brandi said it was crucial to get her shopping bearings. In a city, women gave directions using the malls as guideposts, the way farmers used old oak trees a hundred years ago. "You know where the Ridgmar Mall is? Well from there, you go west on I-30 . . ."

They shopped at three different sporting goods stores before they found the right trampoline. They paid extra for delivery and setup. The clerk said it would take less than a week. Shane complained to his wife about the price.

"It won't feel like home until it comes," Brandi countered.

Shane spent his time trying on cowboy hats and boots. He settled on a broad-rimmed brown Stetson and a pair of dark brown, pointed-toe boots on sale at Cavender's. Maybe they should move out to the country and get a horse, Shane suggested. Maybe you should get a different wife if you want to be a farmer, Brandi replied.

They made it home by four. Agent Sam Parcelli showed up precisely at five.

Parcelli looked around the barren house, made a few wisecracks about their interior designer, asked Shane about his ribs, then pulled out the paperwork so they could review it on the kitchen counter. He slid one copy of the memorandum of understanding to Shane and another to Brandi.

This had been their first opportunity to meet with Parcelli since the federal government had whisked them out of town last Friday, mere hours after the explosion that appeared to claim their lives. While onlookers focused on the front door of the mob headquarters as Walter Snead and a few triad members emerged, FBI agents led David and Stacie Hoffman out the side door of the van—the side opposite from the civilians and local police—and twenty feet away into a waiting sedan with tinted windows. A few seconds later, the explosion occurred.

The couple decided to start life over in the Lone Star State. Shane had always thought of himself as a cowboy.

"These are basically the same terms your attorney discussed with Mr. Carzak last week on your behalf," Parcelli said, working them over with the stone-cold stare that was his trademark. Today, the sunken eyes looked more sickly than ever, as if the man had just emerged from his casket to handle the paperwork.

"This memorandum, as usual, starts with the recitation of facts leading up to our agreement," Parcelli continued, glancing at the provisions as he summarized them. "On Wednesday, April 9, Mr. Walter Snead, acting as your attorney, called the U.S. attorney's office and suggested the basic terms of this memorandum of understanding. He called after he had spoken to you about the kidnapping of Jamie Brock by the Manchurian Triad.

"Mr. Snead proffered an agreement whereby you would lead us to the triad's headquarters and help us apprehend gang leaders in exchange for complete immunity and new identities under the witness protection program. Mr. Snead did not provide any details of the plan at the time, saying those details were confidential. The U.S. attorney on the case, Mr. Allan Carzak, agreed to the demands but only if you were instrumental in the apprehension and arrest of triad members."

Parcelli flipped a page and continued summarizing, sounding bored by the process. "Late Thursday night, Mr. Snead informed the U.S. attorney's office that there had been some complications . . ."

Complications. The word sounded so clinical now. So benign. But Shane Peeler, formerly known as David Hoffman, formerly known as Clark Shealy, remembered the panic he felt when Huang Xu discovered the GPS device. And the terror sparked by Huang's threat to conduct surgery without anesthesia. *That* certainly qualified as a "complication." David and Stacie had planned for the possibility of the triad discovering the GPS device, but it made things exponentially more dangerous and gave the couple no room for error.

At the time, David had wondered if his prayers were falling on deaf ears. He had his answer now. While he considered how fortunate he was just to be alive, Parcelli rattled on about the negotiations between Walter Snead and the FBI. Snead had told the federal agents to be on call Friday, ready to move in on the triad's headquarters. But the FBI had pressed for details, Parcelli explained, and Snead wouldn't provide any.

Of course, Shane thought, *because we didn't provide* him *with any.*

"Snead did tell us that he was supposed to meet you two at the Sheraton on Fourteenth Street," Parcelli continued, no longer looking at the document. "So of course we staked out the hotel."

Which is precisely why we didn't give Snead any more details, Shane thought. People couldn't seem to keep their mouths shut. Shane and Brandi had decided to trust no one except each other. And sometimes, out of necessity, the idealistic young law students.

"You came through on your end of the bargain," Parcelli said, ad-libbing and barely consulting the papers in front of him. He was reminiscing now, not just reciting facts. "Surprised the heck outta me. You delivered Huang Xu and had your law student heroes drive us right to the triad's headquarters." Though Parcelli's lips were not smiling, and maybe were not even capable of smiling, Shane thought he noticed a spark of life in the federal agent's eyes. "For our part, we decided to stage your deaths in conjunction with the raid, rather than take you straight to the airport as you had planned with Snead. That way other mob members wouldn't be trying to hunt you down in the future."

Parcelli hesitated, seemed to return to the present, and fixed his sallow gaze on the document again. He squinted as he glanced through some additional provisions, then emphasized the requirement that Shane and Brandi sever all ties with the past. "You cannot

contact anybody you knew in your prior life ... and I mean *anybody*."
He paused long enough to accuse them with the silence: *We wouldn't
be in this mess if you hadn't tried to sell the algorithm.* Then he quickly
reiterated the benefits that the federal government was providing—
new identities, complete with prior work histories and educational
credentials, assistance with finding one new job for each of them, as
well as a housing and furniture allowance.

"Any questions?" he asked. He shoved the documents toward
them. "You need to sign all three copies."

"Can you make me about five years younger with my new identity?" Brandi asked. "It's only fair since this whole affair cost me about
ten years off my life."

"No," Parcelli replied, demonstrating once again that FBI agents
had no sense of humor.

Shane shrugged and began signing the documents. Brandi looked
at the barren cupboards and counters and asked Parcelli if she could
borrow his pen. She signed the same name with three different styles,
apparently trying to figure out how her new signature should look.

Parcelli watched their every move as if they might somehow try to
defraud the government by signing bogus names. Shane felt a need to
fill the silence.

"What's your theory on Snead?" he asked.

Parcelli frowned as if trying to make up his mind. "Might have been
playing both sides, but I doubt it. Too many things don't add up. For
example, if he was a mole for the triads, why did he get caught inside
their headquarters? He knew the FBI was preparing to raid the place.

"On the other hand, I don't buy the theory that the triad kidnapped
him, thinking he might have the code. There was no sign of struggle or
break-in at Snead's house; he wasn't tied up when we stormed the headquarters." Parcelli sighed. "To be honest, I don't have a good theory."

"He didn't have the code," Shane said.

"And he wasn't working with the triad," Brandi added. She had been
adamant about this point every time she and Shane had discussed it.
"Shane and I ... well, I guess at that time it was technically David and
I ... anyway, we knew that the triad would have to think they captured

368 || FALSE WITNESS

David unaware or they would suspect a setup. Why would they follow David to the bank in that case? Somebody had to 'snitch' on David and tell the triad where to find him. That way, when David broke down under pressure and told them about the safe-deposit box, the triad members wouldn't suspect a trap. That's what really bothered us about them finding that GPS device—that they might figure out the snitch was actually working with us."

As Brandi spoke, Shane watched Parcelli take it all in. Parcelli had his poker face on, which by itself told Shane something.

"We asked Snead to make that phone call to the triad—to make it look like he was betraying David," Brandi continued. "If Walter Snead was really working with the triad, he would have warned them it was all a setup."

"I understand that," Parcelli said, "but how do you explain his presence at the triad's headquarters?" It was the same question Shane had been asking himself the past three days.

"It's a mystery," Brandi said. "And it will probably remain a mystery. But I can't buy the theory that Walter was working with the mob."

Parcelli shrugged and placed two signed copies of the documents in his briefcase. "Some secrets go to the grave," he said.

He took a deep breath, and his eyes shifted from husband to wife. "I think you know the real reason I'm here. A first-year assistant U.S. attorney could have handled the memorandum of understanding."

Parcelli pulled another contract out of his briefcase. "Have you had enough time to think it over?" He was referring, Shane knew, to the offer Parcelli made at the Atlanta airport last Friday. One million dollars in exchange for the encoded algorithm.

"That formula is a matter of national security," Parcelli pressed. He tapped the document. "Think of this contract as a hundred stacks of money. Each stack contains a hundred Ben Franklins."

Neither Shane nor Brandi moved a muscle. They had prayed about this next step, rehearsed the alternatives, and endlessly debated the ethics of what to do.

"It's caused you nothing but grief," Parcelli continued. "From what your attorney told us, you can't even decipher it."

Shane looked deep into the man's hollow eyes, trying to discern whether Parcelli could really be trusted. Out of the corner of his eye, Shane could feel Brandi staring at him, her intense gaze reminding him of how she felt about this. Through the years, he had learned to ignore her and ask forgiveness later.

This had the potential to be the biggest con of his life. Two hundred thousand for him and Brandi. One point eight million for Pastor Guptara and the Dalits in India. And he would never have to part with the real algorithm. There could be another windfall later if he sold that.

In the meantime, all it required was one final bluff and a little white lie.

87

THE SUCCESS OF ANY STING depends on the setup. In magic tricks, they call it "the turn," the place where you do something extraordinary, like make the bird disappear. The reemergence of the bird—"the prestige"—is only climactic if the turn has been executed to perfection.

In Shane's opinion, there had never been a more flawlessly executed turn.

All of the events of the past few days had been pointing to this one final meeting, a perfect setup to sting the government in its own game. Though Brandi had resisted at nearly every step, Shane saw it as the only way out.

Nearly two weeks ago, when they first formulated Plan B, Shane had spent the better part of three days substituting random numbers in the Abacus Algorithm for the ones that had been originally provided by Kumari. Nobody would ever break this encryption "code" because it wasn't a code at all, just random numbers meaning nothing. Thinking ahead, they had placed two different bogus copies of the formula in two adjacent safe-deposit boxes. If Plan B worked and the triad leaders were captured, Shane and Brandi knew that the government would demand production of the real algorithm. The feds would undoubtedly assume that a second document, in a different safe-deposit box than the first, would contain an authentic copy of the formula. They would work at breaking the encryption for years.

True to form, the government had demanded production of the authentic algorithm. Shane had asked what they were willing to pay for it. The opening offer had been one million. Shane knew he could negotiate two.

The money would be nice, but it was about more than the money. Shane's and Brandi's covers in the witness protection program had been blown when somebody sent a letter to Johnny Chin and revealed their whereabouts. Who would have done that other than the government? In trying to convince Brandi that they should go through with this sting, Shane argued that it was the only way to guarantee that the government would leave them alone and not rat them out again in an effort to shake the algorithm loose. If the feds thought they had gained possession of the authentic algorithm, they would leave Shane and Brandi alone.

In response, Brandi had quoted Bible verses. "'A false witness will not go unpunished, and one who utters lies perishes.'" She argued that they could put their trust in their own cleverness or put their trust in God.

Shane said she was trying to overspiritualize things. "And what about our promise to Professor Kumari?" Shane had asked. "What about the children who need this money to have a chance in life?"

"Why don't you call Pastor Guptara and ask him if he wants tainted money?" Brandi suggested.

◁▷

"Two million," Shane said, meeting Parcelli's stare.

The sunken eyes bored into Shane, the same stare that had unnerved him four years ago, when he was lying in a hospital bed, disoriented from his first violent encounter with the Manchurian Triad. But this time, Parcelli's gaze struck no fear.

"I'm prepared to sell the algorithm," Shane said slowly, decisively, "but not because it's a matter of national security. And not because we can't decipher the code. I'll sell it because our own government hung us out there as bait once before to pry loose this formula. You're the ones who wrote that letter to Johnny Chin, starting this whole mess a second time. And we've got every reason to think you'd do it again."

When Parcelli didn't flinch, Shane had his answer.

Parcelli said he needed to make a call. After he stepped outside, Shane blew out a breath. "I hope this works," he said.

"It'll work." As usual, Brandi was the strong one. Her faith gave Shane an extra dose of courage.

Two days ago, immediately after their phone call to Guptara, they had agreed on a new course of action. Guptara said he didn't want any money tainted by a lie. He sided 100 percent with Brandi, urging Shane to do the right thing.

"You have to choose," Guptara had said, "between the old Shane and the new Shane."

After hanging up, Shane suggested a plan that shocked even Brandi. They would sell the algorithm to the government, but it would be the real algorithm, not the bogus one. If the feds didn't know the key was contained in Pastor Prasad's Bible, how would they ever be able to decode it?

"We never wanted to take that chance," Brandi reminded him. "The government can bring all kinds of resources to bear on cracking this code."

To an extent, she was right. It was the very reason Shane had not sold it to them in the first place. But the more time passed, the more he appreciated the brilliance of Professor Kumari. Would the man really use a code that even the United States government could crack without access to the key? And couldn't God confuse the minds of the government cryptologists, if that's what it took?

"That's why they call it faith," Shane had said to Brandi. He relished the rare opportunity to stake out the spiritual high ground. "I say it's worth a chance."

Shane's thoughts returned to the present when Parcelli came back in the front door, holding a revised contract for two million. He promised that the government would be watching Shane and Brandi every second to make sure that they didn't try to resell the algorithm to anyone else.

"And how do I know that this is the authentic code?" Parcelli asked.

"You've got to trust somebody," Shane said. And then, to put Parcelli's mind at ease, Shane pulled out his computer and went into his e-mail archives. He showed Parcelli the e-mail he had received four years ago from Professor Kumari, a few short days after Kumari died.

"I'm sure the government can check the original servers and verify the timing and origination of this e-mail," Shane said.

Parcelli asked a few questions and made a few notes. He appeared satisfied, promised that the money would be wired into Shane's account, and left with a copy of the encrypted Abacus Algorithm.

◁▷

On the way to the airport, Parcelli called Carzak. "They sold it," he said. "Two million. I had to get approval all the way up the chain."

He could almost hear Carzak smiling from three states away. "What changed their minds?" Carzak asked.

"They really think we're the ones who wrote that letter to Johnny Chin," Parcelli said. "They think we'd rat them out again if we didn't have the algorithm."

"Interesting," Carzak said. "Who *did* write that letter?"

"I think I'll find out at my next stop," Parcelli said.

◁▷

Shane and Brandi called Pastor Guptara and told him about their decision. He seemed a little nervous about the United States government possessing even an encrypted version of the algorithm, but he understood Shane's reasoning. From everything Guptara had heard about Professor Kumari, he agreed that the code was probably unbreakable. He prayed on the phone that the government would never figure it out. Then he thanked Shane and Brandi for fulfilling the professor's dying wishes and promised to spend every dollar they sent him on education for the Dalits. He urged Shane and Brandi to keep their focus on Christ.

"Remember," Pastor Guptara said, "the government can give you a new identity, but only Christ can change your life."

When they hung up, Brandi and Shane toasted the day's events. The more Shane thought about the bet he had placed on Professor Kumari's ability to encrypt the algorithm with an indecipherable code, the more his confidence grew.

He and Brandi touched plastic cups full of diet soda. "Here's to the witness protection program," Brandi said. "One of Uncle Sam's finest inventions."

88

PARCELLI INTENTIONALLY showed up late at the Breakers Hotel, a five-star luxury resort covering 140 oceanfront acres in the heart of Palm Beach, Florida. The lobby decor featured thick Persian rugs rimmed with light blue and burgundy hues, marble porticoes, overhead arches lined with crystal chandeliers, and a constant flow of white Southern aristocrats with tanning-parlor skin and five-thousand-dollar face-lifts.

On his government per diem, he could barely afford to set foot in this place.

At 10:10, Parcelli strolled into the restaurant, feeling out of place as the only patron wearing slacks instead of shorts, his shirt tucked in, and his face showing his age. He was a runner in the midst of a golf resort, a lower-class working stiff in a hotel that privilege built.

He scanned the tables and did not see the man he was supposed to meet. He thought about that old adage that some people would be late for their own funerals. That was definitely the case here.

Parcelli had the maître d' seat him where he could keep one eye on the door. When the waiter came, Parcelli ordered an orange juice. He ignored the ocean view, deep in thought about the convoluted events of the past several days, events that led him here to consummate this deal with the dark side.

It was just last Tuesday that Parcelli had called U.S. Attorney Allan Carzak and explained his unconventional plan. The Brock girl had lost her dog and been threatened by the triad, the government had lost track of Hoffman and had no hard leads on the triad leaders, and Snead had filed his multimillion-dollar lawsuit. Parcelli's plan was unprecedented, but so were the stakes.

They could stage the kidnapping of Jamie Brock, telling nobody. They could immediately suggest to Hoffman's lawyer that Hoffman needed to cooperate with the feds in a sting operation in order to save Brock and obtain future protection for himself. Basically they would use Brock's kidnapping to obtain Hoffman's cooperation and then turn around and use Hoffman as mob bait. The end game: nab the triad leaders and buy the algorithm from Hoffman as part of the deal.

After a few initial objections, Carzak warmed to the plan. Parcelli promised that the feds would inflict minimal trauma on Jamie Brock. The kidnapping went off flawlessly. But then, as usual, the lawyers fouled everything up. Since Carzak and Parcelli couldn't find Hoffman, they had to work through Walter Snead. The savvy old codger saw this as an opportunity to feather his own nest and possibly keep his sorry carcass out of jail. Snead proposed a package deal—"two for one," as he phrased it. He would talk Hoffman into working with the government to nab the triad leaders, but Snead also wanted a secret side deal.

And it was a doozy.

Snead would testify in secret grand jury proceedings about corruption in the Los Angeles court system. A small band of lawyers, including Snead, had been bribing judges on civil cases so that they could win enormous verdicts. On criminal cases, those same lawyers provided only token defenses, basically throwing the cases so that criminal defendants whom the judges wanted to nail ended up serving time in prison. Snead would provide details as well as the names of lawyers and judges. The FBI had been investigating this corruption ring for nearly two years, and now Snead could give them proof.

Snead would also talk Hoffman into working with the government on his case and, even more important, would try to pry the algorithm out of Hoffman's greedy little hands so it could be sold to the government. Snead explained to Carzak and Parcelli that the algorithm was encrypted with a code nearly impossible to decipher without the government's enormous resources. But Snead had a plan, he said, that might get the algorithm into Wellington Farnsworth's hands. If that worked, the government would have to pony up about one and a half million dollars into an offshore account in exchange for the encrypted algorithm. Parcelli was pretty sure where that money would go.

But Parcelli had done everything he could to intimidate Farnsworth and had come to believe that the kid probably never received a copy of the algorithm. In any event, that issue became moot on Monday, when the Hoffmans agreed to sell the algorithm directly to Parcelli for two million dollars.

It was time to wrap up the loose ends on Snead's deal. The lawyer had insisted on keeping his deal secret even from his own client. He had liked the government's suggestion that they could stage Snead's death when they apprehended the triad leaders. Things got complicated when Hoffman wouldn't tell Snead the details of Hoffman's plan to nail the triad leaders. He would only tell Snead to meet him at the Sheraton Hotel on Friday morning.

As a result, Parcelli and his fellow agents had been forced to improvise. All things considered, Parcelli thought the improvisation—having Snead secreted into the triad's headquarters after the triad members had all been arrested, staging the shooting as Snead left—had been nothing short of brilliant.

Parcelli checked his runner's watch: 10:20. He didn't understand people like Snead, people who always showed up late, people who presumed on other people's time. He especially couldn't understand *lawyers* like Snead—ones who sold out their clients' interests to further their own.

That was the problem with the witness protection program. To convict the Satans of the underworld, you had to hold your nose and cut deals with Satan's demons. Parcelli tried to console himself by thinking about all the judges and fat-cat lawyers they would convict in the Los Angeles corruption sting. He reminded himself that they would be putting Huang Xu and Li Gwah in prison for a very long time, something like three consecutive life sentences. Maybe even the death penalty. He reminded himself of these things just in time, right as big Walter Snead came ambling across the dining room, heading straight for Parcelli's table.

The FBI agent did not bother to rise. And Walter Snead did not bother to smile.

"I don't understand your insistence on the formality of a meeting," Snead began. No pleasantries, no "thanks for saving my hide," just begin the meeting with the usual Snead complaints. "I can read the agreement on my own."

"It's procedure," Parcelli said flatly. He waited for the waiter to appear and for Snead to order a Bloody Mary. At 10:22 in the morning. Parcelli slid the memorandum of understanding across the table. Walter Snead was now known as Archibald Holmes. His background: a retired state court judge from Nevada. That way, Snead said, he could insist that his new friends address him as "the Honorable Archibald Holmes" in any formal invitations.

"Did you get the algorithm from Farnsworth?" Snead asked. He leafed through the memorandum and scribbled his signature on the last page of all three copies.

"That won't be necessary," Parcelli said. "Hoffman agreed to sell us the original."

Snead snorted. "Traitor wouldn't even give his own lawyer a copy, and he sells it to the feds?" He shook his head. "How much?"

"It's confidential."

"You probably paid too much. You know that thing's encrypted."

"We'll figure it out," Parcelli said.

The waiter reappeared with Snead's drink. Both men declined breakfast.

"Here's your subpoena for the grand jury," Parcelli said, handing a second document to Snead.

Snead read it quickly. "Next week," he said. "I think I'm busy."

"Your continued protection under this memorandum of understanding is contingent on your truthful grand jury testimony and the truth of all the factual recitals in the memorandum of understanding."

Snead waved him off. "I know all that. What else you got in that magic little briefcase of yours?"

Parcelli handed him the second-to-last document. It was a dismissal order from a federal court judge of Snead's lawsuit against the government for allegedly disclosing Hoffman's location to the mob. It was one of the benefits of the deal for the federal government.

"It's a shame my client had to go and get blown up," Snead said. "That would have been a heckuva lawsuit."

Parcelli ignored the comment—this was the hold-your-nose-and-get-the-job-done part—then pulled out the last document. "As part of our investigation into that L.A. corruption ring, we obtained a warrant to search your home and office. Figured you wouldn't mind, being dead and all. Of course, we had to tell the magistrate that you were actually in the program."

Parcelli took a deep breath and sipped his orange juice, savoring the only fun he would have on this entire trip. "This warrant covers all of your personal belongings as well. I know that when we sent you out of town, you took your laptop and a briefcase with you. I'm going to need to follow you up to your hotel room and secure that laptop as potential evidence."

"Let me see that," Snead said, snatching the document from Parcelli. Snead read the warrant carefully. When he finished, he allowed himself a thin smile, perhaps remembering that he had already negotiated complete immunity for any crimes associated with the L.A. corruption ring or the Hoffman algorithm.

"Suit yourself," Snead said. "It'd be hard for me to win a motion to quash that subpoena anyway, given the fact that I'm not technically alive."

He took a long hit on his Bloody Mary and broke into a full-toothed smile. "Go right ahead, Mr. Parcelli. Knock yourself out."

89

BY TUESDAY MORNING, Wellington was sick with worry. He was scheduled to testify in front of the grand jury on Wednesday and didn't know if he could handle the pressure. He knew that Carzak would ask about the algorithm. And Wellington's research on the attorney-client privilege was not encouraging. Even if Wellington could object to testifying about any conversations he had with Stacie Hoffman, which was questionable since he wasn't technically a lawyer, he would still have to answer whether he was presently in possession of the algorithm.

His client was dead. There were national security interests at stake. And Carzak would argue he needed the algorithm to prosecute the triad members. Wellington was pretty sure a judge would compel him to answer Carzak's questions.

Wellington was no longer worried about giving up the encrypted algorithm. When he had finally discovered how to decrypt the formula, he realized that nobody would ever be able to figure it out without Pastor Prasad's Bible.

If Professor Kumari had only used the encryption system that Wellington first suspected in church on Sunday, somebody might conceivably have been able to figure that one out without Prasad's Bible. Especially if the federal government had put hundreds of cryptologists on the assignment. Somebody might have guessed that the sequences of five numbers somehow referenced the words in a book or document. Somebody else, knowing Kumari was a religious man, might have suggested the Bible. From there, it wouldn't take long to check all the versions.

So Kumari had used another twist. Sometimes, the sets of numbers would be pinpointing a character in a particular verse in the English translation of the NLT Bible, and sometimes the numbers would be pinpointing a symbol in a particular verse in the Hindi translation. And the *only* way to know which translation to use would be to check Pastor Prasad's Bible, where Kumari had underlined the verse on one translation or the other. And just so it wouldn't be obvious, he had underlined a number of other random verses as well.

When Wellington had figured this out, he downloaded some software to help him translate the Hindi symbols and resulting words. After that, the entire algorithm fell into place.

What scared Wellington now wasn't the prospect of being forced to produce the encrypted algorithm, but being forced to answer questions about it. He knew that Carzak would ask whether Wellington had ever seen the key to the encrypted code or if he knew how to decrypt the algorithm.

Which was why Wellington had hardly eaten a thing in the past three days. He couldn't lie—not after taking an oath to tell the truth. The attorney-client argument looked weak. And he didn't want to go to jail for refusing to answer.

He sent another text message to Jamie Brock—**Have you heard anything yet?**—and said another prayer.

How did I ever get myself into this mess?

◁▷

No.

Jamie typed the one-word text message and sent it to Wellington. She understood why the kid was nervous, but he was driving her crazy.

Jamie had finished the paperwork on Monday. She wanted to meet first thing Tuesday morning with the U.S. attorney, but Carzak the Magnificent couldn't squeeze her in until late afternoon. Wellington would just have to endure a few more hours of panic attacks.

She arrived at Carzak's impressive office precisely at four and he offered her something to drink. When he shook her hand this time, he seemed shorter than he had when she'd first met him in federal court. The effusiveness she once construed as friendliness she now viewed as unseemly, even sleazy. She wanted to wipe her hand on the side of her skirt.

She refused his offer of something to drink. When Carzak offered his condolences for everything she had endured, she nearly laughed in his face. She sat down in front of Carzak's massive oak desk, crossed her legs, and looked him straight in the eye.

"That's actually what I'm here to talk about," she said. "The U.S. government's condolences for what I've been through. I'll spare you the details of how I found out, but I think a million dollars might be the appropriate tangible expression of those condolences."

Carzak gave her a pleasant but sideways look, the condescending kind reserved for family members with mental disorders. "Jamie, you've been through a lot. But it's not the federal government's job to compensate you for that—"

"Spare me," Jamie cut in sharply. "It is when you orchestrate the kidnapping. When you stage the whole thing. When you tie up a law-abiding citizen and put her in fear of rape."

Jamie watched Carzak carefully, impressed by the man's ability to maintain a thin, neutral smile in the face of stinging accusations. But it was no longer natural. Instead, Carzak pulled it into place by careful use of every one of his well-toned smiling muscles.

The look infuriated Jamie.

"How can you sit there and defend this conduct? My own government—threatening my life?" She pulled her smoking-gun document from the file and handed it across the desk. "It's an affidavit from Drew Jacobsen."

She still hadn't forgiven the man, still didn't trust him, but at least he had done this much.

Even Carzak couldn't smile through this. He read the document, frowned, then interlaced his fingers on the desk. "Jamie, I don't know what to say. If Mr. Jacobsen's affidavit is true—"

"It's true, Allan. You can drop the hypothetical charade."

"Are you going to let me finish?" Carzak asked.

"Please."

"Okay. If what Mr. Jacobsen says is true, I'll help you get to the bottom of it. People will lose their jobs over this. And I'll personally ensure that you receive fair compensation under the Federal Tort Claims Act."

Jamie sat up a little straighter. She knew she had him, but the money wasn't the only issue. "You've subpoenaed Wellington Farnsworth for the grand jury tomorrow," she said. "Drop that subpoena and agree not to pursue his testimony."

Carzak scowled. "Are you blackmailing me—using a threatened lawsuit to force me into releasing a witness in a criminal investigation?"

Jamie couldn't believe what she was hearing. Carzak staking out the high moral ground? "You sound pretty sanctimonious for an attorney representing a client that just got finished kidnapping me," Jamie said. "I'm threatening you with the truth. A million bucks and drop the subpoena, or I'm going to the press."

Carzak got up from his seat and walked to his window, like a troubled monarch gazing down on his fiefdom. This time, he talked with his back to Jamie. "Assuming this is true, I offer both my apologies and also a sense of perspective. If you were detained by the federal government, it would have been to protect you from the Chinese mafia, criminals who would stop at nothing. The stakes in this case were unbelievably high. We're talking about an encryption-deciphering algorithm that could literally throw the Internet into chaos and expose some of our national secrets."

He turned toward her, his face serious and drawn. Carzak looked as tired as Jamie felt. "Sometimes, in the interest of a greater justice, in the interest of serving and saving millions of innocent people, compromises are made. That's the whole purpose of the witness protection program in the first place, really.

"I want to make it up to you, Jamie." He hesitated, then added, "Assuming for the sake of argument that what you say is true. But I can't recommend a million. You don't get a jury under the Federal Tort Claims Act. In a post-9/11 environment, I can't see a judge giving you more than a few hundred thousand for this claim. Without a reasonable number, I can't get the settlement approved by the deputy attorney general. And believe me, he will need to personally authorize this deal."

"Will you drop the Farnsworth subpoena?" Jamie asked.

"We just wanted to know if he has the algorithm."

"Will you drop the subpoena?"

Carzak waited and thought. After a few seconds, he shook his head ever so slightly as if he was still convincing himself. "We may be able to obtain the algorithm through other means. Tell you what. If you're willing to settle for two hundred and fifty thousand and agree to a confidentiality order, I'll release Wellington's subpoena."

"Seven fifty."

Carzak frowned and shook his head. "Jamie, I think a judge might be somewhat sympathetic to our predicament. If this algorithm had made it into the hands of the mob, it would have been a complete disaster. I can recommend five hundred thousand but even that's a stretch."

Jamie hated this. It seemed like she and Carzak had just sat down at a Vegas poker table, both trying to bluff the other, as if justice were some kind of game. To Jamie, justice was anything but a game. It was a calling. A chance to avenge some very personal losses. A sacred thing.

But definitely *not* a game.

"Seven fifty," she repeated. This time, she meant it. She would blow this whole charade wide open, expose everything the government had done, if Carzak dared to offer her one penny less. She didn't even care about the money all that much, although she wouldn't turn it down. There was something far greater at stake than money changing hands.

Carzak must have read it in her eyes. "I'll see what I can do," he said.

"That's not good enough," Jamie insisted. "Do you have the authority to approve this deal, or do we need to get the deputy attorney general on the phone?" She paused, unblinking. "If I walk out that door, the deal's off."

"Give me ten minutes," Carzak said. Jamie nodded and left him alone in his office.

Fifteen minutes later, he ushered Jamie back in and told her they would have the paperwork and check ready by the end of the week. He reiterated the confidentiality provisions and had her sign a brief statement. Carzak agreed to release Wellington's subpoena. Jamie agreed to release all claims arising from the kidnapping and agreed not to talk with anybody about the incident.

"*Anybody* means just that," Carzak reiterated. "No exceptions—public or private. We can't, of course, keep you from testifying about these events if you're compelled to do so in some kind of criminal case by a court subpoena. But the final paperwork will require you to contact me if you ever receive such a subpoena. That will give me a chance to have the court quash the subpoena based on national security interests. Are those confidentiality and release terms acceptable?"

Jamie assured Carzak she understood. They shook hands, and Carzak told her that she was going to make an outstanding lawyer.

"One last question," Jamie said, watching Carzak's face for any hint of the answer. "Assuming, hypothetically, that it was my government who kidnapped me—would that idea have come from the FBI agent involved or from this office?"

Carzak didn't blink. "The government didn't kidnap you, Jamie; the mob did." He lowered his voice a notch, his face oozing sincerity. "But if the government had done this, I can assure you that it would not have been initiated by this office."

She knew the first statement was a lie. *But if he's lying about the second part,* Jamie thought, *it's a world-class performance.*

She should have left celebrating. Wellington didn't have to testify. The key to the algorithm would never leave his hands. Jamie could wipe out her student loans with a fraction of the settlement and still have enough to live on for ten years. If money could buy justice, Carzak had just provided a nice down payment.

Yet somehow, Jamie felt like she had been played. She hated this feeling of compromise, of feeling like she'd sold her soul one little piece at a time. Beating the government at its own game brought no real satisfaction. She wanted to be able to trust men like Carzak, prosecutors sworn to uphold the law and protect the citizens.

When Jamie became a prosecutor, things would be different. She would bust the bad guys, all right, but not sacrifice her own morals in the process. She would not break the law in order to convict criminals. There had to be a line, she decided as she walked away from the federal building. A line she wouldn't cross.

A person had to determine where that line was before she started practicing, or the temptation would be too great in the heat of battle. Especially for someone like Jamie—a crusader, someone who hated to lose, someone with some very personal reasons to combat crime. Jamie would never cross that line, she told herself.

But something inside her didn't quite believe it. She knew in her heart that she would use any means necessary to make sure her mother's killer, now sitting on death row, received his ultimate punishment. She would continue to do whatever it took to ensure that the men who killed Snowball got what they deserved.

That was different, she told herself. Personal tragedies. As a prosecutor, she would maintain a professional distance from the crimes. She would be vengeance personified, a scourge on the criminals, but she would not compromise integrity or ethics just to achieve some misguided notion of justice.

She beat back that skeptical voice in her head, the one claiming that the system *required* those kinds of compromises. She buried it someplace deep in her own subconscious. If she couldn't walk the line, then why even become a lawyer? Why become a prosecutor especially—with all the power of the state at her disposal?

Jamie had learned advocacy well from her law school professors. By the time she climbed into her 4Runner, she had convinced herself it was true. Jamie Brock, representing the people of the state of Georgia, would never compromise just to get a conviction. There were some things in life more important than winning.

PART V

THE WITNESSES

There is no honor among thieves.

A MODERN PARAPHRASE OF AN OLD
ENGLISH PROVERB THAT ACTUALLY SAYS,
"EVEN AMONG THIEVES, THERE IS HONOR."
MAYBE TIMES HAVE CHANGED.

90

AS WALTER SNEAD'S grand jury testimony ground to a conclusion, Allan Carzak had to admit that the law school professor made a formidable witness. In the last two days, Snead had painted a graphic and detailed picture of justice for sale in Los Angeles—crooked lawyers buying verdicts in civil cases and simultaneously selling out their criminal defense clients. He had a nearly photographic memory, testifying without notes about the particulars of cases and meetings from four or five years ago. His details always checked out with the corroborating documents that Carzak and his team had assembled from Snead's computer and legal files.

Getting the grand jury to indict would not be a difficult matter. Defense lawyers weren't even allowed in the grand jury room—all of the proceedings were conducted in secret. Carzak had often claimed he could have indicted the pope if he had wanted to. Thanks to a wealth of damning testimony from Snead, this grand jury had more than enough to issue blanket indictments that would shake the Los Angeles legal community. Plus, the feds in California had already used Snead's particulars to flip another crooked lawyer, one who would testify at trial in the light of day as part of his plea agreement.

These were the best of times for the career of Allan Carzak. The big shots at justice knew about his role in helping to procure the Abacus Algorithm, though thus far the encrypted code had proved impenetrable. He was personally handling the Atlanta grand jury proceedings that would generate additional indictments against the Manchurian Triad members and several of their cohorts. At the same time, he had been asked to question Walter Snead in front of this Los Angeles grand jury, since Carzak and his team were the ones most familiar with Snead's testimony, the ones who negotiated the deal requiring Snead to testify in the first place.

As Thursday afternoon drew to a close, Carzak turned to his last area of questioning: the deal between Snead and the federal government.

Carzak had warned Snead and the U.S. attorney for the southern district of California that he would cover this ground. Carzak always informed grand jurors of plea bargains and deals that might be used to question the credibility of a witness. That way, when the defense attorneys eventually got their hands on the grand jury transcript, they couldn't attack the prosecutors for a failure to disclose exculpatory evidence. Plus, it only served to make the grand jurors trust Carzak more—he appeared so forthcoming.

Snead handled the questions about the deal without flinching. Yes, he had been granted immunity. In fact, he had insisted that the government enroll him in the witness protection program. He couldn't provide details of where he had relocated, of course, but the government had given him a fresh start in exchange for testifying here today. Snead even admitted, rather arrogantly in the opinion of Carzak, that his deal included the proviso that the government could not call him as a witness at trial. He was only required to provide this grand jury testimony before he disappeared forever.

But Snead was adamant in saying his testimony had not been bought. It was all true, he claimed, looking the jury dead in the eye. Every word of it.

Carzak nodded his affirmation, then took a few steps toward the witness. Carzak didn't appreciate crooks who tried to game the system. It was one thing to negotiate a deal with the government—such dealings greased the wheels of justice every day. But it was *the way* this deal got cut that stuck in Allan Carzak's craw.

"You understand that your immunity applies to any criminal activity associated with the practice of law in Los Angeles and in particular the allegations of bribing judges; is that correct?"

"Yes."

"And you also understand that you have immunity with regard to any dealings you might have had with Mr. and Mrs. Hoffman and the Chinese mafia; is that also correct?"

"Yes."

"But you do know, Mr. Snead, that if you testify falsely today or have misled the government in any way about these events—in other words, if you have defrauded the government in the process of obtaining this deal—you don't have immunity for those types of actions."

Snead took a drink of water. He stared at Carzak as if trying to read the man's mind. His Adam's apple bobbed up and down. "Of course not."

Carzak brought out a personal laptop computer and had the court reporter mark it as a government exhibit. "Is this your laptop, Mr. Snead?"

Snead took the computer and inspected it, snarling at Carzak, undoubtedly wondering why they had departed from the script. "Without turning it on to make sure, it appears to be."

"You will recall that the government seized this computer pursuant to a search warrant issued last week. Is that your recollection?" Carzak smiled as he asked the question. He knew how much Snead hated the smile.

"Yes, I believe that's correct."

"Did you know, Mr. Snead, that your computer hard drive retains evidence of every document produced and a log of every website ever accessed?"

"I don't doubt that, though I fail to see the relevance of it."

Carzak loved this moment. He studied Snead's face. The scowl lines were carved deep into the man's forehead. Snead probably knew that Carzak was now toying with him, but he obviously hadn't figured out the details just yet. Carzak glanced quickly at the jurors, giving them a watch-this look. "You know, Mr. Snead, there was one thing that always bothered me in the case against the Manchurian Triad. You have any idea what that was?"

"No, Mr. Carzak," Snead said sarcastically, "I'm afraid I left my mind-reading crystal ball at home."

"After four years of hiding out, why would David Hoffman write a letter to Johnny Chin and try to sell the algorithm to the Chinese mob?" Carzak started pacing in front of the witness. He was no longer technically in question mode, but this was a grand jury. There was no judge to rule him out of order, and Snead knew better than to start an argument here.

"If Hoffman wanted to sell the algorithm on the black market—even the encrypted algorithm—would he really pick the one organized-crime group that already had a grudge against him for killing several of its members? And even assuming that Hoffman sent the letter, how did the Manchurian Triad find him? The only people who knew where he lived were his wife, the federal marshals, the FBI, and his attorney. That would be you, Mr. Snead."

Carzak stopped and turned toward Snead. The man had a look of false bravado, but Carzak saw sweat beads on his forehead. "I knew the marshals and the FBI wouldn't turn Hoffman over to the mob. Heck, we didn't even know he had kept the algorithm. And it sure didn't make sense for Hoffman to turn himself over either."

"Is there a question in that parade of sentences?" Snead growled. "Or are we all just here to watch you grandstand?"

Carzak gave the witness a pleasant but condescending look. "Okay, Mr. Snead, here's a question. And keep in mind that my computer techs can access *every* document ever created on your hard drive, including ones you thought you had deleted." Carzak paused to study the witness. Snead glared back. "Did you or did you not create and send the letter to Johnny Chin that purportedly came from your client?"

"I most emphatically did not."

Carzak smiled. His computer techs had, in fact, searched in vain for the letter on Snead's hard drive. But Carzak wasn't finished. The witness was feeling cocky. It was time for the counterpunch.

"Did you or did you not, on February 14 of this year, exactly twelve days before Mr. Chin received that letter, access the website for the Federal Bureau of Prisons and use the inmate locator function to determine where Johnny Chin was being held?"

"Which proves nothing," Snead countered without hesitation.

He shifted in his seat so he could address the jury directly. "Since the attorney-client privilege does not allow me to reveal the details of any conversations with my clients, allow me to pose a hypothetical. Let's suppose that Mr. Hoffman was concerned that the Manchurian Triad might find out about his renewed efforts to sell the algorithm to legitimate companies. Suppose he expressed that concern during one of our meetings. Wouldn't you expect to see a federal inmate locator search on my computer, not just for Johnny Chin, but for every other member of the Manchurian Triad who had been convicted four years ago as well?"

With the question hanging in the air, Snead turned back to Carzak. "Why don't you tell the jury the total number of names you found associated with that search, Mr. Carzak? Why don't you try telling the jury the *whole* truth?"

Carzak wiped the pleasantries from his face. Snead had indeed been careful—probably typing the letter on some obscure computer, even covering his tracks when he searched for Chin's address. "The whole truth," Carzak repeated, nodding. "Fair enough. You represented the Hoffmans. You tried to sell the algorithm to legitimate companies but could not because it had been encrypted. At the same time, you started feeling the heat from the Los Angeles investigation. You stood to lose everything—your career, your freedom, your money." As he spoke, a genuine anger sharpened Carzak's words.

This was why lawyers had a bad name. *This man*—selling out his client for his own self-preservation. A breach of the nearly sacred trust given to lawyers. A man who treated clients like commodities, justice like a game. And Carzak was stuck with *him* as a witness.

He had to use Snead. But he didn't have to like it.

"Then it dawns on you, Mr. Snead. The feds would probably do anything to get their hands on this algorithm. If you put your own client in harm's way and let the feds know this algorithm was still out there, you could probably work out a deal where you end up getting immunity along with your client. So you send a letter to Chin under Hoffman's name and contact the Manchurian Triad to let them know the general area where Hoffman is living. Then you have the audacity

394 || FALSE WITNESS

to sue the federal government, committing fraud on the court by claiming that *we* were the ones who sent the letter to Chin. At the first opportunity, you propose a deal that will give you immunity and make you part of the witness protection program. How am I doing, Mr. Snead?"

"*Alice in Wonderland*, Mr. Carzak. You spin a wonderful fairy tale."

"Do you deny under oath that you contacted the Manchurian Triad, Mr. Snead? Do you deny telling them about a scheduled court appearance by Hoffman?"

It had all come to this—Snead's moment of truth. Carzak's long speech really had just one purpose: to frustrate the witness and rile him up. To throw him off-balance and make him more likely to react. Snead was right—the computer evidence was circumstantial at best. But on this pending question—whether Snead contacted the triad to tell them about Hoffman's location—the evidence was direct. If Snead denied it, Carzak would have him for perjury. And that would only be the start.

How could Snead even make contact with the Manchurian Triad? Carzak had wondered. *What conduit did he use to inform them about Hoffman's location?* It wasn't through Chin—he had only received the typed letter that didn't say anything about Hoffman's court hearing. It dawned on Carzak late Monday afternoon, after hours of rehearsing Snead's grand jury testimony.

The plastic surgeon—Dr. Silvoso. He had worked with the triad to facilitate Hoffman's first kidnapping. He might know how to get a message through to the mob.

When Carzak squeezed Silvoso, the surgeon squealed. Yes, Snead had recently contacted him. Yes, Silvoso had passed a message on to some members of the Manchurian Triad. The rest of it Carzak had pieced together on his own.

"Do you deny it?" Carzak pressed. "Do you deny that about three weeks ago Mr. Hoffman came to you with a routine legal matter? Do you deny telling him that he could save some money by going through legal aid and you would still oversee the matter? Do you deny not only sending the letter to Chin but also sending a separate message to the

Manchurian Triad, through a plastic surgeon named Dr. Silvoso, about Hoffman's scheduled court hearing?"

This time Snead paused, his brilliant mind churning through the possibilities. "I'm asserting my Fifth Amendment rights as a U.S. citizen, Mr. Carzak." The rage darkened Snead's face as he spoke, his voice a mere growl. "I refuse to answer these ridiculous questions."

91

ALLAN CARZAK, U.S. ATTORNEY for the northern district of Georgia, and Eva Salazar, his counterpart for the southern district of California, coordinated their announcements of the groundbreaking indictments under the Racketeer Influenced and Corrupt Organizations Act and various other federal statutes. An Atlanta-based grand jury had returned multiple indictments against eleven members of the Manchurian Triad, including Huang Xu and Li Gwah. State charges, including crimes punishable by death, were expected to follow. A Los Angeles–based grand jury indicted seven prominent L.A. lawyers and three California state court judges.

For all the hoopla, there was no indictment against Walter Snead. It was Carzak's decision, and despite the protests of Parcelli and several other FBI agents, Carzak was comfortable he had made the right call. Snead had been smart enough not to perjure himself during the grand jury proceedings. Carzak probably could have built a case against Snead for defrauding the government, but an indictment against Snead would divert focus from Carzak's main prosecution of the triad leaders. Even worse, it would give the triad's defense lawyers some ammunition for their arguments and might jeopardize the entire grand jury proceeding.

Plus, Carzak didn't want to set a precedent for prosecuting government witnesses who provided vital information under the witness protection program. Carzak would go after the big fish. He had wanted to put the fear of God into Snead. Nothing more.

◁▷

SATURDAY, APRIL 26
SEMINOLE, FLORIDA

Walter Snead celebrated the indictments by gambling the night away at the Hard Rock Hotel and Casino Hollywood, a Seminole casino located an hour from his waterfront condo in West Palm Beach. He arrived home a few hours before the sun came up, somewhere around 4:00 a.m. As he climbed out of his three-day-old silver Mercedes, parked in the soft lighting of his own driveway, he took a sniper's bullet to the base of the skull. The coroner concluded Snead was dead before he hit the ground.

Allan Carzak found out about Snead's assassination through a phone call from Sam Parcelli, who didn't seem the least bit distraught as he recounted the events. "One day we discover that Snead defrauds the government so he can get immunity. Next thing I know, somebody shoots him in the back of the head. Clean shot from nearly two hundred yards away. Sounds to me like a professional hit man."

The casualness of Parcelli's description, the lack of concern in his voice, the way he practically gloated over Snead's death—it was all too much for the normally unflappable Carzak.

"We can't lose witnesses like this," Carzak said sharply. "I don't care how much you dislike the guy; it's your job to keep him alive. The entire witness protection program is only as good as our ability to protect witnesses. And frankly, Sam, you and the marshals' office have done a miserable job on this one."

"I hear you," Parcelli said drily. "I'm all broken up about it."

"Doesn't sound that way to me," Carzak fired back. He took a deep breath and calmed down a little. Allan Carzak wasn't the type to lose his cool or hold a grudge. What good would it do? His success ultimately depended on good relations with FBI agents, including agents like Sam Parcelli who happened to be first-class jerks. Carzak hadn't come this far by burning bridges. Instead, he built trust. He couldn't let the death of one crooked lawyer tear down the trust he had spent years nurturing with his counterparts at the FBI.

Carzak lowered his voice and adopted a much more conciliatory tone. "For the record," he said, "if anybody asks, I reamed you out good on this one."

"And for the record," Parcelli said, "this was my response: we haven't lost a witness yet unless he violated the terms of his memorandum of understanding or lied to get the agreement in the first place."

Carzak wanted to get along, but he just couldn't let that one go. "What's your record on the others?" he asked. "What percentage do we lose if they're careless enough to violate provisions of their agreements?"

"Nobody keeps records on them," Parcelli said.

"Well, maybe somebody should."

The phone line was quiet for a few moments, and then Parcelli spoke. This time, he was the one who toned it down a notch. "Look, Allan, I don't like it any better than you. But despite all of its flaws, the witness protection program is still one of the best things we have going."

"Try telling that to Walter Snead."

92

THE GRAND JURY ROOM in Rabun County was a far cry from the grandeur of federal court. The room was cramped and humid, a large window AC unit working furiously to complement the overtaxed central air system. Even so, Jamie estimated the indoor temperature to be in the low eighties.

The county prosecutor was Rex Stafford, a zealous law-and-order advocate in a county where they still believed in shooting the bad guys first and letting God sort them out later. Rex was a former basketball star for the Rabun County Wildcats and coached at the school as a part-time assistant to help make ends meet. He wore cowboy boots and a white shirt with the sleeves rolled up to the elbows. His suit coat was flung over a wooden chair. Like everyone in Rabun County, he was a friend of Jamie's brother, Chris.

Rex had agreed to pursue this case for two reasons. First, he didn't like the feds. And second, Chris had called in a favor. But Rex warned Jamie that the evidence was pretty thin even for the low standards needed to get an indictment. "Grand juries up here have minds of their own," he said.

Jamie settled into the witness stand, slightly unnerved by the stares of the sixteen grand jurors. They seemed intrigued, if a little skeptical, by a third-year law student from the big city. Rex walked her through the background information—how she came to represent David Hoffman, the threat by the mob to herself and Snowball, the hearing in federal court requesting a new witness protection deal for Hoffman. She was careful not to mention anything about the algorithm. The jurors were at least interested, she could tell that much. This was a far cry from the trespassing and disorderly conduct disputes that formed their normal fare.

Interest turned to sympathy when she testified about the poisoning of Snowball. A few of the grand jurors, undoubtedly dog lovers themselves, seemed to be tearing up. Jamie surprised herself by remaining stoic, even when she talked about burying Snowball and placing her favorite pair of Chacos in the grave.

Rex walked to the end of the jury box and stood next to the rail as he considered his next question. This way, it would be natural for Jamie to look right at her audience.

"Did there come a time," Rex began, raising his voice to emphasize the importance of the question, "when you began to suspect that the federal government, not the mob, had poisoned your dog?"

"Yes."

"Please tell the members of the grand jury why."

Jamie swallowed hard, cognizant that a lot was riding on the next few moments. Jurors didn't like indicting law enforcement officials. "First of all, there was the note on the windshield of my 4Runner immediately after the judge announced her ruling on our federal court motion. That entire proceeding was under seal, and it seemed highly unlikely that the mob could have found out about it so quickly."

"Was FBI Agent Sam Parcelli aware of the proceedings?" Rex asked.

"Yes, he testified at the hearing."

"Proceed."

Jamie needed to be careful. She couldn't mention the kidnapping because of the terms of her agreement with Carzak, yet she had to provide the jury with some reason why Parcelli would do such a thing. She believed that Parcelli had done this—poisoned Snowball and blamed it on the mob—so that Carzak would go along with Parcelli's scheme to kidnap Jamie. But how could she explain a plausible motive to the jury?

"I also knew that the federal government desperately wanted to find my client," Jamie said softly. "For the reasons I mentioned earlier, they wanted to use him as bait in order to apprehend more members of the Manchurian Triad. But first, they had to find him." Jamie paused, realizing how far-fetched this all sounded.

"They wanted an excuse to put a tail on me since I was Hoffman's lawyer. They hoped he might try to contact me. They also wanted me to trust a local law enforcement guy named Drew Jacobsen, who was actually working with the FBI. They hoped that I would confide in him about Hoffman's location. The ironic thing is that I had no clue where Hoffman was hiding. Basically, they wanted to use me to get Hoffman. That's why they poisoned Snowball."

Rex circled back and had Jamie explain her reasons in more detail. He looked worried. Some jurors looked skeptical. It was time to play the trump card.

"Is there anything else that made you suspect it might have been this Parcelli character who poisoned Snowball?" Rex asked.

"Yes," Jamie said. "A couple weeks ago, I went out to dinner with Drew Jacobsen and asked to use his cell phone. When he wasn't looking, I wrote down the numbers in his call history and the times and dates of each call."

"Why did you do that?"

"On the night that Snowball died, Drew was the first law enforcement officer I called. Afterward, he told me that he had called the local sheriff's office and the FBI. That's when Agent Parcelli made this a federal case and told Drew and the other local authorities to back off."

"What time did you call Mr. Jacobsen?"

"The conference call with the judge took place at about two. I found the note on my windshield a little while later. The earliest I would have called Drew was probably three o'clock."

"And what did you find on his call log?"

"Numerous calls earlier that day, and several the previous day, to a number that I later called myself."

"Whose number was it?" Rex asked.

Jamie hesitated, just as they practiced. "The number belonged to Agent Sam Parcelli."

A few jurors sat forward in their seats. Others furrowed their brows. Not exactly a smoking gun, but it was the best Jamie had to offer.

"Can you think of any legitimate reason Drew Jacobsen would have been calling Agent Parcelli before Snowball was poisoned?" Rex asked.

"No."

Rex must have sensed the lingering ambiguity among the jury members, a sense that there ought to be something more substantial to justify indictment of an FBI agent. The prosecutor went straight to a question that was not in the script. "Did you also have a chance to listen to any of Mr. Jacobsen's saved messages?" he asked. "And if so, were any of those saved messages from Mr. Parcelli?"

Stunned, Jamie tried to quickly process the implications. Rex might be a country boy, but he was also a savvy prosecutor. He hadn't raised this question during preparation. That way, he couldn't be accused of soliciting false information. He would say that he really didn't know; he just wanted an answer.

But in reality, it was a road map to a sure indictment. Jamie could claim she heard a recorded message. She could make up the damaging content, secure in the knowledge that it would simply be her word against Jacobsen's and Parcelli's. At trial, Rex would argue that Jacobsen had erased the message once the indictments came down. There was enough suspicion raised by the very existence of the phone calls that a jury would probably believe Jamie.

The perfect setup. Snowball avenged. Justice guaranteed. She took a sip of water, stared at Rex for a moment, and thought about the pain Snowball must have endured in those final hours as he fought for his very life.

"No," Jamie said firmly. Decisively. She felt a weight leave her shoulders as she did so. "I didn't listen to any recorded messages."

93

ON TUESDAY NIGHT, Jamie joined Wellington and Isaiah for a celebration dinner. They toasted the indictments of the triad members and the corrupt L.A. lawyers and judges. They toasted the fact that Wellington had not been called to testify at the grand jury. They toasted the indictments of Sam Parcelli on cruelty-to-animal charges and Drew Jacobsen as a coconspirator.

Rex Stafford had called Jamie late Monday afternoon with the good news. Following the indictments and his call to Jamie, he had placed courtesy calls to Parcelli and Jacobsen. Soon, he heard back from their lawyers, and the negotiations began.

The indictments would remain under seal. The two men would plead no contest to a Class 1 misdemeanor, pay fines of a thousand dollars each, and agree to six months' probation. They would both be suspended from their jobs for six months. Rex asked Jamie how she felt about the terms. Given the sparse evidence, she told him it was probably the best they could do. Nothing could bring Snowball back. But at least Parcelli and Jacobsen wouldn't get off scot-free.

Before Wellington left that night, he thanked Jamie one last time for helping quash his grand jury subpoena and gave her an awkward hug. Isaiah volunteered to tutor him on proper displays of affection with the female sex. Jamie smiled at them both. She couldn't ask for better friends. Wellington Farnsworth: nineteen-year-old whiz kid and keeper of the world's most powerful secret. Isaiah Haywood: defender of the downtrodden, a man who risked his life for a client he barely knew.

There were still good men in the world, Jamie realized. Decent men. Men who cared about justice as much as she did.

After dinner, Jamie returned to her condo and decided to catch up on some coursework. Her professors had been incredibly accommodating, telling Jamie she could even postpone her final exams if she wanted, but that was not Jamie's style. She had been studying for about two hours at the kitchen table when she heard somebody knock.

The knock, loud and insistent, startled her. Jamie didn't get unannounced visitors. The kidnapping wounds were still fresh. The death of Snowball was still a gaping hole in her heart. She pulled the gun out of her backpack, double-checked the safety, and headed for the door.

Would she always answer the door with a gun? Would life ever return to normal? Could she ever learn to trust people again?

She knew the answers would take time. She had survived tragedy before.

She peered through the peephole. Nobody.

Strange.

Curious, she unlocked the dead bolt and cracked the door open, her gun ready. She still didn't see anybody or anything . . . until she looked down. There was a small, white plastic crate with a wire-mesh door. She opened the apartment door, knelt down, and looked inside.

Big brown eyes peered back, like two bright stars surrounded by the black night sky. Jamie had to press her face up to the metal grate to see the little guy. A black Lab puppy! Wagging his little tail. Standing at attention in the crate, his oversize tongue hanging out the side of his mouth. His enormous paws made him look like a little black clown.

Instantly, the nightmares of housebreaking and crate training and teaching a puppy not to eat everything in sight came flooding back. But so did the companionship, the spirit and loyalty of this breed. This incorrigible, wonderful, frustrating, irrepressible breed.

She noticed for the first time the card on top of the crate and picked it up. *I need a good home,* it read. *I like playing Frisbee.* Jamie felt tears forming in her eyes. *My name is Casper Haywood.*

Casper made a high, squeaky noise, a let-me-out-of-here bark, and clawed at the front of the cage. Jamie loved her friends. And she would learn to love this puppy. It wouldn't be all that hard, if past experience was any guide.

But she had her own ideas about names. "Casper Haywood, huh? "I think I'll call you Justice for short."

A NOTE ABOUT
THE CHURCH
IN INDIA

THOSE OF YOU who read the original version of *False Witness* probably noticed many substantial changes. Most were designed to bring the story more in line with the original vision for the book that came to me at my friend's funeral. But one set of changes was for a different reason altogether—I wanted to highlight the challenges of the church in India.

I did this for two reasons. First, I believe that most Western Christians are unaware of the persecution of the church and the miraculous things happening there. And second, I believe that India is at the center of the greatest human rights struggle of our generation.

India is a land with two faces. To the outside world, there is "shining India"—the world's largest democracy, a growing economic force, and a land with admirable civil rights laws. But for the hundreds of millions of Indians in the lower castes, and for a large segment of the Christian church, there is a darker side to India. Anti-conversion laws are used to imprison pastors. Some radical Hindu groups intimidate and abuse Christians and Dalits (formerly called untouchables) often without repercussions from the government. For the 165 million members of India's lowest caste, India is a land of civil rights in theory but oppression in fact. Human trafficking in all of its barbaric forms is rampant, and equal enforcement of the laws is still a dream.

During my first trip to India a few years ago, I saw firsthand the systemic oppression of the Dalits through the Hindu caste system. I was astonished by the fact that the world's largest democracy was also a breeding ground for the world's largest human-trafficking operations, that it would allow the exploitation of 15 million children in bonded labor, that it would tolerate temple prostitution and other forms of sexual slavery, and that it would foster economic and social systems that oppress nearly 25 percent of its people.

But for the people of God, there is a silver lining. At a pivotal human rights rally in Delhi in 2001, Christian leaders apologized to the Dalits for ignoring their plight and promised to stand with them in the future. Thereafter, when the Dalits were abused or attacked, Christians helped publicize the events and called for government intervention. A bond was formed and the Dalits began asking the church to help educate Dalit children. Hundreds of schools sprang up, providing thousands of Dalit children with an English-based education (critical to landing good jobs) and newfound self-respect. The church also offered help in other areas: social justice, economic development, and health care. The result is that millions of Dalits and other Indians are learning that Jesus loves them and that the ground is equal at the foot of the cross.

What can we do to help? For starters, I'm donating every penny from the sale of this book to the Dalit Freedom Network. By buying this book, you've been able to help sponsor a child at one of the Dalit schools in India, including the costs of meals and health care. If you'd like to sponsor a child for a full year, you can do so for less than a dollar per day through the Dalit Freedom Network child sponsorship program (www.dalitnetwork.org).

During one of my trips to India, a Christian leader explained to me that it takes two generations to abolish systemic slavery or oppression. The first generation gains legal freedom through the courts and the legislative process. Much of this has already been done. But it takes a second generation to really grasp the mind-set of freedom and equality. And this can only be done if the children are given a chance through education and economic opportunities.

"It is," the leader said, "the struggle for the soul of a civilization."

I was moved by the plight of these beautiful Dalit children, struggling to throw off the yoke of oppression and replace it with real freedom and dignity. I committed to do my part. I've never asked my readers for a favor before, but I'm asking for one now.

Won't you consider helping out?

◁▷

A truthful witness saves lives . . .

PROVERBS 14:25

ABOUT THE AUTHOR

RANDY SINGER is a critically acclaimed author and veteran trial attorney. He has penned ten legal thrillers, including his award-winning debut novel, *Directed Verdict*. Randy runs his own law practice and has been named to *Virginia Business* magazine's select list of "Legal Elite" litigation attorneys. In addition to his law practice and writing, Randy serves as a teaching pastor for Trinity Church in Virginia Beach, Virginia. He calls it his "Jekyll and Hyde thing"—part lawyer, part pastor. He also teaches classes in advocacy and civil litigation at Regent Law School and, through his church, is involved with ministry opportunities in India. He and his wife, Rhonda, live in Virginia Beach. They have two grown children. Visit his website at www.randysinger.net.

ALSO BY RANDY SINGER

Fiction
Directed Verdict
Irreparable Harm
Dying Declaration
Self Incrimination
The Judge Who Stole Christmas
The Cross Examination of Oliver Finney
False Witness
By Reason of Insanity
The Justice Game
Fatal Convictions

Nonfiction
Live Your Passion, Tell Your Story, Change Your World
Made to Count
The Cross Examination of Jesus Christ

www.randysinger.net

CP0232